The Rx Conspiracy

Ted Culbertson

AmErica House
Baltimore

First printing

ISBN: 1-58851-160-X
PUBLISHED BY AMERICA HOUSE BOOK PUBLISHERS
www.publishamerica.com
Baltimore

Printed in the United States of America

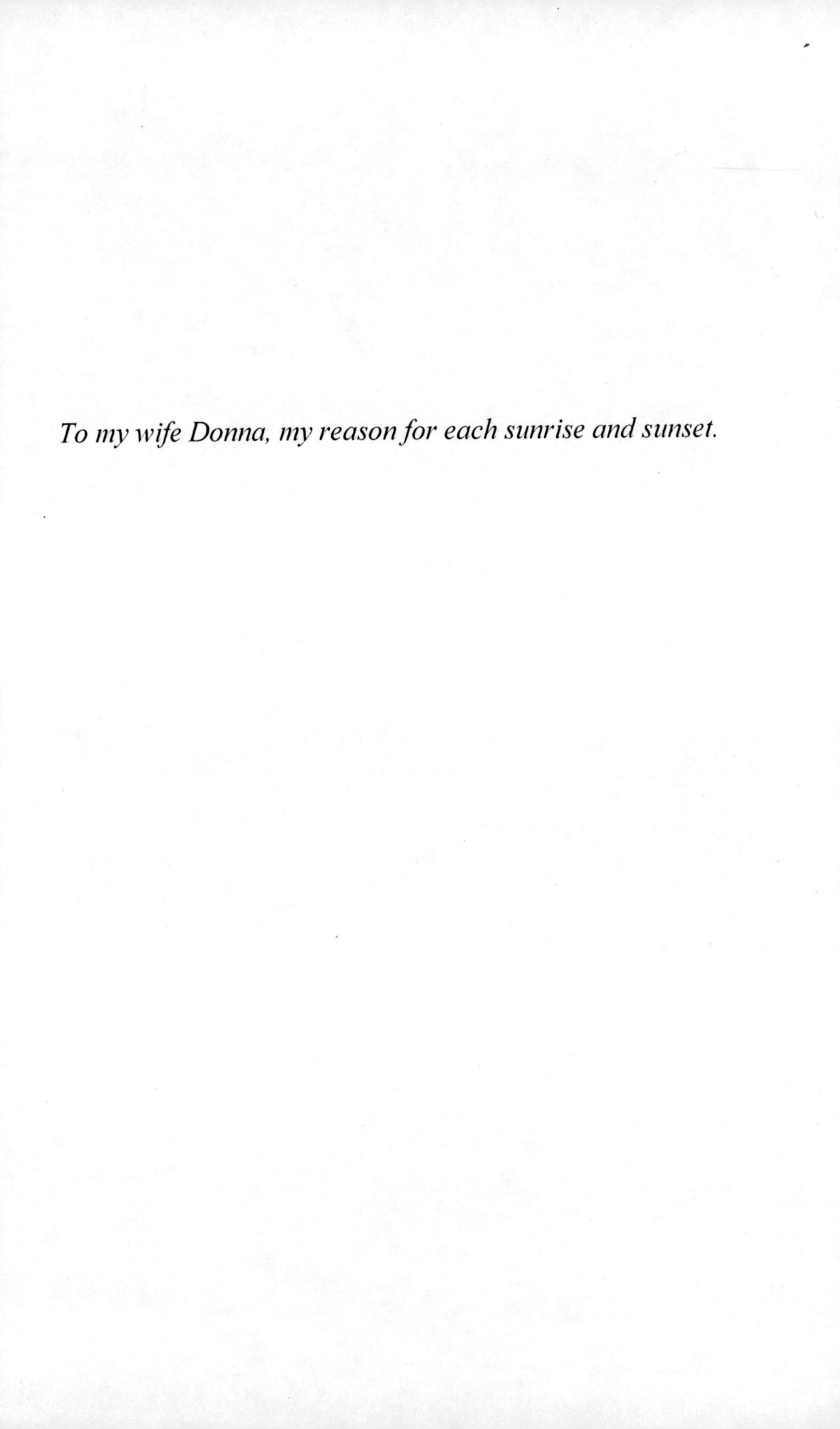

To my wife Donna, my reason for each sunrise and sunset.

In The Memories Of
Murial R. Culbertson
James H. Judge
and
Cuddles

---- Chapter One ----

Brad Claxton pulled the laces of his Nike running shoes tight and neatly tied them with loops of equal size. He rose from the slip-covered wing back chair and walked over to the full length mirror on the back side of the closet door where he kept his wardrobe of suits and jackets. He adjusted his headband, pulling it upward slightly, just above his thick eyebrows. His running suit was dark blue, Ralph Lauren's latest design with the Polo signature on the upper-left pocket. With both hands, he lightly brushed over his short blonde hair, combed straight back with no part. His eyes were the color of the blue Mediterranean Sea on a perfect day. His cheek bones were high. The face tapered downward to the full mouth and prominent jaw line. He decided to pick out the ensemble he'd wear to the office after his five mile run. That's the way his mind operated, disciplined and well organized.

He grabbed the dark brown, double breasted, Armani suit from a row of fifteen and placed it on the silent valet near the entrance to the master bedroom bath. After pondering over the stack of cellophane wrapped, freshly laundered shirts in his perfectly arranged dresser, he made his selection; solid white, button-down collar, with his monogram stitched in chocolate brown, block letters on the left French cuff. Returning to the closet he quickly chose a brown and tan colored tie and slid the drawer open for some socks and underwear. He reached down to the shoe rack, picking his oxblood Bally penny loafers, polished to a high luster the night before. His selection for later in the day was complete and ready to slip into when he returned. While more comfortable in sweat clothes, his position as Director required him to play the part to the hilt.

Once again in front of the mirror, he began his daily exercise routine which would loosen his muscles prior to his one and a half hour jaunt. In the mirror he noticed the reflection of his bedroom. Every woman he had brought into the house *oohed* and *aahed* over the color scheme, furnishings, and accessories. A young, good looking doctor of internal medicine, Brad was one of the most sought after bachelors in the area. He'd never started a private practice and had no patients, but, holding the position of Director of the Center had launched him into a position of prominence. He *was* in demand.

The entrance to his bedroom was the normal six-panel door, not a revolving one, but, with the covey of women pursuing him, it could have been. And, probably would have been if the inroad of sexually transmitted diseases hadn't placed a damper on such a lifestyle. Although, Trojans were within easy reach in the burled oak box on the nightstand beside the bed, Brad remained selective. Different, attractive young women frequented his bedroom for an evening, some more than once, but, there were no commitments. A permanent relationship wasn't part of his plans for the immediate future. The various ladies in his life found his present focus to be different than theirs. Their agendas simply didn't match, but, they didn't seem to mind. Being seen with him increased their own stock in the tight knit circle of the community's elite.

He gave a local designer carte blanche and a $200,000 budget to do her thing. She was good. “Damn good,” he had told her. With very little input from Brad because of his busy schedule, she had given him exactly what he wanted. *What a pad*! The entire decor was fabulous and reeked of money. Nice, easy to maintain and comfortable. It had a certain style and tasteful grace that was just him, simply put. While it had cost him a pretty penny, it was under budget and he was more than pleased with the result.

Warm-up exercises complete, he left the room, turning out the light behind him. He took the carpeted stairs silently, two at a time, down to the foyer. As he reached for the front door knob, the grandfather clock began to chime. Brad was right on schedule. The coffee would be brewed, thanks to a timer, the minute his morning exercise routine was completed.

As he stepped out to the dark gray slate porch, he glanced upwards to check the weather. He felt the coolness of the misty light rain alighting on his face. It looked as if it were trying to stop. He gave his muscles one final stretch and proceeded down the four steps and along the front walk leading up to his townhouse. He glanced around to check. The blackness behind the dormer window of the master bedroom assured him he hadn't forgotten the lights. He waved to a neighbor depositing his trash cans at curbside for 7:00 A.M. pick up. He began his slow trot down the sidewalk, proceeding over the same route he'd taken hundreds of times, his black and white Nikes cushioning every step.

*****

"This damn light mist is really screwing things up. It's hard as hell to see anything."

"Turn on the *damn* wipers then," the passenger said.

"We're not trying to look obvious to the neighbors you know. We parked here before sunrise wanting it to look like the car has been here all night. Were trying to fit in. Remember?"

"Do I ever. It's too damn early to suit me. The assholes in this neighborhood are too concerned about where their next dollar is coming from or getting to their health clubs on time to notice anything out of the ordinary."

"Is there ever a good time of day for this kind of shit."

"Not really, but it pays the bills. My lifestyle creates a few. I sure as hell could use a cigarette."

"That's ironic."

"What?"

"Someone... that does what you do, smoking. You know how bad it is for you. Why do you still do it?"

"Most people say it's a habit. It is! But, I enjoy it at the same time. Besides, they're probably going to find a cure for Cancer soon. At least that's what I'm banking on."

The driver was squinting hard to see through the water-covered windshield. "He should be coming out any second from what I've been told." He strained his eyes as if they could then see better. "*Damn.* There he is. Right on time. Just like clockwork."

"God damn if *he* isn't. He's a fuckin' slave to habit. How can people stand to have such a rigid schedule? The son-of-a-bitch probably knows exactly where he'll be at two thirty-five in the afternoon, six months from now." Returning to the immediate problem, he continued, still frowning. "Personally, I prefer to do a solid day's work, like today, and get the hell out of the country for a month's vacation."

"In your line of work, it's probably the best course of action. You'd better get going."

"Give him ten minutes more. Make sure he hasn't forgotten something."

"It's your call."

*****

Brad had jogged through the streets of Georgetown for the past couple of years on, nearly, a daily basis. But today, he was proceeding slower and being more cautious than usual because of the conditions. It was the first week of November in the Nation's capital and it had been a longer, hotter summer than ordinary; the leaves only recently beginning their lazy drift downward to their final resting place. The pre-dawn drizzle made it very slippery, but, to a disciplined runner like Brad, the conditions were tolerable. The light rain had almost stopped.

He had become as regimented as his schedule would allow him to be in his efforts to keep his 30 year old body in shape. The unfortunate skiing accident in the 1988 Winter Olympics had prematurely ended his being a member of the United States Ski Team. He would, however, never accept the end of his career with the team as an excuse for being out of shape.

During his early morning runs, his thoughts often returned to his last competitive downhill race in Calgary, Alberta. Because of his aggressive style, he had been favored to win his second gold medal for the United States. At that time of his life, the thought of representing his country was pretty heady stuff. For six months prior to the actual competition he was on a constant high.

When the time arrived for the event, the weather was quickly deteriorating as a front slipped over the northern extremities of the Rocky Mountains. Postponement of the race was a distinct possibility. Prior to the actual start, he'd made the run a dozen times in his mind. His concentration was complete. The making of each turn. The approach of each flag. All the jumps that "downhillers" try not to make but are inevitable. Staying as much in a tuck position as possible to maintain a high speed. Crossing the finish line. He had memorized each move and then had gone over them a hundred times. They were now part of him. The course was his!

More than for himself, Brad wanted to make a good showing for his father's benefit. His dad was unable to attend the games in person because he had been fighting cancer and unable to travel. He was in a hospital near their home outside of Denver, Colorado. Thank the Lord for 24" television sets. Knowing his determination to see his son compete in the Olympic Games, Brad was not surprised his father had lived so long with such a horrific disease. And see his son compete, he did, because Brad had won the Gold Medal in the Giant Slalom the day before.

After the medal presentation ceremony, Brad's father called. "It was a wonderful win son, congratulations. I wanted to see you compete, not embarrass the Italians and Austrians with the best performance of your life," he said jokingly from his hospital bed. "They'll probably start World War III over it or, at least, break off diplomatic relations with us. Now son, go get another one for the good old USA." When his father told him, "I love you son," it was more important than any win. Those words would be the last he would hear from his father, but, Brad didn't know it at the time. The Cancer, which he had been stricken with for years, would finally end the life of a great man.

As Brad began his downhill run in the pursuit of his second medal of the games the visibility wasn't real good. It probably should have been postponed until the following day, but, the television network providing coverage to millions of people throughout the world would be very upset if it were canceled due to the weather, or any other reason. Keeping sponsors of events happy and market shares high obviously meant more than the risk to the athletes competing under hazardous conditions.

As Brad approached the midpoint of his downhill run, he had entered a section that had been nicknamed by previous skiers, "leaps and bounds". Speeds of 80 miles per hour were not uncommon in this section of the downhill course. It involved a slight rise with an abrupt fall off and then a very demanding turn to the right followed, soon after, by a second turn to the left. The result for the downhiller, regardless of expertise, is that he becomes airborne for approximately 150 feet. He immediately has to make a right angle turn followed with another turn to the left. Brad always assumed the nickname was derived from what the skier must look like while trying to complete these maneuvers. It must appear that he "leaps" into the air and then, ends up out of "bounds".

The personnel responsible for setting up the television cameras obviously knew where the best skills were required by the downhillers. The network had three cameras focused on this particular area and used them to provide various angles from which the racing could be viewed. Immediately prior to the "leaps and bounds", a radar gun, similar to those used to see how fast a pitcher was throwing a baseball, was used to determine the speed of the skier. This information was made available to the announcer so he could create more excitement broadcasting the ski coverage to his audience.

This section of the downhill race was also very popular for crowds attending the games because of the reckless speeds and hair-trigger turns. The racers, to have any chance of winning the event, must throw caution to the wind. As Brad was "leaping" into the air and sighting his landing area 150 feet further down the mountain, he noticed through the nearly blinding snowfall, a spectator crossing the course for a better vantage point on the other side. His attempts to avoid the person were successful but, his angle of approach to the turn had necessarily been altered drastically. Not only did he crash, but, he also missed the crash fence designed to protect the skier from going off the course. Brad had experienced a few bad spills in his career, but never one like this, involving large rocks and trees.

The quote of the old airline pilot of, "any landing you can walk away from is a good one," certainly applied in Brad's case. He did walk away from the crash, with some help; however, the damage caused to his upper torso was extensive enough to end his career. When Brad viewed the video tape, he agreed that he was lucky to be alive.

After being airlifted to the Calgary hospital, he was informed by the Canadian doctors that he had suffered a broken shoulder, a broken collar bone, separated the other shoulder, broken one arm in two places, fractured numerous ribs and broken a wrist. Brad remembers stating, as straight-faced as possible under the circumstances, "I think I"ll have to get a second opinion." It cracked the doctor up with laughter. There was only incidental damage to Brad's lower extremities, which again proved, the ski bindings designed by his father had done their job.

The team coach told Brad that the remainder of the downhill event had been canceled for the day because of poor visibility and that Brad's intermediate time was the best of the day. Brad advised his coach that there had been a spectator on the course and it wasn't the weather conditions which brought about his accident. He replied that the films indicated the same and there was already an investigation in progress. It was unfortunate as hell. He probably would have won the Gold.

His coach, at the same time, made Brad aware that his father had finally passed away in Denver. He felt fortunate that his father hadn't seen his terrible spill. He would have been terribly upset. Although his death had been anticipated for some time, it was still not easy to take. For years Brad had wondered how a nation can land a man on the moon in 1969 and still not have a grip on a cure for cancer decades later. Brad did make it back home in time for the funeral.

*****

Samantha Sawyer stood in front of the full length, mahogany framed mirror in the bedroom of her small home located in Georgetown. She reached for the red fabric-covered elastic band she had clenched between her perfect, snow-white teeth. Still looking in the mirror, she took the red band and wrapped it around her long auburn hair to hold the pony tail in place. She inspected her face and then smiled, checking out her teeth for the thousandth time since removal of her braces eight years ago on her sixteenth birthday. Everyone she knew told her at one time or another she was beautiful, but, they were friends and family. Their compliments were anticipated, almost expected. She was never quite certain they weren't prejudiced in her favor.

She leaned a little forward to do a closer examination. Plastic surgeons would go bankrupt waiting for a mandate to change those features. Her eyebrows were full and capped the clear, wide blue eyes. The nose was one which was the hidden envy of countless women in their endless pursuit of beauty. The sensual lips, lightly colored with Crimson Red lip-stick, her favorite color, surrounded an inviting, generous mouth. The lightly tanned skin, naturally pink at the high cheekbones, was velvet smooth to the touch.

She always had beautiful facial features but now, the body had caught up. The loose fitting sweat suit with the words, *ATHLETIC DEPARTMENT*, plainly visible on both the shirt and long pants, hid the development that her body had made over the past few years. While Samantha knew what was there, *very few men did.* And, she *preferred* it that way. A teenager with beautiful facial features had turned into a woman with an unbelievable body in a mere five years.

She had always attempted to stay healthy. Not a total health freak but, at the same time, Samantha tried to maintain a proper diet. She paid more attention than most to the nutritional labeling now provided on products thanks to current legislation. She was also a strong believer in exercise, something she was preparing herself for at this very moment. Jogging. How boring! But, at least, it would give her the opportunity to get acquainted with the neighborhood she had just moved into.

Samantha approved of her reflection as she prepared to leave for her morning run. She made her way from the bedroom, through the dining room with its oak hard wood flooring and immense fruitwood table. She must do something about that centerpiece. She didn't care a whole lot for it. In fact, she hated it. She put the thought in the back of her mind as something she would take care of later when she had the time.

She reached the small, but ample, foyer and took one final glance at the ornate, gold leaf mirror hanging on the wall. She methodically put one wisp of hair back in place, noticed the full lips curl into a smile of satisfaction and proceeded out the front door.

"Good morning...Samantha, isn't it?" came a voice from her right.

Turning, she saw an older, nice looking gentlemen, probably in his early 70's. His silver hair blew slightly in the breeze as he tucked the morning paper under his arm. He was a fairly renown, semi-retired romance novelist still having one published every year like clockwork, instead of the contractual obligation of four per year he had laboriously endured during the last five years. He was noticeably admiring his new neighbor as if, in his mind, casting her to be the feminine character of his next manuscript. Possibly about a dirty old man's affair with his zestful, young and attractive next door neighbor? Samantha had no idea!

"Good morning to you Mr. Johnston. And yes, you did remember. It is Samantha."

"You're out and about pretty early this morning, aren't you, young lady?"

"Going to do some jogging. You know, stay in shape."

"I think I'm the one that needs to go jogging. I had trouble bending down to get the newspaper," he replied, now waving the *Washington Post* in the air as if it were a trophy.

"You're welcome to join me if you want," she invited, already knowing his answer.

"I'll have to pass on that one. Thanks, just the same."

"By the way, Mr. Johnston. This is my first morning to run since I moved in. Should I head in any particular direction? Any monumental views I should take in?"

"One direction is as good as another, Samantha. Just be careful. There was an early light rain this morning so it's going to be slightly wet and slippery out there."

"Thanks for the warning. See you later."

Walking slowly to the sidewalk passing in front of her home, Samantha took a few moments to stretch out her muscles. Now, which way to go? She could have flipped a coin, but her Georgetown University sweat-suit had no pockets. Being right handed she turned to the right and began to trot down the smooth, recently replaced sidewalk. Seemed like good enough reason for her.

*****

The man opened the passenger door of the charcoal gray Mercedes and quickly slid into the leather seat, totally obscured by the darkly tinted windows. He loosened his tie and sank back into his seat. Slightly out of breath and with a sigh of relief in his voice he said to the driver. "All done."

"Didn't take you long," came the reply.

"When you don't have to worry about breaking and entering, it goes pretty quick."

"It was open then?"

"Unlocked. Just like they said it would be. Wide open."

"Naive assholes. When are they *ever* going to learn?"

"*His* lesson starts in less than an hour. Then school's out," replied the passenger, smiling slightly at his little play on words.

"That clock on the dash right?"

The passenger glanced at his watch, then, back at the green, pulsating, numbers on the instrument panel. "To the second... and counting."

"German engineering. Hell of a car." Looking at the passenger's watch with the distinctive gold band, he asked. "Is that a real Rolex or a wannabe?"

"It's a Rolex. Remember I said, for the kind of work *I* do, they pay pretty good."

"They must."

"They do! Barbados, here I fuckin' come," he stated, dreaming of an island rum drink garnished with wedges of pineapple and orange to give him relief from the hot tropic sun.

*****

Brad turned a familiar corner on his daily route and stopped off at the neighborhood deli for his daily takeout order... a dose of quick energy. The sound of the bell tinkled loudly in his ears as the glass-paned door quickly slammed shut behind him. "Joey, the spring on that door is too damn tight. I'm surprised it doesn't break when it closes."

"Your running a little late this morning Brad," the older customer with the droopy jowls commented with a smile and a shake of his head as he passed him on his way out.

"It's a little slippery out there, Ralph. Had to slow down a little to be careful."

"Joey probably didn't hear you. He's somewhere in the back. Wouldn't do anything about it anyway. I've told him about the spring a dozen times."

"Maybe if he hears it once, from twelve people, he'll do something. There's power in numbers."

"Doubt he will."

"If I know Joey, you're right. Have a good one, Ralph."

Ralph was right. Joey wasn't in sight. Brad's statement had been yelled over the cacophony of voices, there already being a number of different, animated conversations between the regular, early morning customers. Some of them acknowledged Brad's entrance with a wave of the hand or a friendly grin. Nothing, but, nothing could interrupt their discussions.

He made a quick study of the clientele. Mostly professional people. Some young, on their way up. Others, older, possibly thinking about retiring in a few years. Regardless, these conversations were not the so-called power breakfasts where each person wanted something from the other. Those conversations were reserved for the fancy establishments where you needed reservations for both lunch and dinner... big deals and peoples' futures were made there. Here, people just enjoyed themselves and got caught up on the latest news and sports. Monday morning quarterbacks were a dime a dozen.

Joey's Delicatessen, owned and operated by Joey Salmon, had been there for years and was one of Brad's favorite places. Years ago, it had been opened as an ice cream parlor by Joey's father, but, had been changed over the years to one of the area's best deli restaurants. Overhead, the original ceiling fans lazily made their hypnotic, rhythmic turns. They were anchored to the embossed brass ceiling, now aged with a patina revealing an unusual design. Crown moldings, milled with a rarely seen profile, and carved, statuesque white columns, shining like they were still wet from the most recent covering of paint, seemed to lend it support. The black and white checkered marble flooring was cracked and aged from years of use. Scratch marks were visible in its polished surface from years of metal footed chairs and tables, having red and white checkered cloths, being moved about. Dejavu of years gone by. Ones, to which a large extent, would be worth returning to.

The parlor had been renovated in the early eighties into a booming deli business, the tablecloths, although new, the only remembrance of its original appearance. People really liked Joey. The food was really good and not too expensive. It was the kind of place to go after a Friday or Saturday night movie. There was a comfortable counter which would seat nearly twenty people at one time on armless chrome stools, padded with maroon vinyl. The large brass, antique Cappuccino machine held a place of prominence at one end, the foaming hot brew still available for a dollar and worth every penny. The counter itself was wooden and newly installed. There was also an attractive dining area that seated about 60 people, maybe 70, but it was a bit crowded with that number.

Didn't matter. People came here now from areas as far away as northern Virginia and Baltimore, normally on their way home from work or during the lunch hour for the scrumptious omelets or to pick up the legendary sandwiches offered as carryout. A meal in themselves. And, every bit as good as The Stage or Carnegie in New York City. A variety of breads baked daily in ovens, out of sight in the rear, are piled high with the best deli meats and freshest vegetables available.

You were greeted with cheers by your friends or family when you entered a room holding a bag with Joey's logo on it. Each day, they had a limited number of specials and you better get there early because they went awful fast at dinner time.

With a pat on the back or a high five, Brad acknowledged all the familiar faces seated at the counter, sipping the piping hot coffee and finishing off their breakfasts. They all knew him. And, he knew most of them. A prominent partner in a DC law firm chatting with a brick mason doing construction work near by. It was a great place. All dressed in their attire for the day. From thousand dollar suits to paint-stained work clothes. Conversing about the more important things in life such as the Skins playing their last season at RFK Stadium before John Kent Cook moved them to their new facility.

As he approached the last seat at the counter, Brad put his arm affectionately around the shoulder of one of his favorite regulars, giving him a playful squeeze. His antics were rewarded with a wide grin from Gus, one of Joey's many, long-standing customers. Probably his best customer. Every weekday, as far back as Brad could remember, Gus saved the same stool for him to sit on while waiting for his hot bagels. They'd become good friends and during the ten or so minutes he spent in the deli each morning, they'd converse about whatever was on their minds, the subject seemingly not mattering one iota.

"Gus, my man. How we doin' this fine morning?" asked Brad grabbing the rock hard biceps and sitting down.

Gus Triandos was a large, muscular Greek man in his late forties. He was six foot two inches tall, weighed in the neighborhood of two hundred twenty five pounds and claimed to have only eight percent body fat. No one knew that to be true for certain. But, then, no one was going to argue the point with him. His dancing eyes, set deep in his boyish face framed by thick, black, curly hair, were a light blue and his full mouth broadened slightly as he smiled and brushed the crumbs from Brad's stool. Gus had owned a string of thriving, body-building centers in the city for nearly twenty years. Beginning with the original center near the Silver Spring beltway exit, he'd added nine more in Maryland and Virginia, spotting them along the heavily traveled roadway surrounding DC. His physical appearance served as a testimony for their use.

"Good morning my man. Running a little late aren't you. I'll have you know I beat the shit out of three people to save you this seat."

"At the same time?"

"One was alone. Two were together. They were easy."

"Single guy give you some trouble did he?"

"To the point that I had to hit the son-of-a-bitch with his God damned cane."

"Guy had a bad leg huh?"

"Hell no. *He was blind as a bat.*"

"Gus, you're too damn much. You're a real trip." replied Brad laughing. "By the way, how's Sanderson doing?"

"He's supposed to play this weekend if his hamstring pull continues to improve. He's getting lots of physical therapy. His knee is probably eighty five percent. He was afraid that last pass route he took across the middle was his last. With the hit he took from the linebacker, it damn sure could've been."

Sanderson played wide receiver for the Skins. He was currently going through extensive physical rehab under the watchful eye of Gus, the weight trainer for the team. He'd been given the position five years ago in return for a small salary and game tickets. The salary wasn't important. The tickets, a premium commodity in the DC area on game day, were.

"Not a hundred percent?"

"Let's just say... he has a damaged wheel but the damn tire is a long way from being flat."

"Hell of a way with words, Gus. Where the hell is Joey?"

"Saw you coming in the door and went to the back to get your morning bagels. You eat those damn things every morning don't you and you never get constipated? They lay in my stomach like a load of Al's bricks over there," he said, motioning towards the mason standing to leave. "I eat one of those and I can't shit for a week."

"I get them whenever I can. They're the best I've ever had. Even better than in New York City. And, they don't constipate me. I love 'em."

"I've never had New York bagels, but, I don't doubt you're right. They can't produce anything that's worth a shit. Christ. Look at the Jets this year."

"They're after the first round draft choice next year."

"I think they've got it wrapped up."

Brad noticed the old, Philco, black and white television above Gus's head displaying the sports news. *Sorta nostalgic,* Brad thought. *Was it even possible to buy a black and white television today?* Brad had no idea. Regardless, on its screen was a familiar face to say the least. The Coach of the US Ski Team. Older than when they had first met, but certainly recognizable.

"That's ironic as hell. Just before coming in here, I was thinking about him."

"Who?"

"Him," replied Brad, pointing to the screen.

Before answering Brad, Gus turned and jokingly yelled to the back of the deli, "Hey, Joey. Get out here and fix the damn color on this relic, will ya please. And, don't forget Brad's bagels." Turning to Brad he continued. "Who is he?"

"Tony Carlisimo. He was my Coach on the US Ski Team."

"When you won the gold? Hell, he must have been pretty young back then to be a Head Coach."

"Thirty six."

"*Damn*. Name sounds Italian. He even looks it."

"Born and raised in Italy. A town somewhere near the foothills of the Alps, I think he said Bolzano but I'm not sure."

"Probably where he learned to ski."

"You're right and he's *damn* proud of it. He still thinks that the only skiers in the world that are worth a damn, learned in the Alps."

"Well, I'd say you were fair, winning the gold and all that shit. In all the time we've known each other, you've never told me. Where the hell did you learn?"

"Shit. Where else? The Alps. The Southern Alps."

Gus, not being a geography buff, asked. "The ones in Italy? Just like him?"

"Not exactly. The Southern Alps are in New Zealand."

"You're shittin' me? You lived there?"

"No I'm not. And, yes I did, to answer both your questions. Tony and I still joke about it all the time."

"You guys still stay in touch after all these years."

"By phone most of the time. Hell, we were friends before he was my coach. I met him my freshman year in high school. He was *real* close to my dad."

"Don't tell me. They met when your father operated on him at some time, right?"

"Wrong. Good guess though. They met through my father's association with the team, but, not as a surgeon. He'd developed a binding system to help prevent injuries. They eventually bought it. Hell, the whole damn world ending up buying it. He was a brilliant man."

"Sounds like it."

"Tony was a *damn good* friend of my dad. Guess what he did?"

"What's that?"

"He promised my father, who was close to death at the time, not to tell me if he died, until after I completed my Olympic competition. That takes a *hell* of a friend to do that."

"Your dad knew how much it meant to you. It takes a *hell* of a father... to make the request."

"That he was. One *hell* of a father."

*****

Samantha Sawyer was enjoying her new neighborhood unaware of a lurking problem as she continued her morning jog. She had no idea where she was, where she had been, or for that matter, where she was headed. She was enthralled with some of the most unique, turn of the century architecture she had ever seen. Intriguing designs. Gorgeous stained glass windows. She found herself straining to see through the windows, wishing she good get a real glimpse of the interiors.

She noticed the weathered brass plaques on some of the brick and stone buildings dating back over a hundred years. The plaques denoted them as part of the Historical Society and would save them from future demolition, an eventual fate, as time went on, which would befall most of the others. Progress sometimes could be shameful.

As she eyed another Historical Society building it happened. She tripped over something and landed head first on the manicured lawn in front of the building. Not one to swear very often, she said the "S" word under her breath anyway. "Shit."

She jumped up quickly, completely embarrassed and hoped that no one had seen her clumsy fall. Or, heard her. She looked behind her for the cause. She'd stumbled over the raised and cracked concrete. She quickly surmised the stately oak tree was at fault. As old as the building at which she had been looking, the roots of the ancient tree had grown so large they were beginning to break up the sidewalk.

She glanced at the front of her jogging suit. It had changed to a much deeper color. It was wet. Not damp. Wet. The sweat shirt acted like a sponge against the grass, soaking up the moisture from the pre-dawn rain as if preparing for a crossing of the Sahara. Her hands went quickly to her face to brush away her tousled hair.

Looking up into the expanse of the oak tree she saw the curious face of a squirrel looking down at her, chattering loudly. She had obviously interrupted his chores, especially that of scourging for acorns and burying them for the winter months. He was shaking his tail and loudly scolding her for the act of clumsiness which had interrupted his activities.

"Sorry," she mouthed up to the squirrel, smiled and trotted off down the street.

At the end of the street she saw a small building with "Joey's" written in lighted, neon script across the side and above the parked cars in the lot. What kind of place was this? Didn't matter. It would have a washroom and at this point, that's what held her interest.

She slowed down her jogging pace and now approached the front window, the Busch Bavarian sign, revealing the familiar mountain scene, lighted and hung well above eye-level. She saw her reflection in the glass. Hair messed up. Dirt on her face. Stained and wet clothing. She looked so bad there was no way she would enter, even to go to the rest-room. Samantha Sawyer didn't want anyone to see her looking like this.

"God," she uttered under her breath. Another swear word and in less than five minutes. And, this time, it was the "G" word. She left the window hurriedly wanting to get back home as quickly as possible. She knew the streets in certain parts of DC and the surrounding area were built on circles. Because of this, a mere trip around the *block,* could turn into a real adventure. Not to worry. She would simply retrace the route she had taken. Turning and heading up the street, in the direction from which she had come, she hoped the squirrel was off burying his bounty some place.

*****

"Did you see that?" asked Gus.

"See what?" replied Brad.

"That girl at the front window. You didn't see her?"

" 'fraid I didn't." The sportscast was just ending. "What about her?"

"Hell of a looker, Brad. One *hell* of a looker."

"You know me Gus. Don't have the time for that kind of stuff. I'm on a mission."

"That's the best one I've heard in a while. You've always got some rich bitch hangin' on your arm. Brad, get serious. I've heard there are tons of women after your ass."

"That's the point. *They're after me*. I haven't found one yet that *I'd consider* going after."

"You'd change your mind in a heartbeat if you'd seen her. Looked like she was a jogger like you. Took off the same way you're headed. Probably catch up with her if you wanted to."

"Don't think so."

"Don't think you could catch her or don't think you'd want to?"

"Take your pick. Where the hell is Joey?" Brad questioned, trying to change the subject.

"Here they are Brad," said Joey coming through the swinging doors of the kitchen in the nick of time. He was holding up a bag of warm, fresh bagels bearing the familiar "Joey's" logo on its side.

"Thanks, Joey. You put the creme cheese and raspberry jam in there?" Brad asked, taking the bag from him.

"Do I *ever* forget?"

"Great. Put it on my tab until Saturday. I don't even have time to eat one here. I'm already late."

"So I noticed."

"He doesn't have to go," interjected Gus. "He just wants to chase down that honey that was staring in the window a minute ago."

"What honey?"

"For Chrissakes, you missed her too? You guys never notice the finer things in life."

"Some girl who, according to Gus here, is going to replace Lady Godiva at her next public appearance," said Brad. "She was going to come in until she saw this shady character sitting here drooling."

"Lady Godiva. We should be so lucky," proclaimed Gus. "Can you imagine some nude broad riding horseback on the streets of Washington, DC? The politicians in this burg would go nuts, especially our horny President."

"God Gus, give it a break. Go lift some weights or something." Brad said laughing. "Got to run, guys. By the way, Gus. I don't think a piece of masking tape with your name on it can reserve that stool for you tomorrow morning, can it Joey?"

Looking down, Joey spotted the two inch wide by four inch long strip of masking tape fastened to the chrome. On it was written in block letters, *Don't Cuss, This One's For Gus.* How long's *that* been there?" asked Joey.

"Judging by the faded letters and turned up edges of the tape, quite a while I'd say. Wouldn't you, Gus?" asked Brad standing up and turning to leave. He would let Gus and Joey have the looming discussion without him.

As he was leaving, Brad heard the national weather forecast being projected over the ABC television network. Snowstorms were expected in the higher elevations of Colorado and Utah. *Lucky bastards,* he thought.

Brad, with Joey's bagels in hand, again began to jog up the street. He couldn't be certain, but he thought he caught a glimpse of the now infamous Lady Godiva turning a corner about two blocks distance away. No matter. He didn't have the time to chase her and he was headed in the other direction. His thoughts immediately returned to the discussion he had with Gus about actually living in New Zealand. It was quite an experience.

In 1975, at the age of 35, Brad's father, who was an avid skier, had taken a hiatus from his medical practice on the outskirts of Denver, Colorado. He took a position to teach some medical courses at the University of Canterbury in Christchurch, New Zealand. The year before, his father had suffered through reconstructive knee surgery as the result of a skiing accident. He realized the injury could have been prevented with better equipment.

While in New Zealand teaching, he developed a revolutionary ski binding system. It allowed the skier to change the settings of the bindings himself as terrain and weather conditions dictated. The new binding system was licensed to all the leading equipment manufactures in the world and made Doctor Bill Claxton a very wealthy man.

Brad had the typical nine year old's reluctance about the move to New Zealand. He was in a foreign country where all his classmates, not him, talked funny and they played "dumb" things like soccer and rugby instead of baseball. They did play football, but, there was no resemblance to the game as it was played in Colorado. His feelings, however, were tempered by his parents telling him it was only a temporary move and he would probably be returning to his friends and the familiar surroundings of Colorado within a few months. No one in the family anticipated they would be spending the next three years in New Zealand. He quickly adjusted to his new life, however, with the help of the parents of one of his new friends, Evan McCardy.

As difficult as it was, the move proved much easier on Brad than on his sister, three years his senior. She was soon to enter her teenage years and begin dating. Chantal, his sister, was entirely against the move from the get-go. Although not allowed to date until her thirteenth birthday, she'd "left the love of her life" behind in Colorado. She'd never see Tommy again and would never allow her parents to forget what they'd done to their only daughter. It just wasn't *fair* to be up-rooted at this time in her life.

She was placed in an environment where everything was different than she was accustomed to. How dare they? Coming from a very good and expensive private school in Colorado, in Christchurch she found herself behind in studies for her age, something even her parents weren't pleased with, but, for different reasons. All that money and she was behind. New Zealand, apparently took the education of its youth more seriously than the States. As if her accent wasn't hindrance enough, her wardrobe was totally wrong and she stuck out like a sore thumb amongst her classmates in the school she attended. They weren't the foreigners, she was. And, she hated it.

Then, it happened. No sooner had her parents bought her the proper dress attire, than *William* appeared on the scene. A year older, and *much* wiser as a result, he was willing to take a chance on this very attractive, twelve year old, blonde, bombshell from the United States. Chantal was awe struck that an "older man" would show her any interest. William quickly replaced the love of her life back in Denver. Tommy who?

Chantal's life had just flip-flopped one hundred and eighty degrees for the better. She joined the school's cheerleader squad and became an instant success, her popularity growing daily. She'd even caught onto the local jargon for burgers and a Coke. Her life was back in full swing and she was enjoying it to the extent her parents would allow. Denver where?

*****

Retracing her route from the deli had not proven easy. Samantha glanced around as she jogged home, not recognizing anything. She had made a wrong turn somewhere. But, where? Looking ahead, she saw a man that would have all the answers she needed.

"Excuse me," she said as she approached the mailman. "Could you please help me?"

He was in his mid-fifties, slender from the daily walking of his route, black and wore the customary US Postal Service gray-blue with black shoes appearing to have rubber soles two inches thick. As he turned smiling, his white teeth flashed against his black face.

"I don't sell stamps miss." Then, with apparent concern after surveying the damage the fall had done to Sam, he asked. *"What happened to you*?"

"Long story and, *do I look like I'm in the need of a stamp*?"

"Sorry, miss."

"No. *I'm* sorry. Sincerely. I *shouldn't have been* so abrupt with you. I'm just frustrated."

"What's the problem?"

"I guess the problem is that I don't know how to get home from here. Now, *that's really* embarrassing. It's just... I've *just* moved into the area and this is my first morning jogging. I'm lost, dirty and wet from a fall, and would like to get home to clean myself up. Maybe, if I had a stamp, I could put it on my forehead and mail myself home," she concluded trying to make light of the situation.

The mailman laughed and after calming Samantha down, found out her address and gave her explicit directions of how to get home. She was on his route so he knew exactly where she lived. He'd even described her house.

She apologized once again, thanking him for the help, turned and jogged off, again back in the same direction from which she'd come.

*****

Brad took a swipe at his headband with his forearm as he jogged at a steady clip further along his route. It was damp from perspiration. His thoughts returned to the weather report he'd heard when leaving Joey's. New snow fall in Colorado and Utah. Cold weather. Skiing. Those lucky bastards. His thoughts, as if drawn by an unknown magnet, returned to his earlier family days.

During the family's stay in New Zealand, Brad's mother did not work. It was more important to make certain her children were comfortable in their new environment. She did so by keeping Brad and his sister very involved in their school work and introducing them to sports and other extracurricular activities.

Brad was first introduced to snow skiing by his mother and father while living there. This was *his* sport from day one. It didn't seem as though Brad could ever get enough of the slopes. Living in Christchurch, New Zealand had been one of the most pleasurable times of Brad's life. As busy as his father was teaching three classes at the nearby university and conducting his research and development of the ski binding system, there was always time for skiing.

A short distance to the west of Christchurch were the Southern Alps and the majestic Mount Cook. It was the tallest peak in New Zealand, rising 12,349 feet above sea level and virtually snow covered throughout the year. Most people, Brad found, knew very little about New Zealand. He also became aware that the majority of New Zealanders, preferred it to remain that way.

Brad often was questioned about learning to ski in "such a remote" area. His reply was, "it certainly beats waiting in the long lift lines at some of the resort areas of the United States, like Aspen, Sun Valley or Stowe." People commented, "I'm not even certain where New Zealand is, let alone that it has decent mountains for skiing."

As was his nature in dealing with such people, Brad carefully attempted to have them, in their own minds, solve their short comings. He would kindly ask them a series of questions, in reality offering them the answers at the same time. He would carefully lead them down a path to the conclusion that New Zealand offered some of the best skiing in the world.

During his father's tenure at the University of Canterbury, the family returned to the United States, but only infrequently. While these trips were intended more for business than pleasure, Brad became introduced to the Dillon, Colorado area. It was in the midst of a snow ski region commonly referred to as the "Summit", named after the Colorado county. Resorts such as Breckinridge, Copper Mountain, Vail, Keystone and Arapaho Basin were all within an hours drive. He became familiar with the resorts and their numerous ski slopes; each presenting a different type of challenge. He quickly ascertained that they all had a uniqueness and collectively offered some of the best skiing in the world.

Smaller resorts were pocketed throughout the area and the "powder" snow was renown as providing some of the most excellent conditions anywhere. His first encounter with powder revealed that it's virtually impossible to make a snowball. The snow was, in essence, dry. At his age, he felt it important to build a fortress from snow as well as ski on it. Never did he give a thought to the scientific rationale of why both could not be simultaneously accomplished. Over the years, he gradually inherited a love for powder and still enjoyed the thrill of skiing virtually waist deep, only the tips of his skis visible.

He became particularly fond of one resort which offered night skiing on parts of its mountain. At that age, he wasn't a morning person. The night skiing allowed him the opportunity to advance his skills since the slopes were not as crowded as during daylight hours. This was the arena which set Brad's life in motion. He became fast, agile and daring. His expertise progressed to the point of the 1988 Olympic Games and an eventual Gold Medal.

Brad's thoughts, as he jogged along toting the carryout bag, were interrupted by the sounds of a squirrel high above in an ancient oak tree. Stopping to look up, Brad spotted him. There he was. Perched on a branch, squawking up a storm and flapping his tail wildly.

"You're really pissed about something aren't you fella." Looking to his right Brad noticed the indentations on the manicured lawn. Obvious, someone had fallen. And, not too long ago. Some of the grass had been damaged where the person had put their hands in an effort to break their fall. The torn up sod reminded Brad of two large divots created by a couple of futile, wedge shots on a plush golf course fairway.

Looking back at the squirrel, Brad said, "I'll bet whoever did this is the one that has you so upset. When I leave, you can come on down here and try some of this." He reached into the bag and ripped off a piece from one of the bagels, placing it on the raised and cracked sidewalk. He then resumed his paced run up the street. Turning around, he saw the squirrel pick up the piece of bagel and scurry back up the tree. He *wasn't* going to bury that goodie... he was too hungry.

A mail truck passed him going in the opposite direction enroute to some destination in the neighborhood. The driver was obviously happy, lip-singing a song coming from the small portable radio perched on the dashboard, his white teeth clearly visible against his black face as he smiled in a wide grin.

*****

Samantha couldn't believe it. Either she couldn't follow directions worth a damn or she hadn't listened carefully enough to the mailman's detailed instructions. Didn't really matter at this point. She was still lost, and getting tired of jogging. It *was* boring. And, *frustrating*. She found herself wishing Mr. Johnston had come along. At least he'd know the way home. Might even make a good chapter in his next book.

Looking ahead, she noticed a young man jogging, with apparent ease, across the intersection. Maybe, he'd be able to help her. He probably lives somewhere close by and would recognize her street. She didn't know if she could catch him, but, she was certainly going to try. He must have been jogging for years to maintain the speed he's going.

*****

Brad checked the traffic long before arriving at the intersection. The only thing he noticed was a distant woman jogger, her pony tail flapping in the wind. Brad wondered if was Gus's Lady Godiva. He immediately dismissed it from his mind. She wouldn't be coming from that direction unless she was lost. And, of course, that was highly unlikely.

Brad turned his attention to the Norwegian Maple trees lining both sides of the street ahead of him, their branches becoming more barren with each passing day. Two weeks earlier, a row of a sixty foot diameter balls of bright yellow leaves provided a majestic contrast to an early morning blue sky. The only Maple leaves Brad had seen larger were those on the Canadian National Flag. Brad noticed a break in the straight row of enormous single-ball topiaries. One was missing and had been replaced with another, trying in a never ending saga to achieve the same grandeur. The symmetry of the line was forever broken due to a lightning strike from a violent, summer storm passing through the area.

It wouldn't be long now and colder weather would be upon everyone in the DC area. Problem though. This area never received enough snowfall to cover winter's harvesting of the beautiful fall foliage which made the area look alive... and livable. His mind drifted to the beauty of winter, resorts, and, of course, skiing.

In the summer of 1978, the Claxton family had moved back to Denver. The design of the ski bindings was complete and the prototypes were produced in Wellington, New Zealand. Brad's mother, Natasha, a name that

Brad was going to suggest for his first daughter, used her experiences as a CPA to help set up the family business. The manufacturing business was established in New Zealand, because the import-export laws were more favorable.

Brad returned to the Denver area and began his freshman year of high school. Over the next four years, Brad became the most noteworthy high school snow skier in Colorado history. Later, he attended the University of Colorado on scholarship, studying pre-med to follow in his father's footsteps and become an orthopedic surgeon. That's when a close friend of his father, named Tony Carlisimo, suggested to Brad he try out for the United States Ski Team. The story of the 1988 Olympics is history.

His sister, Chantal, graduated from high school in 1980 and entered Colorado State University. There, she met her husband, the soon to be Doctor Phillip A. Bowers. In 1984, she received a Bachelor of Arts degree and Phil, three years older, graduated the same year and began his internship at the Greater Denver Hospital. He planned after one year to take a residency in internal medicine. The couple were married in a June wedding in 1986.

As sibling relationships go, Brad and Chantal were closer than normal. She attended the Olympics in Calgary and witnessed Brad's fateful accident. It was a small blessing she was there since she'd helped Brad return to Denver in time for their father's funeral. After the funeral, as family and friends gathered at the Claxton estate, Brad told Chantal he had changed his mind about being an orthopedic surgeon. Concerned, she reminded her brother, "you always wanted to be a doctor like Dad." Shocked by her brother's pronouncement she asked, "why have you suddenly changed your mind?"

Chantal would never forget the answer to her question. "I didn't say I wasn't going to be a doctor," Brad replied, "I'm changing to internal medicine and research because of Dad. I *will* find a cure for cancer."

Brad's decision became the driving force of his life.

*****

This guy has to be some sort of athlete, thought Samantha as she determinedly pushed herself even harder. Her attempt to catch up with the other jogger seemed as futile as finding her damn house. Looking down the front of her sweat shirt she was able to read *ATHLETIC DEPARTMENT* and realized she had *no* business wearing it. She certainly didn't feel like an athlete at all. Right about now she'd prefer to be home taking a luxurious, hot bubble bath. The guy in front of her was still almost a block away. While she was starting to catch up with him, she had no idea how long she could maintain the killer pace. She was struggling. Whoever claimed they enjoyed running, had *no idea* what a good time *really* was.

Maybe, she should just stop and ask for directions. No, not after all this! She was more determined than ever. She was going to catch this guy or die trying, even if she had to follow him through the front door of wherever he lived.

*****

The driver violently hit the steering wheel with his balled up fist. Looking at the clock on the dashboard tick away the last few minutes of what soon could become a bungled job he growled, "Where is this *damn* guy. *For Christ's sake*. He's almost *twenty* minutes late now," he said, checking out his watch this time.

"I see him coming," said the passenger finally. "What the hell's he carrying in the fuckin' bag?"

"His damn morning bagels. This is going to be close," he added looking at the dashboard once again.

Noticing the driver turn the key in the ignition, he asked. "*What the hell are you doin'*?"

"I have to start rolling. Can't be sittin' here at curbside when this thing goes off." The Benz's engine started quietly. Not bothering to check traffic, the driver slowly inched the parked Mercedes into motion and swung out into the street towards the row of townhouses. "I think we're going to need some luck on this one."

"If you had your shit together on this guy, he'd already be inside. *Jesus*, I can't believe this shit. I used to think you guys knew what the fuck you were doin'."

"We've been at this for over three God damn weeks. He's *never* been this late before." He continued driving slowly ahead, looking at dash board clock again. "How accurate is that damn thing of yours."

"*More accurate than your fuckin' information on this guy's schedule.* I've used the same kind before and it's plus or minus five seconds on accuracy."

"Damn, this is too close for me," the driver said, his heart beginning to pound in his chest.

*****

Brad continued to jog at his normal pace, the brown bag swinging freely from his hand. Oblivious to Samantha's struggle to catch up with him, taking place less than a block behind him, Brad approached his townhouse. He noticed what appeared to be a black embassy town car approaching toward him from further down the street.

Common cars in the Washington, DC area. He'd seen many embassy town cars before, most of which were black or dark gray Mercedes. Four doors and large. Weird, diplomatic license plates, probably coded to conceal the nationality. It wasn't normal for one to be in his neighborhood though, especially, this time of the day. In the overcast, early morning light, he could barely make out the letters of the oval shaped plate. *AMWQRS*. As usual, it didn't mean a damn thing to him.

He thought he heard someone yelling to get his attention, but, never turned around to acknowledge the source. He was already late and behind schedule. As Brad started up the four steps to his townhouse, he imagined the aroma of the freshly brewed coffee steaming on his kitchen counter. Instead, he was greeted by an explosion and a large flash of light.

*****

Her mouth dry from her exertion, Samantha made an attempt to stop the young man before he entered the townhouse. "Hold it. Hey. Before you go in, I have a question for you," she tried to yell, but, it came out as a hoarse whisper.

He hadn't heard her. After all this agony. He didn't hear her. He was going inside and she was still lost. *I'll just knock on his door and ask him.* Then, something happened.

A deafening sound accompanied the explosion blowing off the front of the townhouse. The force knocked the young man backwards, propelling him against the large tree by the street. He lay there, motionless. Large stone pieces of the structure were flung high into the air, landing on the car parked at curbside. Pieces of the once stately townhouse were falling all around Samantha. She realized she was ducking, her arms held over her head for protection.

With her heart in her throat, she paid little attention to the Mercedes as it sped past her. She no longer remembered her tiredness as her adrenaline kicked in and she raced over to help him. She finally had caught up with him!

*****

"Do you think he could live through that?" asked the driver.

"I *don't* think it's possible that anything could live through that kind of explosion. *Christ*, it blew his ass all the way to the street," answered the passenger. "*You saw it*. There would've been no question if he'd *just* gotten inside the *damn* door before it went. He'd *damn* sure be dead."

"But, *he didn't*. Stranger things have happened. For your sake, I hope you're right. You know they don't like fuck-ups. You should have used an electronic detonator you dumb ass. Then you'd have been sure he was inside."

"Don't *sit over there* and try to tell me how to do my fucking job you dumb asshole. Do you want trace evidence of the damn detonator in case the arson squad checks?"

"No. Of course not."

"That's why the acidic fuse is the best way to go. The acid eats all its housing and then blows. Nothing left that's traceable. *The son of a bitch was just late. And, that's your department you arrogant bastard.*"

"You're right. I'm sorry. We'll check his status a little later," came back the somber reply. "Hopefully, at the morgue."

---- Chapter Two ----

John moved slowly down the narrow, burgundy-carpeted isle, making certain not to bang his laptop against the first class, fabric covered high-backed seats. He was trying to match the number on his boarding pass to those dimly lit on the overhead bulkheads. The interior of the Boeing 747 was much larger than the aircraft he flew on hopping around from one location to the other in the States. This was definitely not a commuter flight, John having arrived two hours earlier on one from Melbourne.

It was crowded, probably sold out, as was normal for this particular flight from Canberra to Los Angeles. The flight originated in Wellington, New Zealand arriving nearly an hour earlier. Passengers with business in the Australian capital had deplaned, flooding into the airport and, now, final boarding for the long flight to LA was underway.

As he followed the slow moving pack of people in front of him his eyes gazed about the cabin. What a mix, but one you learn to expect on international flights. He approached a smartly dressed fight attendant in her mid twenties, standing to one side and leaning over one of the large, over-stuffed seats. She was offering seating assistance for storage of carry-ons, seating assignments and refreshments to passengers. John wondered how many languages she could speak. Probably four or five fluently not to mention the most important, as he viewed her from the side, she was damned attractive and well built.

John finally arrived at his row, stowed his carry-on luggage in the overhead and made his way to his seat assignment. From further back in the aircraft, in a familiar, English accent came a voice.

"John? John Sipel?"

There could be many Johns on board, or Ralphs, Bills or Bobs *but, not many John Sipels*. He quickly looked back in the Business Section of the aircraft and spotted the voice, his arms crisscrossing in a waving motion. *Son of a bitch, Evan McCardy. What the hell was he doing here?* Acknowledging him, John picked his way back to the next section in the cabin. After making some arrangements with other passengers, aided by another flight attendant, John shook Evan's hand and plopped down in the seat next to him.

"Couldn't you get a seat any further back for Christ's sake? Maybe in tourist or even the luggage compartment?"

"You know me. I hate this flying crap. I've heard it's one of the safest places onboard."

"Who'd you hear that from, some survivor?" John mocked.

The plane was taxiing now, getting into position for takeoff, the flaps lazily moving up and down as the pilot gave them one final test. Evan was looking out one of the small, oval shaped windows that lined the interior of the aircraft. He didn't bother to answer John's last question but asked a couple of his own.

"Those damn windows are made out of plastic. Did you know that?"

"I'd heard it somewhere before."

Referring to the wings, he continued. "As big as they are, you'd think they'd just fall off. Wouldn't you? Look at the weight of those things bouncing up and down. What the hell holds 'em on?"

Realizing how nervous he was, John tried to change the subject. "You talking about the wings, or the flight attendant?"

Evan looked back at John with a confused look on his face, then looked again at the flight attendant and began to laugh. "I told you, I don't like to fly. You're going to have to put up with my rambling until we're safely in the air and on our way. I'm nervous as hell. As soon as the in-flight bar opens, I'll be fine."

"I'm looking forward to a drink myself. What the hell are you doing here? Shit, we could have made arrangements to fly together if I'd known you were coming down here."

"Personal business back home. It came up suddenly. Had to leave in a flash," he replied, in the English accent one gets accustomed to with New Zealanders.

"Speaking of flashes, do you think he's going to make it?"

"After what I've heard, I honestly don't know. You heard anything from anyone?"

"Nothing. One way or the other," came the reply. "It's been over two weeks."

The four turbofan engines roared, hurtling the 747 and its four hundred passengers down the runway. The aircraft lifted off and began climbing to an altitude of 39,000 feet which it would maintain at a speed of over 550 miles per hour during the long journey to LA.

John looked at his Rolex. Yes, they were right on time and should arrive in LA sixteen hours later.

*****

He entered the room and noticed the rather bland decor which was so typical of hospital rooms all over the world. Someday a hospital administrator would acknowledge the positive effect a bright, cheerful room can have on a patient.

Doctor Phillip Bowers had been in the room before, many times, conducting his rounds at the Georgetown Medical Center. The only change was the patients. He and Chantal left the Denver area in the fall of 1990 so he could establish a medical practice in Bethesda, Maryland. Chantal took a position as an assistant curator at the Smithsonian Institute in downtown DC.

He walked to the eighth floor window, tilted the blinds allowing the early morning light to flood the room and saw the Potomac River, meandering on its southeasterly course through the District of Columbia. A US Air, red-eye flight was flying above the river, snaking its way on final approach to Washington International. The tri-engine aircraft flew low over the 14th Street Bridge, treating its passengers to a bird's eye view of area landmarks such as the Capitol Building, the Washington Monument, and the Lincoln Memorial.

Staring, trance-like, at the landing plane, from the corner of his eye he noticed movement to his right. He turned quickly to look at Brad lying in bed. Nothing. No movement. Maybe it was his mind playing tricks on him because for weeks he had looked for *any* indication of improvement, no matter how slight. He checked the bedside monitor. No changes in the readings. He walked to the end of the bed, pulled the patient chart from its plastic jacket and began scanning it. There were new entries, but, none indicated any change. Replacing the chart, he noticed a slight movement of the sheet covering Brad's feet. This *was* real! Not imagined. He quickly went to the side of the bed, pushed the call button and placed his hand on Brad's shoulder, shaking it gently.

"Brad. Brad, can you hear me? Wake up. Brad."

"Yes, Doctor. What are you calling about," came the voice from the intercom behind the headboard.

"Get some ice in here fast," he ordered.

"Right away," the nurse replied.

"Brad wake up. Can you hear me?" Phil continued, still gently shaking the muscular shoulder.

Within seconds the nurse entered with some ice. She went to the side of the bed, placed the Styrofoam cup on the table beside Phil and as instructed, rubbed an ice cube across Brad's forehead.

Hoping the coldness would jar him into consciousness, Phil continued to massage Brad's hand. "Brad, wake up man. Give me a sign."

"I think his breathing is more regular," said the nurse excitedly. "And, we're getting an increase in heart rate on the monitor."

Glancing at the bright red, digital readout of the monitor Phil raised his voice. "Brad, if you can hear me squeeze my hand. Let me know, give me a sign. Brad, squeeze my hand. Please pal, do it." Thinking he felt some slight pressure, he continued. "Brad, don't be such a wuss. That wasn't a squeeze. Break my damn hand if you can!"

This time, the pressure was real. Not a hard squeeze, but, Phil definitely felt the effort. Phil's forehead broke out in a sweat and he could feel the dampness of perspiration under his arms. "He did it!" Phil said, more to himself, than anyone else. "Brad, that was good. Real good! Do it again!" Again, a responding pressure. His feet under the sheet moved again. "Great, now try to open those big blue eyes."

Phil anxiously stared at Brad's face as water from the melting ice cube trickled off his forehead down across the bridge of his nose. The facial muscles slowly began to twitch. Finally, a flutter of an eyelid. Then, slowly, ever so slowly, Brad's eyes began to open, wincing from the brightness of the overhead, neon lighting.

"Brad, try to focus. Do you know me? Focus, pal! Do you know who I am? Squeeze my hand if you know me?" Stronger pressure than before. "Squeeze again if you know me." Again, pressure. "Good. Now try to say my name. Say it," he ordered.

"Ph ....Ph.... Phil," Brad forced through parched lips.

"Now take your time. Try to collect your thoughts. Stay awake. Concentrate, Brad, on staying awake. Listen to my voice."

As his eyes closed again, Phil would've been concerned if not for Brad's arms and legs showing constant movement. Brad turned his head towards Phil. His eyes opened again, wider this time. He blinked, often at first, as his eyes became accustomed to the brightness and then, at a more normal rate. A good sign. His eyes moved away from Phil to the smiling face of the blonde nurse. Without moving his head, his eyes looked at her hand holding the ice cube, the action creating wrinkles in his forehead. He was becoming more alert. His lips parted slightly as he forced a weak smile, showing his gratitude. It was the best he could muster.

Turning his attention back to Phil and barely audible, he said, "Thirsty."

"What?" responded Phil, turning his head to hear better.

"I'm... so... thirsty," repeated Brad, the tip of his tongue trying to moisten his dry lips.

Reaching over to the cup on the table behind the nurse with a plastic spoon, Phil retrieved a small chip of ice. "Try this for now," he said, placing it in Brad's mouth. "Betty, please get some ginger ale in a cup with a straw," he said to the nurse.

Brad's eyes went back to the nurse as she removed the melting cube from his head and hastily left the side of the bed for the items the doctor had ordered. His eyes returned to Phil with a puzzled look.

"Brad, do you remember anything?"

Brad raised a tired, left arm, examining the limp hand as if making certain it was his. The hand went to his face, the fingers first touching the bandage and then massaging his eyes. Red from rubbing, his eyes returned to Phil. "What did you say?" he asked in a weak voice.

"Do you remember anything?"

"Remember anything? About what?" Brad responded, noticing the nurse returning.

"Take a sip of this, Brad," Phil said, taking the cup from the nurse and placing the straw between his lips. He noticed the ginger ale fill half the straw and then drain back into the cup. "Good try. Try again." On the second try, Brad felt the cool wetness enter his mouth and continued drinking until Phil removed the straw.

"I'm still thirsty. I feel like I... haven't had a drink in a week."

"Try two weeks, pal. Do you remember how you ended up here?"

"Where's here?" came the weak reply.

"The hospital."

Brad's face became blank, his eyes staring off in the distance, his mind trying to forge answers for questions not yet asked. "I'm in the hospital?"

"Afraid you are, pal."

Brad's confused expression matched his mind-set. "For what?"

To test his brother-in-law's legendary sense of good humor, Phil said, "Well, you're certainly not pregnant."

"That's a hell of a relief," said Brad, his speech becoming easier and forcing a grin. "I'd need an agent if I were, not a doctor."

"I see you're sense of humor is still intact."

"I don't see one thing funny about any of this," Brad said, his voice getting stronger by the second. You said something about... not drinking for two weeks. I've been here for two weeks?"

"A little over."

"Doin' what?"

"Absolutely nothing. Believe me. You've been completely knocked out."

"Phil, I'm confused as hell," Brad said, his hand moving to his forehead and touching the bandages as he closed his eyes.

"You don't remember anything? About jogging or getting home?"

Removing his hand, Brad began to organize his muddled thoughts, his eyes remaining tightly closed. "I...I was jogging. Went to the deli... like I do every morning I jog. Ralph was just leaving. Saw Gus as usual. And, Joey."

"Then what?" Phil coaxed from him.

Brad envisioned arriving at his townhouse and continued. "I ahhh... I got home. Was on the porch. I reached for the door knob." After a pause, he concluded. "That's it. That's... all I remember."

"Do you recall seeing anyone following you?"

Brad carefully tried to remember, his forehead pulled together in a frown as he tightly squinted his eyes. "I didn't see anyone. No one at all," he finally said with concern.

"No explosion?"

Astonished by Phil's latest question, Brad replied with one of his own. "There was an explosion? I don't think so. I remember everything. Like it happened this morning. If there was an explosion, I'd remember it."

"There was a humdinger, pal. A really *big* bang. Guess that's where your memory stops. Understandable that it would though. We were concerned with total amnesia, but, it appears your memory is good. A young woman was jogging about fifty yards behind you and saw the whole thing. Right as you reached the front door, your place blew all to hell."

"The townhouse?"

"Yep."

"Two weeks ago?"

"Yep," Phil repeated. "If it wasn't for the girl's quick actions and her call to 911, you might not be around. When you get right down to it, she probably saved your life. She told me the force of the explosion knocked you all the way from the porch, across the lawn, to the tree at curbside. You must've hit your head on it. Either the concussion of the blast or hitting your head on the tree put you in the coma."

"Damn. I... I don't remember any of it. Who was the girl?"

"Samantha Sawyer. She'd just moved into your neighborhood."

"I'd like to thank her for what she did."

"You'll get your chance. She's been coming here everyday since it happened. I guess she feels kind of responsible for you. She'll be in later today, I'm sure. But, for right now, I want you to take things slowly. I'm going to get the neurologist to run some tests on you and have Betty here," he said motioning towards the nurse, "do some reflex testing with you. Keep you awake for a while and functioning for a change. Are you hungry?"

"I hadn't really noticed before, but, I think so. I'm not quite sure yet."

"I'm going to put you on liquids for the time being to see how you respond. Soups, juices, Jello. That kind of thing. Keep it down and maintain those readings where I want them," he said pointing to the array of monitors at bedside, "and then I'll let you begin with something more substantial. I don't want to rush this." To the nurse he said, "Betty, have the television switched on in here. I want his mind awake and working."

"Right away, Doctor Bowers."

"Brad, I'm going to finish my rounds and then come back. Should be back in less than an hour. We'll continue where we left off. Ask me anything and I'll try to fill you in."

"Thanks, Phil."

"Brad, welcome back. And, don't forget where we left off."

"You got it."

*****

The phone on her desk was ringing off the hook. Shoeless and standing on her tip-toes she hurriedly crammed the last piece of documentation in the over-filled top drawer of the filing cabinet. *Where was the government Paper Reduction Act when you needed it?* It was the receipt for the latest artifacts she'd inventoried that morning on loan from the Egyptian government for the upcoming show, Treasures of the Nile. At least, she was involved in unpacking the items and got a close-up look at the priceless items from the various dynasties. The craftsmanship was fantastic.

Pushing the heavy drawer closed on its over-taxed rollers, she quickly moved across the short-napped, jade green carpet to the back side of her oak desk, reached over the stack of filing trays for the still ringing telephone and broke one of her freshly polished nails.

"Damn it," she said in disgust, looking at the splintered nail. She watched the phone cord sweep two neatly stacked piles of papers from her desktop to the floor, put the receiver to hear ear, and heard the familiar dial tone. They'd hung up!

"I don't believe it," she said to herself. Replacing the receiver on its cradle, she walked around the side of her desk, picked up the now disorganized pile of papers spread across the floor and placed them back on the desk. She flopped into the ladder back desk chair, gave a disenchanted sigh and began to suck on her throbbing finger. The telephone rang again.

"Hello, Assistant Curator's Office."

"Chantal?"

"It's me, hon. Why the call at this time of day?" she asked, the frustration of her first hour of work evident in her voice.

"Sounds like your not having a very good day. What's wrong?"

"Phil, you have no idea. I'm exhausted getting ready for the Treasures of the Nile showing. The shoes I picked up a Nordstrom's the other night are absolutely killing my feet. Someone just called and I broke a nail trying to get to the phone before they hung up. Need I go on?"

"Not really."

"That wasn't you on the phone that hung up, was it?"

"Not me," Phil fibbed, not wanting any part of the return conversation and knowing he would be blamed for all that had gone wrong with her day. "But, I think I'm going to make your day."

"You taking me to lunch at Joey's?"

"Nope."

"Your taking me to dinner then?"

"Nope."

"Then, what?"

"Brad woke up about ten minutes ago."

"What!! He's awake! Does he remember things?"

"Calm down. I only talked with him for about ten minutes. He's weak as hell, but, getting stronger. I ordered some tests. He remembers everything right up to the time of the explosion. Amnesia *isn't* going to be a problem."

"I'm coming over."

"Chantal honey, he's got to take it slow at first. I want him to get some strength together. Get something into his stomach."

"Your saying I shouldn't come? My brother's been in a coma for over two weeks and I shouldn't come? Phil, how..."

"Chantal, hold it a minute. Your husband agrees with you. However, Brad's doctor doesn't."

"They're one in the same."

"I know that. Honey, relax. I don't think there's going to be any problem. He's a little confused, but, remembers everything. He has to have a while to get stronger. Give him the day. Come over after you're finished at work, like normal. I'll tell him you wanted to come sooner. Believe me, he's going to be fine. The nurse already did some reflex testing and he passed with flying colors."

"I've waited for this day for so long, but, you're probably right. I'll be there when I get off. Maybe, a little sooner," she said, thinking of an early departure. "Phil?"

"What?"

"I'm sorry for being so ahhh..."

"Don't apologize. Just remember, the doctor knows best."

"So does the husband. Thanks for calling right away, honey."

"Anything for the girl I love. See you later. Bye."

"Bye, bye."

Chantal grabbed the pile of papers from her desk that she'd picked up from the floor and threw them into the air. As they fluttered their way back to the floor, she yelled, "Yes!" She knew her excited, spontaneous action just created a couple of hours of work, but, it didn't seem to matter. A minor problem, considering the weight that Phil's news had just lifted from her shoulders.

*****

As he entered, Phil held the eighth floor door open for the departing neurologist who'd completed his examination and was confident Brad was on his way to a complete recovery. He directed a thumbs-up sign at Phil, reinforcing his prognosis. Brad was alert, responsive, had no apparent amnesia, and was starving. All good signs, even the last one.

Phil noticed the television was turned off and asked, "Brad, you're supposed to be keeping your mind occupied with something. If not the television, something else."

"I'm not a Regis and Kathy Lee type of guy," he replied in a near normal voice. "It's about the only thing on right now. I'd be watching ESPN of CNN if the damn hospital would spring for cable. Besides, there's been so many doctors in and out of here, poking and punching me, you'd have to be dead not to have you're mind occupied."

"Sounds as if you're getting back to normal. You feeling okay?"

"I feel fine. Had a slight headache a little earlier, but, the neurologist said it was a normal reaction. I'm hungry as hell though. That soup and Jello entree didn't do much."

Phil read over the chart at the end of the bed and eyed the monitors. "Things look normal enough. Amazing," he said as he took Brad's blood pressure, "the mind is really something. I'm *going* to allow you to order lunch from the menu. Now Brad, *don't* over do it the first time you're on a normal diet because, *if you do*, I'll be the one ordering your dinner. Feel like talking a little?"

"I sure do. I've got a few questions. Early this morning when I woke up I wasn't that coherent. Maybe we can go over some of this again."

"Fire away, pal," Phil said, sliding a chair over to bedside.

"You said I was here because of an explosion. I don't remember any."

"Well, my friend, there was. A hell of a gas explosion."

"Gas caused it?"

"So they say. A young woman, I mentioned her to you this morning, found you and called 911."

"Samantha something right?"

"Your memory is back. Right. Samantha Sawyer. She probably saved your life. You were rushed to the ER here and admitted. You've been in a coma until about two hours ago," he said, looking at his watch. "You've pretty much recovered physically; but, I was actually more concerned about the mental part."

"No shit?" Brad said softly.

"No shit," Phil repeated. "That bandage on your forehead is a lot smaller now than when you came out of emergency. The girl saw everything. That blast *threw you* into that large oak tree in front, the one down by the street. There was a blood stain on it. Probably where you hit your head. Other than the gash it caused, and some minor scrapes and bruises, you looked normal. The concussion and the coma were the big problems."

Showing a little more patience and more interest in what Phil was explaining, Brad said, "I remember now. Vividly. I was within a few feet of my front door." With a puzzled look on his face and after some thought, he continued in a slow, determined voice. "That means I was thrown *almost fifty feet*."

"It's no wonder you were in a coma. Hell, you should be dead. Damn lucky as far as I can see."

"No argument there, that's for sure. How's mom taking this news?" Brad inquired, always his first concern since his father's death.

"She's here. Doing as well as can be expected, with her only son lying around in a coma. Chantal called her the minute she heard from me you were brought into the ER. Matter of fact, mom flew here the next day from Colorado."

"Knowing mom, I'd expect it."

"She's been staying with us since she arrived. We decided, because of your situation, to have Thanksgiving dinner at our place instead of at the estate in Colorado. My parents are flying in this afternoon and I have to pick them up at Washington International."

"Your dad's a pilot. Why didn't he just fly the lear jet?"

"It's in for a scheduled maintenance check on the engines. I'm taking the subway to the airport and catch a taxi to bring them back here. We're going to pick up Chantal and my car here, about seven. Chantal's been taking the subway to the Foggy Bottom Station every day and sits in the room with you until I finish up my work. She's probably going to be early today if I know her at all. I already called this morning and told her you were out of the coma. She wanted to come right over, but, I told her there were tests to be run and I wanted you to get some strength back. Looks like you have, pal."

"Can't wait to see her."

"My parents and I'll check the room after we get back to see how you're getting along. I'm going to be pretty busy the rest of the day, but, I'll see you later on this evening."

"Sounds good to me Phil, and thanks, friend, for looking after me. I'm sorry for being such a problem for you but I..."

"Don't apologize," Phil interrupted. "I'd more than likely be the same way if I were in your shoes. I know you must be confused as hell and you have two weeks to catch up on. A million questions! Don't worry. We'll get you the answers. And oh, you don't have a home anymore. The explosion caused major damage. For safety reasons, a wrecking crew tore down what was still standing. See ya at seven or so."

"That's just *great* news. I loved that place," Brad muttered as Phil left the room, thinking of his designer's efforts. He laid back and closed his eyes, trying to remember the details of what Phil had just told him. Putting news like this into perspective is no easy task. Makes a person drowsy.

*****

Samantha sat quietly, turning the pages of *Cosmopolitan,* but not concentrating on the articles in front of her. She'd been here nearly an hour and was constantly looking up from the magazine. Her mind was preoccupied with uncertainty. *Was she nervous?* Maybe just a tad because her imagination was running wild. Her fingers turned another page which hadn't been read.

Brad had dozed off, but, started to wake up when he heard the shuffling of paper, causing him to open his eyes slightly. Peering through sleepy eyes, he focused on the most gorgeous girl he'd ever seen. Seated in the chair facing him, he looked at the curves of her long, slender legs, crossed while she was reading. Unaware her skirt had inched up to her thighs, she made a wonderful sight for a sick patient. She was slender. Her body, what he could see of it, appeared hard, in a feminine sort of way. Probably one hell of a jogger. Brad found it difficult to keep his eyes off the long auburn hair that flowed dramatically over her squared shoulders As she noticed Brad looking at her, she lowered the magazine to her lap.

With a body that should never be covered with clothes, the girl was fabulous. *What a figure. Dyn-o-mite!* After staring, for what Brad thought was an eternity, he finally asked, "Am I supposed to take some medicine or something?"

The time had come. Samantha had thought at length about their first conversation. If, in fact, there was ever to be one. She'd found out a lot about this young man, the one she'd desperately tried to catch that morning jogging, and wanted very much for him to like her. She'd rehearsed in her mind what she thought he'd want to hear. Rehearsal was over. She was on stage in front of a live audience. And, she'd forgotten her lines. With disaster looming, in a southern drawl that would have made Daryl Zanuch, the producer of *"Gone With the Wind"* proud, she said, "I wouldn't know." She nervously continued, "I'm not your nurse. Or a doctor. Do you want me to get one for you?" She was still in a state of shock finally hearing his voice for the first time.

Brad was now growing concerned. *Brad, you do have amnesia? Is it happening? You better hope so. You have no idea who this gorgeous creature in front of you is.* He wanted to believe he did know her, but had forgotten. *Brad, this woman could melt frosted glass.* In the past, women have affected Brad, but never like this. He was thinking crazy thoughts all ready. Not answering her question and having some of his own, he asked. "What're you doing here?"

Mesmerized by his deep blue eyes for the first time, she stammered, "I'm ahhhhh... I'm in my final semester of law school at Georgetown University. My actual home is in Charleston, South Carolina." *This isn't going real well, Samantha. Your lines aren't fitting. He must think you're a nut case or something.*

That explains the accent. "No, you don't understand. What are you doing in this room?"

"Ohhh, visiting you." *That's obvious to him. Why would you say that.*

"Do I know you?" asked Brad, hoping like hell he did and that she'd stay for a while. Change that. God, let her stay forever.

"No, ahhhhh... not really. We've never... really met before."

Damn, you don't know her. "Then explain to me... why I would be visited by someone I've never met. Who are you?"

"I'm ahhh... Samantha Sawyer," she replied, a bit sheepishly and giving her lower lip a small bite. *Samantha, he has a nice voice.*

"You're Samantha Sawyer!" Brad exclaimed loudly. "Damn!"

In shock from his last statement, she stood, as if preparing to leave, and said, "I guess I shouldn't be here."

"No, no, no. Don't leave. You don't understand. Please, sit. I knew that a girl named Samantha Sawyer saved my life, but, didn't realize it was you. Never put the two together."

Sitting down on the edge of her chair, Samantha said, "I didn't exactly save your life."

"That's not what I heard this morning. I heard that if it weren't for your quick actions, I'd probably be dead."

"Ohh, I don't think so," she argued lamely with a sheepish grin on her face.

"Well, I do and you know what that dude over in China says."

"Who?" she asked, not really understanding.

"Confucius, or whatever the heck his name is. A proverb that goes something like, if you save someone's life, you're responsible for that person for the rest of yours."

"I really don't think I did anything out of the ordinary."

"You were the only one there that saw or did anything weren't you?"

"As far as I know, yes."

"Well, if you don't mind, how about giving me an eyewitness account. I'll be the judge of whether you saved my life. Okay?"

"Okay. Where do I start?"

"Wherever you please."

"Okay. I was jogging like you were. Well, not really, you're much better than I am. I saw the horrible explosion and what it did to you. I called 911 from a cell phone in a damaged red car parked along the curb."

"I didn't even see you. Where were you?" *How on God's green earth could you have missed her?*

"I was about a half a block behind you trying to catch up. I even yelled to you just before the accident." *Now he's probably wondering why you were trying to catch him. That didn't come out the way you rehearsed it.*

"Why were you trying to catch up with me?" *If you'd only known. Shit, you could've slowed down, faked a fall, anything.*

"Nothing that important. Just wanted some directions. I was lost," she said, completely embarrassed.

"Lost?" he asked, disappointed at the response.

"I'm sorry. I don't really want to go into that now. It was kind of an embarrassing situation."

"Okay. Go ahead with the story."

"Okay. Where was I? Oh, I was holding your head in my lap, trying to stop the bleeding, when the ambulance arrived and took you to the emergency room. That's it," she concluded.

"That's all there is?"

"Well, yes. Other than, I've been checking on you every day for over two weeks to see how you're doing and everyday, it was the same story, no change. Until today that is. I certainly didn't mean to alarm you and hope you don't mind me being here. I was concerned for you and, besides, your sister Chantal and her husband, Dr. Phil, said it would be okay. The doctors told me today, after I arrived from my classes at school, that you'd come out of the coma. I just wanted to hear your voice to make sure for myself. I'll ahhhhh...go if you want me to." *You "just wanted to hear his voice." How stupid can you sound, Samantha?*

He took less than a nanosecond to reply to her last words. "No, no don't go! Please." He'd been watching this ravishing beauty as she recounted the episode and would do anything, short of tackling her, to have her remain. Hell, he might even do that. *Why don't you just plead with her to stay, Brad. Not a real macho approach. A girl that you don't even know.* "I really wish you'd stay for a while so I could continue to talk. It may help me to remember and keep me from having a relapse." *That was a dumb thing to say. She'd see through that in a second.* He waited anxiously for her reply.

I think he's trying to get you to stay, Samantha. Even though you want to, it's time to shift gears. "The doctor didn't want me to stay too long and I promised I wouldn't. Maybe a couple of minutes more."

"What the heck do doctors know anyway? Minutes or decades, who's counting?" joked Brad. "You live up the street from me?"

"Yes. How did you know?" she asked with a slight smile on her face and her confidence growing with each word.

Brad was encouraged by the smile and in reply to her question said, "My brother-in-law, Dr. Bowers, mentioned something about it. I've never seen you around the neighborhood. How long have you lived there?" As she was about to say something, with a pained expression on his face, Brad let a groan escape through his clenched teeth. He prayed to all saints, even future ones, she wouldn't realize it was done on purpose for sympathy so she wouldn't leave.

"Oh my, you're in pain. Can I get anything for you, maybe a nurse?" she asked with genuine concern in her voice.

Grimacing, he moaned, "Well maybe, help me rearrange these damn pillows, if you could. They're really uncomfortable now."

"Stop trying to do it yourself. Let me help you with those," she responded as she got up and approached the side of the bed.

As she rose from the chair, Brad noticed she was probably five foot, nine inches tall and dressed in a short skirt, which vainly tried to cover her gorgeous ass. It didn't stand a chance. Her waist, at the point that the stylish silk blouse was tucked into the skirt was so small, Brad didn't even attempt a guess at a measurement. No sand was getting through that hour glass. The blouse, a solid emerald green color, was fashionably unbuttoned one more than the designer had intended. As Samantha reached across Brad to fluff the pillows on the far side of the bed, the whiteness of her full, rounded breasts became visible. Brad thanked the designer a thousand times over. Her perfume was driving him crazy. Noticing his eyes widening, she said, "I'm sorry. It would've been easier for you had I walked around to the other side of the bed. Is that any better now?"

"Yes, that's much better. Thank you."

"Good... but you know, I don't think you're up to all this conversation when only this morning you were totally comatose."

"Don't worry about it, I feel much better. By the way, I didn't thank you for calling 911 for me. You *really* held my head while the ambulance was coming? That's something. Me being a complete stranger. And, the concern *you've shown* by coming to the hospital. Thanks Samantha. I guess that Confucius guy was right. You feel responsible for my life."

"I'd do it again," she said, her full, sensuous lips breaking into a smile. "Brad, call me Sam, all of my close friends do." she said. "Is Brad short for Bradley?"

"Damn! I'm sorry. I never introduced myself to you! No, it's short for Bradford. Bradford Claxton. I haven't been called that for so long, I don't remember the last time. How much do I owe you for the clothes I messed up?"

"What do you mean?" she asked with a puzzled look on her face.

"Weren't you holding my head in your lap when I was bleeding? I must have ruined whatever you were wearing at the time. I insist on taking care of your expenses. That's the least I could do for you."

With a very pleasant laugh, she answered. "Don't be silly. You don't owe me anything. It was only something I wear to run in." As an afterthought, she added. "It was kind of messed up to begin with."

"Then dinner sometime after I'm out of here. I won't take no for an answer. Okay?"

She shyly responded. "We'll see. Right now, your main concern should be getting better and out of this hospital."

"Sam, you mentioned something about a cell phone in a damaged car out front. What kind of car was it?"

"I wasn't really paying that much attention to the car at the time. It was an older car. Red. I think a two-door with white interior. Why?"

"It was my '65 Mustang. Which, I cherish. How badly was it damaged?"

"I don't know. It didn't look in real good shape. I think some of the house, when it blew up, landed on it. The windows were smashed. The roof was collapsed. I had to squeeze through one side to reach the phone!"

Envisioning Sam squeezing though anything could caused his fantasies to start up again. He forced the vision from his mind. "I can't believe it. First the house is a disaster. Then, my car. I shouldn't have gotten out of bed that morning."

"I'm *glad* you got out of bed. If you hadn't, you'd have been inside and probably killed. I'd never have met you. By the way, I went jogging two days later and your car wasn't there. It must have been towed."

"That's great. I had some important papers in the trunk. No house, no car, and no answers," Brad said in disgust.

"Look at it this way Brad. You do have a new friend," Sam said soothingly as she placed her hand over his.

"Of course, you're right, Sam," he replied, the warmth of her touch rushing through his entire body. "And, thanks for being a friend. I only hope we become good friends."

"I think it might be possible. Dinner's on, if, you're still buying," Samantha quipped. *Perfect timing. Samantha, you are smooth. Real smooth.*

"That's a date, young lady from the South, and I'm going to hold you to it," Brad responded, determined to make it happen.

"I'd better be on my way before the doctors get angry and throw me out. I'll see you tomorrow afternoon," she promised as she stooped down and gave him a friendly peck on the cheek. She walked towards the door like a model down a runway lined with photographers. *Samantha, show him what you've got. Leave him with something to think about.*

Brad had seen women from a large part of the world during his traveling days with the US Ski Team. None could come close to Samantha Sawyer for pure beauty but, oddly enough, that wasn't even important to Brad any longer. More importantly, she was a very sweet person who was, it appeared, somewhat fond of him. He touched his cheek and looked at his finger tips. Crimson red. *Things don't get any better than this, Brad.*

*****

Chantal rounded the corner before the veneered elevator door closed behind her. Never, in her thirty-three years, could she remember being in a bigger hurry. The gentle breeze blew the long blonde hair away from the sides of her slender face. Dressed in a navy blue, business suit, her high heels accentuated the shapeliness of her calves above slender ankles.

She was nearly running now and paying no attention to the pinching agony of new shoes. Down the long corridor, past the nurse's station, around a custodian, she hurried on. She bumped into a metal cart being pushed from a room, made her apologies to the nurse's aid and finally arrived at the patient's room, one she'd entered far too many times over the last three weeks.

Brad's thoughts were still on Samantha Sawyer when Chantal entered the room, in obvious good spirits and a little out of breath. "Hi little brother. Howya feeling today?" she asked as she kicked off her shoes.

"Do I know you?" Brad said with a somber face. She'd stopped smiling and, instantly, registered disappointment. "I'm sorry sis, that was bad joke. Actually, I feel great. Get over here and gimme a big hug."

She nearly ran to the bed and kissed him on the cheek, grabbing both shoulders for a giant hug. "Bradford, I've been coming here everyday knowing *if* you woke up, you might not remember anything. You looked so *healthy*, but you just *wouldn't* wake up. Shoot, you looked worse in Calgary, but at least I could talk with you."

Brad saw her eyes well up and once the tears started, there was no hope. The last time she'd called him Bradford she'd been very upset with or about him. He couldn't recall which, but this time it was both and he was in deep trouble. Brad was never deliberately mean to his sister, only devilish. Searching for a way out of the situation he'd created, Brad began to laugh slightly as she continued to pout.

"What's so funny?" she demanded to know.

"Sis, how many times have I told you. The word "shoot" is merely the word shit spelled with two O's." He hoped this tactic would remove the threat of rain. Hell, he'd made her laugh at his outrageousness before. It had the same effect on her this time too.

"Brad, you haven't changed a bit," she responded hugging him again.

"Isn't Phil with you?" he asked.

"He's checking some tests done on you this afternoon. Said he'd be right along. Mal wanted to see the hospital's new laboratory set-up so Phil's giving him and Sibyl a quick tour. Brad, for me. Please, please try to get along with Mal. He's my *father-in-law* you know. He's really a nice guy when you get to know him."

"Sis, I *promise* I'll try. I have no problems with his wife, Sibyl, but *he* tends to rub me the wrong way."

Mal was a man with no apparent common sense, a transplanted Texan to Colorado Springs with a six year lay over at Harvard Medical School. He was naive enough to believe people called him Mal, short for Malcomb. Rumor had it that his name was short for malpractice. Regardless, he'd been involved in so many law suits he couldn't afford the insurance premiums, and so entered into the world of medical research.

Mal was a portly man. After picturing him in his mind, Brad quickly changed the image to porcine. His small eyes were set in a piggish face, highlighted by enormous cheeks and jowls. He'd have to lose a hundred and fifty pounds to return to a more respectable, two-chin appearance. His suit jackets looked painted on and he used touch, rather than sight, to fasten his Texas Long Horn belt buckle. The act of crossing his legs caused heavy breathing and he burped incessantly. And whether Mal wanted to own up to the guilt didn't matter. When no one in a room could identify the source of a foul odor, all knew it was Mal letting go one of his wicked SBD's, Silent But Deadlies.

Sibyl, on the other hand, was the complete opposite being petite and always dressed to perfection. She presented herself in a manner to maintain her status in the elite society of Colorado Springs. She was involved in many clubs, the Junior League, volunteer activities and had been president of the area's prestigious Bridge Club for years. She was a Master Player and well know around the world, traveling abroad to play in competitive tournaments. However, one incident tarnished an otherwise flawless reputation. She was rumored to have had an affair with one of the cadets at the United States Air Force Academy shortly after her marriage. With one look at Mal, who'd have blamed her?

The door to the room flew open, its knob hitting the wall. In a loud Texas drawl, which should've disappeared years ago, Mal bellowed. “Accident kind of cramped your style. Right boy?”

“Not really, sir. My time in bed is about the same now as before the accident.” Brad looked at Chantal and noticed a frown forming. As she held his hand, he continued. “Only one difference now. I'm alone.” After the last remark, Chantal's thumb dug hard into the back of Brad's hand.

After a small burp, Mal replied. “You're sure a party animal, boy.”

“Not really sir. How have you been getting along?” Brad asked pleasantly, now remembering his sister's request.

At that moment, the door opened again and the woman of Brad's life entered the room flanked by Sibyl. Brad's mother, Natasha, although two years older than her late husband, maintained her five foot, four inch body magnificently.

During her younger years, her long blonde hair surrounded a face of defined, classic beauty as it would blow slightly in the breeze. In later years, she'd wear her hair much shorter, adding an air of sophistication to her features. Her near-perfect figure always received wolf whistles from the men and stares of envy from the women at the Country Club pool. According to his mother, she “had not gained a pound since her days as a Hawkeye cheerleader at the University of Iowa”.

In 1960, she was a business major in her senior year when she met Brad's father, a pre-medical student in his junior year. They'd fallen in love quickly and married right after his mother's graduation. She took a position with a local CPA firm, her husband finishing medical school four years later.

Upon his graduation in 1965, the couple moved from Iowa City to Denver, Colorado, his mother taking a position with another CPA firm as Bill Claxton completed his residency as an orthopedic surgeon in a smaller hospital specializing in sports injuries.

The couple wanted to wait for children and tried to plan accordingly but, God had a couple of ideas of his own, ones that turned out for the best. When they decided to make the move from Iowa City to Colorado, Chantal was three years old and her mother was already seven months pregnant with Bradford.

Natasha was as beautiful as ever with her stylish blonde hair, stunning figure, unblemished skin and unforgettable smile. She was smartly dressed in a dazzling, sapphire blue suit, accented with simple, yet stunning, pearl jewelry. Her eyes had their normal, crystalline sparkle. "*Mom*, it's great to see you. I'm sorry I messed up plans for Thanksgiving dinner at home."

"Bradford, stop being silly. You *couldn't* help what happened," she said, bending to kiss and hug him. "Besides, I'm looking forward to a Holiday back east for a change anyway."

"How'd you get here from Chantal's house?" Brad inquired, realizing that in less than ten minutes, fifteen tops, his full first name had been used twice.

"Chantal called me from her gallery to tell me that you were out of the coma, but to wait until this evening to come. Later, I called a taxi, threw on some clothes and came down from New Market," she answered.

"Mom, it's not my gallery," Chantal jokingly corrected.

"Mom, you never look like you just *throw* on clothes. You look great," praised Brad.

The next hour or so was spent on reunion type of talk, the "remember-when, kind of stuff". There were discussions about the Smithsonian, Phil's practice, snow skiing in Colorado, Mal's research, and Samantha Sawyer.

About 8:30 everyone agreed they should leave and allow Brad to get a good night's rest. Oddly, Brad recalled, there was little discussion about the accident. After everyone left, he realized he was very tired and was not surprised he drifted off to sleep rather quickly. His thoughts immediately returned to Samantha. Beautiful! Even amnesia wouldn't make him forget her ... not that he wanted to.

---- Chapter Three ----

The noise from the busy corridor woke him early. Patients were supposed to get rest and quiet. If that's a correct assumption, he couldn't understand why the hospital staff continuously awoke people for blood pressure readings, medications, blood samples and a thousand other little things. It would seem they could pick a better time than 4:30 or 5:00 in the morning and, at least, do them *quietly*. But, it appears that nurses and interns always have a lot to discuss .... and, in loud voices.

Brad was angry with himself for not asking about Samantha's class schedule at Georgetown University. He had no idea when to expect her next and it was driving him a little crazy. He missed talking with this girl from Charleston, her southern accent adding to her charm. Just the thought of her put him in a near frenzy.

It was 9:30 AM and from what Brad had heard, he'd temporarily need a place to hang his hat. He had never realized that a major shift back to metropolitan living was in full force and that, consequently, housing in the area was in such high demand. This morning's real estate section of the *Post* didn't help much in his search either. He folded the newspaper and tossed it to the table near the window. He missed. He'd *never* make Washington's NBA team, the Bullets.

For the past three years, Phil was Brad's personal physician and until he regained his strength, Phil, simply put, wouldn't allow him to go anywhere. Phil, a stickler for details, would know every gram of Brad's food intake and use it as factor in determining a suitable release date. With the thought of release in mind, he'd already downed his selections from what the hospital mistakenly called the Breakfast Menu. He'd cleaned his plate.

Phil entered the room and noticed the clean plate on tray in front of Brad. With a broad smile on his face he said. “A little hungry after that tubular feeding, huh Brad? Ate all they had to offer and wanted seconds, so they tell me. That's a mighty good sign, pal.”

Brad replied, with a slight grin, “If I don't eat, you'll never let me out of here, willya Phil?”

“Correcto, buddy. Chantal would never forgive me if I discharged you too soon. I want you to stay here for a while for observation and get your strength back. All of the tests run have been read by the neurologist and he sees no problems. Personally, I doubt there'll be any relapse. The longer you're out of a coma, the less likely you'll go back into one. You noticed anything going on I should know about?"

"None. I've been up and about, not for long, three or four times this morning. The first time, I felt a little dizzy, but nothing like that since."

"That was probably because you got up too fast and aren't used to being on your feet. If it happens again, let me know. And, *Doctor Claxton*, you have to take it easy at first. You of all people should know that."

"What's up with the Doctor Claxton shit, Phil. No one calls me that. Only when their pissed about something?"

"Only that what they say about doctors being the worst patients is true. You're a *doctor*, Brad, or *did you forget*?"

"I haven't forgotten for Chissakes. What's the problem?"

"You weren't supposed to be out of bed, *Doctor*. I heard about your little unauthorized excursion this morning with the chair."

"Oh that. It was nothing. Sorry."

Brad had wanted to test his stamina so, without permission, he'd gotten out of bed for a little exercise, but, light headed, flopped into one of the two chairs facing the bed. Thanks to the hospital garb, his bare ass had touched the cold vinyl causing him to jump like a startled cat. No one had seen him, however, a nurse passing by his door had heard his yell of shock and entered the room. Laughing as she'd left, she couldn't wait to get to the nurse's station to relate the story to the staff.

"Speaking of excursions, is it necessary I be walked to the bathroom?" Brad asked trying to change the subject. "The nurses insist on following me instead of leading me. Phil, I may appear stupid, but, I saw in the mirror what I look like from behind in this damn gown. Can't they get their jollies at someone else's expense."

"Women seeing your ass never bothered you before. Getting a little private about your privates?"

"Give me a break."

"Relax. I already told them you don't need their help any more. You had any head aches or shooting pains through your head."

"No, just the light-headed feeling the first time this morning. Other than the pain in the ass this whole thing has become, no problems that I know of."

"You've lost a little weight but, I don't see that as a big problem. You continue devouring the food like you did this morning and your weight will be back up in a flash. Not bad for a hospital food, is it?"

"It's better now than when I did my residency here, but it could still use some improvement. They really do need to do something about the eggs. They taste okay but, just don't look right."

"You going to lodge another complaint, Doctor? What do you mean?"

"Phil, they looked like a couple of piss holes in a snow bank."

"I've had more than a few complaints about 'em, but none with your eloquence," Phil laughed and continued. "Your best bet is to order them scrambled. Then, they *may* resemble what you expect."

"I hate scrambled eggs," Brad joked.

"Brad, now is as good a time as any. I have some questions about the explosion that morning. They claim a gas leak from your furnace in the basement caused it," Phil stated hesitantly.

"What do you mean, they claim?"

"Did you smell any gas before you left to go jogging?"

"No. Not that I remember."

"It's been pretty warm this fall for the most part. I know you like to keep your house cool. Have you even turned on your furnace this year?"

"No. I even sleep with the windows open. During the day, I'm not even there, so why would I turn it on?"

"Did you leave windows open when you went to jog?"

"I think so. It was raining as I remember, but not hard enough to close them. By the way, I had that furnace serviced in October. Everything was fine then."

"How long were you gone that morning?"

"The normal. Probably one and a half hours," Brad replied and then corrected himself. "No, wait a minute. It was wet that morning and pretty slippery, so I took a little longer than normal. I was probably gone closer to two hours."

"That's interesting."

Brad could tell that something was bothering Phil at this point. "That's all you have to say, "that's interesting?" Christ, what the hell's going on?"

"Sorry Brad, I was thinking."

"I noticed. About what?"

"Your stove is electric. Right?"

"Right."

"The only gas you use is for heating?"

"Two for two."

"Hot water?"

"Electric."

"Bear with me for a minute." After some more thought, Phil continued. "How does gas from a recently serviced furnace and not turned on this season, build up enough to cause an explosion? Especially, in a house where the windows are open?"

"I don't know. Maybe some pipes were bad. Or connections."

"Brad, you just had it serviced last month. Do you honestly believe they wouldn't have noticed a bad pipe or connection?"

"Shit happens, Phil. Maybe they missed it. How long does it take for a pipe or connection to go bad? I sure as hell don't know. Do you? What the hell are you trying to say?"

"I'm not sure. You know, everyone is saying your house blew up, right?"

"I haven't talked to everyone. How the hell would I know what they're saying. Shit, I've barely talked to anyone since it happened."

"I know, I know. I went by your place the next day to salvage what I could for you. Something bothers me about the damages."

"What?"

"Yours is a townhouse with at least one unit on each side, correct?"

"Yeah. So what?"

"Your house didn't blow up, Brad. It blew out. Straight out."

"What the *hell's that* supposed to mean?"

"If the source was from gas accumulating in the basement, the direction of the blast would have been up. This was towards the front of the house. The basement area didn't look like a blast was centered there. The houses on each side weren't damaged much. If the blast was up in direction, the roof would have been blown off, but, it collapsed down, replacing the part blown out towards the street. I think the explosion originated on the first or second floor."

"Christ, Phil. What are you now? A damn explosives expert. What, on the first floor, or second floor for that matter, could possibly cause an explosion? Hell, Phil, you've been there a number of times and you know there's nothing at my place to blow up except gas."

"If that's right, then, what caused a first floor explosion or what ignited it?"

Brad was beginning to get the drift of this conversation and was not enthusiastic about its direction. He thought it should be brought out in the open to clear the air.

"Christ, Phil, it sounds like your suggesting it was a God damn bomb. Come on, Phil. Get real. You think I blew up my own house? Why? For insurance? Or maybe, I was pissed at the damn designer? Now there's a good reason. No it's not. I like my designer," he concluded adamantly.

"Of course not. I don't think any such thing. It's just been on my mind. Brad, I'm sorry. I guess I allowed my imagination to get away from me. Did you notice anything strange that morning before the blast? Anything at all, however slight?"

"You're *sorry*, but you're continuing this nonsense? You sound like a damn detective!"

"Hell, Brad, I owe it to you to continue. Strange things have happened since the explosion. For lack of a way to put it mildly, I'm going to say it outright. Sure, I'm concerned about your health. Christ, I'm your doctor. I'm just as concerned about your safety, because you're a damn good friend of mine, not to mention being my wife's brother."

"What are you saying? Someone's after me for God's sake. You're *way the hell* out in left field now, Phil. You don't even have a damn ticket to the ballpark. You're suggesting that someone is trying to *kill me* with a bomb? *Hell*, I never came out of the coma. I'm dreaming all this shit."

"Brad, think what you will, but try to hold your voice down a little. I don't want anyone to overhear what we're saying."

"You," Brad whispered, "don't want any of those bad guys out in the hall to know we're on to them, right? Or maybe, you don't want anyone to know how *God damn nuts you are*," he added, his voice rising.

"Look, *pal*, give me the damn *courtesy* of listening to what I have to say *before forming any opinions on my sanity. All right*?" Phil responded in the same manner, his voice rising.

"I'm sorry Phil. I don't quite know how to handle all this James Bond shit. Please, go ahead with your CIA, cloak and dagger theories. I'll listen."

"As I asked before. Do you remember *anything* at all out of the ordinary that morning?"

"Nothing at all, other than it was wet," Brad answered. A thought then entered Brad's mind that made him very uncomfortable. Something Samantha had said the day before. He continued slowly, picking his words carefully.

"Phil, assume *this* was a bomb. It would probably be on a timer of some sort. Right?"

"Are you asking your brother-in-law or are you asking an explosives expert?"

"Touché."

"Good possibility it would be on a timer of some sort," said Phil, his head nodding in agreement.

"That means, if it had not been wet that morning, I would have been right on schedule. Inside the house when it went off." The thought of how close he'd come to actually being killed, whether by accident or on purpose, finally struck home with the force of an out-of-control locomotive.

"You're starting to see what I'm talking about."

"Phil, what you're suggesting is no joking matter. It could be *real* serious," Brad said softly.

"I agree. Now you know why I'm concerned."

"You mean there's more?"

"You bet. I mentioned some odd things happening since the explosion."

"Right." Brad replied slowly, not certain he wanted to hear what was coming.

"Remember, you found out from Samantha your car was towed away."

"Yeah."

"It was apparently picked up by someone, towed up Wisconsin Avenue past the beltway and dumped off on a side street."

"Why?"

"Don't have the foggiest. The local police found it, checked the registration and contacted me through the hospital."

"That's weird."

"I'll say it's weird. I called Bernie over in Baltimore. Told him to pick it up and to make repairing it, his number one priority. I wanted it done when and if you woke up. By the way, he delivered it to me early this morning. Damn thing looks brand new. I know what that car means to you, Brad."

"Thanks a million. You know, Dad bought that car brand new in 1965 right after I was born and really loved it. We had some damn good times together in that car. I'm just happier than hell he left it to me in his will."

"I know how close you two were. Believe me, if anyone deserved something special from your dad, you did. What a sight that was at his funeral. You, barely able to move, bending over the casket and placing the Gold Medal you'd won around his neck to be buried with him."

"Let's not get sentimental here, okay." Returning to the conversation at hand, Brad asked. "What do you mean, the car was dumped on a side street. Why would anyone tow a car to another location and dump it?"

"If someone wanted to ransack the car, they couldn't very well do it in front of a house that just blew up."

"Blew out, you mean." Brad corrected and noticed Phil nod in agreement. "The car was ransacked then?"

"No. That's another strange thing. Everything was in tact. All of the stereo equipment, radio and even the cellular phone was still there."

"Damn. Maybe they were interrupted before they got a chance."

"Possible. It certainly wasn't kids doing this unless they stole a tow truck. The car couldn't be driven. What'd you have in the car?"

"Other than my briefcase with some notes from the research center, nothing of any importance. Hell, John could replace those for me in a matter of seconds. That son of a gun is something else on that computer. He's a real trip! If I didn't know him so well, I'd think he was crazy most of the time."

Brad's mind returned to when he'd re-enrolled at the University of Colorado after his father's death. John Sipel was his roommate at the Sigma Chi fraternity house, quickly becoming like a real blood brother to Brad and filling the void left by Bill Claxton's death. They did everything together; ate, skied and even studied together. The only time they weren't seen as a pair was while they attended classes. John pursued his computer science degree and Brad focused on becoming a medical doctor.

John would sit up 'til wee hours of the night in their room "playing" on his computer. However, playing wasn't what Brad thought of it. He'd tell John, "when you end up in jail for that shit, don't waste your one phone call on me to bail your ass out." John, simply, was a hacker. And, a *very* good one. He'd claim, "There hasn't been a system built I can't get into." Most people thought it was bravado, but, Brad knew better. Brad's only rule was that he never wanted to know which systems he'd cracked or the ones he was trying to. When John gained entry, there was always a loud "yes." This utterance would be followed by comments such as "no way," "holy shit," "look at that crap," or some other earth-shattering vocalization.

John took a position with the National Security Agency (NSA) at Fort Meade, Maryland only because, Brad believed, it had one of the largest computer complexes in the world. A better playground didn't exist for John to expand his knowledge. Brad never knew John's responsibilities at the agency, only that he'd advanced rapidly to a supervisory position due to his knowledge of computers and an uncanny ability to get along with people.

Brad knew the FBI was chartered for domestic problems and investigations, while the CIA handled foreign operations. Where NSA fit into the scheme of things, Brad never knew and never pressed the issue with John. It seemed to Brad there were only two choices, foreign and domestic, and both were filled.

The only time Brad was physically at NSA was to pick up John so they could catch a flight to Salt Lake City for some skiing. At the direction of a snap-to-attention MP, he'd driven around the entire complex pulling in front of one of the four gate houses. The place was mammoth and looked like a highly guarded prison, having three or four tiers of different types of fencing, apparently electronic in nature It was designed to keep people out, not in. The only entry or exit points were at the gate houses, or guardhouses as Brad preferred. NSA was doing something of a very secretive nature and on a very large scale.

John's career was on a constant upswing to the point that it was becoming a personal problem. His next promotion would take him away from the hands-on computer work, something he loved, and place him in a supervisory position. But, Brad had saved him from his boring fate by hiring him with the promise of complete control of the Center's computer operations. It wasn't a hard sell because, being best friends, each believed strongly in the other's abilities.

With input from directors of prestigious cancer research and treatment centers around the world, such as the Mayo Clinic, Johns Hopkins and Cambridge University in England, the two had spent many hours formulating the Center's standard operating procedures. Since the promise made at his father's gravesite, Brad felt that to expeditiously find a cure for Cancer, a central processor was necessary to pool global information.

However, a basic problem with the Center's operation had to be overcome. The cure, when found, had to be affordable to those in need of it. Therefore, the Center wanted subscribers whose main focus was on finding a cure, not the monetary rewards to be reaped once it was found. Established on the premise of a non-profit entity, the Center would maintain an overall data base of cancer research projects and disseminate the information to its subscribers, effectively reducing their costly duplication of effort and providing them with future guidance.

Monthly payments for the Center's services would come from the subscriber's existing sources such as research grants and private funding. Of major importance was the research community's ability to communicate and sell the concept to its members. Simply put, the more subscribers on-line with the non-profit operations of the Center, the less the monthly charge per subscriber. The money saved by the Center's inputs to the individual efforts would be more than ample to offset the costs. In return, the Center would maintain irrefutable records and documentation in accordance with FDA guidelines to speed up the approval cycle and reduce the resultant governmental price tag. Arrangements for streamlining the process had been made with the FDA and, once found, facilities had been earmarked for the cure's production.

Production and cost of the cure would be controlled by the Center with profits, held to a minimum, being distributed to subscribers on a pro-rata basis. The distribution of income realized by the facilities would hopefully be applied to research efforts of other diseases such as AIDS or MS for which the Center would, once again, be the focal point. But, from the get-go, the Center opened as a central processing point for the eradication of Cancer. This would remain its primary focus until the cure was discovered.

Funded in its entirety by the estate of the late Bill Claxton, in the fall of 1993, the Center became fully operational with some research centers and labs immediately becoming subscribers. Some were apprehensive and others were entirely against its inception because of professional jealousy, infringement of patent laws, copyrights and so forth. Big business was rearing its ugly head again, much the way it had during the Vietnam War. The war was a boom to the economy; but, what the country really needed was a good kick in its economic ass to shake off its lethargic approach to business problems. The politicians controlled the country's war involvement and were stuffing money into their pockets as fast as their greedy little fists could rake it in. John used to say, "there was two differences between a computer and a politician. First, a computer has a sincere personality and second, a computer provides information at a much cheaper cost."

Subscribers to the Center gradually increased, even the skeptics were won over, but, those adamant about protecting their financial interests continued to operate in an isolated mode. John was solely responsible for getting the Center on-line and installing the security measures for the system.

Brad's thoughts were interrupted by Phil rising from his chair. “Brad, I hope all of this is just a stretch of my imagination. It may well be, so let's keep what we've been talking about between the two of us. In the meantime, try to remember anything that might be important. By the way, I'm having a phone plugged in for you to make some calls if you want.”

“I should really give John a call at the Center to see what's going on. Thanks for the phone. Phil, you wouldn't happen to have Samantha Sawyer's number, would you?”

“That's a switch. Usually, it's women asking for your number. Showing a little interest of our own are we? No, I don't have it. Don't worry, you'll see her again,” he said and added teasingly, “eventually.”

“I'm not sure what's going on here Phil. I don't *ever* recall having this kind of feeling about someone. I'm really, I mean *really*, attracted to her.”

“You *must* be slippin' back and forgotten what she looks like,” Phil responded in disbelief. “She's a magnificent woman with a charming southern accent and lots of brains to boot. That's why you're attracted to her.”

“It's not just her looks Phil. It's her,” Brad responded slowly searching his memory for the right words. It's her... her whole persona. I adore the girl. And, I've only known her for one day. Is that normal?”

“It's love, pal. And, at first sight yet. It's possible you know,” Phil stated emphatically.

“*Bullshit*. Love at first sight. *That* never happens. Only in the movies,” Brad said defiantly. Then with concern he continued, “What if she doesn't feel the same way?”

“Well, pal, don't worry about it until you know it's a problem. Hell, it took Chantal and I about six months for it to sink in. It may take Samantha a while to realize the type of guy you are. When she does, you'll be okay. Is she stopping in today?”

“Yeah, she's supposed to be in after her law classes at Georgetown, but I don't know her schedule.”

“She'll show. Don't worry. I've got to run and finish up some things. By the way, I arranged for you to be released the Wednesday before Thanksgiving. A little sooner than I prefer, but what the hell, it's a holiday and if no complications set in, you should be ready. I expect you to be staying with Chantal and I at New Market. Your mother and my parents are there."

"I have to stay in here that long? Hell, I'm ready now."

"Slow and easy Brad," Phil reminded with a serious shake of his finger for Brad's benefit.

"Right. Thanks for the invite. If you let me out of here, I'll show up. I'm looking forward to it," Brad replied, thinking to himself of how enjoyable could a Thanksgiving dinner be looking across the table at Phil's burping dad.

Phil departed, leaving Brad to ponder their discussion. All Phil said appeared on the surface to be idiotic, but yet after mulling it over in his mind, an uncertainty remained in the back of Brad's mind. But, he soon rationalized there was no reason for him to be anyone's target, therefore, it was an accidental gas explosion. Plain and simple!

A candy striper entered his room with the promised telephone, placed it on the table within his reach and plugged it into the jack. Brad thought immediately of placing a call to information for a listing of Samantha Sawyer, but discarded the idea as a bad one, not wanting to appear aggressive. Instead, he dialed the number for the Center, hoping to get in touch with John.

*****

She sat, thumbing through the latest issue of Research Today, with the tips of her toes barely touching the floor because the desk chair was adjusted for someone much taller than her five foot, two inch height. She'd just hung up the phone, politely informing the caller they had a wrong number, when it rang again and a different button flashed on the phone system. Not realizing it was the Director's private line, she answered with a slight irritation to her voice.

"Center. How may I direct your call?" responded Abigail Hoffman.

She was a petite and slender blonde with a bust size that would look wonderfully sexy on a woman eight inches taller. Her voice echoed that of a young woman with a personality full of enthusiasm for life itself.

She was a joy to be around and the term, youthful exuberance, described her perfectly. In twenty-six years, she'd developed a well-disciplined, educated personality that suited the strict requirements of medical research.

She had worked side by side with John Sipel on data base development and maintenance. Thanks to their efforts, the Center had compiled an extensive data base. Over a period of months, they had also developed a warm, intimate relationship that possibly suggested marriage.

“Abbey, where's Susan?” Brad inquired about the Center's receptionist.

“Brad, is it really you?” she responded excitedly, her voice changing right on cue.

“Yes it is.”

“How are you feeling? Are you okay? When did...”

Brad interrupted the never ending string of questions. “I feel great. I'm fine, as far as I know. I woke up yesterday after the longest sleep of my life. Phil says he's going to release me the day before Thanksgiving. How come you're answering the phone now, not enough to keep you guys busy?”

“Oh yeah, sure. It's Thanksgiving, and Susan took some time off to go home to Wisconsin. She'll be back on Monday. You said she could have some time because it was going to be slow anyway. Remember?”

“You're right, I remember. I've just lost two weeks of time, that's all. Is John there?”

“He sure is, he just came in from the airport five minutes ago. Let me buzz him for you.”

“Airport?”

“Dulles Airport. His flight just arrived from LA about an hour ago. He called and told me he had some data from the research center in Melbourne and to meet him here.”

“Damn. That's right. I forgot about that trip. I was supposed to go with him. Did he take anyone else with him?”

“No, he went alone.”

“Hell, Abbey, you should've gone with him in my place. It'd have been good for both of you to get away together for a change.”

“Always trying to match us up, aren't you Brad?”

“You two are doing a pretty good job yourselves.”

“You think so, do you boss?” she replied humorously. “Let me buzz him for you.”

“Thanks, Abbey,” he said, picturing her trying to find the correct button on the large switchboard.

After about five buzzes, John finally answered, “Hello.”

"Christ, I take a couple of weeks off to get some rest and you leave the country on vacation. What the hell do you ..."

"*When the hell did you wake up* asshole?" John interrupted with a guffaw.

"Yesterday morning buddy," a smiling Brad replied.

"You're all right then? Everything going to be fine?"

"According to Phil, sounds like I'm fine. No amnesia, which was his biggest worry, aside from the coma. Only a small bandage on my forehead now."

"Jesus, man. You really had us all worried. If you could've seen the damage to your place. You're damn lucky you weren't inside."

Thinking of his discussion with Phil, Brad replied slowly, "Maybe, I was supposed to be."

"What the hell does that mean?"

"Nothing. Forget I said it. I'm not thinking too straight yet, missing two weeks and all. How was the trip to Melbourne?"

"The Australian Research Institute has decided to become subscribers. I think talking with Jennings from the Moffit Center in Tampa helped finalize their decision. He must have told them the amount of money we saved them. It appears the lab over there, or down there as you would say, is getting some good results. I have to put the information into the data base and have the BRT check it over. "

The BRT, short for Biological Research Team, is responsible for verification of data forwarded from centers around the world. As standard procedure, prior to any feedback being allowed from the Center's secure data base holdings, the team makes certain of the data's credibility. This was a fundamental part of the Center's protocol and allowed truly dedicated research professionals to compare notes.

"By the way," John continued, "I flew back with Evan. I didn't know he was going home. I got on the flight in Canberra and there he was. Told me his mother died suddenly and he had to go to Christchurch to take care of the arrangements and put the family property up for sale."

Evan McCardy was Brad's best friend when he attended school in New Zealand, a true New Zealander with the distinctive English accent to prove it. They learned to ski together with Brad's family, making frequent trips to the mountains west of Christchurch. Over the years, they maintained their friendship, Brad seeing him on trips back to New Zealand with his father.

Evan had graduated from the Victoria University of Wellington, entered the foreign service and, eventually, received the assignment he'd long been waiting for, the New Zealand Embassy staff in Washington DC. Living together again in the same city, their friendship flourished as if never interrupted.

"Damn. Sorry to hear about his mother. I really liked her. She was a big help to me getting used to some strange surroundings when I first moved down there."

"He thought you'd be upset. Evan and I were discussing," John continued, "your being in the hospital and our plans for next month. We decided, if you weren't available, everyone would cancel the trip and do it next year instead. I think Phil feels the same way. It wouldn't be the same with just the three of us."

"Look, John. Evan chose last year, you chose in '94 and Phil got his choice the year before. It's mine this year and I've been working on this for about nine months. You guys aren't getting out of it that easy. I feel fine and, shit, by the time Christmas rolls around, I'll be ready for anything."

Each year on a rotating basis, one of the four would select something adventurous to do between Christmas and New Years. Whatever the choice was, the other three agreed to do, providing it was legal of course. In '93 Phil decided to go to Aruba skin diving. In 1994 John decided they'd go winter camping in Utah, the finale, a bungee jump off a bridge spanning a gorge. Last year, Evan joined the group, the newcomer showing his enthusiasm for the ritual by selecting Acapulco for sky-diving and para-sailing.

"I've been pretty limited," Brad continued, "because of the new rules you guys agreed to. I can't believe wives and girl friends *have* to be included. I *know* Chantal pressured Phil into that one. And, you, *you wuss*, probably got some pressure from Abbey. Evan and Terri still together as a couple?"

"In a big way, she's the one going with him."

"Jesus Christ. How did he *ever* get hooked up with the Ambassador's daughter?"

"Have no idea. She thinks quite a lot of him though."

"She must be nuts. I think that guys opening line with a girl is "pull my finger" and then, it's down hill from there."

"You know these diplomats. They have a way with women."

"I guess they do, but, Terri is so refined, having traveled all over the world with her parents filling appointed positions for the New Zealand government. He's so... hell, I don't know. How Evan latched onto her, I'll never know. Shit, his *own* choice for last year's trip scared the hell out of him. He's got a *real* phobia about heights now."

"Serves his ass right," said John with a short laugh. "I don't think I appreciate heights anymore myself. Speaking of this trip, we have a total of seven people committed already."

"What do you mean, seven people?"

"There are three couples and a singleton. You, Brad. What're you doing about some female companionship for the trip?"

"Don't worry about me, John. I've just got to make up my mind which socialite I think I can stand for more than one night at a time," Brad lied with a superficial smirk.

"That's great. Just don't wait to long to pick one. When are you going to get out of the hospital and where are you going to stay?"

"Phil thinks I can be discharged Wednesday, the day before Thanksgiving. I'm going to try and talk him into an earlier release, but, you know him. I'll probably stay with he and Chantal out in New Market until I can find a place closer in."

"You're welcome to stay with me in Laurel if you want. It's closer than New Market. The only problem is that damn Parkway traffic every morning and then the north bound on the beltway. It's a real bitch."

"Thanks for the offer, buddy. I'll consider it. Why don't you and Abbey take off and go do something. That data insertion can wait."

"Would like to, but, you know how Abbey is. If there's something to do, she won't rest 'til it's done."

"Yea, I know. She's great but, she works too damn hard. I'm going to change the locks on the Center so she can't get in for about a week."

"That's the only way to keep her out."

"I think this trip next month will do her a lot of good. Talk to you later."

"Glad to hear you're up and around, buddy. See you later."

"You bet."

*****

He flipped the still-lighted cigarette into the shrubbery amongst the dry leaves blown there by swirling winds and entered the Georgetown Medical Center. If his actions started a fire, tough shit. He followed the signs hung from the ceiling and proceeded to the door with the words, ***Admitting Office,*** printed in bold, black letters across its glass. The gray, metal framed door closed silently behind him.

"May I help you?" came the question from Ms. Patterson, her name visible on the hospital identification badge pinned above the left, breast pocket of her white uniform.

"I certainly hope so. I just flew in from Europe and was on my way to the hotel. As we passed the hospital, I realized this is where he's admitted. I believe he's in a private room. I don't have time right now to see him, but thought I would stop and check to see when visitin' hours are. The cab's waitin' out front."

"Visiting hours are at the discretion of the doctor for patients in private rooms. They depend on how well the patient is progressing."

"I know, Ms. Patterson. I've been travelin', so don't really know how well he's doin'. That's why I came to the admittin' office instead of going to the information counter out in the lobby. I'm kinda in a hurry and thought you could get the answer faster."

"What's the patient's name?" she asked, trying not to make the man uneasy about his speaking problem. He appeared to be well educated and was dressed to kill, so his omission of the letter "g" at ends of words was probably a childhood habit.

"Bradford Claxton."

"Oh, you mean Brad, Doctor Bower's brother-in-law?"

"Yes. I believe so. You know him."

"Only for about five years or so is all. He did his residency here before he opened up the Center downtown. Real nice doctor. Shame what happened to him. Let me pull his record up on the screen." Ms. Patterson's fingers moved quickly over the keyboard, "his status was just updated. It says here, he's allowed visitor's between 9 AM and 9 PM."

"Any change in his condition? The last I heard, he was still in the coma."

"Appears he's doing much better from what's on the screen. Yesterday was my day off, so I missed the excitement."

"What excitement?"

"He came out of the coma yesterday morning. That's great news! Doctor Bowers has tentatively scheduled him for release the Wednesday before Thanksgiving. That would be the 27th. I'll give you directions if you want to go up. He's on the eighth floor."

"Like I said, I don't have the time right now. I'll stop by later today. Thanks for your help."

"You're welcome. May I tell him who stopped by?"

Pretending not to hear Ms. Patterson's parting question, he left Admissions in search of a phone. Eyeing the bank of telephones across the lobby, he walked at a brisk pace towards them. His route took him past the entrance to the lobby where, in his haste, he ran head-on into a young woman, also in a hurry.

"Sorry miss. I didn't see you comin' in the door."

"It's okay," she said. "It was probably my fault anyway. I'm just in a hurry."

"Let me get that for you," he said, reaching to the floor and retrieving a large canvas satchel. "What the heck is this? It weighs a ton."

"Oh, it's called a book bag."

"You must have a lot of books in it," he said, laughing and handing it to her.

"I do. Thank you sir and, I'm sorry I wasn't watching where I was going."

"No problem," he said as she left in a rush.

He continued on his route and, in the privacy of the phone booth, dialed the number and anxiously waited for someone to pick up on the other end.

"Hello," came the answer to the ringing.

"The son of a bitch is going to make it. He came out of the fuckin' coma yesterday and he's bein' released on Wednesday the 27th. I can't believe this shit. This is my first miss in fifteen years."

"Shit," came the reply.

"Guess my trip to Barbados is on hold until it's taken care of."

"I would think so. Remember, the follow-up attempt is at our discretion. At least, the *when* of it. It's *got* to look like an accident and we can't have a bunch of them happening to the same guy too close together. Might raise some eyebrows."

"I agree."

"We'll let you know. You stay in contact with him to find out where he's going to be staying. He sure as hell can't go home. You took care of that."

"You got it! Remember what I said? If he lives, I'll set it right and at *no* cost."

"Money isn't that important to us. Getting rid of him is."

"He's fucked up my reputation. Now, this one's on me."

"Have it your way. I don't give a shit. But, *you bide your time* until we say it's a go."

"I understand," he answered hanging up the phone. He glanced at his Rolex and pulled a Camel from a half empty pack, placing it between his lips as he left the phone booth. Passing by a No Smoking sign, he lit up and then, walked through the automatic front doors to a light drizzle outside. "Lucky bastard. I'm really pissed," he whispered, sucking a mouthful of smoke into his lungs.

*****

With all the liquids Phil prescribed for him, he slowly got out of bed and picked his way carefully to the bathroom. Taking his second leak in an hour, he glanced into the chrome framed mirror over the sink. He didn't look half bad considering what he'd been through. His blonde hair needed a visit to Smitty, his barber, and he looked as if he hadn't shaved in a couple of days, and he was right. Prior to coming out of the coma, someone must have done it for him. Who? He had no idea, but, they sure hadn't been around lately. Flushing the toilet and moving in front of the mirror he noticed his drawn and ashen colored face.

From behind him, came a soft "Hello." He turned around and found Samantha standing in the open entrance, her heavy book bag casually thrown to the floor next to the bedside chair. Brad was still dressed in the hospital gown and his buns were bare-assed naked.

"I'm sorry Brad, I should have knocked. I didn't mean to embarrass you. I can come back later if you want."

"No, no, no. I'm fine if you're okay," Brad floundered, but continued. "Sam, do you know how to snow ski? Ahh...don't bother to answer that, Sam. You're right. I was flustered. I was trying to change the subject."

"Okay," she chuckled. "Did you ask me if I knew how to snow ski?"

"Yes, I did. Do you?"

"Well, for what it's worth, I do now how to ski. Daddy taught me in the North Carolina mountains. He took me a couple of times to the Poconos in Pennsylvania and I loved it even more. The slopes there are wonderful!"

"Really. That's great," said Brad, thinking the mountains she'd skied wouldn't make good foothills for the slopes he'd conquered.

"By the way Brad, Daddy wanted me to ask if you're the guy they show every week in front of that sports show on television. The guy crashing in the Olympics?"

"Yeah, that's me. My claim to fame."

"Sounds like a sore subject."

"Still is in a way, but I'm getting over it. Heck, that was in 1988. I guess I *should* be over the incident by now. It's just, some idiot was on the run and avoiding the guy caused the accident which ended my competitive racing career."

"1988?"

"Yeah, why?"

"How old are you?"

"Thirty. Just had the big one."

"Geez Brad, I thought you'd be closer to my age."

"And what might that be?"

"Twenty-four."

"You thought I was twenty-four?"

"Not exactly, but close to it."

"You mean twenty-two?" Brad asked smiling.

"No, more like twenty-five. You look a lot younger than thirty. Especially from behind. Whoops," she said, moving her hand to cover her growing smile.

"Ahhhhh ha. How long were you standing there?"

"Long enough to get an appreciation for your... age."

"My age?"

"I have a twenty-five year old brother and he looks similar. Well, you know what I mean."

"Believe me, Sam, I completely understand," Brad said in jest. "So, when are you going skiing with me?"

"I don't know. When did you have in mind?"

"Leave here on December 23rd, spend Christmas with my mother in Denver and go skiing the 26th through the 28th. On some real mountains."

"You're kidding, right?"

"I thought you'd say that."

"You're not kidding?"

"Right. To a point."

"What do you mean?"

"I don't know why so don't ask me, but, I feel very comfortable around you. What I'm suggesting is, we should have dinner when I get out of here. Get to know each other better. Then, maybe go skiing in West Virginia for the day. It should be opening soon if it's not already open. Just spend some time together. Meanwhile, you can get acquainted with the people also going on the trip to Colorado. See what you think of them. You already know Phil and Chantal. They're going. No commitments now. Kind of a wait and see what develops sorta thing." After a thoughtful pause, Brad continued, "I can't believe I suggested this. There must be something wrong in my head. I'm not normally this forward with..."

"Sounds like a good plan to me, Brad," she responded, breaking in on his feeble apology. "First things first though. Let's concentrate on getting you out of here."

"Great!" Brad said, trying not let Sam know how happy he was. As she stepped aside, Brad tripped over the book bag, and, walking backwards, made his way to the bed, climbed in and pulled up the sheet around him Samantha had a deep smile on her face highlighted by a small dimple on her left cheek.

"What's so funny?" he asked, only his head and fingers holding the sheet across his neck visible.

"It's just that you're a very shy person behind all the bravado and I like that very much."

Changing the subject, Brad wanted to continue the discussion about the trip. "Sam, getting back to what we were talking about. You know, getting to know each other better."

"Yes."

"I'm going to my sister's place in New Market for Thanksgiving dinner. Would you like to go along? My mother is here from Colorado and it'd be a good chance for you to meet the most important person in my life."

"You mean you'll be out of here by then?"

"Phil says the Wednesday before. It may be sooner, if I have anything to say about it."

"I'd love to go, Brad. I was going home but, at the last second my parents decided to fly to Europe. As a result, I don't have any definite plans other than staying around here."

Looking at the young woman seated in front of him, Brad knew what he saw in her. There could only be *one* Samantha. Intelligent, beautiful and a gorgeous shape. For the first time in his life, the young, handsome, suave, prestigious and rich doctor was unsure of himself. She was the first woman he *really* desired, and not just sexually, but rather as a companion as well. All the other women, and there had been plenty, had chased him. He'd simply allowed himself to be caught. This was *much* different. "Sam, let me ask you a stupid question."

"All right."

"Why are we, seemingly, getting along so well when we don't know much about each other?"

"Well, Brad. In my case, I know more about you than you might think."

"How so?"

"First, I wanted to know more about you because I was concerned about the accident. Then, the more I found out from Phil and Chantal and the rest of the staff here, the more curious I became. I continued to ask questions. It was like, you know, everything I found out was about a good person. I just wanted to know more."

"Just how much *did* you find out?"

"Enough to know you're sincere in all that you say and do. From what I've heard, I feel that you can be trusted and that's very important. You're a very good, loving person and one that has an unending drive to accomplish his goals. You founded and own the Center downtown. You loved your father very much and would do anything to make your mother proud of you and happy. You're a great brother and brother-in-law. And finally, you haven't been seriously involved with a girl in years because of your devotion to the Center. Quite frankly, I haven't found one negative thing about you."

"Sounds like you've been talking to Chantal and Phil. You realize, anything they have to say about me is highly prejudiced in my favor. Maybe not, the more I think about it," he said, a frown taking the place of a smile.

"See? What you just did shows you're very sensitive about what people think of you. I said earlier that you were shy. We *both* know that's not the truth. *Shy* people don't accomplish the types of things you have. *Confident* people do. You just keep it hidden as part of the facade you display to people you don't know well. Mr. Innocence. You don't have to rely on others to give you an A+ Brad. Your actions do it for you and, I guess, they intrigue me."

"Honest?"

"See?"

"Okay, okay, I see what you mean. And, by the way, I don't really own the Center. Well, theoretically, I guess I do, but, I don't really look at it in that light. The Center was established to find a cure for Cancer, not to make money. The charges to subscribers only cover the salaries to the staff and myself and normal operating expenses. It's non-profit, so, you see, any owner wouldn't get anything out of it except personal satisfaction."

"Do you get satisfaction from it?" Sam asked.

"Not that much yet, but it'll come. It's just taking a tad longer than I'd hoped it would."

"I really don't have a clue about what's done there. Only, that you're attempting to find a cure for Cancer."

"That's true as far as you've taken it. I'm not attempting to find a cure. I *am* finding a cure. A better way of putting it might be, I'm helping others find a cure."

"See? There's that confidence that I mentioned oozing out again. You mentioned it was taking longer than you'd anticipated. Are you working on a time frame or something?"

"Not a time frame per se. I just want, very much, to get my goal accomplished. People are dying every day. The time spent so far has been productive, but, all the data we've collected from various sources hasn't been associated with cancer alone. There's a lot still to be culled out and interpreted. And, we've run into some road blocks that weren't anticipated."

"I'm not sure I understand what you're saying," Samantha said. "What kind of road blocks?"

"I'm probably not saying it very well, but, it has to do with how some people in this world view things. Let me put it this way. For example, let's assume you're working for a pharmaceutical company and they've developed a cure for the common cold, which, by the way, probably won't happen."

"If it did, the company would make a fortune, that's for sure," Sam interjected.

"You can bet on it, Sam. One roadblock you have as a company, keeping in mind it's a corporation controlled by stockholders, is you have to market this product to the population. In the United States, it's unlikely to occur in less than ten years because of the Federal Drug Administration and there's about a ten million dollar price tag."

"Why so long and expensive?"

"The FDA makes certain the drug won't have a negative effect on someone's health, even though it'll cure the common cold. It requires the agency's own biological research efforts, including testing on animals; rats, guinea pigs, and so forth. Finally, there's testing on a small sampling of humans for case studies. The process takes money. Lots of it. And, time. Human testing can take as long as four or five years itself."

"Sounds as if it's an irresolvable problem. How does the problem get fixed?"

"Overnight, it doesn't. In the long run, the FDA *must* be able to rely more on data offered by the research facilities doing the original development. The situation now is so bad, the FDA can't even trust the data supplied to them. There've been cases of outright fraud by companies trying to get early approvals. And, the research centers that are guilty, are still operating. Shit, some of the government..." Brad stopped abruptly, then said, "I'm sorry, excuse my French, Sam, I kind of get carried away at times. Especially on this subject."

"It's okay, Brad, I have a brother, you know. Besides, I've been forewarned by Chantal," she said with a smile. "Keep going. Please. This is interesting."

"I'm still sorry. Where was I?"

"Something about the government."

"Oh yeah. Some of the government funded," he repeated and continued, "research programs being conducted pull the same crap. Grants are given to Universities, independent labs, pharmaceutical companies and the such. As long as they continue to turn out something, their funding is continued each year like clock work. Doesn't matter if any progress has been made. Just make certain the documentation and accompanying data look as if something fruitful *is about* to happen. *Bait* the government into the next year's grant."

"It's really that bad?"

"Samantha, I mean Sam, I've barely scratched the surface. I'm not suggesting every lab in the country does this. Only, that it happens. Biological and chemical researchers enjoy very lucrative careers, some earning in excess of the famous three digit income. Yet, the programs or labs they've been associated with over the same period of time, haven't fostered a damn thing that's concrete. These researchers, both men and women, simply move from program to program, lab to lab, and penthouse to penthouse. It's a big game with people like this. Stay ahead of the Jones, regardless of the consequences to the population in general, the same folks who are funding their rise up the social ladder."

"That's terrible, Brad. It can't be as bad as you're saying."

"I didn't used to think so myself, but, since we started collecting information at the Center and sifting though what we have, I've changed my mind. I think I've gotten a little off track here. Back to your cure for the common cold. Considering your stockholders, what do you do? You have to protect what you've found against other guys trying to profit from your discovery. You've got to patent the formula used to make the drug. It's good for seventeen years."

"That means no one else can legally make the drug, right?"

"Right. Now, turn it around and use the profit motive. It means you have seventeen years to make as much money from the drug as possible. It may cost you only ten cents to make the pill. Doesn't matter. You charge based on its demand. Obviously, you can't charge ten dollars per tablet to cure a cold. People may be required to take three or four daily for up to a week, You're talking about," Brad paused to make the calculation and continued, "$210 to $280 to cure a cold and, at the end of a week, without any medications, colds are generally history. People would say bullshit. They'd rather gut it out and drink the chicken soup. Now, if the ten cent tablet was a guaranteed cure for cancer, people would probably spend $1000 per pill."

"It never crossed my mind to look at it in this light before. This is something."

"Keep in mind, you only have seventeen years," Brad continued in a disgusted tone, "to make as much money as you can. After that, there's competition for your product from other companies because you're no longer protected by the patent laws. Someone can copy your formula and come out with a legal, generic drug. Are you following me?"

"Yeah. It kind of makes me sick to my stomach a little. To think people are such money-mongers. And in effect, they're really denying medications to people who need them but, can't afford them," Sam said softly.

It didn't matter what expression Sam had on her face. Brad knew it divulged her inner most feelings. Her look reflected deep-felt concern and Brad was appreciative. She understood the inherent problems in society and showed a remarkable caring for the welfare of those less fortunate. She was beautiful, beyond words.

"And to top it off," Brad went on, "one thing is ironic beyond belief. The people that bitch the loudest about the cost of medications today, are the very same stockholders waiting for their inflated dividend checks in the mail."

"Serves them right!"

"Only, if they understand what the basic problems are. The health care problem in this country, isn't the fault of the insurance companies. It's the costs of everything from the aspirin up to and including the heart transplant. The whole gamut is overpriced and the insurance companies are expected to pay these inflated charges on the whims of a bunch of high rollers. No wonder the insurance companies charge premiums like they do. Shit, they have no other choice."

"I get your drift. They really don't have a choice, do they?"

"Don't get me wrong, there are good and bad insurance companies just as there are good and bad medical research organizations. The point being, the bad ones are the guys making a lot of dollar profit at the general public's expense.

"Can't someone do something about all this?"

"The only way to do something is through Federal legislation. These guys have such a large lobby effort in congress, I doubt there's a chance. The public needs the knowledge of precisely what's going on. Then, and only then, through elections will the right people get to congress and some action be taken."

"That's years away. Isn't it?"

"Appears it is. Unfortunately. Getting back to your cure for the common cold. Let's say you knew a natural cure for the cold existed, one found in nature. It didn't have to be developed through chemical and biological research, was abundantly available in a natural state, and didn't require the ten year and ten million dollar FDA approval. Would you promote its use? Keep in mind, of course, that you want to make money off the cure you've found."

"*I'd certainly make people aware of it*," Sam replied with a bit of hostility in her voice.

"Don't get upset here. I know *you* would. The point is, a CEO making those decisions and responsible for the corporate bottom line *may not*. He may even go to extremes to prevent people from finding out about its existence. It may be in conflict with his biologically founded cure. He may attempt to keep profits up by not divulging it."

"If I knew that a natural cure existed for something, I wouldn't even do research into the area."

"That's good Sam. But, what if you were the only one that knew the natural cure existed. It could provide you short cuts to formulating an artificial or biological cure. One you could charge millions for?"

"Gee Brad, I don't know. This is getting pretty deep."

"I know, I'm probably boring you to death. It's just things I think about."

"It's definitely interesting. No *way* am I bored."

"I could go on with my theories, but, I think you've heard enough of my rambling for the day. Maybe at dinner sometime."

"That's right. The day you get out of here, remember?"

"I haven't forgotten."

"Have you had any luck finding a place to stay?"

"Not yet. I'm really not in that big of a hurry. I can always stay with my sister or John."

"John who?"

"John Sipel. He is my right hand man at the Center and my best friend in the world. He's one of the people going on the ski trip to Colorado I mentioned earlier."

"I'd better be going, Brad. They told me not to stay too long. I'll see you tomorrow and bring you a copy of Renter's Guide. Do you want me to bring you anything else?"

"Some clothes if you could arrange it. And a razor."

"What type of clothes do you want?" she asked, moving towards the door.

"Anything with a zipper all the way up the back," Brad joked. "Sam, thanks for coming. Thanks a lot."

"Got you covered, big guy," she replied with a suspicious smile on her face. She let the door close behind her and left Brad lying in bed, a bit confused and wondering what she meant by "big guy". He wasn't *all that* tall.

---- Chapter Four ----

Brad tossed his toothbrush and travel size Colgate, both purchased at “bargain prices” in the hospital's gift shop, into the see-through, clear plastic bag which the hospital, in its *overwhelming* generosity, provided. Its inflated cost would undoubtedly wind up on his hospital tab as a $5.00 item. Nothing's free at a hospital, including the proverbial box of Kleenex tissues that is a part of each room's decor. The small bag offered no privacy for his personal cache and he'd spent five minutes stretching it to its limits with the few items brought by family members.

He quickly went to the waste basket, looked down and sighed in relief. Joey's carryout bag, evidence of Brad's not adhering to Phil's strict dietary requirements, was completely covered and he needn't worry about last minute troubles with the staff. Gus, on his way to Redskin's training facility the past two mornings, had smuggled him a daily ration of bagels and, this particular morning, had also informed him that Samantha and “Lady Godiva” were one in the same. She'd been frequenting the deli for the past week to keep the regulars abreast of Brad's progress and delightfully fitted in with the early morning regulars. That's all Brad needed, Sam chatting with the likes of Gus, Joey, Ralph and all the others. His reputation was probably shot to hell.

Sam had brought him a jogging suit which he'd taken an instant liking to. Her brother had given it to her for her twenty-fourth birthday and, finding it too large, she'd worn it only indoors for comfort and something to lounge around in. Brad believed Samantha had another reason for not wearing it in public.

She and her brother had attended the University of South Carolina for their undergraduate studies and the over-sized jogging suit was from their alma mater. Sam had probably looked unfavorably on wearing the nickname of the South Carolina school, *Gamecocks*, plastered across her ample chest. Brad hadn't asked her specifically, but graciously accepted the gift. He had no inhibitions what-so-ever about wearing it. In fact, he rather enjoyed the double meaning and attibuted it to her wonderful sense of humor.

It was Tuesday, two days before Thanksgiving, and Brad's spirits were higher than a kite dancing in March winds. His strength and weight were near normal, all tests were negative and he was no longer wearing a bandage on his forehead, only a minuscule scar remained visible where the stitches had held the gash together. With his resolve returning in full force, he'd coerced Phil into a one day early parole from the big house. *Were the nourishing delicacies prepared daily in the hospital kitchen responsible for his early exit? Very doubtful.* Probably the pizza Sam had smuggled past the staff in her book bag two nights ago, a definite no-no on Phil's list of cuisine for his patient.

She was definitely his type of girl, a true, free-spirited, party animal. They'd been seated, legs crisscrossed, on the bed facing each other and the pizza box open between them. Brad had devoured most of it, when the asshole across the hall, the same guy who snored all damn night, had begun bitching that he hadn't gotten pizza for dinner. Putting her nose to the wind like a Louisiana Bayou coon-hound, the nurse had followed the scent to the party in Brad's room. The festivities had ended abruptly and he'd been reprimanded by Phil the next day for his antics. Probably the main reason he'd agreed to an early pardon for Brad. He was proving too much to handle and feeling too good. Albeit, Brad was being sprung today and, to top it off, he was being picked up by Sam. *Life* was great!

Brad had grown desperate in his attempt to locate temporary quarters while his townhouse was being rebuilt. Only one listing in the local papers and renter's guides showed any promise so, Sam and he'd made a three o'clock appointment with a local Realtor for a look-see. First however, they were going to White Flint, an upscale shopping mall, for Brad to pick up some clothes and have lunch. Some *real* food!

There'd been little discussion about the explosion since Phil's numerous questions had been left unresolved. During brief moments of privacy, they'd tried to make some sense of their discussions but this inquisitive probing led only to frustration. They'd finally agreed to let the Fire Department's report stand on its own merits.

The idea of leaving the hospital with Sam made thinking of anything else impossible. Pulling the shades up and looking outside, Brad noticed billowing gray clouds hanging low over the city and moving rapidly towards the east. A storm was brewing, possibly a thunder storm. Brad's eyes followed the clouds down to the horizon, across the expanse of metropolitan DC to in front of the Georgetown Medical Center, eight stories below. No grayish-white vapors were being emitted by cars passing on the streets so it couldn't be that cold. His new *Gamecocks* sweatsuit would be fine, he thought, as he heard the door open.

"Good morning," said Sam as she entered. "Are you ready?"

"Never been more ready for anything in my life," Brad replied. "You look great this morning, as usual." Great wasn't the proper word to describe this girl, but hell, one didn't exist in *Webster's* anyway. She was wearing a Washington Redskins's jogging suit and had her hair pulled back in a pony tail and tucked through the back of a matching cap. She was simply dressed, but, beautiful none the less.

"You're wearing that?" She asked as she took notice of what Brad was wearing. "I thought it was more for around the house and indoors, you know?"

"Of course I'm going to wear it. Not only do I like it, but, I'm strongly thinking of becoming a *Gamecock's* fan."

"South Carolina's sports teams haven't done real well the past few years you know," she stated shaking her head from side to side.

"Precisely, they need all the help they can get, including publicity. I wouldn't feel right if I didn't do my part and, besides, you said the only reason you didn't wear it was because it looked too large on you. This is a perfect fit," Brad said as he slowly turned, parading back and forth, imitating a high fashion model on a Paris runway.

"Don't walk like that," Sam said laughing, "it's not ahh...very masculine."

Brad turned quickly, crouched downward and began stalking her. He advanced slowly towards Sam like a leopard after its prey, with his arms and hands held outward and fingers bent like claws. "This any better?" he asked, getting closer.

"I don't know... yet," she responded with the smile fading from her face. Her sensuous lips were slightly parted as her seductive eyes met his.

He grabbed her waist, pulled her close to him and asked, "Well?"

"Much better."

They accepted the fact that the casual friendship was over, being replaced by a craving neither had experienced before. In a tight embrace, their lips met, each trying to show their true feelings, the ones they had from the first day, from the first moment. Brad prayed the emotion was the same for Sam. Their lips parted and with their eyes locked together, Brad said softly, "I'm sorry Sam, I shouldn't have..."

Cutting him off in mid-sentence, she replied in the same tone, "Don't apologize big guy. I've been looking forward to this." She lovingly placed her hand on the back of his head and pulled him towards her again. He responded, their lips meeting again, tongues exploring and their two bodies becoming one. The emotion of the second kiss was unbearable for Brad. He felt like telling Sam he loved her, but, couldn't, afraid it would be pushing things. Hell, he'd only known this girl for a week his mind told him rationally, but, love can happen quickly. *Phil* had told him so!

As their lips reluctantly parted, Sam said softly and somewhat shyly, "Brad... I think I love you."

"What?" Brad said loudly, startled beyond belief.

"I shouldn't have said that. I'm sorry. I put you in a bad position," she replied to his outburst.

"*No, no*, no... *what* did you say? I just want to make sure I heard you right. And, don't apologize for the position that we were in. I kind of liked it."

"You're just mocking me. Making fun."

"Believe me, *that's* not the case. By any stretch of the imagination."

Again, softly as before, her eyes drifting away, she said, "I think I love you."

"I can't believe this," Brad blurted out with an astonished look on his face.

"I know Brad, it's way to soon to even think of something like..."

Brad quickly cut her off before she could apologize. "You don't understand what I mean. Let me finish."

"Okay."

"What I can't believe is...as we were kissing, I wanted to tell you so much I loved you, but, was afraid to because I thought it would be rushing things." With a look of relief on his face, he continued. "I'm just dumbfounded we were thinking the same way about our feelings. I do love you Sam, very, very much. *Damn*. I mean, how could I *not* fall in love with you?" he asked as he looked down at the word, *Redskin*, written across her chest.

Following his eyes and slightly blushing she said, "That word should be on my forehead. I can't believe we've known each other for less than two weeks. But, I feel I've known you all my life. I never thought of myself as a romanticist. Is this really possible for the two of us to feel the same way... so soon? I mean, one of us possibly, me for sure, but both?"

"Of course it is! Let's face it! We know it's possible because it's happened! We have a lifetime together ahead of us. During that time, I'll know you longer, but, I don't think it's possible I'll know you any better. As stupid as that sounds."

"It doesn't sound stupid to me. I know *exactly* what you're saying."

Their romantic feelings for each other finally spoken, their lips touched in unequaled passion and as Brad was lowering her to the bed, he heard the door to the room open behind him.

"Ah hem... feeling better are we?"

"Shit. Great timing Phil," Brad said as he stood up, leaving Sam prone on the bed, and turned around. "Don't you know enough to knock, even in the hospital?"

"Sor... ry fella. I only came to help you get out of here."

"I know Phil. You just caught me at a bad time."

"A bad time was it," echoed Sam as she sat up on the bed with her long legs dangling over the side and an ear to ear grin on her flushed face.

"Not a bad time, a good time. I mean... Hell, you both know what I mean."

"Exactly," said Phil. "Let's just get you out of here before that nut across the hall wants to join *this* party." All three of them were now laughing, not a bit embarrassed at the interruption.

"Roger that," Brad said as he looked back at Sam.

"Double roger that," said a beaming Sam with a sparkle in her eyes as she jumped of the bed making the Redskin Logo bounce. She noticed Brad watching the action. "Sorry," she said clenching her teeth in a cute, devilish sort of way.

"No more apologies. Okay?" Brad said, winking at her.

"You got it, big guy."

*****

Brad had said his good-byes to the hospital staff and the asshole across the hall as he'd been chauffered from his room to the hospital's lobby in a wheelchair by an attractive nurse's aid. He'd been pushed past the fourteen-foot, Blue Spruce Christmas tree adorning the center of the lobby, where volunteers were helping youngsters from the children's wing put final touches on its decoration. Ms. Patterson had even come across the lobby from the

Admissions Office to wish him well. The small, spoked, front wheels of the wheelchair touched the black rubber mat and the automatic doors swung open. Freedom, at last!

The air was cooler than Brad expected from looking out the eighth floor window and a light rain was beginning to dampen the hospital grounds. Compared to the antiseptic odor of his room, it smelled wonderful. The familiar scent of burning leaves was in the air and the pine fragrance of Junipers used to landscape the front of the hospital added a distinctive, aromatic fragrance. Brad inhaled deeply, taking in the mixture of fall scents. Even the billowing cloud of black exhaust from a diesel bus pulling away from the nearby stop sign smelled good.

He turned and looked up at the enormity of the coral-colored, marble building, trying to identify the window of the room he'd occupied. Impossible to do so, he walked slowly down the front steps not bothering to use the hand rail to his right. With the back of his hand, he wiped the light sprinkles from his cheeks.

Ahead of him he saw a circular fountain with symmetrical patterns of brick inlay. It had already been drained as a safeguard against freezing temperatures. Wind dried leaves were blowing around the circular basin and creating a kaleidoscope of colorful, changing patterns.

To his right was a twenty-five foot high black, granite monolith rising from the concrete. It proudly displayed the stone cutter's work, *Georgetown Medical Center*, emblazoned on its surface. Like a giant tombstone, for all those that would enter the front doors only to be carried out the back, it stood there, dark and cold. Brad moved slowly past it, looking at its intimidating size and wondering how many people died before their time because researcher's couldn't find answers. Far too many.

The sound of metal hitting metal caused his attention to turn to the left. The brass fittings of ropes to raise and lower the flag were banging against the pole in the strong breeze of the coming storm.

At curbside, a school bus was unloading elementary students for a field trip of the Medical Center. In single file, leashed together with a light-weight tether, they proceeded past him leaving in their wake the usual high pitched chatter of excited children. They reminded him of multi-colored Christmas tree lights, new from the box and untangled. They appeared to be well-behaved, disciplined kids and no doubt had explicit instructions from their teacher bringing up the rear, hemp reins in her hands.

He stood by the street having heard, seen and smelled similar things numerous times before, but, never with the same appreciation of someone that's been so close to death. From his right, he noticed a bright red car approaching. Sam was driving and had a joyous smile on her face. As beautiful as that '65 Mustang looked to Brad, it was no match for the driver.

She brought the car to a skidding stop on the damp pavement and rolled down the window. “Where're you headed, big guy?” she asked in a sexy voice batting her long eyelashes.

“Trying to pick me up?”

“Only if you're buying.”

“Can't. Don't have any money on me,” said Brad, crossing the street and bending down to the open window.

“I'll take plastic.”

“Kind of a play now, pay later plan?”

“Is there any other kind?”

“How much of a tab can I run up?”

“Unlimited credit. Sky's the limit.”

“Sure as hell can't argue with that. It's a deal,” said Brad looking around and beginning to laugh. Brad took a step backwards to get a better view. “Damn, *look at* this car. From what I've heard about the damages, Ernie did a *hell of a job*.”

“Who is Ernie and what job are you talking about?” she asked with a puzzled look on her face.

“Ernie, the guy from Baltimore that's always worked on my car. He only works on Mustangs. *Look at this thing*. It looks brand new.”

“Oh, that job. You're right, he did one helluva job and it does look like it came right from the showroom. And remember, I *saw* it before he got his hands on it. Now that I *really* think about it, he did do an *amazing* job. This thing was a mess.”

“You know, restored antiques and classics are becoming more popular these days. They're becoming status symbols. Hell, look at what's going on in Hollywood. Drive a classic. Doesn't matter which one, just so long as it's old, but looks new.”

“How old is this?” she asked, thoroughly checking out the car for the first time.

“It's thirty years old, two months younger than me,” Brad responded proudly.

"Brad, sweetheart, I know I got the car from the lot to pick you up out front, but, can I drive, can I, can I?" she pleaded. "I always wanted to drive a classic."

"Sam, you *are* a classic. Believe me. Okay, you can drive. Just remember though, this car *isn't* just a classic to me. I love it because it was my father's and he willed it to me. I don't want anything else to happen to it. Please?"

As Brad was sliding into the passenger side of the car and closing the door Sam said, "Don't worry about the car. I'm a good driver and besides, with a craftsman like Ernie available, who cares? Where are we headed?" she asked as Brad heard the squeal of tires spinning against pavement.

With his heart pounding in his chest, Brad closed his eyes and simply hoped for the best. Suddenly, as quickly as she'd started, she stopped the car and let out a laugh.

"What's wrong?" Brad questioned. "I didn't say anything."

"I know you didn't, but now I know what your face will look like when you're really scared. I don't drive like that. I was teasing you to see what you'd do."

"*Thank God.* If you would've kept driving like that, I would probably have said something. Or, be going back through those hospital doors with cardiac arrest."

"You wouldn't have said anything and you know it. Be honest. Remember Brad, I've got you pegged. I told you up in the room that I knew more about you than you think. And, that's why I love you so."

"Caught me again, didn't you. I love you too Sam, very much," Brad answered, leaning over to give her a playful kiss on the cheek.

Turning her head toward him, Sam offered her luscious lips instead of her cheek. Brad took full advantage. A few seconds passed and the sound of a car honking behind them interrupted the moment. The impatient driver behind yelled. "You two should get a damn room!"

Both smiled at the crude remark, but neither offered a response. Sam, in a much more controlled manner, began driving to the hospital exit. "As I asked before, where are we headed?"

"The No-tell Motel. Closest one." Brad replied as straight-faced as possible.

"Trying to satisfy the whim of every Joe Blow on the street and look for a room?" asked Sam, beginning to laugh.

"Joe who?"

"Never *you* mind. The No-tell Motel, did you say? Where'd you come up with that?"

"You've never heard of them? Biggest international outfit on the planet. At least one location in every burg in the world."

"Do they cater to unmarried people?"

"Are you kidding? You know what the desk clerk's motto is?"

"I've never been to one, so don't have a clue," replied Sam, playing the straight man for Brad's routine.

"It's simply, Motel spelled backwards."

"And what's that?"

"*Let 'om,*" Brad responded in a deep voice.

"That's a good one," said Sam, holding back her laughter. "Are these motels very big?"

"Hell yes they're big. Banquet rooms and everything. Huge marquees for advertising out front along the roadways of America."

"They actually advertise?"

"*Of course* they advertise. The last marquee sign I saw, read, " Have Your Next Affair Here."

"Brad, you're too much. I think there's something seriously wrong with you to come up with these things all the time."

"Maybe, we should check in, so you can check me out. And, by the way Sam, I wasn't trying to satisfy Joe Blow's whims. Just mine." Brad replied, gently rubbing the nap of her neck.

"Brad, the therapeutic massage is wonderful, but, we have plenty of time for that later. And besides, there is a three o'clock appointment with the Realtor."

"There's *never* going to be *enough* time for *'that',* as you refer to it." Realizing defeat was at hand, he continued in a dejected tone. "I guess, go out Wisconsin Avenue and head towards White Flint."

"I love White Flint. It's got fabulous stores."

"Good restaurants too," Brad said hungrily.

"Clothes first," insisted Sam.

"Why?"

"Because."

"Does this jogging suit bother you *that* much?"

"Just the nickname a wee bit."

"So *that's* the reason you wouldn't wear it outside. The size didn't really have a thing to do with it."

"It is too big on me, though."

"Sam, I know our relationship is ahhh... not that old, but, am I ever going to be allowed to make a decision?" Brad asked, playfully.

"Of course you will. Eventually. Especially the big ones."

"Like what? Whether we go to war with China or something?"

"Precisely the one I had in mind."

"Thanks lady."

"Your welcome sir. Well?"

"Well what?"

"Are we going to war or not?"

"Not today. Okay, if it bothers you that much, clothes first, then food. And, I don't care what kind of food either. Just so it's not from the hospital. That stuff's running a close second to airline food. You know, the best food I had in the hospital was the pizza you smuggled in the other night and the bagels Gus brought me."

"I shouldn't have done that. I don't think Phil was too happy. The staff was pretty upset about it when the guy across the hall had them sniffing us out."

"Don't mind Phil, his bark has always been bigger than his bite. Besides, he's only a doctor on staff and it's obvious he's got no pull. I had to ride in a damn wheelchair. Hell, he's my brother-in-law and has seen *me* do a lot worse things than what *you* did."

"Good. I don't want him to be angry at me for it."

"Don't worry Sam. He's not angry at you. Hell, he didn't say a negative word when he found out it was totally your idea."

"*Brad*! How could you tell him that! It was your idea and..."

Cutting her off in mid sentence, Brad said, "Just playing with you. Like your spinning tires in front of the hospital. I think we're even now."

"Fair enough," Sam said, looking into the rearview mirror to check the traffic behind her. She was a safe driver.

*****

With the biggest retail shopping day of the year the day after Thanksgiving, Brad wondered why the parking lot at the mall was so crowded two days before. Sam was having a difficult time finding a place to park. "There's one!" Brad pointed.

"Where?"

"Down at the end of this lane."

"I see it." Just as Sam was approaching the empty space, a Mercedes raced in front of her. "Darn it," she said with an air of disgust in her voice. "Why are people like that?" With her face beginning to redden slightly, Sam continued. "I can't believe how a guy like that frustrates me. He knew we were going to that space and he pulls in, right in front of me. These so-called rich people, driving their status symbol cars and thinking they're more important than anyone else, really drive me crazy at times."

"Sam, first of all, being rich and nice doesn't necessarily go hand in hand. And, second, we're the ones in a status symbol. This '65 is a classic. He's just a peon."

"You're right. I forgot." Noticing a puzzled look on Brad's face she asked, "What's wrong?"

"I think I've seen that car before."

"Where?"

"I believe it's the car I saw just before the explosion at my townhouse."

"You're mistaken."

"Let me ask the obvious, Sam. *How* do you know that?"

"I saw the Mercedes on the street that morning too and it had a different license plate."

"Sam, I know it's the same plate. I remember the black oval with the white letters inside."

"It's *not* the same car, Brad. I'm positive."

"Enlighten me, if you will. How are you so positive?"

"It's not the same plate."

"I'm to believe you remember the plate being different? Sam, what game are you playing with me?"

"Okay. Don't look back at the plate right now and I won't either."

"All right."

"What are the letters inside the black oval?"

"Hell, I don't remember the letters for Christ's sake. I only looked at the plate one time. You would have to have a photographic memory for that."

"Precisely."

"You're trying to tell me that you have a photographic memory? That you can recall the letters on that plate?"

"Yes."

"Come on Sam. You expect me to believe that? You got lost jogging, 'Lady Godiva'. Couldn't remember where you were."

"Lady Godiva? Why'd you call me that?"

"It's ahhh... Gus's nickname for you. He saw you looking in the window of the deli that morning. I didn't know until this morning that you were the same girl."

"You were in there too?"

"Sure was. Talking to Gus. Had my back to the window."

"Ohh. I hope he means it as a compliment."

"He does. Believe me. Well?"

"Well what?"

"What are the letters of the license plate over there?"

"S...T...R...V...R...L...S," Sam replied with determination in her voice. "Am I right?"

Brad glanced quickly towards the car in question and read STRVRLS. "Yeah, you're right! How'd you do that?"

"I told you. I have a photographic memory. I can just remember most things I see. Except, where I've been," she replied, thinking back to that morning and laughing.

"You're putting me on, right?"

"Wrong."

"Okay, what were the letters on the car that morning?"

Closing her eyes, Sam responded more slowly, "A...M...W...Q...R...S."

"You're sure?"

"Yes, I am."

"You're playing with me, right?"

"Maybe later."

"Sam, Sam, Sam! Why do you say things like that? Let's leave," Brad coaxed.

"Realtor, Brad, remember?"

"How could I forget? All right, getting back to this game."

"What do you mean, game?"

"Well, you could've made up those letters, and being the *gullible, dumb-ass* that I am, I wouldn't know the difference. And, besides, you only said six letters and the plate over there on that car has seven letters. Caught you didn't I?"

"Not really. I only said six letters because that's all there were on the car the other morning."

"Come on," Brad said. "Are you serious?"

"Okay. The green car next to the Mercedes has a Virginia license plate, DGR397 and by the way, it's an expired tag. The renewal sticker shows it is valid through the tenth month of 1996. That's October, last month, Brad."

Brad quickly glanced over, himself not remembering a green car let alone its license plate. Right again. "*God damn*! Is there anything else I don't know about you? You aren't *psychic* or something else weird are you?"

"No, nothing else. Just the memory thing. And, *it's not weird*!" Sam answered, laughing.

"That's incredible! It must be nice to have that ability."

"It certainly comes in handy. Especially, going through law school and having to remember case law citations. You probably noticed, I don't spend much time studying. I've already taken my finals for this semester. The only thing I have left now is the bar exam."

"Speaking of a bar exam, I could certainly use a drink."

Proceeding on through the parking lot, Sam found another parking place in the next lane over. They locked up the Mustang and walked, hand in hand, towards the mall entrance. "Look, over there." Brad quietly said, not wanting to draw any attention. "There's the asshole who stole our parking place."

"Where?"

"Over there, talking to some other guy in a car. He's looking at us now. See him?"

"Oh yeah. Why do you think he's looking at us?"

"Probably thinks were going to say something about what he did. Maybe I should."

"Don't bother Brad. Ignorant people never get the point anyway."

"You're right and, I might add, as usual."

"By the way, did you notice?"

"Notice what?"

"The man he was talking to in the car. His car had the same type of plate, a black oval. The letters were H...C...K...R...S. Not seven letters, not six letters, but, only five letters."

"Didn't even notice. They must be staff at some embassy, though."

"What makes you think it's an embassy car?"

"Don't really know. Guess it's the look I expect an embassy car to have from the movies I've seen. Kind of a Hollywood stereotype. Who else in this town would have license plates with black ovals and a series of letters that don't make any sense? Hell, you ought to see the damn plate on the New Zealand Embassy staff car Evan drives around. It doesn't make any sense to me either. I asked him about it once and *he* doesn't even know what it means."

"You're probably right. Wherever those two guys work, they seem to know each other fairly well. At least it wasn't another Mercedes. I think it was a Cadillac."

"It was a Cadillac. Still dark gray though. What a drab color. When are those embassy dudes gonna start driving red classics?"

*****

"Looks like they're going shopping or getting something to eat," said the Mercedes driver. He was bent over talking to the man behind the wheel of the Cadillac. They go anywhere from the hospital other than straight here?"

"Nope," came the response. "I followed them all the way from the hospital, once they stopped makin' out in the middle of the fuckin' street. Didn't stop anywhere else. You're probably right about what they're doin' here."

"Think we should go inside to make sure?"

"I'm sure as hell not. What the hell else would they be doin' at White Flint?"

"I'm just trying to make sure they don't go out another exit and board the subway or get a taxi."

"Why would they do that? They don't have any idea what's goin' on here. If you want to play it safe, go on in. Just keep in touch with me. I'm sittin' here. From what I've heard, he isn't about to go anywhere without that damn Mustang of his. Even if he leaves, he'll eventually be back to pick it up."

"After that screw-up over three weeks ago, I wouldn't want to be a party to another one."

The man grabbed the steering wheel tighter. "*That wasn't anyone's fault*! The son of a bitch was just late! Besides, all we're supposed to do right now is find out where he's stayin' and try to determine if he has any suspicions about the explosion. He'll get his sooner or later!"

"I'm going to head in just to make myself feel better. We ought to just blow his ass away and be done with it."

"You know we can't do it like that. Has to look like an accident."

"What form's the next accident going to take?"

"I don't have the slightest idea. But, that's not for us to figure out."

"I really don't like this shit. Just blow 'em away. Make it look like a robbery or something. I'm going on in. You want anything while I'm in there?"

Lighting up his last Camel and crumpling the package tightly in his fist, he threw it out the window to pavement of the parking lot and watched it blow away in a gust of wind. "Get me some more smokes," he barked.

"You got it."

The man slid lower in the seat, resting his aching neck against the headrest. Looking in the rearview mirror, he saw his companion making his way across the lot to the mall entrance. He adjusted the driver's side mirror to have a full view of the '65 Mustang parked one row over and stared at the reflection with hate in his eyes for its owner, the only miss in his fifteen year career.

*****

"I love this time of year. Don't you?" asked Sam not waiting for an answer. "All the hussle-bussle, crowds, shopping, decorations and songs. I just love it."

"Bah humbug," he replied.

"Brad!"

"Just kidding. I'm really a sentimental nut this time of year. Probably the one thing I enjoy most is getting gifts for everyone. To me, it's the thought behind what you give a person rather than how much you spend on them."

"I already have what I want for Christmas," said Sam giving his hand a squeeze.

"Ditto", Brad replied. "Why in the hell are we in a mall for Christ's sake? The way I feel about you, we should be somewhere else. *Anywhere else!* Holiday Inn, maybe. No-tell Motel!"

"Phil told you to take it easy. After all, you did just get released from the hospital you know," she said, turning and giving him a peck on his cheek.

"I know, I know, but, I feel like I'm about to explode just being near you! You don't know the effect you have on me."

"Oh, but I do, young man. *I know exactly* what you're going through."

"Let's leave."

"No. You need some clothes."

"Food."

"Clothes first."

"Okay."

They'd spent about thirty minutes milling around in the men's wear department, when Brad normally spent about a minute and a half shopping for a particular jacket, pair of pants or sport shirt. He always knew ahead of time why he was there and what he wanted. Women, never seemed to know these things, having to look at everything two or three times. It takes a real knack to waste so much time. There *must be* a class, only open to females, called Shopping 101. Sam was no exception.

"How do they fit?" asked the salesman anticipating the sale.

Sam was finished outfitting Brad in the men's department from the shirt on his back down to the shoes and socks on his feet. Standing in front of the mirror, he was fascinated with her selections, especially, considering how she'd put up with his grumbling the entire time about how famished he was. Before he could answer and to the salesman, Sam ordered, "They fit fine. Cut the tags off. He'll wear 'em."

Trying to catch Brad's attention in the mirror, the salesman didn't respond. Brad purposely avoided the salesman to see what he'd do. He merely stood there with a blank expression, doing nothing. Brad turned around. "Let me ask you a question. And, give me an honest answer."

"Yes sir."

"What would you rather wear, what I have on now or what I had on when I came in?"

"You mean the jogging suit?"

"Yes."

"What you have on sir. Now."

"Okay, I know you want to make the sale. Consider it sold. Doesn't that change your answer?"

"Not in the slightest, sir. I'd still go with the lady's choice."

"Obviously, you aren't aware. The jogging suit was her choice as well. She gave it to me as a gift. Still the same answer?"

"Without a doubt, sir."

"By the way, do you remember what school that jogging suit's from?"

Without batting an eye, the amused salesman replied, "The University of South Carolina, Gamecocks, sir. Cocks for short."

"Give that man a cigar. You are very observant my young man. I can't believe that..."

"Thanks, Chuck," Sam interrupted.

"No problem Samantha," the salesman responded cutting the tags off the new purchases.

"You two *know* each other?" Brad asked in disbelief.

"Classmates at Georgetown for about the last year and a half," replied Sam.

"It appears, I was set up."

"Gotcha," said Sam smiling. "Aren't you hungry?"

"You're not allowed to change the subject, Sam."

"Is this the guy I've heard so much about the past couple of weeks?" chimed in Chuck.

"This be him," Sam said proudly.

Sticking out his hand, Brad questioned, "Chuck is it? Brad Claxton. Good to meet you."

"Pleasure's mine."

After a good laugh, Brad found out Sam had set him up for some new clothes to assure he wouldn't be wearing the Cocks outfit when they left. Even complaining that Samantha was wearing one from the Redskins didn't help. Chuck suggested that Samantha's fit her better, a point which no one could argue. Shit, anything she wore looked good on her. "Have a great Thanksgiving Chuck, and a good Christmas if I don't see you," Sam said.

"That's right, I may not see you. I wish I had my finals over with like you do. Of course not everyone has a memory like yours."

"You know about her photographic memory thing?"

"Sure do. You've got a smart girl there, Brad. Us peons, that can't remember anything, will be spending the holidays getting ready for finals. She's already completed hers. Passed 'em all. And, maintained her 4.0 average. Must be nice."

"Well, again Chuck, it's been great meeting you. And, by the way, in all seriousness, you'd prefer to wear the jogging suit, right?"

"I wouldn't touch that question with a vaccinated telephone pole. Besides, I prefer a jogging suit from Georgetown University with the Hoyas logo. You know, the Bulldog."

"Ya know something? I went to Georgetown after Colorado and I still don't know what a damn Hoya is," replied Brad.

"Neither do I! See ya."

"Bye Chuck," said Sam with a little wave.

"Brad, what is a Hoya anyway?" Sam asked with a puzzled look on her face. "It's not a type of bulldog is it?"

"I don't think so. I think it's an acronym for Hang Onto Your Ass or some such thing because of the cost of tuition there."

"Brad, you're impossible."

"Not really, try me."

"I plan to later."

"*Shit, why do you do that to me?* Let's leave!"

"Can't."

"And why not?"

"Because, now, I'm hungry."

"We'll do it your way," Brad said in a dejected voice.

"Thanks."

*****

Jerome walked to the podium style counter at Gate 22. "How long is the delay going to be?" he asked, evidencing a little disgust in his voice.

The ticket reservationist, a smaller man and slight of build, looked at the monitor beneath the counter. "According to what's coming up on the screen, you have at least eight hours before your flight leaves for London, Mr. Sawyer."

"Damn. That's about six hours longer than was scheduled."

"I apologize for the inconvenience, sir. The flight's been delayed in San Francisco. We've been authorized to give you and Mrs. Sawyer a voucher to use in the International passengers lounge if you'd care for a cocktail or something to eat, perhaps? It's the least we can do. Try to make you comfortable during the wait."

He tried to compute in his mind when they'd arrive in London. Time now. Projected departure time. Time in the air. Time zones. Too damn many factors involved. *Would a drink help? A free drink. Not really.* Thoroughly disgusted with the turn of events, Jerome returned to where his wife Mildred was patiently waiting and guarding the carry-on luggage. "Eight hours. What do you want to do, Millie?"

"Let me call and see if she's home."

They proceeded to the nearest pay phone, Jerome now guarding the luggage while Mildred placed a call to their daughter. She returned and offered a shrug of her shoulders. "No answer."

"You leave a message?"

"No. I think with an eight hour wait, we should just jump in a cab and run over there. Take a chance she's home when we arrive. It's the least we could do. She was planning on coming home for Thanksgiving and then this trip came up. What do you think?"

"Let's go. She probably leaves a key in the same place we do at home. At least we'll get a chance to see her new place even if she isn't there. We'll leave her a note that we stopped by if we have to."

The two left the international terminal of Dulles in search of a taxi to take them to the Georgetown address Mildred pulled from her purse.

*****

Samantha and Brad attempted to find a place in the mall to eat, but, the wait was too long. They'd left the mall and proceeded a short distance to a well known and locally owned street side restaurant and were seated immediately, but weren't served for nearly an hour. This restaurant was known for its food, not its recognizable appearance like so many of the national chains. There were no golden arches here. It could seat nearly 300 guests and the menu choices were prepared at the time of order, not filled from a production line manned by teenagers. Brad claimed at one point, if the place was any slower, it'd be going backwards but, when the food finally arrived, it was well worth the wait.

The interior of the place was spotless and simply done to the point that a design theme was indistinguishable. Numerous Formica topped tables were placed in the center of the large dining area with booths lining the exterior walls by the windows. Sam and Brad were seated in the comfort of a booth designed for a party of four facing the parking lot.

The view could've used some improvement however, they were having a great time just being together, away from the confines of a hospital room. They could talk freely, the anxiety of saying the wrong thing no longer a hindrance. The question of their mutual feelings was answered at the hospital a few hours earlier and now their uninhibited love for each other was evident by their display of pleasure from just being together.

They were approached by a retired couple from Dallas, in their seventies, maybe early eighties. They were visiting in nearby Silver Spring and were in the midst of taking their great-grandchildren to the Washington Zoo to see the Pandas.

Prompted by the logo on Sam's sweatshirt, initially the conversation was all about the Dallas Cowboys destroying the Washington Redskins. The idea of why this old fart would've noticed the logo on Sam's chest began to bother Brad, but, his irritation was considerably less when he remembered the logo was also on her cap.

Brad was now disturbed at how possessive he'd become lately. People were going to think Sam was a gorgeous young woman with a fantastic shape. Plain and simple. He thought back to the first time he'd seen her seated in the chair facing him in the hospital. Hell, he was no different than anyone else. Realizing people, both men and women, would stare at her because she was a captivating woman, he put his thoughts to rest and promised himself he would cope with jealousy on a much more positive basis in the future. He rationalized that Samantha would always garner attention because of her outstanding looks, fantastic intelligence and charming manner.

The conversation with the elderly couple and the four kids lasted only five minutes, but was enjoyable. The gentleman's wife said Sam and Brad shouldn't wait too long before starting a family. They become the "joys of your life," she'd said, motioning with her hand to the good looking crew beside her. Brad jokingly asked if she felt getting married first would be the proper thing to do. She'd replied, "not necessarily, sonny." They all had a good chuckle at that comeback. Their parting comment was, "don't ever change what's in your heart." After their departure, Sam and Brad made a solemn oath to live by the quote.

"Are you going to finish that?" questioned Brad, referring to the few pieces of broiled fish left on Sam's plate.

"You want this?" Sam replied in amazement with a look of disbelief on her face.

"Well, yeah. That is, if you're not going to finish."

"Oh, *I don't want* anymore. I'm *really* stuffed. It's just... I don't understand where your putting all of this food."

"I haven't eaten all that much."

"I've already checked under the table three times to see if you had a doggy bag under there."

"I don't have a dog."

"I know," replied Sam. "I'm just teasing you."

"*Come on now*. Think about it. What've I eaten?"

"Well, let's see. You started off with a Greek salad, according to the menu large enough for two people."

"You saw it. It really wasn't that big."

"Two people, Brad," she said, holding up two fingers.

"Okay."

"Next, you had those chicken thingies."

"Thingies?"

"Right. Those little pieces of deep, and *I mean deep*, fried chicken in the basket."

"That was only a side order, like a small, *very small*, appetizer, my dear young woman."

"You may believe what you're saying to be true, young fellow, but, the basket was large enough to be passed around a table designed to seat twenty."

"That's good. That's real good Sam. Okay. Let's keep this going... I'm *really* enjoying this."

"Very well. The next item on the agenda. Let me think. Was it the side order of onion rings, again deep fried or, was it the wedge of coconut creme pie which looked like it was cut from a two foot circle."

"I don't remember which came first and besides, isn't two feet stretching it a little?"

"Not really. That's how much your going to stretch your stomach with all you've put in it. By the way. I've never seen anyone eat a dessert with their meal. *Why* do you do that?"

"I want to make sure I have room for it."

"*Good grief.* Obviously, you did. It's gone! So are the hula hoops the menu refers to as the onion rings. Need I continue with the main entree?"

"Please do. Your choice of analogies intrigues me," he said trying to concentrate on the conversation instead of imagining Sam working out with a hula hoop.

"Before I do, look at that," Samantha said.

"At what?"

Nodding towards the window she said. "Out in the parking lot. Looks like that guy's messing with the Mustang."

Watching for a few seconds, Brad said, "He's not messing with it, he's only looking inside. It happens all the time. People can't believe how great a '65 looks so they want to see if the inside's in as good a shape. See, he's leaving already."

"Okay, I suppose so, but, I have the strangest feeling I've run into that guy somewhere before. I just can't seem to place my finger on where I've seen him."

"You know something?"

"What?"

"I've never really thought about it too much but, that photographic memory of yours could probably drive you nuts sometimes. Maybe you saw this guy before, maybe you didn't, but, this memory of yours is telling you that you should know who he is. You know what I'm saying?"

"I know and, I think at times you're right about it. Sometimes, I wish I didn't have it but, unfortunately, I can't just turn it off and on. I do know one thing."

"What's that?"

"It may be pretty nippy outside after that storm passed through but, this afternoon sun coming through the window is too warm to suit me. Feel the vinyl upholstery on the bench."

Brad motioned to their waitresses passing by with a loaded tray of food held high on her shoulder. As she stopped by their table she smiled and asked, "May I get you something else, sir? Would you like to see our desert menu?"

Stealing a quick glance at Sam, Brad replied. "No, I don't think so, I've had plenty. Could you draw the blinds to block out the sun, it's getting kind of warm here."

"No problem," said the waitress beginning to giggle. "We normally do it this time of day anyway but, it's been so busy, we haven't gotten to it yet."

Noticing the amusement, Brad asked. "What's so funny?"

"Oh, nothing. I'm sorry. It's just that the two of you have been acting so cute together since you came in.... well, I guess it just kinds of rubs off on people. At least it does on me. I like seeing people happy."

After the waitress had closed the blinds, Brad turned to Samantha. "Hon, where were we?"

"I believe I was about to describe your cheeseburger."

With a short laugh, Brad replied. "That's right. Continue on my love."

"That's simple enough, I suppose. From a distance it approximates the size of the dome for the rotunda on the US capital building. The order of fries that came along side this monstrosity of a burger, could've been used in construction of a pontoon bridge across the Potomac. Then, George Washington could've retrieved the silver dollar he supposedly threw across. How's that?"

"He did."

"*Who* did *what*?"

"Washington did throw a dollar across the Potomac."

"Brad, sweetheart. Now, *you're* trying to change the subject. And, besides, did someone on the other side catch it and give it back to him as proof?"

"Always the counselor aren't you Sam? Need proof of everything."

"Brad honey, it's never been proved."

"A 4.0 GPA, huh?"

"*What*?"

"Chuck said you had a 4.0 GPA at Georgetown."

"Yes I do, but, it's got nothing to do with what we're talking about, darling of my life. You're *still* trying to change the subject," she huffed crinkling up her adorable nose.

"Damn, the best semester I ever had in my life was probably a 3.5."

"The memory helps."

"Yeah, I guess so. There isn't the slightest possibility you're going to forget what we're talking about. Is there?" he laughed slightly pinching her cheek.

"No way, Jose."

"Well Sam, if you don't want to share your lunch with the man you love, then there isn't much I can do about it."

"You clown. You don't give up do you?"

"Never. Pass me the ketchup please."

"*For the fish*!"

"No, love, for the rest of my pontoon bridge. I'm not *that* weird. But, you know, when I'm with you, I feel so at ease and happy I just might start doing crazy things."

"You already do, but I know what you mean. I don't normally ramble on like I just did. I guess I'm aware of who I'm with and abnormal behavior seems to be apropos."

"Are you insinuating that I'm abnormal?"

"Of course not, big guy," she said with a smile. "Only that I feel that I can say or do anything I want when I'm with you and not end up with a guilt complex."

"Precisely what I was trying to say; however, put into better words."

"Here's your ketchup," she said, passing the nearly full bottle.

Brad examined the label. "You know, when I was a kid in New Zealand, our first dog was named Heinz."

"German Shepard or Schnauzer?"

"Neither. It was a mixed breed. You know, 57 varieties," Brad replied, smacking the bottom of the bottle trying to get it to pour.

"That's funny," Sam said smiling. "Having a little trouble with the red sauce there, are we?"

"No more than usual. When these damn bottles are full, you can never get anything out of 'em."

"Tap the bottle on the 57."

"*What*?"

"Tap the bottle where it says the number 57. It pours easier."

"You're kidding me," said Brad, beginning to tap anyway.

"Not on the label. On the neck of the bottle where the 57 is."

"Shit, I didn't even know there was a 57 there." Holding the bottle up so he could see better with lighting, Brad proclaimed, "*Hell, it's right in the glass*." Lowering the bottle to his plate, he began to tap the bottle again. After about five taps, the catsup began pouring with ease. "I don't believe it," Brad proclaimed, "they should put directions on the damn label. You learn something new every day of your life, don't you?"

"Stick with me, sweetie," Sam replied laughing, "and you'll learn a lot, at least about the more important things in life."

"I am planning on staying with you. I can't comprehend *not* being with you. I love you so much, it'd be unbearable."

"Likewise. Brad.... the other day at the hospital, you were saying some things that were very upsetting to me. I can't get them out of my mind."

"I'm sorry. I didn't realize. I didn't mean to do anything that would..."

Cutting him off, Sam continued. "No, no, I don't mean anything on a personal basis."

"Then, what?"

"You remember, the story about curing the common cold and how money-hungry people are gouging others."

"Oh yeah. Upsetting?"

"Yes, very much so. Actually to the point that I find myself thinking about it quite often."

"Now you know the frustrations I 've been going through for the past couple of years."

"I really don't know how you can cope with the situation."

"It's difficult, believe me. Are you aware that in the states that border Canada, people actually charter buses to take them across the border to purchase medications?"

"*It's that bad*?" asked Sam, once again shocked.

"Sure is. Some medications in the US are five times the cost they are in Canada. Even after paying for the charter, these folks come out ahead. Way ahead!"

"Is it legal for US citizens to purchase drugs outside the country?"

"Hell, you're the lawyer and your asking me? I honestly don't know. I think it's legal, providing the drug's been approved by the FDA. I'm sure crossing the border with a prescription drug that hasn't been approved occurs every day. That's probably illegal. But, I'd imagine, the risk of being caught doesn't matter much to the people doing it. A lot of these people don't have insurance. Regardless, they still have to purchase the drug where it's available and that's why there's a continuous trek across the border to the promised land. Michigan, New York, Minnesota, Washington... that's only a few of them."

"Does that mean drugs sold in Canada that aren't approved for sale by our FDA are unsafe?"

"Not necessarily. We just have stricter standards than most countries. Doesn't mean our standards are better, they're just more protective of the consumer. Other countries' procedures may be more streamlined. The FDA and the Canadian counterpart receive drugs from all over the world, especially the European nations, such as Germany and Switzerland. These companies want to recoup their investments, or gouge the public, whichever may be the case, as soon as possible after development. The sooner they market them, the better off they are. Remember, when they submit one of their products for approval the seventeen year international patent right's clock begins ticking."

"That's really sick, Brad."

"I know it is Sam. But, the worst part about the entire dilemma is the people who are forced into these predicaments are legitimately sick and require the medications."

"Unbelievable. Those that suffer the most can afford it the least. I remember you saying you had a goal to accomplish. How's it coming?"

"Well, Sam, it's like I said before. When I first started the Research Center, the idea was to help find a cure for cancer. It's really mushroomed. I have a personal vendetta against cancer because of my father's death, but, feel as if it's almost selfish on my part when I take a long, hard, focused look at what's really happening. The whole picture in the health industry appears out of whack to me."

"How do you mean, out of whack?"

"Okay. From the information we've accumulated, there're some questions that must be answered. *Serious* questions! Like, why has funding for certain projects been halted and shifted to other studies which have just begun? Or, to those, showing no promise of providing any valid results?"

"Do you have any of these answers?"

"Not yet. That's what the overseas conference in January is supposed to accomplish. Not necessarily the answers, but get the questions in front of the research community. On the table for discussions so that they might be answered. What time is it?"

"Two-thirty."

"Oh shit!"

"What?"

"We were supposed to meet that real estate woman at 3 o'clock to look at the place I wanted to rent."

"Don't worry about it."

"One thing Sam. However busy I might be, I pride myself on being prompt. Especially for business meetings. This woman is trying to make a living and could be spending her time with someone else."

"I agree completely. That's why I already took care of it. I took the liberty to cancel your appointment. Told her you would call back in a few days and reschedule it."

"When did you do that?"

"While you were in the fitting room trying on your new duds, Chuck let me use the telephone in the men's department to call her. Okay?"

"Yeah, that's a relief. *Wait a minute. What* the *hell* am I going to do about a place to stay now. I'll *never* get another chance to look at that place until after Thanksgiving. I guess I'll stay at Chantal's out in New Market."

"I've already thought about that and made arrangements for you."

"Where might that be?"

"At my place."

"You're kidding me. Are you certain about this?"

"Of course I'm certain. I love you. I have two bedrooms because Daddy didn't want me to live alone. He felt I'd be much safer having a roommate."

"You're inviting me to stay there for protection?"

"Not really, big guy... *just bring some*," she said, noticing Brad's blue eyes widen. "I think, even with you there, I still might look for a roommate." Sheepishly, she continued, "There's still going to be an empty bedroom."

"Can we get out of here now?" asked Brad. "Right now?"

"What about my left-over fish?"

"All of a sudden, I've lost my appetite."

"I hope not all of it," she said with a smile spreading across her entire face.

"*Damn, Sam*, I simply *love* your southern accent," Brad said, their eyes again meeting and connecting with each other's thoughts.

"I think we should go," she said coyly, purposely highlighting her accent.

"I agree," responded Brad trying in a poor imitation to mock her southern drawl.

*****

As he pulled out into traffic on the busy four lane road, he heard his call answered over the cellular phone held to his ear.

"What's up?" asked the voice.

"Just wanted to let you know they're rollin' again."

"What'd they do at White Flint?"

"What's his name, Samuel, followed them into the mall and, get this, he *thinks* they bought some clothes. Well, *no shit* Sherlock. I don't think this Samuel character working for you is real bright, ya know?"

"Why?"

"It's kind of fuckin' obvious he bought clothes when he comes out wearin' something different than when he went in."

"Whatever. Any idea where they're heading?"

"Nope. Just followin' 'em to find out. By the way, the broad he's with looks kinda familiar. I think I've run into her before. Just can't remember where."

"Maybe the hospital?"

"Damn, I think you're right. In the lobby."

"Anything else?"

"Only that when this shit's over with, if his car is sold, I want it. That damn thing's in good shape. Looks brand new, even the interior."

"First things first."

"Ya got it. Talk to you later."

*****

"What the hell's that?" asked Brad, nearly jumping out of the passenger seat.

"It's only the cell phone ringing. I thought you'd need it, so I put it in the glove compartment for you at the hospital. It's the same one I used the morning of the accident to call 911."

"Christ, my heart is in my throat. I usually have the phone on the seat beside me. I guess I sorta forgot about it. That *damn* ringer has always been too loud to suit me." Brad removed his hand from Sam's knee, opened the glove compartment in front of him and picked up the phone. Sam was driving because she *now* knew the way to her place and he didn't. Strange turn of events considering a little over three weeks ago, she'd been totally lost.

"Would you rather have the phone or me on the seat next to you," Sam said jokingly.

"You of course. You're much better at conversation," Brad responded quickly rubbing her trim leg next to him and giving her a lecherous grin.

"You'd better answer before they hang up."

"Don't you know "they" can't be calling. That implies more than one person's calling. Only one person can call at a time, Sam. You should have said, before he or she hangs up. You *must* learn to be grammatically correct."

"Could be a conference call, smart ass."

"Wow. Such language from one of the South's finest ladies."

"Brad, answer the phone."

"You expecting an important call my sweet?"

"No, I'm not," she replied, checking the rearview mirror for traffic with her gorgeous eyes. "Please, answer the phone."

"Hello," Brad said, pressing the "send" button.

After a few seconds, Sam asked, "Well, who is it?"

"He or she hung up."

"I warned you that would happen."

"Not to worry. If I hit this button, right here," Brad replied, "it'll automatically dial back the person that just called."

"Then press it."

"It's ringing."

"Wonderful."

"Hello," the voice on the other end said.

"Phil?"

"Brad?"

"Yes."

"I just tried to call you a minute ago. On your cell phone. Where are you?"

"In the car."

"Why the hell didn't you answer?

"Sam was giving me some lip," said Brad, winking at Sam as she quickly glanced at him with a look of total disbelief on her face. She then went back to the business of driving with a smile on her face.

"Lucky boy."

"What?"

"Sam? Giving you some lip? Lucky boy," he repeated.

"Not that kind of lip." Now Sam began to laugh a little. "Where are you calling from? I didn't recognize the number."

"I'm at the hospital. You and Sam having a fight or something?"

"On the contrary, things between Sam and I couldn't be better. Believe me," he responded, reaching over and patting her on the leg again as she was breaking for a red light. "And Phil, I'm not coming back to that damn hospital. I'm fine."

"Believe me Brad, I don't want you back here after your antics of the past couple of days. That's good news to hear you and Sam are getting along so well."

"Thanks."

"Now I have some good news for you."

"What's that?"

"You remember me telling you that your car was picked up in front of your house that morning and towed up Wisconsin and dumped off?"

"Yeah. And then something about the police contacting you and then you having Ernie pick it up and tow it to Baltimore. That's still a mystery to me."

"Well, it's not a mystery anymore."

"Why?"

"I made some phone calls. Apparently, the truck that picked it up was from Virginia. The driver couldn't tow it to Baltimore, not licensed for Baltimore County or some such thing. At any rate, they dropped it off, put in a call to a company in Baltimore, gave the location and told 'em to pick it up. The second company never showed. That's why the hell it was sitting there."

"I guess your theory about cloak and dagger shit isn't going to hold up. But, you know something? It is kind of exciting to think you might be involved in something like that. Phil, I understand now. It's part of the Georgetown Medical Center's rehabilitation service. A way to jump-start a patient's heart, right?"

"Hardly."

"Seriously Phil, I'm not a person in any position to demand *that* kind of attention. Shit, man, I'm your basic nobody. You know what I'm saying?"

"I wouldn't go that far, but, I know what you're saying. Well, you can rest easy now."

"Thanks for the feedback, Phil. I haven't been thinking about it all that much anyway, but, it's definitely been in the back of my mind."

"I knew it would be. That's why I did the checking. Sorry about ruffling your feathers for no reason."

"No apology necessary."

"Are you going to stay at our place?"

"No, but thanks anyway. I've made other arrangements."

"Staying with John in Laurel?"

"No."

"Oh, that's right. You were going to look at the rental place in Georgetown. How's it going to work for you?"

"Haven't been there."

"Later on today?"

"No."

"When?"

"*What is this*, twenty questions or something? I've *made* arrangements! *You* don't have to worry about it."

"Touched a nerve, did I? Testy, testy, Brad. Does the wittle man need a wappy nappy?"

"*Come on*, Phil."

"Wait a minute. Just *how* well are you and Sam getting along there pal? *You're* staying at her place, *right*?"

"You caught me."

"You foxy devil you."

"Phil, she asked me. She has an extra bedroom and that's all there is to it."

"Is she still going to have an extra bedroom after you move in?"

"If it's left up to her she is," Brad lied feeling that it was no one's business what he and Sam did.

"I'll bet."

"Get serious."

"You certainly are."

"If it's of any consequence, there's some truth in what you just implied."

"I knew it. When I caught you two this morning just before you checked out, I could tell from both your reactions, there's more than meets the eye in your relationship with her. That's great, pal. I didn't mean to be so prodding. I'm just glad you've got something in your life besides the damn Center. She's a great girl Brad."

"Believe me Phil. I know how lucky I am. Say 'hi' to your parents for me, and, to Mom and Chantal. Sam and I'll see you on Thursday."

"Right, Thursday it is. Bye."

"Bye Phil."

"What was all that about?" questioned Sam.

"Oh, Phil was just making sure I had some place to stay until mine was fixed up."

"I got that part. What I didn't understand was the talk about some cloak and dagger stuff," she said, making a left turn.

"It's nothing to concern yourself with, Sam," Brad responded. Attempting to distract Sam from the subject at hand and making certain she noticed, he threw the cell phone out the window. He watched it slide down the drainage gutter along side the curb and continued, "Phil thought there was something suspicious about how my car was towed away. As it turns out, everything's on the up and up."

"Did you just throw your cell phone out the window?"

It worked, thought Brad. "Yes... I did."

"Why?"

"To prove to you I'd rather have you on the seat next to me."

"There's always the glove compartment."

"You wouldn't fit," replied Brad feigning a boisterous laugh, "and besides, three's a crowd."

"Brad, you're really something. Let me pull over so you can go back and get it."

"Never mind. I told you the ringer was to loud to suit my taste anyway. Besides, it's down one of those rain gutters."

Now laughing, she responded, "You're impossible. What'd Phil think was going on with your car?"

The distraction didn't work, and the damn cell phone cost him a good $300. *Was there such a thing as a bad $300?* Probably, but, he hadn't seen it lately. "No biggie, Sam. He thought someone had the car towed to another location so they could strip it. Anyway, he made some phone calls and found out his theory was wrong. Okay?"

"Okay."

"With talking on the phone, I'm not even sure where we are," Brad stated.

"You really have tunnel vision don't you?"

"Why do you say that?"

"Your place is just up here on the right. I thought you'd want to see the progress being made."

"So it is." Sam slowed the Mustang to a crawl so Brad could take a good look at his townhouse as they passed. "Damn! I don't believe that shit. The whole front's gone!"

"I know. You're really fortunate to be alive. Lucky for me you are because I'd never have had the chance to know you, let alone fall in love with you, ya big nut."

"Nor me you and besides, to know me is to love me. I'm *adorable*," Brad exclaimed, "and *you know it*! Incidently, how far is it to your place?"

"Two more blocks, a left and we're there."

Pulling to a stop along side the curb in front of a quaint, bungalow-styled house Sam said, “Isn't much but, it's mine as long as I want it, thanks to Daddy.”

It was a single story house built nearly fifty years ago by a custom builder whose sons had carried on the tradition in the upscale communities in the farmlands north of DC. It had a uniqueness about it, not like one of those ranch houses sitting endlessly side by side in some lesser expensive subdivision with the only difference being the color of shutters flanking the windows.

The red brick had weathered over the years to a deep burgundy color with streaks of black created by aging. It was accented by the white trim surrounding the windows and and high-pitched, black shingle roof. The black lacquered front door had a weathered, brass knocker centered at eye level. White drapes were visible at the dining and living room windows, sweeping from the tops of their centers to the sides and out of sight. The grounds were well-kept, shrubbery as high as the windows showing evidence of recent pruning. The trees would be trimmed in the spring.

“Looks like a nice place,” said Brad with a touch of uneasiness in his voice. He'd never been jittery with any of the other women in his life, but, he'd never been in love with them either. He hoped she didn't notice.

At the front door, Sam said, “Brad, can you unlock this for me? I can't seem to get the key in the lock. I guess, I'm a little nervous.”

“Sure, let me have it,” he responded.

“Do you mean... let you have the key?”

“Samantha, Samantha, Samantha! You *do* have a way with words!” That did it. Now, Brad was fumbling with the key. He felt a warmth rush into his head, not from embarrassment, but, from anticipation of what was coming. Finally, with the door unlocked, they entered the foyer and closed the door behind them. Brad noticed their reflection in the ornate mirror hanging to his left.

Brad turned Sam around and pushed her back against the front door. Slowly, he pressed against her, his arms going around her hour-glass waist and his hands up her back. His body came to rest against the roundness of her breasts. She began to say something. He didn't know what and at that moment, he didn't care. He stopped her in mid-sentence by kissing her. Pulling his head back briefly, he said, “Don't talk Sam, let's just let it happen.”

"I love you so much."

"I love you back," he said. He could feel the heat of her body pressed against him through her jogging suit. He knew the Redskin logo was smiling. Abruptly, she pushed him slightly backward, virtually ripping off his new shirt, the one she'd just picked out for him at White Flint. Crossing her arms, she removed the top of her jogging suit in a single, fluent motion, somehow, the baseball cap disappearing at the same time. The logo was no longer smiling, no longer a part of the action.

Samantha wasn't wearing a bra and her full firm breasts were seemingly reaching out, demanding to be caressed. Her body was magnificent. They embraced again, flesh against flesh, and, with the firmness of her body ever present in his mind, Brad slowly sank to his knees. He kissed her silken body wherever she directed his head with her hands.

She held it tightly against the milky flesh of her magnificent breasts. Sam's breathing was heavy, causing them to swell and subside rapidly. Brad's tongue darted in and out like a serpent, exploring the softness of the prominence. Around and between his tongue flickered as if answering Sam's sensual sighs of pleasure. Brad's hands moved to hold and massage one breast as his mouth tried to devour its roundness. The tip of his searching tongue found her nipple hard from ceaseless examination. Now standing on weakened legs, they embraced tightly and violently kissed, Brad's hands running through silken strands of auburn hair.

Neither could remember who took off what next, but, it didn't matter. He was carrying Sam, at her direction and both naked except for underwear, towards a bedroom. Any bedroom. Kissing as he carried her, Sam slowly pulled her head back and with her eyes flashing fiery passion she said two words. "The table."

"Good, I don't know where the bedroom is anyway."

As he placed Sam on the dining room table, they knocked the centerpiece onto the floor. Too pre-occupied, neither heard the crash. Brad had just laid himself lovingly on Sam, his hardness pressed against her and the roundness of her breasts flattened against his chest, when a feminine voice from somewhere in the house, called out in a southern accent, "Sammie, is that you?"

"*Mom*?" Sam shrieked.

"*Oh shit*," Brad yelled, hearing footsteps coming from the direction of the kitchen and not believing what was about to happen.

Brad noticed Sam, lying beneath him with her head upside down, craning her head backwards, trying to look in the direction of the voice. Brad slowly looked up as Sam's mother entered the doorway with her father closely behind. With nothing much left to say, Brad meekly said, "Hi."

Sam's mother totally freaked out, letting out a yell, the last half of which could only be heard by dogs roaming the neighborhood. It was the most ear-piercing sound Brad ever recalled in his life, a life, soon to be over. A scream, that by comparison, would make the screech of chalk on a sixth grade blackboard sound pleasant. Her father simply exclaimed, "Oh *my God*!" in the same, charming southern accent. And Sam. She simply kept saying, "Mom! Mom! Mom!"

After what seemed like a decade, her father suggested he and his wife retreat to the kitchen so their daughter could make herself presentable. No mention what so ever of Brad. He remembers thinking for a fraction of a second, Sam looked presentable to him. Especially on the dining room table where he was about to enjoy the best main course of his life. When her parents left the room, it didn't take a lot of time to get dressed. Brad, however, had some difficulty with his shirt, Sam having ripped off the buttons moments before.

Brad glanced at Sam. Doing her best not to laugh out loud, she slipped the sweatshirt back over her head and covered the magnificent breasts. Brad's face was still flushed, not from passion, but, from embarrassment. The anxiety of not knowing how her parents were going to react was setting in. Seeing their daughter, virtually naked on the dining room table is one thing. Her having an unknown, nude dude on top of her with some serious intentions between his legs was a whole new ball game. He should've worn his regular underwear home from White Flint. *But, no.* Sam had to buy him and insist he wear the bright red bikinis. Not too embarrassing! It was time for Brad to make some decisions. The United States should definitely go to war with China.

Still trying not to laugh, Sam whispered to Brad, "If I didn't truly love you, I'd be upset also. There isn't a thing they can do or say, that's going to change that."

Somehow, what she'd said made Brad feel better. It wasn't as if this was a one-time fling. It was simply the first time of many to come. They *were in* love. And, *making* love because they were. He hoped her parents had the same viewpoint. They'd gotten caught. That's all. Brad whispered back.

"You know what they say. You only have one chance to make a first impression. How'd I do?"

That did it. Sam began to roar with uncontrollable laughter. Still laughing loudly she answered, "That... squeaky little...'hi' of yours, was fantastic."

Now, Brad became amused with the whole scene and was beginning to laugh when her parents re-entered the room. His laughter was short lived.

"Mom, *what* are you doing here?"

"The question is, what are you doing here? I never..."

"Now Millie, yes you did. And, more than once, I might add," Sam's father interjected before his wife could continue.

"Mom, I was only making love to the man I'm going to marry. You came into the room... no, let me change that, into my house, totally unannounced."

"*You're engaged*?" Millie asked quizzically, her bifocals slightly askew on her nose.

Before Sam could answer and squeezing her hand, Brad said, "Yes, we are." Brad noticed a return squeeze from Sam that he interpreted to mean a yes. This had to be the most expedient proposal and acceptance of marriage in the history of mankind.

"You must be Brad then," her father said, sticking out his hand for a greeting, "the young man that Sam's been calling us about. Thought you were still in the hospital."

"Yes sir, that would be me. It's a real pleasure to meet you Mr. Sawyer. I got out of the hospital this morning."

"The pleasure's mine."

Sure, Brad thought to himself. *You come into a room and see your only daughter spread eagle, in the act of intercourse with someone you've never met, and it's a pleasure to meet this character.* Turning his attention to Sam's mother he said, "Mrs. Sawyer, it's a pleasure to meet you as well."

"Thank you," she responded coolly, adjusting her glasses which had remained askew on the tip of her nose.

"Millie, come on dear. Relax. We shouldn't have come without telling Sammie. It really is our fault that the situation is a little tense right now."

"I suppose you're right," she said in a chilled voice, still annoyed. "When is the wedding?" she asked suspiciously, looking directly at Brad.

"We haven't exactly set a date yet," said Sam attempting to remove some of Brad's pressure. "Mom, how'd you get in here?"

"Remember, we always put an extra key under the third rock to the right of the doorway. Not the normal place that folks supposedly hide keys like under the mat or in the flower pot. There was an eight hour wait for our flight from Washington to London so we thought we'd surprise you. We tried to call from the airport, but, there wasn't any answer. So, we came over anyway. You remembered. There was the key under the third rock outside your door."

"You *certainly* surprised us Mom."

As time passed, the flavor of the visit with her parents progressed from bearable to pleasant, much more so than Brad felt possible considering the circumstances Her mother and father congratulated them both, Mrs. Sawyer wanting, nearly demanding, a typical and truly southern, May wedding in Charleston, outdoors among blooming Azaleas and Magnolias for her only daughter. Brad nearly brought up the idea of a Colorado wedding, but, quickly forgot about even suggesting it after hearing Sam's mother carry on about tradition.

Over drinks, which Brad prepared, the four toasted the engagement and sat in the living room talking pleasantly for over an hour. Samantha's mother began to loosen up a little and showed a bit of warmth towards her future son-in-law, calling him by his first name and occasionally casting a smile in his direction. Brad thought the strength of the drink he'd prepared for her may have helped as much as his good behavior.

Even though both Samantha and Brad genuinely offered to take the elder Sawyers to the airport, they decided to call a taxi as they prepared to leave. As Sam's mother approached the front door, she stepped on something. Hearing a cracking noise on the hard wood floor she pulled her foot up quickly. "Wonder what that was?" she asked.

Brad reached slowly down to the floor and picked up the broken pieces. "Just a button," Brad replied softly, the heat of further embarrassment creeping from his loose shirt collar towards his face.

"Get Sammie to sew one back on for you... son," Mrs. Sawyer replied lifting a ton of guilt from Brad's shoulders. "She knows how to sew."

"I'm sure she does," Brad hesitantly replied as he received a hug from her.

Sam's father gave them both departing hugs as Brad said, "Stop in to see us on your way back from London."

"I don't think we'll have time on the return trip but, we'll see. At any rate son, we're *definitely* looking forward to May."

"Not as much as I am," stated Brad.

The Yellow Cab had barely pulled away from the curb when Sam held up the key to the front door and proclaimed, "It's the only extra key in the world to this place. Where were we?"

The time it took to return to the table and the same position before being interrupted was a world's record in somebody's book. "I will marry you Brad, whenever you want."

"The same goes for me too, Sam."

What transpired until the wee hours of the morning, beginning on the dining room table and ending in the bedroom, could only be described as more passion than either could imagine possible. They fell asleep, she in his arms, both completely exhausted. Completely satisfied. And, completely unaware of events less than 200 feet from their front door.

*****

"It's three o'clock in the damn morning," said the grouchy driver, peering at the Rolex in the dim light of a nearby street light. "The damn Mustang's still parked at the curb. They're *not* goin' any fuckin' place. I'm ready to get the hell outta here."

"Has anyone else showed up since you got there?"

"Absolutely, no one. The only other people in or out of that house were the two old farts that left a few hours ago. Who the hell were they, anyway? A damn taxi picked 'em up."

"We had another car follow them. They went out to Dulles and then boarded a flight to London. Mr. and Mrs. Jerome Sawyer."

"Probably the broad's parents."

"Your right. They're from Charleston."

"Any possibility of their needing to disappear?"

"Looking for business?"

"Not necessarily. Just don't like loose ends."

"Doesn't look like they're involved at the present time. Their departure was delayed. Looks like it was an innocent trip to see their daughter while they were waiting for their flight."

"Then, it's still, only him, that *lucky* bastard," he said, grinning and showing a mouthful of overbite.

"He's the only one *you* worry about and, possibly his girlfriend. It's been decided to issue a separate contract on another party. It's being handled by someone else."

"A contract on who?"

"It's not your concern and right now, I honestly don't think you need any additional workload. Besides, I don't make those decisions, I only pass them on."

"I still can't believe the guy lived through that blast. *Jesus*. I was there! I saw him blown over fifty feet."

"Some folks are just plain lucky."

"Shit, if it weren't for him, I'd be soaking up those warm rays in Barbados instead of sippin' cold coffee like I'm doin' right now. He really fucked up my plans, but I'll get him though. Remember, that's our deal. He's the first one I've ever missed. Never needed a second chance in fifteen years. He's mine! Don't forget that."

"I understand you're doing it for free now instead of the normal quarter mil."

"I'll take it out of his ass. He's screwed up my reputation but good and I don't forget easy. The second time, it's gonna be right. That's why I'm sittin' out here at three in the damn morning. Doin' some of the surveillance bullshit myself. To make sure it goes right."

"How much you do in that regard, is totally up to you. What time do you want someone there in the morning?"

"Have someone here around six. I want to know this guy's every move."

"Six it is. Talk with you later."

He hung up the cellular phone, turned on the engine and slowly pulled away. Waiting until he was a half a block down the street, he turned on the headlights. He reached into his pocket and retrieved a Camel, tapped it on the steering column to pack it tighter and placed it between his lips, lighting it. Seeing the reflecting eyes of a cat on the prowl suddenly cross the street in front of him, he quickly swerved the Cadillac. "Shit, another miss," he muttered under his breath.

---- Chapter Five ----

Brad was driving as if he were under a caution flag at the Indianapolis 500. The amount of traffic wasn't the problem because most people were already settled in where they'd be spending Thanksgiving Day. However, the road was a problem. It was a main thoroughfare heading north from one of the many Maryland towns skirting metropolitan DC. It used to be a four lane road, but now, was reduced to one in each direction because of the widening project. *Shit,* Brad thought, *by the time the six lanes were finished, it'd be outdated.*

They should just make it eight, ten or maybe even twelve lanes, just to get it the hell over with for the next twenty years instead of tearing the crap out of it every five years. Seemed everyone, with the exception of city planners and the DOT, knew where the next boom town of new housing construction would take place. Hell, there're only so many places left for a realistic commute to the DC area. They're not hard to find on any map that's worth a shit and planning roads to get there, without packing an overnight suitcase, isn't brain surgery.

Brad swerved the Mustang sharply to miss one of the small, A-frame, orange and white striped barricades spotted every fifty feet, as far as the eye could see. Like toy soldiers, the endless line guarded the edge of the road to prevent cars from entering the freshly graded dirt to his right, now turned to mud from the rain.

The guy placing these obstacles must've been drunk as hell, not drinking on the job, but rather, about it. *Must be boring as hell,* thought Brad. Get it off the truck and unfold the damn thing. Turn on the switch to light the orange, battery operated, blinker. Get the sandbag off the truck and place it on the supports to prevent the wind from blowing it over. Get on the truck and ride fifty whole feet just to start the same thing all over. And, these damn things were placed on both sides of the road!

Does each one of these barricades come with an envelope containing a diagram and set-up instructions Brad wondered. The sandbags were a joke. A healthy fart would've blown the barricades away. And, to top it off, they weren't even owned by the State of Maryland. Rather, each and every one of them was rented by the state for God only knows how much per day. Bubba's Barricades knew the daily tab, the owner's name evident on each A-frame. How *well* Bubba was doing was anyone's guess. Damn well surmised

Brad as he lost count of the barricades at fifty-seven, or was it sixty-seven?

It was dismal and overcast with a light mixture of freezing rain and sleet falling which had made visibility difficult, so he'd turned on his headlights for safety's sake. This type of down right nasty winter weather, just warm enough *not* to snow, was normal for the Washington DC area; however, for it to arrive this early in the season, wasn't normal at all.

Most people in the metropolitan area detested this type of weather, but, Brad coped with it knowing chances were good that the mountains of western Maryland and West Virginia were getting legitimate snowfall. Snow skiing would be excellent when he and Sam arrived at the Snowshoe Resort this weekend. The storm moving into the area today was expected to dump 12 to 18 inches of *real snow* in the mountains to the west and cover the man-made stuff manufactured by the resorts to build up a good base and extend their skiing seasons. The skiing would be fantastic.

He and Sam had spent the majority of yesterday doing what two people in love do, showing how much one loved the other. Neither had won that little contest, but, Brad was looking forward to all of their future competitions because he'd enjoyed the love making sessions immensely. A discussion concerning her parents' impromptu visit surfaced. Brad knew her mother's name to be Millie, short for Mildred, however, realized that in all of the fiasco of their first meeting, he'd never heard her father's first name. Sam had informed him that it was Jerome; however, most people referred to him as Jerry or *Sawyer the lawyer*. Using a southern accent, Brad had asked if it would be proper to call him Daddy. Giggling at his remark, Sam had suggested he wait until they were married.

Sam and Brad spent a portion of Wednesday shopping for some essentials, returning to White Flint to see Sam's classmate, Chuck, and replace Brad's ripped shirt. He had, again, worn his University of South Carolina wardrobe which had prompted a few humorous remarks. After Brad's decision to go to war with China, Sam had allowed him to continue wearing it, even to the restaurant where they'd eaten the day before.

When he'd ordered a rotunda dome, pontoon bridge and a side order of hula hoops, it had caused quite a reaction from their server. The owners had come forth, wanting Sam to redo their menu, feeling it would add a nice touch for their guests. They'd left, promising the owners they'd return to give them a hand.

The two had entered a small sporting goods store, this time of year stocked with the latest snow ski equipment and fashions. During the summer months, scuba diving and water skiing items filled the shelves and racks. Brad had known the owner for some time, an older gentleman and still an avid snow skier. He had not had any problem replacing the equipment lost in the explosion and didn't know anyone more trustworthy to outfit Sam properly. Proper fit of boots, length of skis, and bindings could mean the difference between having a great time and breaking a leg.

In casual conversations with numerous "experts", Brad would ask if they knew the most common skiing injury. Ninety-nine times out of a hundred, the response was a broken leg or sprained knee. Finding out it was a sprained or dislocated thumb would blow their minds. Brad explained that as a fall occurs, a normal reaction is for people to grab the ski pole tighter. As they're going ass-over-tea-kettle, the pole hits things or digs into the snow, pushing the thumb abruptly backwards and causing the injury. While Sam was being fitted, Brad had informed her of this trivial tidbit.

They'd shopped further, Sam picking out a sweater for herself and Brad claiming it was made from camel hair. Sam had refused to believe him so while she was still modeling it, Brad had laughingly pointed to the two humps in front, claiming it was enough proof for any court of law in the country and the case was closed. Samantha had vehemently denied his claim, stating the sweater was a wool blend. While doing so, she noticed that Brad's face had become frozen as he looked out the windshield of the car.

"Shit," Brad said disgustingly, his concentration returning to driving.

"What's wrong?" Sam asked.

"You can sure tell the asshole that just passed us going the other direction isn't from around here."

"Why, how'd you know?"

"You must not have noticed how fast he was driving. If he was from around here, he'd know better. He sprayed up my windshield real good. *Damn it*, the water kicked up by his car is mixed with dirt from the road. *Look*, it's shit brown. When Ernie repaired the Mustang, he must've forgotten to fill the washer bottle. All the wipers do is smear this crap around. I can barely see. Remind me at Chantal's to put some water in the bottle."

"You'd better slow down."

"I already have. Until enough sleet collects to help clean it, I'll *have* to drive slower." The car behind him was becoming very impatient and irritating the hell out of Brad with his constant honking. Finally, the car passed him on the left, the passenger flipping him a bird. "Nice guy. I'm glad that idiot's gone."

"Amen to that," agreed Sam, "guys like that cause accidents."

"Guys like that *were* accidents back when they were conceived."

Five minutes later, the traffic was beginning to back up and their speed was reduced to a crawl. Approaching a slight turn to the left, Sam said, "I think there's been an accident. There's a car up ahead, over in the ditch, next to the road."

As they approached the scene, Brad exclaimed, hoping Sam didn't notice the slight smile on his face, "It's the idiot that passed me. Look's like he slid right off the road trying to make the turn."

"Probably so. There isn't any other car around."

As they passed by the car, obviously very stuck, Brad noticed the driver and passenger standing along side. Close by, were three orange and white striped, one-eyed, toy soldiers, lying on their backs, winking at the heavens as if trying to lure the next non-stop flight into a landing. The temptation to return the gesture the passenger had so willingly given him entered his mind, but, with Sam in the car, he thought better of it. "Nice guys get theirs. What goes around, comes around."

"They both look okay. I don't think they're hurt."

"Too bad," said Brad softly, noticing the traffic beginning to pick up speed again.

"What?"

"Nothing."

"Brad, did you notice the license plate?"

"I really didn't. I'm kind of busy trying to see out this damn window. Are we back to the photographic memory game thing again?"

"Not really. What a coincidence."

"What's a coincidence?"

"It was the same kind of plate we saw at the mall the other day. I couldn't make them out, but, it was definitely a black oval with white letters. Does that seem at all strange to you?"

"Not really. Whoever it is, they deserve to be stuck."

The precipitation was beginning to get heavier and the windshield cleaner. They entered the New Market area, enjoying the countryside along their route and wondering how many Confederate and Union troops had marched across it on there way to battle, and to death. It was wide-open farmland with gently rolling hills, spotted here and there with stands of nearly barren trees intermingled with an occasional evergreen of some species. They'd arrived. Boom Town.

*****

"This is a beautiful area. How long have Chantal and Phil lived out here?"

"It was early spring of this year, around March, when they moved in. This'll be their first Thanksgiving here."

The area they entered, after identifying themselves to the security guard at the swinging, wrought iron gate, once was a three thousand acre turf farm. Sam found it hard to believe people made a living growing grass, at least the kind used for landscaping and not smoking. Brad told her, all of the sod used to landscape new construction, whether it be for residential and commercial property or highway medians, came from somewhere. The gradual rolling hills of grass cascaded downward to various small lakes and ponds. In the distance, were dense, wooded areas, some of the fall foliage still clinging to the branches as if in a fight for its life.

The area was divided into separate, ten acre tracts with some of the most grandiose homes Sam had ever seen, breaking the contour of the acreage. It was simple to envision those homes still under construction. They'd be beautiful also, as if in direct competition with one another for a featured article in Architectural Digest. There were Georgian Manors, New England Colonials, French styles and English Tudors.

One home in particular caught her eye, an enormous log house. The home wasn't the normal log house used for weekend hunting or fishing trips you see scanning the pages of Field and Stream. And, neither was it built from one of the kit manufactures, such as promoted by Bob Villa and advertised within its pages. It was, simply put, the largest log house Sam had seen, exquisite in its design and nestled amongst a wooded area, on top of a hill, overlooking the vast expanse of the entire development. "Look at that place up there on the hill! *Isn't that gorgeous?"*

"You mean the lodge, as I call it?"

"Yes!"

"You *really* like that?"

"*Do I ever*!"

"I know the owner fairly well. Would you like to see the inside?"

"I'd be in heaven!"

Pulling into the driveway Brad said, "Come on, I'll see if they're home."

"You *can't* ask them to go through their house on Thanksgiving day!" replied Sam, obviously upset with the idea. "We can do it some other time, Brad."

"I know them. They're nice and won't mind. We've got plenty of time until dinner according to Mom and Chantal."

"I can't believe I'm imposing on people like this," Sam whispered as Brad rang the bell. "And, on a holiday to boot."

"You're early," said Chantal, opening the door to greet them.

"*Darn* you, Brad," said Sam.

"Did I interrupt something?" asked Chantal.

"No, not really. I was so impressed with this home when we were down the hill. Brad said he knew the owner and would ask if I could see the inside. I told him not on Thanksgiving, but, he insisted. He never told me it was *your* place."

"I didn't say *one* thing wrong. She's the owner. I know her, fairly well and, on occasion, she can be nice. I think she'll allow you to look around a little bit, even if it is Thanksgiving. Right, sis?"

"By all means, Samantha and what do you mean *on occasion*," she asked, not expecting an answer. "Come on in and get out of that nasty weather. And, by the way, you have to get used to his weird sense of humor," Chantal said, kissing Brad on the cheek. "He does things like this to me *all* the time. How was traffic coming up here?"

"It wasn't that bad. There was one small accident though," Sam said.

"Did anyone get hurt?" she asked, showing some concern.

"No, unfortunately." Brad interjected.

"What do you mean by that, little brother?"

"Nothing. I don't want to go into it."

"Okay. Come on, Samantha, let me show you around."

"I was hoping you would."

"By the way, Sam. Sis *is* a wannabe designer. She's just been too busy at the Smithsonian to pursue it. Everything you see, inside or out, came from her noggin. This splendid array of decor you are about to witness on your tour, stems from ideas she's had for years. I remember her *poor* attempts, *I mean poor to the point of being feeble*, before she could do renderings that looked worth a damn during her high school days. I recognize a lot of her original ideas here."

"You're *embarrassing* me, Brad."

"That's what you get for being too busy to do my place and making me hire a designer."

"Brad, she *did* a beautiful job on your place. You *know* she did."

"I know, sis. I've decided to use her again."

"You've got nothing to be embarrassed about from what I can see," Sam told Chantal. "It's wonderful. One wouldn't expect to see this style of home in an area like this, but, it fits the natural setting among the trees outside like it's been here a number of years. It's more elegant than just the ordinary log home... not exactly what you'd call an Abe Lincoln facade."

"Thank you, Samantha. Living in Colorado for all of those years, I always dreamed of having one. And, just because we chose to move to Maryland, why shouldn't I?"

"I agree completely."

Phil, flanked by his parents, and Brad's mother entered the magnificent foyer with its ceiling towering nearly 30 feet above. They proceeded through the appropriate holiday greetings. Phil's father was glad they'd arrived early because he was famished and ready to carve up the turkey. His wife, Sibyl, to his dismay, told him dinner wasn't going to be ready for a couple of hours. This news caused the blotched skin of his jowls to drop several inches and reveal his disappointment. Brad had warned Sam about this portly fellow, but, for some reason, he was nicer than usual. Not as boisterous. Maybe, with Sam's presence, he was on his best behavior, something which Brad had never witnessed.

As they entered the living room area with the wooden vaulted ceilings and knotty-pine floors, it became evident why Chantal selected the property. The view was, simply, breathtaking. The exterior wall was virtually solid glass with milled, pine framing. It rose twenty-five feet and allowed a view from the loft area above and behind them.

Access to the loft was by a wide, sturdy iron, circular staircase, spiraling upward and connecting to a thirty foot, natural wood, spindle railing. The loft had a second exit for those in a rush. There was a shiny brass, antique firemens' pole, salvaged from a circa 1920 station in Philadelphia, centered in a three foot diameter hole of the loft's floor and extending downward to the level where they were standing.

The property had white, cross buck fencing which gave the impression they were in the midst of the Kentucky Bluegrass region. With the grass of the turf farm still in place, it was a natural grazing area. And, yes, there were horses within its perimeter.

"Horses!" shrieked Sam. "I can't believe it. I love to ride. Who rides? Brad, do you ride? Can we go?"

"Hold your pants on, Sam," Brad interrupted her barrage of questions. He realized what he'd said might be pounced upon by someone as an opportunity for a snide remark, so quickly continued. "Phil and Chantal ride. There are horse trails all over this area and most people living here take advantage of them. And no, I don't ride. I don't even get *near* something with teeth that big." Everyone laughed at that, even Mal. Turning to Sam, Brad asked. "Do you think this crowd has the right to know what's going on?"

"I believe it would be appropriate. My parents know."

"Know what?" Everyone questioned in unison.

"We're engaged to be married, but haven't set the date yet," announced Brad. "I haven't even had time to shop for a ring."

Phil said, "I *knew* it."

Chantal said, "Way to go, little brother. You landed a nice one."

Brad's mother hugged them both and said with her normal grace and dignity, "It's wonderful news. This is the best Thanksgiving in many years."

Sibyl appropriately said, "Congratulations to the both of you. You make a beautiful couple. I'm certain the two of you'll be very happy together."

Mal didn't really say anything but, nodded his approval and gave a thumbs up sign. At least, he'd stopped eating potato chips and dip long enough to acknowledge the occasion.

"Thank you." Brad said, again turning to Sam. "I love you. And, from now on, you're part of the family. Look around, it's all you get."

"Thank you everyone, I'm so happy," Sam said, blushing slightly. "And Brad, I love you. I couldn't have hand-picked a better family to be a part of."

Mal, with his mouth dry from eating the salty chips or maybe the bag of pretzels he'd devoured earlier, said, "I think this needs a toast."

All agreed and after the toast, Chantal took Sam on a tour of the house. Brad heard his sister promise Sam, as they left the room, they'd go riding some day. Sibyl and Brad's mother left for the kitchen to look after the dinner, especially the turkey with its slow-roasting aroma filling the entire house. It smelled like Thanksgiving.

*****

The men retired to the recreation room and began playing pool on the green-cushioned baize, slate topped, regulation table, while they waited for the kickoffs of the traditional Thanksgiving Day football games. The giant screen television was located to the right of the antique wood stove, functionally used for heating some of the house.

Applying some chalk to the end of the cue stick Phil said, "I tried to call you a couple of different times yesterday."

As the chalk made a soft squeaking sound, it brought back the vivid memory of Sam's mother's scream. As quickly as it entered his mind, the thought disappeared and Brad said, "We were out most of the day getting some things I needed. We also had to get fitted for ski equipment. We're heading up to Snowshoe tomorrow for the weekend."

"You're going to Snowshoe with a woman like Sam and you think you need ski equipment? I'll bet you don't get many runs in, pal."

"I think my son has a very good point, Brad," added Mal. "I'll take a little of that betting action myself if you want."

"Come on you two. Cut me a little slack. She *is* the woman I'm going to marry, you know. Besides, we have to do some skiing before we go to Colorado next month on the trip with Evan and John. You'd better get some time in on the slopes too Phil. If you're not in shape, it's going to be a tough outing."

"Are you implying that I'm not in shape, pal?"

"What've you done physically since last year's trip?"

"Played a hell of a lot of pool. Your shot," Phil said as he missed sinking a ball on the break.

"Haven't gotten any better with all this pool you've been playing, have you?" Brad quipped. "I did forget. How insane of me. You *do* get a *real good workout* from riding horses. Shit, the only thing getting in shape, besides the horse, is your ass."

"He does have a knack of putting the truth into words doesn't he son?"

"Dad, are you ganging up on me too? I can't wait for you to have to stretch out for a shot on this table, speaking of being in shape."

"Watch your mouth boy," came the Texas drawl, "I *am* in shape. Just happens that the shape I'm in is round."

Brad even had to laugh at that comeback. Perhaps, Mal wasn't that bad to be around after all. "Phil, why were you trying to get in touch with me yesterday?"

"Just to razz you a little about where you were staying, that's all. With the announcement you two just made in the living room, it would've been a wasted effort anyway. I'm happier than hell for the two of you. There's going to be a lot of pissed off young women in the greater DC area when the word gets out that you're off the market."

"Thanks, Phil. If we're as happy as you and Sis, we can't ask for much more."

"I don't understand something, Brad. What happened to your cell phone?"

"It's broken," Brad said, and really meant it both figuratively and literally.

"Hold on a minute," Phil said reaching for his wallet and pulling out a small piece of paper. Reading from it, he continued, " that's not what a ahh... Sergeant Butterfield at the 47th Precinct said."

"Who the hell is Sergeant Butterfield?"

"He's the cop who climbed down into a storm sewer to retrieve your phone. A number of people heard it ringing, probably when I was calling. They reported it to the police."

"You're shitting me. That damn thing still works?" Brad thought out loud.

"Of course it works. Brad, why the hell was it down a storm sewer? Butterfield hit the recall button and, of course, I was the last one to call, so it rang me. How do I explain to a cop, it's my brother-in-law's phone, but, I don't have a clue as to how it got there?"

"If you don't know Phil... you can't explain it."

"Seems reasonable to me," chimed in Mal, trying not to let anyone realize that he was breathing heavily while stretching out for a shot on the pool table. He also let go an SBD in the attempt.

"*Jesus, Dad. You did it again.* Whew," he said catching the first whiff of the foul odor and waving his hand violently in front of his face. Phil continued, not noticing Brad's silent, controlled laughter. "Dad, come on now. You can't side with Brad all the time. *Damn, that thing's hangin' around here! What the hell did you eat? Whatever it was, it musta died three years ago! Light a match or something! And next time you have to stretch for a shot, use the damn bridge!"*

Mal paid no attention to his son's antics. "Son, he's not the one that insinuated I couldn't reach for a shot on this table. Didja see that shot sonny boy?"

"Phil," said Brad, getting his attention and trying not to laugh. "When you called me the other day, Sam was driving. Right after we'd hung up we were going around a corner and she scared the shit out of me. The damn phone just flew out of my hand, hit the street and slid into that gutter. I thought it'd be broken so, I didn't bother to go back for it. That's all there is to it. *Damn, that is bad,*" he said as Mal passed by dragging the scent behind him. "*Cut that sucker loose!*"

"She a bad driver, huh?"

"The worst," Brad fibbed.

"Well, I told Sergeant Butterfield, you'd stop by the precinct and pick it up. I told him I had a crazy brother-in-law, one who'd probably throw a cell phone away for some stupid reason."

"Yeah, right, Phil. That's a *$300 cell phone*! Like, I'd *really just throw the damn thing away."*

"That's what *he* said."

"Who?"

"Butterfield. He said, anyone that would just throw away a phone would be pretty stupid."

"What'd you say?"

"I said he'd have to meet you and draw his own conclusion."

"Thanks for the confidence booster, buddy."

"You're welcome, I'm sure."

"Mal, how are things going in Colorado Springs at the research center?"

"I assume you're asking about the Cancer studies we're working on."

"Yeah, or anything else that looks promising. You know, when I finally got the Center downtown off the ground, I was trying to focus its efforts on Cancer alone. But, since opening we've been, slowly but surely, collecting data on other types of research. If it weren't for John's ability with the computer system and Abbey's unending devotion of inputting the data ...well, we'd be pretty snowed under."

"I've seen your operation down there and believe me, I can't believe what's been accomplished in such a short period of time. What you're doing, should've been done years ago. More power to you. I don't know if we've forwarded out latest findings to your center or not. They were about to as I left. Through all of the feedback, it seems you may have put us on the right track and saved us a lot of money. Without your input, we'd still be unaware the center outside of Tampa did the same basic research without any favorable results."

"That's the kinda thing our subscribers pay us for. Hopefully, they keep the data rolling in so our feedback can be more and more refined. It's not just the money that's important. The Tampa study took almost two years, so look at the time you saved. In the meantime, people are dying daily from this shit disease. And, when you really come down to it, God only knows if the Tampa group was repeating someone else's research and didn't realize it."

"We're still working on our splitter theory as *we* call it. We feel that we've centralized an enzyme to digest the cancer cell, but, a big problem still remains. Living cells, like cancer, are protected from the enzyme. The membranes can't be pierced as long as the cell is alive. The splitter would allow the cell wall to be cracked open, allowing the enzyme to enter. An antibody that cracks only cancerous cells *has* to be found. Dosage is also a problem. How much enzyme to destroy how much cancer? Ideally, the splitter would crack only the cells you want to attack, kind of a search and destroy battle throughout the body, you know, and then be expelled naturally. Ideally, the enzyme would digest on a hierarchical relationship, first, the cancer cells and second itself, so to speak. The body would be free of Cancer and the enzyme both. That's what we're shooting for Brad, at least in the Cancer area."

"Wouldn't this technology apply to a lot of other areas if it works?"

"I don't see why it wouldn't."

"I'm looking forward to seeing the data down at the center," Brad said, knowing full well it hadn't been received yet or Abbey, in her unending devotion, would've informed him.

"I don't know how you two guys can stand the frustrations and all the dead-ends associated with research. I don't think I'm cut out for that aspect of medicine. It's all I can do to just keep up with my patient load," Phil stated.

"Son, after a period of time, dealing with patients and becoming more and more upset as they die off one by one because there're no cures available, you do what you feel you've got to. *It is frustrating*, but, over the years, there's been some *remarkable* advances made through research and being applied today to save lives. Even, probably, to some of your patients. If you're a caring person, as I know you are, as well as Brad here," he said motioning towards Brad, "eventually; although you should never do so as a doctor, so were told, you build up personal relationships. When they begin to die off, *it hurts*, son. You're *going* to find that out.

Brad on the other hand, has not been involved in a doctor-patient relationship. He's found out though, because of his father's death, there's *pain* involved with losing someone because of no cures. You feel helpless. He's merely negated the pains involved with losing patients and moved directly into research. And, thank God he has."

Brad was listening attentively to what Mal was saying. He didn't understand how this man, who he detested with disgust for the few years since making his acquaintance, was coming off so well in this conversation. Even his exaggerated Texas drawl had subsided to the point that it had become bearable. Mal, as far as Brad could distinguish, had not burped at all. And, only farted once, so far. To his amazement, Brad was enjoying this guy. Sam wasn't even in the room so she had no influence on his current behavior. Phil's father was continuing so Brad again listened with interest to what he was saying.

"Years ago, too many for my liking and not long after you were born Phil, I was in partnership with..."

"Not that many Dad," Phil chimed in trying to protect his own aging and missing another shot on the pool table.

"*Long enough*! As, I was saying, I was involved in a partnership with some doctors, sharing the same facilities. The practices were thriving. I'm fully aware of all the stories, all bullshit by the way, about how I became involved in costly malpractice litigation and was forced into research because of them. Brad... Phil knows all of this. I just wanted you to be aware of the circumstances surrounding my entry into the research area."

"I appreciate the trust," Brad said.

"Don't misunderstand what I'm saying here. I would've ended up in research for the reasons I mentioned earlier. What happened, with regards to the malpractice insinuations, only pushed me there sooner. Although, I could never prove it, even if I was willing to spend the time to do so, the other partners were the ones responsible for my professional demise. The three of them instituted a plan to discredit me by falsifying documentation on patients of mine ranging back over a two year period. They changed the diagnosis and subsequent courses of action to be taken by my patients and leaked the information to the respective families. It opened the floodgates for legal action against me. As a result, I was unable to obtain the insurance protection necessary to continue my practice. That much of the story is true. That shit gets *real* expensive!"

"I can only imagine. Why would they want you out of the partnership so bad to go to such extremes?" questioned Brad, his attention now solely on the conversation with Mal.

"Those three guys, again I can't prove anything, were up to no good. Believe me! I think they realized I was becoming aware of some of the things they were doing and were looking for a way to remedy the situation. They probably felt that if they could discredit me enough, anything I might say concerning their practices would be considered sour grapes. They were involved in some pretty shady endeavors. I strongly believe some of their patients were actually used as guinea pigs for testing of drugs. Without the patients knowledge, of course.

Over the years, these guys expanded their goals and entered the research arena as well. The last I heard, they were fairly high up the corporate ladder at one of the conglomerates in the pharmaceutical industry, somewhere in Europe. Once I got personally involved with the research center in Colorado Springs, I became very narrow sighted, with all of my energies devoted to its efforts. There was no use in trying to prove anything. It was impossible to accomplish. And, besides, I had a young son, a loving wife and I was very happy to be in biological research. My life seemed right, so why mess with it. I have some ahh... other interests, on the side, to keep any idle time I might have occupied."

"Malcomb, we should've had this little talk a couple of years ago," said Brad.

"There never seemed to be an appropriate time with you being in school and followed by your residency at Georgetown University Hospital. Not to mention how busy you've been getting the Center off the ground. Hell, I think you're probably busier than I am. And, Brad, it's okay to call me Mal. I'm fully aware of what some people think triggered the nickname."

"Thanks."

"No problem."

The three men completed four or five games of nine-ball before the first kickoff. It was nearly half time before they were summoned to dinner. Passing through the expanse of the living room, Brad noticed out the window, it was no longer raining or sleeting. It was snowing like hell. Was it possible the forecasters were right for a change, he wondered. What a weekend was coming he thought, entering the dining room. He gave Sam a peck on the cheek as, smiling and winking, she placed the snow covered Himalayas on the table. Mashed potatoes to the novice. *Him...will...lay...ya.... later*, Brad thought, smiling at his private joke. Maybe Sam's right and you *are* disgusting. He didn't really care.

*****

Conversations, none of which were of a serious nature, during dinner were very entertaining and there was lots of laughter around the table. Everyone felt at ease and were having a wonderful time. At future family gatherings, it would be referred to as often as any other get-together.

Mal offered a tale of woe and his audience enjoyed it immensely. He and five or six of his best friends, all seniors in high school, had piled into a Volkswagen and driven the 50 or 60 miles to the Texas State Fair. And, considering they'd lugged a pony keg of beer with them, it was very cramped quarters. They'd gone to the fair with one purpose in mind. One of them was going to win the Texas State Fair Chili Eating contest. Being football jocks, all were built quite bulky and could hold their share of food.

They'd carefully mapped out their strategy. No matter how spicy the chili , under no circumstances would they eat anything other than chili, not even a saltine cracker. Considering how worldly traveled and full of knowledge seventeen and eighteen year olds have historically proven to be, swallowing anything else would simply take up space that could be used for chili.

They'd been seated, along with nearly two hundred entrants, at wooden, picnic-style tables and the sponsor of the event had provided each with a place mat. Mal had taken a quick glance at the *Texas Fire Brand Chili* advertisement on his placemat and realized the company's logo had been a chili bean with little arms and legs. It had been depicted running across the mat with fire coming out of its ass, or at least the proximity of where a bean's ass might be, and had possessed a horrified look on its face, mouth wide open and obviously yelling in pain. Rightfully so Mal had recalled a few moments later. The copyrighted saying, *Chili So Hot, It Cooks The Beans After You Eat 'Em*, had been scrawled out in an arch across the top, the letters simulating flames. Mal, at that moment, had *strongly* believed he and his friends *might* be in trouble.

Seated across the table from Mal, had been a man who had a face like a bulldog and a body to match. The only differences were his arms and legs were shorter and he must've tipped the scales at 350 pounds, minimum. He'd sat there, casually eating a hot-dog with a shit eatin' grin on his face. "You in this contest?" Mal had politely asked.

"Yeah," had come the gruff reply, "just warming up with a couple of dogs. Did the same thing last year when I won it."

Thoughts of winning had disappeared from Mal's mind faster than the hot-dog he'd seen the bulldog devour. He and his friends had decided to see how well they'd do anyway. *Shit, they'd entered, why not give it a shot?*

None of the teenage entrants had come close to winning and two dropped out after only five dishes claiming their mouths were on fire. Mal had been the last teenager to become an also-ran in the contest and hasn't touched chili since.

The bulldog, seated across from him, had finished the last half of Mal's thirteenth bowl and, grinning the whole time, had ordered what easily must've been his twentieth. He'd won again that year and as Mal and his friends had retreated, they'd looked back to see the asshole ordering some dessert.

The young men felt so horrible they'd decided the fair had nothing more to offer and piled into Volkswagen for the return trip home. To quench their thirst from the chili, they'd polished off the pony keg, now warm from sitting inside the closed up bug. What had transpired on the way home was funny at the beginning, but quickly turned into a serious situation.

The combination of beer on the way to the fair, the chili, and, then, the warm beer before they'd left for home, had begun to work wonders. Nobody admitted who'd let the first fart fly, but, six large guys trying to get fresh air out the windows of a Volkswagen bug at the same time, can prove to be difficult. Especially when the back windows don't roll down. This phenomenon had lasted for about thirty miles, everyone admitting to being the culprit on no less than six occasions each.

One of Mal's friends said, "I just had the biggest surprise in the world guys."

"What's that?" they'd all wanted to know.

"A wet fart with a lump in it," he had informed them.

"No way!" had come the response in unison. As if sworn in to testify before the grand jury, he'd not been lying. In less than ten minutes, everyone had begun lumping more than farting.

To explain the extent of diarrhea which erupted would fill a complete chapter in a medical book on the subject. The driver of the bug had to sell his car, the interior was that bad. And, he hadn't gotten much for it either.

The story took quite a while to recount and laughter interrupted its flow often. Sibyl laughed, even though she'd heard the story told a number of times before. Mal had pre-warned Sam about the contents of the story, which Brad appreciated. She said it wouldn't bother her and it hadn't. She'd laughed throughout as much as anyone, if not more.

*****

At the conclusion of dinner, Sam couldn't believe what happened. As if on cue, Phil placed a portable television on the kitchen counter. The men then, set forth cleaning up "the mess", as they called it. They completely cleared the table and washed, dried and put away all of the dishes, including the pots and pans. They worked in near silence as they watched the Detroit Lions and Green Bay Packers play their traditional Thanksgiving Day game on the small TV. Probably made their task more bearable for them!

The women, on the other hand, after laboring for hours preparing the meal, would adjourn to the family room of the house to relax. *What a wonderful tradition and a great family!* Sam took the time as an opportunity to coax Chantal outside in the snowfall to pick out her horse.

Later, Mal taught Sam the finer points of shooting pool. Amazing, Brad thought, yesterday he *wasn't* looking forward to dinner with Mal. Even though he had burped a few times since dinner, he'd excused himself to go out on the front porch to supposedly get a breath of fresh air when Brad knew full well it was to let go another SBD. In the period of a few hours, he'd grown to like the man and, he knew Sam did as well.

After a few games, she'd become remarkably good and challenged Brad. To his astonishment, she was fantastic at bank shots and the angles involved. Brad felt her *memory thing* must have had something to do with it. With his win streak in jeopardy, Brad decided they'd better join the family for some parting talks. Samantha didn't say a word, simply smiled and followed him into the family room

Phil's parents and Brad's mother were planning to fly back to Colorado Monday as Natasha was anxious to begin the traditional Claxton estate Christmas decorations. She wanted it perfect for everyone's arrival in late December. Brad told Sam that when his mother decorates for the holidays, she *really* decorates... *in a big way*! He'd long since lost count of the number of lights and displays that she'd collected over the years, but, she'd see what he meant when they arrived. Samantha learned that neighbors drove from all over the area, even as far away as Denver, to see the estate when it was completed.

"Brad, you haven't forgotten about the Christmas gala at the Embassy have you?" reminded Phil.

"No, not at all. It just hasn't been in the front of my mind, that's all. I've had a few more important items on my agenda lately," he said eyeing Samantha.

"Is this something I should be aware of?" questioned Sam.

"If you're going to attend with your future husband, you should," Brad responded.

"Wherever you go, I go. Which embassy is holding this little shin-dig?"

"The New Zealand Embassy," chimed in Chantal. "Every year, since Evan got his position on the staff, we've been invited, and, I might add, it's quite an honor to be on the guest list."

"It's *that* big a deal?" asked Samantha beginning to show some concern. "Who goes to this thing every year?"

"Only the first ten pages of Who's Who in DC, that's all," added Phil. "Folks like other Ambassadors, foreign dignitaries, corporate CEO's, the usual assortment of politicians and the like may attend. It's in two weeks pal," Phil directed at Brad. "I can't believe you've never mentioned it to Samantha."

"Like I said, I've been a little pre-occupied lately or have you forgotten?"

"I can appreciate that," stated Mal as he watched Samantha's skirt slide higher on her thigh as she crossed her shapely legs.

"Who else is going that we know?" Samantha further questioned.

"Like Chantal said, she and Phil. Of course it goes without saying that Terri and Evan will be there. And, Abbey and John get a yearly invite."

"Chantal, I'll bet you already have your dress, right?"

"To tell you the truth, I've had it for about two months. I hope it still fits after today's dinner. I've found from past experience that you can't wait too long to shop, especially this time of year. There's a lot of other festivities going on."

"Damn. What am I going to do?" asked Sam, now showing signs of shock and revealing the normal womanly traits. "I've got absolutely nothing to wear."

Brad noticed Mal's eyes widen at Sam's last statement but, gave it little attention. He realized where this was heading and was determined to head it off at the pass. "Sam, honey, I've got it all figured out."

"I sure hope so," came the quiet response.

"Believe me, I do. We'll stop in New York City on our way to Lake Placid. You take as much time as you need to find the gown you want. You should be able to find something in the Big Apple for the occasion. How's that?"

"You'd do that?"

"Of course," replied Brad, knowing he had no other choice and continued, "it's the least I can do for being so forgetful. Then it's settled?"

"You bet, sweetheart. You said on our way to Lake Placid. Why are we going there?"

"I thought we'd tie a trip to see Tony in with the shopping spree. We should get as much skiing in as possible before the trip out to mom's. We don't have to if you don't want to."

"No, Brad. That sounds perfect to me. I'm looking forward to it."

Everyone continued to sit in the western-style leather furnishings, chatting and watching the fire burn in the enormous, natural stone, fireplace. Brad rose and said, "We'd better be a goin'. We have a long drive in front of us tomorrow."

"You're probably right. I just hate for the day to end," answered Sam as she extended her hand to Brad for him to help her up.

"It's probably not over yet my dear," said Mal, winking at her as he watched the auburn-haired beauty rise.

"You're probably right," she said, returning the wink.

They said their good-byes to everyone and as Brad was opening the door to leave, Sam said, "Water."

"What? Are you thirsty?" Brad asked.

"No. You wanted me to remind you to get some water for your windshield bottle or whatever you call it."

"That's right. I can't believe the memory of this woman," he said, a little embarrassed he'd forgotten. "I don't think I'll do it now. It's getting pretty cold out there and it might freeze and crack the container. I'll pick up some actual washer fluid when I stop for gas tomorrow on the way to Snowshoe."

As they departed, Sam looked back over her shoulder towards the log house and said, "Beautiful home and an even more beautiful family. I really feel a part of it. Thanks, Brad, for a great Thanksgiving."

"One of many to come, my love."

*****

The trip back to Sam's house was enjoyable enough. Both couldn't wait to get there, for obvious reasons. Sam was sitting close to Brad, his arm around her and his hand placed on her camel hair sweater, massaging her lovingly. The arrangement was somehow accomplished in spite of the center console and her tight skirt. She effortlessly shifted through the four gears for him as they proceeded home and playfully, at times, grabbed the wrong gear shift. The one in his lap.

They didn't talk much early during the drive, each trying to warm up before the Mustang's heater took over. Both were tired and Brad was still regaining his strength after his recuperation period in the hospital. It was still snowing and beginning to accumulate, about three inches Brad guessed as he swept the snow from the windshield with his arm before leaving.

"How early do we have to get up tomorrow to leave?" she asked.

"Whenever we decide to get up... will be early enough."

"You want to leave for Snowshoe before Sunday don't you?"

"You sex-craved little devil you. We'll make it to Snowshoe tomorrow. Sometime. Probably late," he said as he thought about being with Sam.

"I'm not really that good you know."

"The hell you say. I don't know how you could be any better," he said, applying more pressure to her breast and feeling her nipple become hard.

"God Brad, not at that. I meant at snow skiing."

"Oh!" Brad exclaimed, realizing the error of his thinking. "If you pick up on snow skiing like you do shooting pool, you'll be fine. This trip to Colorado isn't a big deal. If you're in shape, which you are, and a very good shape I might add, you'll be fine. Don't let it worry you. It's not the Olympics and I promise not to race you. All right?"

"Okay. You think I'm pretty good huh?"

"I've never seen you ski."

"God Brad, not that. I mean the other. You know."

"Oh!" Brad again said, realizing her play on words. "At that, you are undoubtedly Olympic quality. A Gold Medal winner."

"I think the partner I have for the pairs competition has a little to do with it."

"I think we're fairly good together. As I recall, the last performance was voted a perfect ten," he said, his voice rising slightly as she grabbed the gear shift in his lap.

The word games continued past the single-file line of blinking, orange and white striped sentries guarding the road. Through Silver Spring and into Georgetown. Brad brought the Mustang to a skidding stop in front. He was in a hurry. He got out of the car and noticed Sam, not even waiting for him to open her door. She was already out, moving quickly towards the house, her heavy breathing visible in the cold night air. She was in a hurry too. He caught her on the front porch and watched her shaking fingers insert the key in the lock.

"Did you lock the car?" she asked, opening the door for him.

"No. Who gives a shit. There's nobody around this time of night anyway." He slammed the door behind them and pressed her against it like he'd done only two days before. She, once again, began ripping the shirt off him. "Do you have something against the shirts I wear?"

"Yes. They're in the way," she said, dragging him towards the bedroom.

While Brad was in tow through the dining room, he attempted to pick up the centerpiece still on the floor. "Leave it there, big guy," she said, slowly, carefully undressing him. Brad returned the favor a bit more feverishly than Sam. Gently pushing Brad backwards onto the dining table, Sam began to kiss him from head to toe. She allowed Brad's passion to rise to an unbearable height. The tormenting over, she climbed onto the table and, softly, lowered her young, firm body on him.

The only lighting was coming through the window from the street lights in front of the house. As Sam put her hands on the table and pushed slightly away, arching her back, Brad got a full appreciation of her perfection. "Thank you for the greatest day of my life Brad," she moaned quietly, feeling his hardness inside her.

"Sam, the best day of my life will always be the next one I spend with you." Their lips met and nothing further needed to be said. Life was fantastic.

*****

"The love birds are back," he said into the phone.

"Jesus Christ. I thought this damn guy was a schedule freak. Now all of a sudden, we don't know where he's going or when."

"Odds are, he's goin' to be hangin' his hat at the broad's house every night," he said lighting up a Camel. "They just arrived and ran into the house. I don't think it's because it's freezin', fuckin' cold out, either."

"You okay there?"

"Me? Fine. Rentin' this room across the street makes this surveillance shit pretty easy. Beats the hell out of sittin' in a fuckin' car and freezin' your ass off. And, I can smoke whenever I want. I'm just getting anxious to get the damn job over with and move on."

He looked around the darkened room. Not much there to be proud of. The chair in which he was seated had cracked and missing spindles and the painted table where he rested his elbows while maintaining the surveillance vigil with binoculars was beyond repair. Two matching side tables, covered with a light brown Formica veneer and cluttered with Playboys and copies of Travel, flanked a chocolate-colored, worn-out, three-seat sofa. The white shades, now yellow from aging and missing the screw-down finials, hung loosely on the harps of two beige, ginger-jar lamps. The furnishings had the appeal of antique K-Mart, but, they were his digs, for the time being.

"We lost track of them for most of the day. One of our cars ended up in a damn ditch."

Blowing a series of smoke rings towards the ceiling of the small room, he replied, "I heard about that earlier. Probably at his brother-in-law's all day anyway. Like he'd planned."

"He was. That's where we picked him up on the way back."

"I'm goin' to hit the sack. I've got the alarm set for five just in case. I have a feeling I'll be looking at nothing for a long time though."

"By the way, for your information, the other contract was on for tonight."

"Who was it?"

"Read about it in tomorrow's *Post*. There's was one hell of an accident on the BW Expressway."

"Who did it?"

"You don't know him. He's from out of town."

"So am I. I might know him."

"Not this guy. It's the first time we've used him. He was an up-an-coming race car driver until he had an accident at Darlington Speedway which nearly cost him his life. It did cost him his nerve. Doesn't race anymore, but, said he could pull this off. We'll check it out later and see how well he did. If there's any movement from the house during your watch, let us know right away," the voice ordered.

"You got it." He pushed the antennae in on the cell phone and crushed out the cigarette in the over-flowing ashtray. Slowly, very tired, he walked over to the roll away bed, rented locally under a fictitious name, and climbed in. Before going to sleep he muttered under his breath, “that lucky bastard. His contract is over. Wish mine was.”

*****

It was roughly 3:30 on Friday afternoon as Brad finished mounting the skies on top of the Mustang in preparation for their late start to Snowshoe. They'd spent all last evening practicing body language skills with Sam winning a Gold in every event. Considering they didn't wake up until after eleven o'clock or gotten out of bed 'til about one-thirty, they were moving right along getting ready to leave for Snowshoe.

During the night it had snowed almost two inches in the metropolitan DC area, but, it was melting now, as a light, misty rain fell. At Chantal's, about forty, maybe fifty, miles north, it was still snowing with an accumulation approaching eight inches. The mountains were receiving more snow than forecast as the weather front had stalled and was dumping more white stuff than predicted. Historically, there's one chance in seven of the DC area having a white Christmas. Finding the ground covered the day after Thanksgiving is a skier's dream come true.

Sam approached Brad from behind as he finished securing the ski poles. “Heh, big guy, is it raining or snowing?”

“What we have here, my dear, is light rain. But, you can bet when we get out of the city, it's going to change to snow.” Turning, he was nearly speechless. “God, you look great. Like you're ready for the chair lift.” Sam had one of her “outfits” on from the ski shop and looked nothing short of terrific. “I told you to buy it when we were in the shop. You look fabulous in black. Turn around and let me see all of it.”

Sam put her arms parallel to the ground and slowly revolved 360 degrees. “How's that? I know you told me this is a new generation fabric used in ski attire, but, Brad, don't you think it's a little tight? You're sure it's going to keep me warm enough? It's pretty thin?”

“I love the lime green diagonal stripes across the front of the top and repeated across your fanny. It *really* shows off your shape. The way it should.”

“You mean, it really makes my boobs and ass look good?”

"Sam!" exclaimed Brad, looking around to see if anyone heard. Seeing no one, he continued more quietly, "where'd you pick up that language?"

"Nowhere in particular. It must be the company I keep," she said laughing. "That's something I've always wanted to say, but, being a refined southern lady, never quite... had the balls to say."

"Sam!" repeated Brad. "You sound like a lady of the night," he continued, teasing her.

"Only if you're the one making the offer," she said batting her eyelashes at him.

"Maybe, we should leave tomorrow," Brad suggested.

"No way. What I went through to get these pants on goes beyond description. I had to, lay flat on the bed and pull these things up, inch by inch. This top, when you hold it up, looks like it was designed for a Barbie Doll. Not, someone five foot nine with 37-22-35 measurements. You can't imagine."

"Oh, believe me, I most certainly can. I can visualize every tug and pull."

"Brad, you're making fun. Stop it."

Putting his hands on her shoulders, Brad asked, "did you say... 37-22-35?"

"Yes," she answered shyly. "You don't believe me?"

"I think I do."

"You think you do? Look," instructed Sam as she inhaled deeply and sucked in her waist even further.

What that did to the diagonal stripes went beyond description as the maneuver stretched the fabric to its maximum. The manufacturer's warranty was about to come into play in front of Brad's eyes. Lucky warranty, he thought smiling, remembering the night before. "I think thirty-seven and a half would be more accurate."

"What?"

"Look," Brad said, directing her with his eyes.

Looking downward to the lime green coloring, Sam noticed her nipples protruding beyond the curvature of her breasts, in a slightly upward angle, stretching the fabric even further. In a deep, southern accent, she said, "Dat do make dem boobs look good. Don't it?"

"*Dat*, it do. Dey look like a *matched* set to me, from where I'm a viewin' dem," mocked Brad, both of them laughing.

When their laughter had subsided a little, Sam said. "I can't really wear this, can I? It looks like it's been painted on."

"Damn lucky artist," Brad responded and continued. "Honestly, Sam, that's what's being worn on the slopes these days."

"Getting into it is a problem, but, you know something, as tight as this appears, it doesn't really hamper any movements."

"Told you."

"The only concern is how warm am I going to stay?"

"Don't worry, Sam. As a matter of fact, you shouldn't really wear that outfit inside for that long. You may even be sorry you wore it for the drive up there."

"I wouldn't go so far as to say that, Brad."

"Okay. I warned you."

"The final problem then, as I see it, or them, is this extra half inch you so kindly pointed out to me."

"Shit, Sam, the half inch pointed out at me. Directly at me. And, quite proudly I might add."

"Brad, you're terrible. What can I do about it?"

"If you're that embarrassed, put something over them from the inside. Would that work?" he questioned in all seriousness.

"Tell me you're not thinking of something like a... like a pasty."

"It *doesn't have to have tassels* you know. Something... ummm... simple, like a round BandAid or something." Brad replied, thinking he had struck upon a good idea. Continuing he said, "Sam, a bra would never look right."

"Brad, darling of my life... I... don't... even... own... a... bra," she said in a determined voice. "And, my love," she continued, "I would never consider applying adhesive of any type or gluing anything to my body, not... even... a ... BandAid, where you're suggesting."

"That's my girl. I couldn't agree with you more. Go as you are. No hidden touches. Only, when you're talking to people, you should have your back to them, so they can do this." Spinning her 180 degrees, Brad reached under each of her arms, softly grabbing the lime green diagonal stripe in his hands and pulled her gently backwards until their bodies touched. He kissed her on the neck, and asked, "should we call and make our apologies to the reservationist? Tell 'em we're going to be a day late?"

"I think you have a winner of an idea," came the response.

"You must promise me though, we'll get an early start tomorrow."

"No. No promises," Sam said softly.

"You're a shrewd business person, lady. It's a deal." Brad said. They headed towards the front door and the dining room table beyond, still clear of its centerpiece.

The man in the second story window across the street was watching as Brad had grabbed Samantha from behind. He abruptly stood and wiped the cold, just spilled Budweiser from his lap he'd knocked over while viewing the action of the young lovers. The freshly opened can rolled across the floor, leaving a trail of foaming, yellow brew. He quickly glanced out the window. They hadn't noticed him. The nearly full pack of Camels lying on the table was soaked. "Shit!"

---- Chapter Six ----

After a couple of ordinary bagels for breakfast, Sam and Brad made their way to the chair lift for their first ski run which they'd originally planned for late Friday or early Saturday. It was now, Sunday. Time flies when you're having a good time and, that, they'd had. They had arrived late, real late, Saturday night; however, the time spent together was worth their tardy arrival. They'd left Georgetown at four o'clock in the afternoon and driven slowly due to the treacherous conditions of the roads, some of which were still in need of a visit from the resident snow plow.

The activities of the past two days brought a smile to Brad's face. The description Sam had forged in his mind, of putting her ski pants on, was, *absolutely*, no joke. While watching her tussle with them this morning, he'd laughed the entire time. Getting them off, he'd discovered Friday, was much easier. She'd simply rolled them down, like panty hose, from her 22 inch waist, over her 35 inch hips and to her ankles. Getting the top off had proven to be an entirely different story as her breasts exploded out of the tight fabric with the force of an A-bomb test in the New Mexico desert.

They'd spent most of the day on Saturday catching up on much needed sleep and had promised each other when they woke, they'd immediately depart for the ski trip. The promise, of course, had been broken, but, neither showed the slightest bit of remorse. They had received a number of calls but, had decided not to answer, not wanting anyone, especially Phil, to know they hadn't left. Why let someone conjecture that an insatiable sexual appetite had delayed their departure. *Hell, so what if it is true, why spread the word around?*

Sam had fallen to sleep midway through the long drive to the West Virginia mountains. Waking on occasion, she'd look at Brad, briefly smile, touch him as if assuring herself he was still there, and then, close her eyes once again. It was the first time he'd seen her sleeping and noticed her soft breathing, a sign he'd taken to mean she was pleased and happy.

It was now late morning and beautiful. A high pressure system from the west had finally bumped the storm over the Atlantic and left clear, sunny skies and an aftermath of 32 inches of new snow. Resort personnel had groomed the slopes overnight and they were in perfect condition for a great day of skiing. Brad was very anxious to see how well Samantha would do.

Dressed in a burgundy and gold ski outfit, the same style peeled off on Friday, she looked sensational. Brad caught a few folks, mostly men, but also a few envious women, stealing looks and checking her out, but, remembered the promise he'd made himself and maintained his composure. She did look sensational, however.

They found the lift line wasn't all that long because the severity of the storm with near blizzard conditions had dampened the spirits of the holiday weekend crowd. The resort had been closed to skiers until this morning so, most ski buffs had left early. Brad had decided to extend their stay until Tuesday afternoon, one of the perks he was entitled to as Director of the Center.

He noticed Sam was easily moving on the level ground with the aid of her poles, not an easy task for a beginner. She *must've* been skiing in North Carolina with "Daddy". Only three couples remained in front of them when Brad heard a familiar voice from behind shout, "Brad. Hey, Brad!"

"Who the hell?" Brad said turning around to look. A short distance behind and near the end of the line was John with Abbey at his side. Both were smiling and waving frantically.

They waved back and as he pointed to the summit with his ski pole, Brad shouted, "See you at the top."

Abbey and John nodded agreement as the lift approached from the rear and Brad and Sam sank backwards into the chair causing it to rock slightly. With the swinging motion creating a stir in her stomach, Sam said, "Ooooh, I forgot how that felt. It's always easier, though, than it looks to get in one of these things."

"You're acting like an old pro at this, Sam. How long has it been since you've skied?" Brad questioned as he gave John and Abbey a departing wave over his shoulder.

"The middle of last year's season. I took a weekend up in the Poconos. I wonder when John and Abbey decided to come."

"It must have been a spur of the moment decision. What's hard for me to believe is... *Abbey is actually here*! I'm surprised she's not at the Center working as usual."

"It's Sunday, you know. And a holiday weekend to boot. Are you some kind of slave driver or something?" Sam asked playfully.

"No, it's *not* that! I've tried to encourage her to take time off but, she always refuses. Total devotion to her work at the Center is always the excuse. Hell, when I couldn't go to Australia with John because I was in the hospital, I told Abbey that she should've gone in my place. Of course she didn't. Wouldn't *hear* of such a thing. Too much work to do! You know, all the usual excuses for spending twelve to sixteen hours a day at work. I've even mentioned it to John trying to get him to have some influence on her and help get her a social life. Doesn't do any good. That's why I'm kinda shocked to see them. More so *her* than him. I'm anxious to see them at the top and find out what's going on."

"She's a vibrant little thing isn't she?"

"*That* she is, *without* question!"

The lift carried them above tree top level. The newly fallen snow had collected on the branches, causing them to majestically arch downward. Below them, skiers snow-ploughed their way down a beginner's slope and looking closely, Brad could identify families skiing together. The beginners, not quite sure of themselves yet, were slowly learning to traverse the slopes.

Brad's thoughts went back to his learning days in the Southern Alps and his mother leading the four of them down the numerous trails. She'd always been followed by Brad and Chantal, in that order. And, his father had *always* brought up the rear to "pick up the broken pieces." It had been a follow-the-leader learning process and as he watched this scenario unfolding below him, his eyes suddenly welled up with the memories.

"Something wrong?" asked Sam.

"No, why do you ask?"

"Your eyes look a little watery."

"Just the cold breeze causing it" Brad responded, sliding his goggles down to hide his eyes. But, he then realized, she was the woman he loved and could be truthful with her. Hell, he *should* be truthful with her. "Actually, seeing all the people down there brought back some wonderful memories. It just got to me a little."

"Memories of your father?"

"Yeah. The whole family thing."

"There's nothing wrong with that Brad. Most guys I know would try to hide their feelings instead of letting the emotion come out. Saving their manly image and being macho, you know? I appreciate your honesty, as well as your manhood." she said playfully placing her gloved hand in his lap and elbowing him in the side.

"Thanks."

Approaching the top Brad said, “Careful gettin' off.”

“Brad, I've done this before. Stop being so protective.”

From their attempts to board the chair lift, it was evident the couple riding one chair in front of them were beginners and, attempting to steady each other as they stood up from the double chair, they both fell. In a frenzy, they made futile attempts to get up-righted and out of the way, but, at least, they were laughing about it. Brad was worried about Sam, but, gradually, with ease, she maneuvered her way around to the left of the couple laying spread eagle on the ground. Watching the graceful motions of Samantha, Brad didn't notice the young man's skis which caught him painfully in the shin and caused him to fall.

“Sorry,” the new skier said, still attempting to get up as his girlfriend made it to her feet. “We're ahhhh... kind of novices at this.”

Popping up quickly and back on his skis, Brad responded, “No problem.”

“No problem, hell! How'd you get up so fast? This really sucks!”

“Lots of practice. I fall a lot,” Brad said, beginning to laugh.

“I doubt that!”

“All you have to do is relax, man. Take your time now and try it again...slowly.”

Taking his time, the young man easily go to his feet. “Shit, that wasn't so bad. Thanks for the advice, man.”

“First time skiing?”

“Yeah. Pretty obvious huh? I took some lessons down on the bunny hill. This is my first time up the mountain.”

“*Stick* to the green for a while. I'm glad to hear you took some lessons. Too many people don't and become an obstacle to better skiers on the mountain. Remember one thing while you’re moving down a slope. Always look where you're going, not where you've been. It's the responsibility of the skiers up hill from you to make sure there's no collision. If you feel yourself getting out of control, fall on purpose.”

“No problem there,” interjected the young man with a toothy smile.

Laughing at his response, Brad continued, “The more practice you get, the more you're going to enjoy this sport. Believe me.”

“Thanks again, man. They oughta give lessons on getting off the chair lift too. That really sucks, dude.”

"That's probably not a bad idea. Have a good time. Your lady friend here seems to have her act together. Listen to what she says. Don't try to be so macho. It can be dangerous."

Using a skating motion, Brad moved to where Sam was waiting. As he brushed the snow off as a result of his fall, he asked her, "Can you *believe* that shit? I don't know the last time I fell getting off a chair lift. I sure as hell hope that's no indication how the rest of the day's going to be."

"Ooooh, did da wittle boy fall down on him bottom?" Sam replied in a little girl voice with an exaggerated southern delivery.

"I fell on my ass. *Right on my ass! That's* embarrassing as hell! And, besides, my shin bone *hurts* like hell. Thank God, the guy had rental skis and they don't have any edges. If he had skis like mine, I'd probably have a gash in my leg. Shit, shit, and more shit!"

"Is it *that* sore?"

"Throbbing!"

"Sorry, I didn't mean to joke."

"*Yes* you did," said Brad, beginning to calm down a little and a noticeable smile returning to his face. "And, for good reason. I must've looked pretty damn silly."

"Yeah, actually, you did look funny. A fall that was kinda in slow motion and ass-over-tea-kettle, as you'd put it. *Very* little grace. No style points what so ever. Nothing like the fall you had in the Olympics, but, there's a lot of time left today for you to improve."

"Thanks, Sam, for the compliments," Brad said, as he re-adjusted the straps on his goggles.

"You were very, very nice to that couple who caused it."

"They didn't cause it. *You* did."

"What?"

"Yeah, you. I lost total concentration when I saw your buns in those ski pants, lady. What a sight! I don't think I could follow you down this mountain and live through it!" Brad explained laughingly.

"You can't blame everything on me you know."

"I know, it just seemed like the right thing to say," he said as he grabbed her and gave her a hug.

"I love you," she said.

"I love you back," he said as his hands slid down her back and below her waist, "and", he continued, "I love your buns."

"Brad!" she yelped as he squeezed her shapely fanny with his hands, "you can't do that here."

"At least you didn't say I couldn't do it at all," he said smiling as he gave her a little kiss.

"Okay you two. Break it up," John said as he approached with Abbey at his side.

"John! You old sonuvabitch. What're you doin' up here?"

"Skiing. I was going to ask what *you're* doing here, but, that's obvious."

"Hi, Sam. Hi, Brad," Abbey said cheerfully. "Nice outfit, Sam."

"I was just telling her that Abbey," Brad said.

"How does that fabric feel Brad?" John whimsically asked.

"I wasn't feeling the fabric John," Brad answered quickly, without much thought. He shouldn't have been so hasty.

"I could have sworn you had a handful of fabric when we came up. Must be snow blindness," John responded, shaking his head side to side in mock disbelief and smiling.

"Gimme a break, will you?" Trying to change the subject, Brad continued in a stern tone, "Abbey, why aren't you at work?"

Knowing he was kidding, she said, "I'm sorry Boss. *Most* people don't work on Sundays. *Most* people don't work on holiday weekends. And *more* importantly, *most* people do take a little time off when they get married!"

"You're married!!!!"

"Yes!"

"Not to this asshole," he stated motioning towards John.

"Who else, might I ask?"

"Me, of course. You know that," he playfully replied, getting into the spirit of the exciting news.

"I didn't think you were available Brad," chimed in Sam, keeping with the humor of the moment. "You two are *really* married?"

"Yeah," said John. "I finally bit the bullet!"

"With you two all tied up together, being engaged and all, I figured John was the next best choice," Abbey said. "Congratulations to you two guys on your engagement."

"That's absolutely the best news I've heard... at least in the last hour or so," Brad said kidding.

"Congratulations, you two," Sam said trying to jump up and down in her excitement but realized she couldn't because of her skis.

Brad, not one to miss much, said to her, "Honey, watch the half inch."

As she abruptly stopped her movement and, friskily, gave Brad a punch in the shoulder, John inquired. "Half inch? Abbey and I missing something here?"

"Personal joke." Brad said. "How'd you know we were engaged?"

"I called Phil on Friday, trying to get in touch with you. The last I'd heard, you were staying with him and your sister in New Market until your place was rebuilt. I understand those arrangements have changed just a tad. He told us about your engagement and gave me Sam's number. He said you were coming up here and I might not be able to reach you back in DC. Tried to reach you more than once on Friday. I even called here, but, they told me you hadn't checked in yet. When *did* you get here anyway?"

"Late last night. We had a slight delay in leaving... car problems, you know?"

"Yeah, I know. That's not what Phil suggested yesterday. He said you two would never answer your phone. Something about, you'd be too wrapped up with other, more pressing matters, if you get my drift."

Brad got the drift. Hell, it was a tidal wave. The cat was out of the bag and he knew Phil was going to have a hey-day with him. If an opportunity ever presented itself to ruffle Brad's feathers about his relationship with Sam, Phil would take full advantage of it. Phil had no right to be *so correct* in all of his insinuations. "So we spent some quality time! So what?"

"No biggie. So have Abbey and I. Quality... I mean *quality* time! By the way, before I forget. Congratulations, to both of you. One hell of a lot of exciting news in a short period of time. Where'd you get all the snow on your back?"

As Sam was brushing it off, Brad said. "I don't really want to discuss it."

"He fell... and we haven't even skied yet," Sam piped in.

"How?"

"Getting off the chair lift," Sam said cupping her hand to the side of her mouth, as if she would prevent Brad from hearing. She continued in a lower voice, "You know how clumsy he is. I'm just going to have to take dis wittle boy under my wing until he proves he can stand up on his own."

Interrupting John and Abbey's laughing, Brad asked, "Why were you trying to get in touch with me on Friday? What's so important it couldn't wait until the first of the week?"

“To tell you we were gettin' married. Give you an invite, man. We had a real small ceremony at the courthouse.”

“Sure, you know I would've liked to be there but, I don't understand. What was the big rush? You could've waited.”

“We'd been thinking about it for some time. After what happened Thanksgiving night, we decided we better go ahead and do it while we were still able.”

“What the *hell* does that mean?”

“We were driving back to my place in Laurel after eating dinner in Baltimore. Remember how nasty the weather was that night?” Not waiting for a response, he continued. “Just before the exit ramp to Laurel, some guy in his big fancy car side-swiped us. Forced us right off the road. We stopped, after doing about five 360's, next to a couple of large trees. It scared the shit out of both of us.”

“Damn,” was all that Brad could say.

“When we were finally dropped off by the police at my place, about two hours later, we realized we'd come within a gnat's asshole of being killed. Would've never been married to each other, something we both wanted very much. So, we got married the next day.”

“Either of you get hurt?” Sam asked showing her concern.

“No, we're both fine. Pretty messed up emotionally though. If the shoulder of the road hadn't been so wet from the weather, the damn car probably would've flipped. It really makes you stop and think about what's *really* important in life, you know?”

“Believe me buddy, I can imagine.” Brad said and continued. “Was anyone hurt in the other car?”

“Don't know. The son of a bitch hauled ass. Didn't even stop. Probably drunk or on something and didn't want to face the cops. Probably a bunch of DUI's on his record already.”

“That hit and run bastard. I wish they'd find these assholes, get 'em off the roads, lock 'em up and throw the keys away.”

“They're looking for a dark Mercedes with damage and blue paint from my car along its passenger side. I'm still pissed about it, but, what the hell, the asshole did us a favor. We got married because of him.”

“That's one way to look at it.”

“Sorry you didn't make it buddy, but you know I'm not one for huge, grandiose affairs.”

"I know that John. Don't worry about it. You two *will make our wedding* in South Carolina this spring," Brad ordered. "No excuses will be accepted."

"We'll be there. For sure," John said, noticing Abbey's nod of approval.

"Okay, okay." Brad continued. "You've all had some laughs at my expense and gotten your digs in. I'm ready for some skiing, guys and gals. Is anyone here in favor of that idea?"

"You haven't been down the mountain yet?" John asked in disbelief.

"No way. But I'm finally ready for the first run of the season. Sam, you ready to show me what you've got?"

"After last night, I'm kind of disappointed you don't already know what I've got. You must learn to pay closer attention to what's going on."

"Or coming off," added Abbey.

"God, you all are unbelievable! I would expect it from John, but not my fiancée, or you Abbey! I'm really involved with a fast crowd here and beginning to become a little concerned." Brad said, trying to hold in the laughter. "Hey guys, let's hit the slopes. Any preference Sam?"

"I'll let the pro pick it."

"I think we should start off on a green and depending on how well you do, go to blues or blacks the next time up."

"Don't feel you have to ski greens on our account Brad." Abbey said. "We've had a couple of runs already today. Some folks *can* get out of bed!"

"I've never seen Sam ski. I'm not sure..."

Breaking in, Sam said, "Brad, I've skied black trails in North Carolina. Maybe the mountain wasn't as big as this one, but a black trail is black, regardless of where it is. I'm game. Just don't expect to see a burgundy and gold flash out there. I'll take my time at first and pick up some speed later. Why don't you just follow behind me?"

"That's one hell of a idea, but, I'm not suicidal, Sam. My goggles might steam up looking at your buns."

"Brad, see. You have a mind like everyone else here."

"I'll certainly second that," stated John.

"So will I," added Abbey.

"You can't, I already did. You either third it or, you don't do anything."

"Who... gives... a... *rat's*... ass? Let's get going," said Brad anxiously.

"Right on!!!!!!!" John shouted as the people around them turned to check out the commotion.

The four approached the starting point for the first run with the steepness of the decent not phasing Brad in the slightest. John and Abbey said they hadn't skied this particular run but, it looked pretty exciting. Sam agreed as she noticed it was nearly a vertical drop onto the slope of about ten feet. After the drop-in, the decline became somewhat reasonable, similar to terrain she'd skied before. The trail went down about two hundred yards before leveling off and making a turn to the right. Large moguls created by other skiers making turns to remain under control were spotted around the area. Brad was just beginning to stretch a little and adjust his goggles when he was tapped on the shoulder.

"I believe we're missing someone, buddy." John said quickly.

Turning towards the trail, Brad said, "Shit man, *look* at that girl ski!"

Sam was already on the run with Abbey in close pursuit. The two *macho* dudes stood in total amazement and gawked at their companions as the distance between them increased rapidly by the second. Sam was flying down the trail doing jump turns and crisscrossing the breadth of the slope. She showed the skill of someone other than an occasional skier and at one point used a mogul to become airborne to a soft, steady landing.

Spraying up snow in a large cascade, she slid to a sideways stop, raised her goggles and looked back up the mountain to where Brad and John were standing in total shock. With one fist in the air in total triumph, her other hand, with her ski pole dangling from her wrist, was waving as if urging the two late-bloomers to get with it. Abbey slid to a stop beside her, gave her a quick hug, turned and gave the same sort of wave to the two men standing at the summit. Two hundred yards away, Brad couldn't really see Sam smiling, but, knew she was.

"John, buddy, do you believe that shit? I'm sitting here worrying my ass off about her. I'm thinking she has been skiing a couple of times on a God damn date or something in North Carolina. Turns out, she'd be a damn good downhiller. Christ, she's good, man."

"She's either crazy or good."

"She is crazy, I'll grant you that. She's also a damn good skier. I can tell from what I just saw. I should've known something was up. She kept saying, 'stop worrying about me'. Shit, if I'd known this, I wouldn't have gotten knocked on my ass back at the chair lift. "'Pick up a little speed later', she says," Brad said mocking her southern accent. "Shit, what a little hustler."

"I think you should divorce her," John said laughing.

"I will, right after I marry her." Brad responded also letting out a laugh. "I guess all that waving down there means they want us to join them. Think we should?"

"Hell with 'em. Let's go get a brewski in the warming house."

"We should, but, better not... I guess. At least I know Sam will do okay in Colorado next month. The way she handled the top of this slope here, bowl skiing will be a breeze for her."

"Bowl skiing? Is that what you are planning for the eight of us next month?"

"Yeah. Some and a little cross country excursion."

"Sounds like a great time."

"You have no idea, John, how *great* it's going to be. I've planned this thing for about nine months and believe me, it'll be an unforgettable trip."

"Shit, I haven't forgotten the God damn bungy cord jumping yet. That was a real thrill that I refuse to *ever* do again in my life."

"I'm with you on that one. I still swear, part of my ass fell off when that damn cord reached its full extension and jerked me back up. I can still see it. Brad Claxton's ass floating down that damn river at the bottom of the gorge."

"The look on your face was, well, let me put it like this. You looked like a constipated bull frog that just got relief from an overdose of Exlax. It *was* great."

"I've never heard it put like that before, but, it's probably close." Still looking at the two girls below them on the slope, Brad continued, "they're still waving, I guess, we ought to do them the favor of joining them."

"Right on partner. Lead the way. *Let's go for it*!"

They traversed the decline in front of them, each with the ease of an expert skier. Brad took advantage of a couple of moguls to display some of his own ability to the eyes he knew were glued on him from below. As they approached the girls, Brad could see Sam smiling in her innocent fashion.

As they slid to a stop by the girls, causing a shower of snow, Sam sheepishly asked, "How'd I do?"

"You're crazy, girl."

"She's also very good," John reminded Brad.

"That, she is," Brad said, leaning over to give her a little kiss. "Why'd you lead me to believe you couldn't ski that well?"

“I didn't. You just assumed I couldn't, my being from South Carolina and all,” she responded to his question in an exaggerated accent.

“Shall we push on down the mountain or, are you two girls tired?”

“No way, am I tired,” chimed in Abbey, “and Sam just got started.”

“Did I ever. This is great!”

“Wait 'til Colorado.” Brad said, almost under his breath.

“What?”

“Nothing. Let's hit it. Sam, let me follow you, please, pretty please.”

“Oh Brad, you're terrible,” she said, turning and starting down the mountain. Sam's last comment fell on deaf ears as Brad began following the pair of gorgeous, swiveling, burgundy buns.

*****

At the end of the tiring day, they had showered, changed clothes and met for dinner, each devouring a large prime rib to satisfy their appetites. Sam had proved more than capable of skiing expert terrain and, in fact, did pick up speed as the day went along. John and Abbey both had attacked the various trails in their no-fear, “let's hit it”, styles. Abbey had fallen once, John claiming she was top heavy due to her bust size. With her never-say-die attitude, she'd insisted on skiing the trail again.

They were seated in the oversized lounge chairs, one couple in each, simply chit-chatting. The heat from the roaring fire had caused them to move the chairs further away and for nearly three hours, they'd enjoyed talking and watching the multicolored flames dance. The firebox was a full eight feet across, six feet in height and, at least, three feet deep.

“Abbey, you could stand in that thing and never hit your head,” said Brad.

“Not without burning my ass off,” she replied making Sam roar with laughter.

“I wonder what size logs they use?”

“Brad, they don't burn logs in that damn thing,” replied John. “They burn small buildings in it.”

“Seems like everyone had a good time today?”

"Brad, it was the best," replied John as he flagged down the nearest waiter for another Coors. "Anyone want anything.?"

"Hon, I'll take another one," said Abbey, placing the empty white wine glass on the table in front of her. "Brad, I honestly don't know the last time I've had so much fun. Or, laughed so hard. It's been great."

"Brad sweetheart, it's been perfect. Good friends, make for good times. I don't think I need anything else, John. I still have half a glass of wine," said Sam, holding it up. "My God, Abbey, where *do* you put it all?"

"Tried to tell you, that's why she fell today."

"Never mind, John," broke in Abbey wrinkling up her nose.

"Everyone hates for days like this one to end," stated Brad, noticing everyone concur. His arm around Sam's waist he continued. "I decree, John and Abbey will extend their stay. They will remain here with you and I, Sam, until Tuesday afternoon. I further decree, the four of us will enjoy the next two days more than we have today. Anyone, *anyone, Abbey*, that does not abide by this decree *will be fired*. Any questions?"

"Not from me boss," replied Abbey smiling.

"Brad, you know I'm not going to fight you about it, right? When you decree something, man, *it be decreed*. Now if you'll excuse me, I have some serious ordering to do here. This man's awaitin' mah wishes," informed John, gesturing to the waiter. "Brad, you want another Rolling Rock?"

"Sir?" interjected the waiter.

"What is it my man?"

"Sir, the gentlemen. He's drinking Heineken's."

"You're confused young man. First, this guy is not a gentlemen. He's my flipping boss and just demanded that I stay here with him an extra two, God damn days instead of returning to DC and going back to work. If I don't, he'll fire me. What the *hell* would *you* do?"

"Sir, I'd stay."

"No question in your mind?"

"None at all," replied the waiter, playing John's game.

"At least that's settled. I'll stay. And second, *my God, you're right* about the beer. *All* this time Brad, you told me the only beer in a green bottle you could afford was Rolling Rock. *Woooo,* we do have a *big* spender here. Must've had a good month at the cash register boss." John finished ordering and promised the young man a ten spot for putting up with his bullshit. "If you all would be so kind as to excuse me, I've to go see a man about a horse.

Either of you girls have to go? I know you don't like to go alone," John said getting up from the comfort of the chair with Abbey seated beside him. "Damn! You know, you can't *buy* beer, you can only *rent* it." As John left to find the Stag's Room, the door with a fourteen point buck's rack mounted above it depicting entry for males, Brad and the two girls continued talking, mostly about how crazy he was.

John stood in front of the urinal as a man approached the one to his right. Neatly dressed in kaikai pants, a ski sweater and casual loafers he said, "Water's cold aint it?"

Not one to be outdone, John replied. "Deep too." Nice enough guy, John thought, trying to make conversation. John finished the immediate task at hand and said, "don't eat the big, white mint down there." He walked to row of four sink basins installed in the dark granite counter. He pushed the handle on the soap dispenser and watched the pink liquid flow into his palm.

"Been here long?" asked the man as John watched him approach in the mirror.

"Only got here yesterday. How about you?"

"Same. How long you stayin'?

"We were going to leave tomorrow. Early. Then my boss decided we'd all stay until Tuesday afternoon. Who am I to argue. So, that's what we're doing. How about you?"

"Not sure yet. Like to stay. But, not sure yet."

Drying his hands on the continuous roll of cloth, John said, "I know we're going to enjoy the hell out of it. You should stay if you can. By the way, how do you like yours?"

"My what?"

"The watch, man. The Rolex."

"Ohh, the watch. Love it. Most people think it's fake."

"Yeah, I know. I've got one similar to it. That's how I know it's real. Personally, I think they're more of a status symbol than anything. I wear this damn Timex most of the time. The way I ski, you know? Takes a lickin' and keeps on tickin'. Great little watch. Picked it up for fifty bucks at a drugstore. I've got to get moving. Good talking to you and good luck skiing if you decide to stay."

"Thanks," replied the man as John left, the door silently swinging shut behind him. Under his breath and roughly drying his own hands, the man said, "you're wishin' me luck? You had all the fuckin' luck you're ever goin' to see on Thanksgiving night. Now I've been handed the God damn contract on you because of someone else's screw-up. Stupid idea trying to kill someone with a car. I'll never see Barbados." Reaching under his sweater, he pulled out his pack of Camels, saw the No Smoking sign, swore and rammed them back into the hidden pocket.

*****

Wednesday morning found that the weather had returned to its usual, balmy nature in DC. It was 10:30 AM and after a couple of hours at the Center, Brad had crawled his way through heavy traffic to the 47th Precinct to claim his cell phone. Sam, after taking care of some business at Georgetown University, had planned to meet him later that morning, a little before noon, for her personal tour of the Center.

As he heard the door latch behind him, Brad looked across the lobby to the distant wall. Facing him, *circa 1940's*, a dark mahogany counter covered its twenty-five foot expanse. Was it still possible to find craftsmanship such as this nowadays Brad wondered, even if that quantity of mahogany could be found in one location and wasn't outrageously priced. Its dark granite top, retrieved from a European quarry, was five foot off the floor and its front consisted of delicate, precision-cut moldings and panels. At one end was a swinging door for access to the slightly elevated floor hidden from view. On the wall behind, a picture of President Clinton was hanging, flanked by an American flag and past, high ranking members of the Police Department, probably Chiefs. From the ceiling hung the banner of the 47th Precinct with the motto, *It's Our Duty To Serve And Protect*, scrawled across it in blue and gold lettering. The lazily turning ceiling fans had large opaque white globes in their centers which provided the dim lighting throughout the lobby.

Brads eyes moved back to the counter area, to a highly polished brass sign and the man seated behind it. *That's him,* thought Brad, *the fifty-five year old desk sergeant you see depicted in all the movies.* His hair was aging from dark brown to gray and he was slightly balding. Black, plastic rimmed, reading glasses, no-doubt government issue, hugged the end of his nose. He wore the typical light blue shirt of a policeman's uniform, the numerous chevrons on one sleeve identifying him as a sergeant. Both elbows were on the counter in front of him and the palms of his hands were under his chin supporting his head. He looked like a man ending a shift, not starting one.

He looked a little overweight, his last real workout probably being in the mid 60's when he joined the force. This guy wasn't a man showing enthusiasm, a love for his job, or, one on his way up the ladder of success. He probably didn't really give a shit and was just putting his time in until retiring in a year or two.

Moving past the State Of Maryland flag in the center of the lobby, Brad made his way to the counter and cleared his throat to gain some attention. The man was seated but, because of the raised flooring, was at a higher level. He glanced down through the clear prisms with his somewhat bloodshot eyes which were draped with bushy eyebrows. With Brad now in focus, he asked, “Hep yeh?”

“Sorry?” Brad asked, not understanding either of the two words just spoken, or maybe, it was a single word.

“Kin I hep yeh?” came a slower response.

“Can...you...help...me?” Brad repeated, not certain if he was correct.

“Yeh.”

“I'm here to see Sergeant Butterfinger. I'm picking up a cell phone he found.”

“Ha, ha.”

“What's so funny?”

“Yeh meen, Butterfield.”

“That's the one.”

“I'll get em for ya.”

“Thanks.”

The desk sergeant slowly rose and went through the door behind him, his head shaking from side to side in amusement. Looking around the 47th Precinct, Brad noticed that there was a lack of activity in contrast to the frenzied scene as portrayed for metropolitan police departments on weekly television shows. No druggies were being led through on their way to lock-up, no prostitutes were yelling at their pimps for bail money or no detectives were milling around a blackboard trying to solve an on-going serial killer case. It was quiet and the only other person visible was an oriental woman in her fifties, sitting patiently on one of the old wooden benches lining the far wall. Those benches could tell some stories, Brad thought, wondering how much chewed gum had been rubbed under each of them.

"Mr. Claxton?" a voice questioned from behind him.

Turning, Brad said, "Yes."

An officer with freshly cut, dark hair approached, his holstered 38 caliber swinging from one side and a baton from the other side of the three inch wide, black patent leather belt. The brightly polished buckle in front seemed to give balance to the belt as handcuffs dangled in the rear. His brown eyes were set deep in his young, tanned face. He was relatively short, but, the crispness of his heavily starched shirt and the bright silver badge made you aware of his presence. The trousers looked recently pressed, the sharp edge of the crease visible both front and back. Close to Brad's age, he extended his hand, smiled and said, "Sergeant Butterfield."

"I read your name plate. Sorry for the misnomer, sergeant. Good to meet you." Brad said shakily.

"Quite all right. Abe's probably *still* back there laughing at that one. I have a feeling you've invented a nickname for me."

"Abe, the desk sergeant?"

"That's his official title, but, he's there primarily as a source of information for folks when they come in."

"This may sound like a dumb question, but... does he handle the 911 calls when they come in?"

"Nooo. I understand your concerns about his speech. All those calls are handled at the switchboard in the back."

"Just curious."

"It's kind of long story about Abe. Seven years ago, he was answering a call at a local convenience store. Two people had all ready been killed. The circumstances mushroomed from bad to worse and ended up in a hostage situation with a nine year old girl involved. Abe negotiated with the perp to let him trade places with the girl. Said he'd be easier to hide behind when the guy tried to escape. As Abe was used as a shield, one of the SWAT Team thought he had "the clear shot", you know? The man died instantly from the wound to the head. Problem was, the bullet passed through Abe's throat on the way. The doctors didn't believe he'd be able to talk again but, after three surgeries, he's getting along pretty well."

"Hell of a story."

"Hell of a guy. They tried to force him into early retirement. Turns out, the little girl's father was a Senator or some big-wig from South Dakota. With his influence, Abe was allowed to continue working as a police officer, something that's really in his blood. He'd have made detective long ago, but, with all of the investigative work, question and answer sessions, the speech impediment was a big liability. He gets involved in cases with other detectives, but, it's all on his own time. He's proven to be a valuable asset to the precinct. Real nice guy. Hell of a guy!"

"I'm sure he is. Saved the little girl's life? The bastard would have blown that kid away and not thought twice about it."

"There's no doubt in my mind. I was a rookie with the force when it went down. The guy knew what he'd done and, according to Maryland law, what he'd get. He was going to escape or die trying. The only thing good coming out of it, other than the girl being okay, was the son of a bitch didn't cost the taxpayers anything sitting on death row one appeal after another."

"Amen to that."

"Abe's getting your cell phone out of the property room. It's a little scuffed up though. How the hell did it end up down that drain?"

"It just slipped out of my hand and flew out the window. I never thought the damn thing would still work. By the way, different subject. Have you ever seen a black, oval shaped license plate with white lettering on it?" Brad questioned.

"Not often, but, I do recall seeing 'em on a couple of occasions. Why?"

"Curiosity, I suppose." Brad said, not really knowing why he'd asked the question. "What is it, some plate for an embassy or something?"

"No, I don't think so. I think it's a corporate plate which uses the background of its logo as a backdrop for the lettering. Somehow, they've gotten permission to use the same plate, regardless of where they're located. Virginia, DC, or Maryland. Money talks. You know what I mean? Let me ask Abe when he gets out here."

As if on cue, Abe came through the door, holding up the cell phone. "Dis it, Budderfingah?"

"That's the one Abe, you smart ass. Thanks. By the way, do you know who the black oval plates with white lettering are registered to? Mr. Claxton here is curious. It's some corporation isn't it?"

Abe nodded yes and said a few things Brad found impossible to comprehend. He listened attentively, none the less. Closer examination of Abe, revealed the scar tissue on his neck, a reminder of the event of seven years ago. He'd *never* pre-judge someone again. To hell with Hollywood interpretations in the movies.

"Did you get that?" Butterfield questioned.

"Not everything," replied Brad politely.

"He said they're registered to a company called Bern Industries, but, thinks it's a subsidiary of a conglomerate named Swiss Technologies, headquartered in Switzerland. Through international channels, the US Government allows the corporation to use identical plates wherever their offices or divisions are located."

"God damn, it must be nice to have that kind of pull. What kind of business are they involved in?"

Abe shrugged his shoulders indicating he had no idea and Butterfield said, "I've never really heard anything about them. Hey, excuse me, it's almost eleven o'clock. I've got to get out in the cruiser and on the streets, fighting crime and all."

"I have to run as well. Thanks for gettin' my cellular phone." Turning around, Brad shook Abe's hand, noticed the strong grip and said, "Thanks for your help, Abe."

As he left the precinct Brad felt better knowing some men *are* devoted to their chosen careers. In Abe's case, his advancement was halted in its prime because he chose to do his duty and live by the motto, serve and protect.

*****

Brad hurriedly opened one of the large glass doors, a gust of wind making the task more difficult, and stepped onto the plush emerald green carpeting of the reception lobby. The darkness of the mahogany paneled walls was broken by portraits of medical research scientists, some of Nobel Prize fame. Framed in striking bright brass, their names were etched in brass plaques at their bases and each portrait was highlighted by hooded lamps throwing out light from the top. Ten foot high, silk ficus trees were placed around the lobby in earthenware pots. Two separate conversation areas consisting of sofas, wingback chairs and mahogany tables were available for visitors to the Center. Leaded crystal lamps provided brightness for the areas and the latest issues of medical research magazines were neatly placed on the tables.

"Good morning Susan, how was Wisconsin?" Brad asked the receptionist behind the dark stained desk.

Replacing the telephone in its cradle, she said. "Mr. Claxton, it's great to see you up and about. Must've been some ordeal." She was standing now, dressed in her usual business suit attire. She looked more than proper for her position with the Center and much older than her 23 years. Her main focus was handling the multitude of telephone calls and greeting visitors to the Center, a simple enough task most people would think, but, Brad knew differently.

Her formal training as a medical assistant was a blessing in disguise and allowed her to answer questions, some probing, without having to interrupt the on-going activities of the Center. She was fluent in four languages and could handle a number of the international calls and foreign visitors one on one. She enjoyed her work immensely and was planning on accepting Brad's offer to pay for her completion of medical school.

"Thanks, Susan, how was your vacation in Wisconsin?" Brad asked again.

"I had a wonderful time with my family. I understand congratulations are in store for your engagement," she said, obviously pleased.

"Thanks. Someone *finally* captured my heart."

"I can certainly see why."

"You've met her?"

"Yes. She's been here about an hour. I told her you hadn't arrived yet so she asked for Abbey or John. Abbey introduced me and in only a few minutes, I knew why you latched onto her. How about that crazy Abbey and John getting married over the weekend? I guess it was inevitable. Looks like the car accident pushed them over the edge, so to speak. They make a great couple, as I'm sure you and Samantha will. I love her southern accent."

"That's why I'm marrying her. For her accent."

"I don't believe that for a second. I see your sense of humor wasn't damaged in the explosion."

"Actually, I've never felt better. I'm a little late, I'd better get in there. Did you get enrolled in medical school?"

"Not yet boss, but, I will. I promise."

"Good. Let me know."

Brad walked across the lobby to the door marked Director and entered his office. Much thought and planning was given to the type of image the

Center should market. It should suggest a strong feeling of success, one which other centers around the world would have total confidence in, team up with and provide advanced medical research, and, it did exactly that.

Brad's office certainly kept true to this overall theme. But, the most outstanding thing in Brad's office this particular morning was Sam. She was seated in the burgundy, tufted leather desk chair behind the executive desk. Leaning back in the chair, her feet, crossed at the ankles, were resting on the desk in front of her. Without trying, she looked very beautiful.

"You're late, big guy."

Knowing he was, he took advantage of the perfect opportunity to change the subject. "Did you know you have gum on your shoe?"

"What?"

"You have gum on the bottom of your shoe."

In complete surprise, Sam reached and grabbed her shoe, pulled it off her foot and twisted it to check the bottom. Brad's view of the maneuver as he approached her, sent throbs of excitement through his body. Her already short, red skirt slid further up towards her thirty-five inch hips, revealing where the insides of her long, slender legs joined at the white, silk fabric of her bikini panties.

"Which foot?" she asked, changing feet.

Completely in a trance, Brad asked, "What?"

"Which foot is the gum on?"

"Just kidding, there isn't any, but, I sure am enjoying your reaction. My office never looked so good."

Realizing where Brad was looking, her face become as red as her skirt as she pushed backwards in the chair, its casters easily allowing her to swing her legs from the desk. "You're really a sex fiend, you know it? The *office*, as you refer to it, is *closed* this morning."

"Looked open to me."

"It's closed. You may be the only tenant, but, it's closed this morning."

"Certainly can't be closed for repairs. It doesn't need any."

"It's closed waiting for new management. When it re-opens, I'm the Manager."

Moving towards her as she was standing up, he grabbed her and pulled her tightly against him. "I'm not just the tenant," he said, "I'm the owner. And, being the owner, I can fire any Manager. So, don't take the job." There lips met and they embraced passionately, their arms around each other.

"Mr. Claxton?" Susan's voice came over the intercom.

"Yes, Susan, what is it?" Brad said in an impatient voice because of the untimely interruption.

"There's a Mr. Riddle in the lobby, from BioMed Research in Chicago. He was in town and stopped in for some information about subscribing to the Center."

"I'll be right out, Susan. Thank you."

"Yes sir, and oh...Mr. Claxton, one other thing."

"Yes, what is it?"

Trying to hide the giggles, Susan said, "I think, you may want to turn off your call button on the intercom."

"Shit! Thanks Susan."

No further response, other than the normal click, was given by Susan.

"How the hell did this get pushed," Brad said, pushing the call button.

"I was playing executive at this big desk of yours and... ahh... I guess, I pushed it." Sam said sheepishly as she began to bite her lower lip.

"Do you realize anyone standing close to Susan's reception desk in the lobby heard everything we've said since I came in?"

"We weren't talking that loud. The only one that could probably hear anything was Susan."

"Everything in this Center is state of the art, Sam. Including the phone systems. She wasn't giggling because she was reading dirty jokes."

"I'm sorry Brad. If she did hear something, she understands. She isn't a little girl you know. I met her this morning and she seems to be quite an intelligent young lady. She's seen her share of "R" rated movies."

"You're probably right, Sam. Besides, the chances of Mr. Riddel hearing us are remote." Brad said, beginning to laugh. "Besides, nothing could be worse than when your parents popped in on us."

Sam began to laugh a little, recalling that incident. "Still love me?" she inquired.

"Of course, darling of my life," he said walking to the door. "I'll only be a second. If he wants a walk through of the Center, I'll have John do it. Wait right here for me and we'll start your own, personal tour. Hands off the buttons, please. And, by the way Sam, you're fired as Manager."

"That's all right. I didn't want the damn job anyway," she said, smiling at him as he left.

"Mr. Riddel?" Brad questioned as he approached the young man in the lobby. "Let's go into the conference room over here," he said motioning with his hand to the door on the far wall of the reception lobby, "it's a little more private and, please, call me Brad."

"Brad, it is. Call me Ron."

"Ron, what can I do for you?" he asked as they entered and the door closed behind.

"Are you familiar with BioMed Research in Chicago?" asked Ron taking a seat at the twelve foot conference table.

"I'm a little familiar with the work out there, virus studies or some such thing if my memory serves me right but, that's about the extent of my knowledge. I have my hands full keeping track of what's going on around here. Can I get you something to drink, coffee, juice?"

"Nothing for me, thank you. Where do I begin?"

"Where do you start about what?"

Rubbing his chin in thought, Ron said, "well, we've done years of research and are coming close, at least I *thought* so, to developing a serum for..." Ron stopped in mid-sentence and then continued slowly. "I'm not really at liberty to say at this point."

"Why not?"

"I just... really can't say, that's all."

"Okay, Ron. Then answer me this if you can. You just said that you thought, not we, but *you* Ron, thought they were coming close to a serum. What exactly does that mean, that you personally think it works and the others at BioMed don't?"

"Brad, maybe I shouldn't have even pursued this. BioMed doesn't know I'm here. They think I'm still in Atlanta."

"Pursued *what*, Ron?" Why are you here?"

"I read an article about you and your Center in last month's Medical Researcher and thought that you'd be the one to approach with my problem. What you've done here and in such a short period of time is very impressive and your reputation is above reproach."

"Then, you're here for information about the Center and how to become a subscriber?"

"No. I really *am* at a loss as to ahh... how to approach you with this. I don't even know, at this point, what to ask of you or what you could even do to help me out. It has to do with a virus that ahhh... recently popped up again."

"You're not talking about the Ebola Virus in Africa *are* you?"

"I really can't say, Mr. Claxton and, besides, that's only a part of the problem I'm talking about."

"Brad, remember?"

"Yeh. Look, I'm sorry to be so vague about all this but, I'm not sure who to trust. I'm just nervous as hell about all this shit. If they knew I was here about this crap, who knows what might happen."

"Ron, you could've called me from Atlanta or Chicago if your that nervous, but I'm having a little difficulty with all this. What problem could BioMed have with your being here? For *sure*, I *can't* help you if I don't know what the hell is going on. Sure, I could say trust me, but, I don't think that's what you want to hear. All I'm asking, Ron, is for you to help me, help you."

"I understand the position I'm putting you in, Brad, because of my vagueness but, this story *has* to be told to someone. Hopefully, someone that will be able to do something. What that something might be, I'm not sure."

Realizing this conversation was going nowhere fast, Brad said, "Look, I'm pretty tied up for the next few hours. Would you be available to meet somewhere this evening in a more relaxed setting and then we can spend more time together. Maybe, you'll feel more at ease over dinner."

"Sure, at my hotel. I appreciate your willingness to tolerate a babbling idiot like myself. I'm staying at the Marriot in Crystal City, down by National Airport. You know it?"

"I sure do. How about seven thirty in the lounge and then dinner?"

"Sounds good to me. I'll probably be a little more relaxed by the time you get there, after a couple of drinks, ya know what I mean?"

"You don't mind if I bring someone with me do you?"

"Your office Manager?" Ron said winking.

"Precisely."

"Not at all."

"Seven thirty at the Crystal City Marriot it is," stated Brad as he opened the conference room door.

"Thanks, Brad."

"No problem, Ron. See you later."

Brad watched Ron slowly walk through the lobby and pass through the glass doors. He couldn't be certain, but, it looked as if he was trying to cover his face as he stepped out onto the sidewalk among the flow of pedestrians. As he headed for his office door, Brad purposely didn't engage in conversation with Susan. *Was Brad Claxton embarrassed? Not hardly. Was the Director of the Center embarrassed? Possibly.* He noticed Sam standing with her back to him looking up at the voluminous book shelves and scanning the titles.

"He heard," said Brad, informatively.

"Who, heard what?" she said turning.

"Riddle heard our conversation out in the lobby."

"I'm sorry."

"Don't worry, Sam, he's cool. As a matter of fact, we're having dinner with him tonight at the Crystal City Marriot."

"Sounds good to me. Kind of sudden though, isn't it."

"Yeah. I have to meet with him though. He seems scared about something."

"Didn't Susan say he was with BioMed Research from Chicago? What's he have to be frightened about?"

"I don't know. That's what we're going to find out tonight."

Brad led Sam on the tour of the Center. They began by stopping in John's office, a bit smaller than Brad's, but it was decorated with elegance. Sam understood the great taste in decor when she'd found out Chantal was responsible for most of the Center's appearance. The personal tour was similar to the ones given to prospective subscribers of the Center; however, Brad was taking his time with Samantha because of her zillion questions. He wanted her to completely understand what this part of his life was about.

The walkway, as Brad called it, was a long, U-shaped hall with glass walls. Visible along this corridor was the sterile laboratory, computer applications room, hard copy research library, and the systems' users library. Each had a coded entry system as did the walkway itself. They waved to Abbey in the computer applications center who was busily verifying and inputting data into the Center's system. Spotted every so often were glassed-in atriums, allowing the growth of vegetation, the likes of which Sam had never seen. These plantings, Brad explained were used by the Center's research teams for their own, natural biological studies.

Each room along the walkway, was maintained in a sterile environment, even the hard copy research library, leaving nothing to chance. Anyone entering the walkway was first sterilized and fitted in white over clothing down to hospital booties on their feet. Everyone looked as if they were prepared to perform intricate surgery at the Georgetown Medical Center. Sam was overwhelmed by the operation. She only had cursory knowledge of how all the pieces of the Center fit together, but, Brad knew she was learning quickly by the types of questions she was asking. She understood the high need for security at the Center and teased that John should do something about the call button on Brad's desk. She was moved by the total layout of the Center and how impressive it must appear to would-be subscribers.

One room in particular got her attention, the only entry being through a combination vault door. She guessed it was for work being done on contagious diseases and entry, to those without a need, was strictly denied. The vault provided protection against an accident and, without a doubt, was air tight as were the suits behind the door the workers climbed into prior to beginning their work.

After the tour of the Center, they spent the remainder of the afternoon visiting various members of the Center's staff, Brad proudly introducing her as his fiancee. Of all the people she met, Doc was the one she liked best. In his fifties and the head of the BRT, the Center's biological research team, he was, jovial, sincere and a pleasure to be around. Brad told her, he'd promised Doc the position for the rest of his life. Doc laughed, saying Brad *always* left himself a way out. Sam discovered Doc had intestinal Cancer and was given a year to live when he accepted the position, nearly two years ago. The chemotherapy treatments, which had turned his naturally brown hair to stark white, were halted nearly a year ago because the cancer was in remission. To hear Doc jokingly put it, Brad wasn't counting on the remission as part of the contract.

*****

Looking at his watch as they entered, Brad noticed they were about fifteen minutes early. A man dressed in a tuxedo, with his shirt collar open and a clip-on, black bow-tie dangling precariously to one side, sat at a black lacquered grand piano playing his rendition of Music Box Dancer. A brandy snifter on the piano top had a few bills sticking from it, tips from appreciative patrons. The bartender reached for the half empty bottle of Johnny Walker Red from the mirrored shelving to satisfy the thirst of a customer seated at a high top table who was tapping his fingers to the beat of the music. The hostess at the cordoned off entrance smiled and said they could seat themselves. Scanning the clientele, Brad noticed Ron getting off a barstool and heading hurriedly towards them. Extending his hand to Sam, he said, "Ronald Riddel."

"Samantha Sawyer, Ronald, good to meet you."

He grabbed her hand and gave it a gracious little kiss. To both of them, he said, "Let's move to the booth in the corner. It's a little more private."

Ron ordered a refill on his bourbon and water and Brad ordered two Chardonney white wines for Sam and himself. Ron was still a little nervous, but, nothing compared to that afternoon in the Center's lobby. Ron finished his drink and handed the empty to the waitress as she placed the new round on cocktail napkins in front of them.

"At the Center, this morning," Brad began, "you were saying something about a two stemmed problem and not knowing what I could provide you with or if I could even help. Believe me, Ron, I want to help if I'm able to but, I'm having a hard time understanding where all this is headed."

"So am I. I don't even know where to start."

"You're actions sure have heightened my interest, Ron. Start at the beginning," Brad offered to break the ice and continued. "You mentioned BioMed doesn't know you're here, in a way which led me to believe that you didn't *want* them to know. If what I'm reading into this is true, why shouldn't they know you're here?"

"Well, I don't want to go over anyone's head at BioMed because ahh... career-wise it could be *very* detrimental.

"You were told... *not* to come to the Center?" Brad questioned in disbelief.

"No, nobody specifically told me not to, but, they think I'm still in Atlanta. They don't know I'm even here. It's just I've got the feeling that if I pursue this endeavor, there will be a ahh... high price to pay."

"They'd reprimand you, for merely talking to us?" Sam broke in. "If that's true, aren't you risking quite a bit?"

"It's probably worse. They'd more than likely fire me and make certain my career was over for good. I wouldn't be able to find work anywhere, they'd see to it."

"I don't understand how that's possible," said Sam.

"A close associate of mine at the lab, a promising research assistant, had been there going on four years. He was dismissed last year on grounds of industrial espionage. They let everyone know the reason and from that day on, he was black-balled by every research lab he approached. He eventually broke down trying to fight all of the allegations and committed suicide a couple of months ago."

"That's horrible." said Sam. Brad, said nothing, just listened attentively.

"It gets worse."

"That's impossible," said Sam.

"Believe me, *it's* possible. The research assistant was my younger brother, Richard. I say younger... by three minutes. He was my twin," Ron said, beginning to choke back his feelings.

"Your *twin brother*?" asked Brad, his voice rising slightly.

"Yeah, he ahh... he ahh, killed himself in my garage. He was house-sitting," he said pausing to get his composure back and continued. "He was house-sitting for my wife and I while we were on our honeymoon. He pulled his car into the garage and ahh...killed himself with exhaust fumes. He was found dead the next morning by the mailman who smelled the fumes and investigated their source."

"Oh my God, Ron. I'm so sorry to hear that," Sam said.

"See, I told you things could be worse."

"That's a hell of a nut to crack, Ron. You holding up okay?" Brad asked.

"I guess as well as can be expected."

"You're brother, he ahh... wasn't really involved in any of this industrial espionage stuff then?"

"No, not at all."

"I thought espionage was reserved for the CIA or some other governmental agency," Sam said. "What does industry have to do with it? I don't understand what you're talking about."

"Sam," Brad began, "industrial espionage is an everyday fact of life. That's why I hired John at the Center. To help prevent it. All of the security procedures he's installed at the Center are designed to make sure only people you want to know things, have access to them. The concept is basically the same. Doesn't matter if it's government versus government or two corporations going at it."

"That's pretty well put, Brad." Ron said, adding, "Samantha, it's important to remember one thing. There're those that would rather steal a good idea, be it a recipe for a vaccine or a new engine design, than spend the time, money and effort involved in its development. Some corporations, although it's never expensed on their balance sheets I'll guarantee you, have large fundings for their in-house espionage units. These personnel are hired for no other reason than to conduct covert operations against other corporations."

"The all-mighty dollar surfaces again." said Sam.

"What do you mean?" questioned Ron.

"Oh, kind of thinking out loud about something Brad had told me. The dollar bill appears to influence people, companies, hell, even countries."

"If it's of any consequence, my brother wasn't involved in anything of the sort. They merely used it against him as a reason for his dismissal."

"I understand what you're saying Ron. The question I have is, why'd they dismiss him if he was such a promising research assistant?" Brad asked.

"I don't understand it either. Let me give you a synopsis of what I do know or, what I think I know."

"Fine."

"Late last year, about a year ago, and, months before the outbreak of the virus in Africa, Richard was transferred to a team ..."

"The Ebola virus?"

"Right. He was transferred to a team doing research on a promising vaccine. After the outbreak, Richard became very disenchanted with the people at BioMed. They refused to continue the research efforts or propagate the vaccine. As a result of BioMed's reluctance, for whatever reason, Rick anonymously contacted the CDC in Atlanta. The CDC placed calls to BioMed concerning the vaccine's availability and one thing led to another.

"The entire time, BioMed never acknowledged that any research had been conducted on Ebola. All references to the viral study were erased from the computers, all notes were confiscated and Rick was fired. All he was trying to accomplish was saving some lives and controlling the spread of the virus. Something, anyone in their right mind would do."

"Who is CDC?" Sam asked.

"It's the Center for Disease Control, an agency of the US Public Health Service," replied Brad. "They're staffed primarily to conduct research into the origin and occurrence of diseases and develop methods for their control and prevention. Like Ebola." To Ron, Brad continued. "Do you happen to know if BioMed was licensed to do the work by CDC. Never mind, that was a stupid question. If they were licensed, CDC would've all ready contacted them about the outbreak. Your brother wouldn't have to contact them. They'd be doing the calling. And, BioMed certainly wouldn't have destroyed everything. That's strange as hell."

"You have to be licensed to do research?" Sam questioned.

"On highly contagious diseases, Sam," Brad explained. "CDC, for the safety of the general population, has to control the access to the virus. Especially, one as deadly as Ebola. To do research against the virus, you've got to have some in your possession to test against. That's not allowed until your facilities are thoroughly checked out. CDC maintains the inventory levels of the virus, distributes precisely measured sample amounts of the inventory to research labs, and maintains very stringent controls over its dissemination. If anyone would know of any vaccine testing being done, CDC would." Again to Ron, he asked. "Did your brother say they *had* tested a vaccine against Ebola or that they had a vaccine they *wanted* to test against Ebola?"

After pondering Brad's question for some period of time, Ron answered, "I can't say with certainty. Rick said, they'd performed testing and what I *can* say for sure is, he led me down the garden path to the conclusion that it was developed using Ebola. It still doesn't explain Rick's dismissal and the subsequent smearing he was subjected to as a result."

"That it doesn't. Look Ron, don't take what I'm about to say personally."

"You think I'm a nut case or something, right?"

"No, just bear with me."

"Okay."

"Ron, I really don't know you from Adam."

"Agreed."

"As little as I know about you, I know even less about your late brother, Rick. Correct?"

"Again, agreed."

"Hypothetically speaking now, and please allow me to finish before you respond."

"Okay."

"Is there the slightest chance that Rick may have been involved, without your knowledge, in some sort of industrial espionage or activity which may have been so interpreted by BioMed Research? Anything at all that might be considered damaging to their efforts?"

"No, there isn't. We were twins, you know. There's scientific evidence proving a more than normal relationship exists between twins... kind of a special bonding. Regardless whether it can be proven through science or not, the special bonding existed with the two us. I strongly believe I would've known, without his telling me, if something of that sort was going on."

"I can appreciate that. One other question. Did his behavior change at all after his becoming a research assistant on the vaccine study?"

"*Yes*! For the first time, he was excited about being a part of something so beneficial. That's why he so eagerly spent all of the time after hours; after all, he wasn't getting any overtime for his efforts. Following the outbreak in Africa, Rick became very enthusiastic about his work. This enthusiam wore away, day by day, because of his frustration with BioMed's not informing anyone of the vaccine. The exercise in futility reached the point that prompted his phone call to CDC."

"First of all, we've established that you're not certain there's an actual vaccine for Ebola, or, for that matter, that there was any testing of any vaccine against the virus itself. Right?"

"That's right. We've all ready been over that."

"I understand that. Have you checked to see if Rick actually made a phone call to CDC?"

"You're suggesting he lied to me? I can see where *this* is headed."

"I apologize. I meant to ask if he told you who he contacted there."

"No, he didn't. That doesn't mean he didn't make the call."

"I know. All I can say is, unless BioMed is involved in some pretty shady dealings, Rick must've let it slip at work that he'd contacted CDC. As a result, BioMed let him go because he didn't follow the proper chain of command, so to speak. But, the rationale for depicting him as a covert industrial agent, still doesn't fit. Seems like overkill to me. Ron, just what do you want me to do about this situation?"

"I don't know. I guess... find out something. Prove I'm not really crazy."

"Ron, our Center is not involved, in the slightest way, shape or form, in policing activities of research centers. We're founded on the idea of promoting Cancer research by fine-tuning efforts. We have other data in our system, but only as an aside to the main goal of the Center, a cure for cancer."

"I felt with your Center's high reputation, you might... be able to make some phone calls to shed some light on the problem."

"Let's leave it like this for now. Give me your home number. Or better yet, for your protection, some ahh... secure way to get in touch with you. I'll do some digging, as my time and schedule allows, and be in touch with you. I won't be doing much on it right away. My December looks fairly busy with getting ready for my conference in Australia in January and the Christmas holidays aıe on us. Don't get upset if I'm not in contact with you until the middle of January or so. Just kind of lay low for a while. Enjoy the season with your wife."

"I guess the best way to get in touch would be through my beeper. I can be reached anywhere in the country on it. Let's see ahh... key in the numbers 7734. That'll let me know to contact you."

"Sounds good. Why'd you pick 7734?"

"The digital readout spells "hell" when you look at it upside down. And believe me, I've been going through it since Rick's death."

"That's a deal. Hell... hell is easy enough to remember. I say hell all the time."

"Are you hungry?" Ron said, directing the question to Sam who'd been uncharacteristically quiet.

"Famished."

"Good. Shall we adjourn to the dining room and order?"

"Let's."

The three enjoyed the cuisine of the restaurant like they hadn't eaten in a week. The conversation during dinner, oddly, didn't regress to the subject being discussed in the lounge. All that could be said, had been. After dinner, Ron shook their hands and thanked Brad in advance for anything he could do. Brad and Sam wished him well on his flight out of National Airport the next morning and left the Marriott.

On the drive home, nothing was said between Brad and Sam until they were on the 14th Street bridge, crossing the Potomac. The night was clear, the stars shining brightly and, overhead, the sound of a Boeing 727 could be heard on final approach to National Airport.

"I believe him," Sam said bluntly.

"He's a hell of a nice guy. I don't know who with yet, but, I'm going to do some checking for him. I wouldn't put too much faith in his story though."

"Why not?"

"What he said about bonding between twins is right. I'm merely afraid their bonding was too much for Ron to cope with."

"What do you mean?"

"I think his brother may have been involved, maybe not in espionage or anything as romantic, but, something which caused his legitimate firing by BioMed. His brother's eventual suicide was the straw breaking the camel's back, the camel being Ron. At that point, I think Ron fabricated a lot. Don't get me wrong, he strongly believes in his mind that's it's the truth, and nothing but the truth, so help him God. I think he's trying to convince himself that his brother was the innocent victim of a villainous hierarchy."

"I suppose what you're saying may be true. But, for me, call it women's intuition, someone still has to prove to me what he's saying isn't true. Kind of sounds like a back end approach, but... oh hell, Brad, I don't know."

"We'll check it out."

"Promise?"

"Yes, my dear. We'll get an answer, one way or the other. Don't be upset if it turns out I'm right."

"I'll be upset regardless of how it turns out. If Ron isn't telling the truth, he's got a deep mental problem coping with the death of his brother. On the other hand, if his suspicions are true, who knows where it might lead."

"I see your point."

"I thought you were inviting me out for a nice time, not to have drinks with a guy who can put a damper on the whole evening in a matter of ten minutes. Oh hell, Brad, it's not your fault either. You had no idea what was coming."

"Look, Sam. Let's just drop this for now. There's plenty of time to discuss this at a later date when we have some answers. Okay? Besides, we're almost home now and the party's about to begin."

"What party?"
"The office party."
"Big guy, you are something. Who's bringing the dip?"
"I am. Any other questions?"
"None what so ever. Let's party!"
"Race you to the dining room table, my love."
"If that's where the dip's going to be, you don't stand a chance."
"We'll see."

---- Chapter Seven ----

Sam Haller sat at his desk, watching the smoke ring he'd just blown curl up towards the grid work of the white, drop-in ceiling of his office. It was a window office on the 16th floor, but, not a corner office. That was reserved for someone with a higher status than his, one for which he'd do nearly anything to achieve. Leaning back in the desk chair with his feet propped on the desk top, he brushed a few ashes off his navy blue tie and white shirt. He stood up and walked over to the wall to straighten the picture of his last NASCAR win at the Pocono 500. One beautiful young lady was planting a kiss on his cheek, while another was pouring champagne over his head. He was holding the silver-plate trophy and beaming proudly. Much happier times! He returned to the chair to answer the ringing telephone.

"Samuel, they're in your ballpark now. They've checked into Trump Plaza."

"How do you want me to proceed on this one?"

"Your scrambler on?"

"Yes."

"You do *absolutely nothing* other than keep an eye on them. We want to know everything they do and everyplace they go. If he takes a shit, I want to know how bad it stinks. Got it?"

"That's all?"

"After your screw up on Thanksgiving, consider yourself out of the loop for right now. You told us you'd cause the car to flip. It didn't. Thanks to you, we still have four people to worry about now."

Samuel abruptly slid his feet off the desk, sat upright in the chair, and furiously crushed the menthol cigarette out in the ashtray as if it was the forehead of the man on the other end of the line. "Look, damn it. You asked me if I could and, I said I thought so. I didn't give you an iron-clad guarantee. It was totally your decision to try it, not mine. You know I'm dedicated to the organization or you wouldn't have asked me to try it in the first place."

"Your dedication has nothing to do with anything, performance does. The point is, *you* didn't complete the contract."

"The point is, if it wasn't sleeting and snowing all damn day, the car wouldn't've flipped. The God damn shoulders of the road were slippery as hell. The son of a bitch did about four 360's and stopped short of some trees."

"Where'd you dump the car?"

"Some woods in Virginia. They found it yet?"

"No. Not yet."

"All you want from me on the new contract are my eyes?"

"Not really."

"What's that mean?"

"Nothing. Just stick to them like glue. It's important for your future. There're other things on the agenda. Things coming down the road for you," he lied. "This one's all ready spoken for."

"Someone on a personal vendetta?"

"Something like that."

"Oh, the idiot that fucked up the bombing. Right?"

"You don't have a need to know who."

"How much rantin' and ravin' did you do with him?"

"It wasn't necessary. It was our fault. Look, Haller. You don't have the authority to be questioning my actions. You do what the hell you're told and nothing else. *Follow me?*"

"I follow you," he replied, realizing he'd overstepped the invisible boundary you should never cross. "Just follow them. Right?"

"Right. And, stay close to them all damn day."

"I will. Like white on rice."

"Good. And, Samuel, try not to be so testy. It was your first attempt. And, not a bad one at that. You'll see how it's professionally done soon. See you."

"Thanks. Bye," Samuel said hanging up the phone and switching off the scrambler. "You asshole," he completed. He looked at the family picture on his desk displaying his wife, Joan and their two kids, Shelby and Justin, standing beside the Ford he'd driven in his last win. "I'd do anything for you guys," he whispered. He stood, walked to the door, turned out the light and left his office. Glancing at his watch on the way to the elevator, he wondered if the kids would still be up when he got home. He hoped so.

*****

It was Saturday afternoon, the seventh of December, and Samantha and Brad had arrived in the Big Apple the evening before on a quick flight from National Airport. Time was flying, but, it always did when Samantha and Brad were together, and, when they weren't, they wished they were. They'd been whisked to Trump Plaza by a talkative New York cabby, probably of Italian decent, who acted as if he'd just discovered his taxi had a horn and was endlessly testing it.

Exhausted from compiling information over the past couple of days for Brad's presentation at the conference in Melbourne, they'd selected their dinners from the variety of entrees presented in the room service menu lying conveniently beside the suite's telephone. Their attempt to finalize Brad's presentation had proven futile. Sam was too excited about shopping for the appropriate outfit to wear to the New Zealand Embassy's gala to put much thought into anything else.

She'd spread out the *Daily News* Womens' section on the room's French writing table next to the yellow pages and methodically gone through their contents and made a list of shops and boutiques showing promise of having the "ultimate gown" for the event. Brad had glanced at the list of twenty and suggested she shorten it by as many as fifteen, or at least, put it in an order that wouldn't require crisscrossing the city eight or nine times. If Sam were anything like Chantal and her shopping escapades, Brad was in for a long day.

He was seated in an antique chair, conveniently placed near the changing room, waiting for Samantha to parade in front of him. While Sam was changing clothes, preparing for the "modeling runways", Brad patiently read newspapers or magazines such as *Women's Day, Bride, Comospolitan,* or *Vogue*. He found himself wondering why an assortment of publications such as this was placed beside chairs where men sat, waiting for their wives or girl friends. A collection of titles such as *Skiing, Field and Stream, Sports Illustrated* or *News Week* somehow seemed more appropriate.

The up-scale boutique was decorated on a rich and authentic antique theme. Things looked old, because they were. The furnishings were late 1800's, the mannequins were circa 1920's and there was an antique, brass-plated, National Cash Register Company machine complete with pull handle for transactions. The paned windows of the store front were fitted with a reproduction of yellowing, antique glass which gave shoppers a distorted view and required they enter the shop for a closer examination of the gowns displayed. It proved to be a very smart marketing technique because that's exactly what lured Sam inside.

Brad liked the first gown she'd tried the best, well over two hours ago in the first shop, and, as far as he was concerned, this endless search could've come to a screeching halt right there. The coal black color emphasized the sleek lines of the gown and with the proper touch of jewelry, Sam would be the talk of the ball. The gown didn't really matter that much anyway, Brad felt, because she made the clothes look good, not the reverse.

Another gown had similar lines and graced Sam's proportioned shape magnificently, but, was fabricated in a bright red silk. Deciding it looked too much like Christmas decorations, they'd passed on it. Sam jokingly said, "The only jewelry I'd need is a pine bough wreath for a necklace and a couple of holly candle rings for my wrist and fingers." Brad suggested a mistletoe pendant hanging just above the crevice of her cleavage would be a very nice touch!

Reaching over and picking up Seventeen, the only magazine remaining he hadn't thumbed through, he heard Sam's soft, southern drawl purr. "What da ya'all think, mister?"

Brad looked up from the pages in front of him and was awe struck. The editors of *Harper's* or *Vogue* could *never* find a more beautiful cover than Sam. The gown was a magenta color, the silken lace long sleeves barely reaching the crown of her bare shoulders. The gown swept gracefully downward to a tastefully revealing bust line. It was bare-backed with the flow of the tight fabric beginning just below her waist and draping effortlessly over her curvature to the floor. Split at knee height in front, the slenderness of the skirt made her walk in small steps which created a wonderful effect and accentuated her gracefulness. As she turned, Brad noticed the silken fabric affixing itself to her body like a layer of soft skin with an air of sophisticated innocence. He caught his breath and barely managed a nod to show his approval and excitement.

"You haven't said anything. What do you think?"

"Sam, you certainly make that gown look fantastic. I love it."

"Didn't see anything you liked better in any of the magazines?"

"I *hardly* think so," he continued showing a wide lecherous grin.

With her hands on her hips, Samantha questioned. "Well, should I take it?"

"I don't believe there's any question." Before he could stand up, he had begun to gawk up at her magnificent bodice covered by the magenta colored fabric. Looking down, it was more revealing.

"Too much showing?" Sam asked pulling up the corners.

"Not for me, but, you have a little better view. Need any BandAids?"

"Built-in," came her response.

"Sam, it doesn't look like there's room for built-ins, but, if you say so. Built-ins," he continued, "that's funny. You talk about them as if they're kitchen appliances."

"Not appliances, sweetie, a complete, home entertainment center," she teased casting a sexy smile in his direction.

"I can go for that. Go ahead and get the gown. I won't have it any other way. I love the color."

"It may be too expensive."

"Doesn't matter. Let me make the decision on this one. Something you look that good in, it's just got to be part of your wardrobe," he urged.

"You mean it!!!"

"Of course. I want you to have it."

"It's not too... sexy looking?" Sam asked with concern in her voice as she turned and eyed her reflection in the mirror. "I don't want to appear out of place at such a prestigious, social function."

"Sexy, but in a sophisticated way. Kinda southern sexy, ya know?"

"I'm glad to hear that," she said as she headed back to the changing room. "Southern sexy is good."

"I'll say it is. You wouldn't happen to need any help, would you?" Brad asked.

"Not today... maybe after the gala," she said as she entered the changing room.

A sudden thought entered Brad's mind, his heart began to palpitate and his stomach felt a bit queasy. He knew it was pangs of jealousy about other men looking at Samantha with unadulterated lust. He wanted her to look good, but, not too good. *I've got to find the time to get over to Baumburg's and let Saul help me pick out an engagement ring,* he thought. *He's good at that kinda stuff. Have to get it done soon, too.* The urge to do so reminded Brad of a male animal *marking* his territory. Somehow, he'd feel more comfortable when *his* ring was on *her* finger.

As Brad stood at the front window straining to see through the wavy, antique glass, he noticed a tow truck driver having difficulty backing into position because of traffic. With the help of one of New York's finest halting the heavy traffic, he began hooking up a car at curbside, up the street and to the right of the boutique.

The apparent owner of the car ran across the street, dodged traffic as he raised his middle finger to a taxi driver and shook his fist at the police officer. Brad couldn't hear a word of the verbal exchange, but, from the crowd gathering at the scene and the body language of the parties involved, the man wasn't a happy camper. With a shrug of his shoulders and pointing to a loading zone only sign, the cop motioned with his arm for the tow truck driver to continue. The owner of the car wasn't about to let it go and must've said something which the officer didn't appreciate and took it quite personal.

To the delight of the crowd of the bystanders, he whipped out his book and proceeded to ticket the man. Something else said, the officer dropped his ticket pad on the pavement and forcibly maneuvered the man against the car for a body search. Reaching behind his back for the cuffs attached to his black leather belt, he forcibly hand-cuffed the man and spun him around so they were face to face.

"What's going on?" Sam asked as she joined Brad at the front window of the boutique, sliding her arms around his waist and pressing her breasts against his back. "They're boxing the gown for us now."

"I'm not really sure. This glass is hard as hell to see through. Quite a scene though. I think that guy just got arrested for something. Probably for pissing off the cop."

Before Brad or Sam could say anything else, the scene quickly became one of horror. Gun fire rang out... both the officer and the man being placed under arrest were immediately struck down by the hail of bullets and were dead before they hit the ground. The blood from their gaping wounds formed separate pools on the ground and grew larger by the second until they joined as if resolving the confrontations between the two men.

The tow truck driver, bending down on his haunches and preparing the car to be towed, escaped the barrage; however, some of the innocent bystanders, unable to find cover, weren't as fortunate. A total of five were killed and nine others wounded during the melee.

Brad noticed a man on the sidewalk wearing a ski cap, only his eyes visible, firing an automatic weapon and running towards the car. He was dressed in a dark blue suit, mostly covered by a gray overcoat, and simple, black shoes with his burgundy and beige argyle socks visible as he ran. Arriving at the car, he quickly looked inside and went to its rear. He emptied the remainder of the weapon's magazine into the trunk's lock area which caused the lid to fly open. Then, calmly and professionally, he popped out the spent magazine and inserted another with his gloved hands. There were no prints on the empty magazine dropped to the pavement, nor, on the spent shell casings littering his path, a true professional. The assailant reached inside the trunk, pulled out a brief case and ran up the street, rounding the corner, and out-of-sight. The entire episode took less than a minute.

Brad looked over at a shaken Sam on the floor, her face white with fear. Without thinking, just reacting, he'd pushed her to the floor for safety, below the level of the boutique's front window.

"Sorry to be so rough, Sam. There wasn't much time," Brad said, trying to hold back the rush of adrenaline and remain calm.

"*Damn*!" she stammered. "*Don't* be sorry Brad. Is it over?"

"I *think* so. The man took off up the street," he replied over wailing sirens of the approaching squad cars and screams of people clamoring for assistance. His hand stroking Sam's shoulder for comfort, Brad glanced up and noticed five perfectly symmetrical holes, each surrounded with hair-line, spider-web cracks, in the front window. His other hand tightly gripped the copy of Seventeen, its cover forever wrinkled. "What's this white stuff all over you, Sam?"

She examined herself, finding she was covered with a powder-like, white residue. "I don't have any idea. You've got it on you too. Where'd it come from?"

Looking at the display window, Brad noticed the mannequins displaying the evening gowns for which the shop was famous. "*Look at that shit*!" Brad said pointing to bullet holes in the mid-section of one and another with its head completely blown off. "Probably ricochets off the car."

"*Oh my God*," exclaimed Sam, her southern accent all but gone. "I was standing *right behind* it. If you hadn't pushed me to the floor, I would've *been hit*." she said, the tone of her voice strident. "What *is* this white stuff?"

"I think it's dust from plaster. The mannequins must be antiques." Brad threw the Seventeen magazine aside and began to brush the powder from Sam's clothing. "You even have it in your hair. Are you okay?"

"I think so," she replied as Brad helped her to her feet. They hugged each other tightly, making certain neither was hurt. In Brad's arms, Sam's heavy breathing subsided as his comforting hands rubbed her back and neck and removed the tension of the moment. With her speech returning to normal and trying to make light of the traumatic situation, she said. "I can't leave you alone for a minute, Brad. Look at the trouble you stir up."

"Me? I didn't do anything," he mockingly disclaimed. "I was just standing here minding my own business when this fiasco went down. I don't believe this shit. Now, people might understand why I don't like big cities. *This* was too damn close." Looking out the window to the scene, Brad continued. "They're probably going to want to talk to us. You up to it?"

Noticing the police milling around the scene, stepping over bodies and helping the wounded, Sam said. "If I have to. I've seen dead people before, but, only at funerals. Never like this. I... I guess I'll be okay out there."

During the next hour they were interviewed by various detectives and police officers inside the yellow crime scene tape and away from reporters. Ambulances had come and gone, taking the injured to the hospital emergency rooms as the coroner's wagons were on their way to the morgue.

They were about to leave with the box containing her gown tucked under Brad's arm when they noticed the tow truck driver taking one final survey of the gruesome scene. There were blood stains, still damp and turning to a deep brown color, spilled over on the sidewalk and street. The tow truck operator lowered the trunk lid to anchor it because the latch was blown away and now, the license plate, riddled with bullet holes, became visible. It was a black oval with the white letters, D... A... Y... Y... I... J.

"Do you see what I do?"

"I sure do," Brad said.

"Coincidence?"

"Probably, what else could it be? Detective," Brad called out.

"Yes sir. Did you think of something else?"

"No. Just curious. Who was the man driving this car?"

"No identification on the body. Must've been in the briefcase the guy heisted from the trunk."

"Who's the car registered to?"

"Can't really remember for certain. I think some foreign government. Probably someone's car from the United Nations. They're all over the damn place."

"Swiss Technologies?"

"Yeah, now that I think about it. That's the name that came over the radio. How'd you know?"

"Ohh, we have a few of those plates in the DC area. Thanks. And, get in touch if you need anything else."

"You're welcome sir. Have a nice day, if it's possible after this."

"Thanks. You also."

"Brad, I'm going to ask you the *same* question. Please don't give me the *same* answer you gave the detective."

"What?"

"How did you know the plate was registered to Swiss Technologies?"

"Ohh, that. Abe told me."

"Abe who?"

"He's the desk sergeant at the 47th Precinct where I picked up my cell phone. Hell of a nice guy."

"You asked him about the plate? Why?"

"I was there and just curious, that's all."

"I can't believe how this *same* license plate keeps popping up. It seems kinda strange to me, more than a coincidence."

"What possible connection could there be between seeing the plate in DC a couple of times and this shooting. If we were connected, we'd be on our way to the morgue with the rest of 'em. The guy that did this was a pro, Sam. He was as cool as a cucumber the entire time. Pros don't make the wrong hit. He knew exactly what he was doing and how much time he had to get it done."

"Your probably right. I'm just nervous as all get out from this."

"To make you feel better, tell you what I'm going to do. I'll call Abe when we get back to DC and have him do some digging, if he can. He helps detectives at the precinct with some of their cases."

"I'd appreciate it."

"Consider it done. Maybe those plates have always been around us and we've just never noticed before. Personally, I'm convinced it's one big coincidence. Right this minute, I want to get out of here, get a drink, something to eat and settle down a little. Try to relax if possible, you know? I think we both want to be in front of the television when the news comes on."

"You're right, Brad, let's go, I really want to try and relax after this."

*****

The roar of a departing flight made it difficult to hear so he waited until the 727 was off in the distance, crushing out his third cigarette on the sidewalk with his shoe. He'd tried to call a couple of times before, but, no one picked up. This would be his final attempt at contact before boarding the flight. "Shit, someone better answer this time or they'll just have to wait to hear from me," he cursed.

"Yes," came the reply over the phone. "Who is it?"

"It's me."

"Where are you?"

"Standing at a God damn outdoor pay phone in front of La Guardia. Thought I should check in."

"I understand he's still alive."

"Which he are you talking about? Haller's deader than hell."

"For sure, Haller's dead?"

"No question. Claxton and his girl didn't get a scratch. They're back at Trump Plaza."

"What the *hell* went wrong?"

"Everything went according to plan. Haller followed them like you told him to last night. We were on him and the other two all damn day until the perfect opportunity presented itself. The set up couldn't have been better. Haller, the dumb fuck, got pissed off at the police about his car gettin' towed and a crowd formed to watch the ruckus. It gave us great cover. The guy and his girl come to the front window of the shop they were in to see what the hell was goin' on. It was perfect, man. Right up to the fuckin' point when I was goin' to take them out."

"You... *just missed*? *How the hell's that possible*?"

"The God damn shop had antique glass in the windows. You know, that wavy shit. Distorted the crap out of everything. It was like trying to shoot fish in rippled water."

"*Son of a bitch.*"

"I thought I might as well give it a go. Everyone would think it was stray bullets from the other guy knocking off Haller anyway. You know, just like you and I planned it. If I got the two of them, great. If not, there's always tomorrow in Lake Placid."

"Maybe, after today, they won't go to Lake Placid like they planned."

"I don't think he'll change those plans. He's goin' to see his old coach, Tony... whatever his damn name is."

"You're right. He's still going. If there's *skiing involved*, he'll go.

"Hold on a minute. Another plane's taking off. I can't hear a damn thing."

"Busy place."

"Sure as hell is." While waiting for the latest departure to get some distance from him, he tore off the cellophane from a fresh pack of Camels. After lighting up and inhaling deeply, he continued his report. "I thought we had a winner of an idea. Just didn't work out, that's all."

"At least Haller isn't a problem anymore. He was an obstinate SOB."

"He was definitely a potential problem. Since he screwed up down in DC on Thanksgiving, he's been pretty damn uncontrollable. You made the right decision gettin' rid of his ass. Tyin' the contract on him into an accidental shooting of the other two was damn ingenious. And, it almost worked."

"I know you wanted him because of your first try. This opportunity presented itself, so thought you'd want another go at it."

"I saw the whole thing go down. Damn thing was perfect. Helping to plan it was nearly as good as knockin' off the bastard's goin' to be. I told you he was the luckiest fuck I've ever seen in my life."

"*God damn* antique glass. Must have been a problem. You've made the hits on worse setups than this before."

"God damn it."

"What?"

"It's starting to rain like a cat's ass out here. What about tomorrow?"

"You going up tonight?"

"Right."

"I'm glad your leaving tonight. Killing the cop was necessary, but, it riles 'em up a bit. Sorry about the pedestrians, but, shit happens. As for Claxton and his girlfriend, stay in a holding pattern. Check the place out. Remember, it *has* to look like an accident. You have my permission for a go, if it can be accomplished. Both of them. We're not sure yet, but, looks like the two of them and the other two, the ones Haller missed on Thanksgiving, are going to Colorado soon. We may decide to hold off 'til then. If you get the chance in Lake Placid, that's two down and two to go. Use your best judgment."

"That's the guy I told you about in the restroom at Snowshoe, right?"

"Right."

"I saw all four of them sittin' around and talkin' in the lodge. It's funny."

"What's funny?"

"I normally don't see my clients before I take them out... to dinner. You know what I mean?"

"Yeah, I do. You have a funny way of putting things."

"Shit, it's rainin' harder. I gotta get out of here."

"Check in tomorrow."

"Gotcha. Bye."

He flipped his cigarette into the street and watched the turning tires of a passing car crush it. So simple to extinguish a life. At least it *used* to be before Claxton entered the picture. With his jacket pulled over his head, he turned and briskly walked to the La Guardia entrance.

*****

Both Sam and Brad were very much on edge with what they'd witnessed in front of the boutique and, nearly in silence, only picked at the dinners placed before them in the Trump Plaza restaurant. With their moods as gloomy as the rainy weather outside, they'd decided they wanted no part of strolling New York streets or checking out one of the multitude of restaurants they offered. They both drank two Martinis before ordering, wanting something a bit stronger than a bottle of 1982 Bordeaux to take the edge off their nerves. After dinner, they'd tried their best to relax at the piano bar, listening to some soft music. They'd danced close together for the first time with Sam's head resting on Brad's shoulder. Neither said anything. They didn't have to.

Returning to their suite at nine thirty, Brad placed a quick call to Tony in Lake Placid to inform him of their arrival time the next day.

"Tony, is that you?"

"Sure as hell is, Brad. Good to hear from you. You in DC or New York?"

"New York, wishing like hell I was in Lake Placid."

"You'll be here tomorrow. Still gettin' in at the same time?"

"No changes coach. Late afternoon."

"Tell Sam I've arranged for her to take a trip down the Bob Sled run," Tony said, knowing Sam would be excited.

"Really. She'll be excited about that. Hell, I've never done it myself."

"I think she'll have some fun. You anywhere near the shooting down there I heard about on the radio?"

"The one in New York?"

"Yeah, that's the one."

"Too damn close. Almost got hit ourselves."

"You're kidding me, right?" Hearing nothing but silence to his question, Tony continued. "You're... *not* kidding are you, Brad?"

"I'm afraid not Tony. We were in a store when stray bullets came flying through the window. Five of 'em. They put some great looking mannequins out of their misery."

"Damn, man. You and Sam okay?"

"Yeah, we're fine. A little shaken, but, our nerves are getting back to normal. Of course, the Martinis at dinner helped a lot."

"Whatever it takes."

"I've got to go coach. Does the Fox Television Network have a ten o'clock newscast up here."

"Yeah, they do. I don't know what channel. All depends on the cable company."

"I'll find it."

"I'm going to try and catch it myself. See you tomorrow."

"Right, coach. Tomorrow then. Bye."

Brad returned the portable phone back to its cradle on the French desk, walked to the in-room refrigerator under the wet bar, selected a Bud Light and flopped on the tapestry sofa next to Sam. Donald Trump thought of everything.

"How's Tony," inquired Sam.

"Sounds like he's great. Hell, he always sounds great. He's going to catch the news too. I told him about the incident today. By the way, he's arranged for you to take a ride down the Bob Sled course."

"That's *fantastic*. Did you thank him for me?"

"Didn't have to. He knew you'd be excited as hell."

"I am."

"He wasn't wrong," said Brad putting his feet up on the round coffee table in front of them.

"Speaking of excitement, Brad. Do you think I could try one of those little sleds on the Bob Sled run?"

"You mean the luge?"

"Yeah, that's the one," she replied, in her endearing southern accent.

"Sam... geez, I don't know. Those sleds go pretty damn fast, sometimes over seventy miles an hour."

"Oh, Brad. A little sled can't go that fast, can it?"

"It sure as hell can. They're moving on ice."

"That fast? I had no idea. Maybe... I'd better not."

"Tell you what. If you want to, we'll go double and try to hold down the speed. How's that?"

"If you're on the sled with me, I might try it. Oh, look Brad, it's coming on." Sam said, referring to the news.

"Okay. Let's see what they're saying about this shit."

The commentator was speaking. "Today, at approximately three o'clock, a gruesome scene unfolded in one of the city's busiest shopping districts. During an apparent misunderstanding concerning the towing of his vehicle from a plainly marked, no parking zone, Mr. Samuel Haller, a vice president of market research with Bonn Industries, was gunned down for no apparent reason by an unknown assailant. According to witnesses who had gathered, Mr. Haller became indignant with police officer, Sergeant Dennis O'Keef who had ordered his car towed away for a parking violation. A fourteen year veteran of the force, he was also reported dead at the scene due to gunfire. Reports indicate that while Sergeant O'Keef was placing Mr. Haller under arrest, the assailant appeared and began spraying the area with an automatic weapon. Also dead at the scene were three pedestrians whose names are being withheld until notification of their next of kin. Nine other persons are being treated at area hospitals, all in serious condition. Bullet holes are evident in the windows of the plush shopping district, where fortunately, no one inside was injured. Mr. Haller was of NASCAR fame in 1994 when he was leading in total points for driver of the year and was involved in a near fatal collision. He is survived by his wife, Joan, and their two children. Sergeant O'Keef is survived by his wife, Theresa, of ten years. The O'Keef's had no children."

"There we are. Look."

Brad saw what Sam was talking about, but said nothing, enthralled with the newscaster's words. The video coverage panned to a shot of a man with *County Coroner* written across the back of his jacket. He was stooped down, at one end of a litter, preparing to lift the covered body of one of the pedestrians.

"*The gall of that son of a bitch*!!!!!!" Brad shouted.

"*What*?" Sam asked, jumping from Brad's shout.

"See that guy's feet... there, the one with the beige and burgundy socks. There... there he is again. See him?" Brad said excitedly.

"The guy with the dark blue slacks?"

"Yeah."

"I see him, why?"

"He's the bastard that did all the shooting!"

"Brad, calm down. How do you know that? The guy I caught a glimpse of, before you shoved me down, was wearing gray."

"Sam, did you see the guy below his waist or from the front?"

"No. Only for a split second from the back."

"I did. He had a gray overcoat covering a blue suit and those socks, those damn socks we just saw on the telecast," Brad said. He picked up the remote and turned off the TV. The newscast had shifted to another segment..

"Brad, honey, you think you can identify a ... maniacal killer by a pair of shoes?"

"Sam, not the shoes. The socks. The argyle socks. The beige and burgundy socks. I saw them as he ran past the shop. I remember how stupid they looked. The guy in the news footage had the same ones on. *It was him*!"

"Okay...oookay. Settle down and let's try to decide what to do about it. You know, the only thing *you* saw, Brad, were the shoes and his pants from his knees down. I remember the gray overcoat. I also remember him wearing a knit hat pulled down over his face. How could you hope to identify him?"

"That guy must really be sick to come back to the scene. Probably relishing his day's work. *That's it*!!!!" Brad shouted, physically showing his excitement by clapping his hands together.

"*Brad*, you scared the hell out of me again. What are you doing?"

"Sorry. Don't ya see Sam, that's it. I can get the bastard," Brad rattled with an look of pleasure on his face.

"How?"

"He came back to the scene right?"

"That's what you're claiming."

"He took off his overcoat. He also took off his ski mask, right?"

"If he didn't, he'd be pretty stupid. I'll agree with you, *if he came back* he would change his appearance, but, you still can't ID the man."

"But I can... or least should be able to."

"Brad, for the life of me, I can't understand where you're going with this."

"What we just saw was video tape of the scene. Tape, Sam."

"Ohh, I see what you are saying. The TV station would have the tape and there may be other footage they didn't broadcast. It might show the entire guy. What station were we watching?"

Brad clicked on the TV and promptly said, "Channel 8."

"Brad, even if this station doesn't have any footage, another one might. We should check all the tapes."

"Not we Sam. The police should. I don't want to get in the middle of this kinda shit. I'm going to get hold of the detective in charge of this case and let him know what we saw. Let him handle it. Believe me, with a dead cop on their hands, they're going to want to go full steam ahead with any leads they have."

"You're right. Go ahead and give 'em a call."

Brad spent about fifteen minutes on the telephone discussing his observation of the newscast with the detective in charge. Initially, he thought Brad was a crackpot, but, changed his mind when a second person called, claiming the same thing. Brad couldn't offer any help to the detective's question of why the man would return to the scene. Sam listened to the entire conversation and had one question for him after he hung up.

"Why do the police think this guy would come back?"

"The only thing he said was he might have come back, if it in fact was him I saw on the newscast, to make certain whoever he was after was dead. That being the case, the guy would more than likely be a professional hit man, an out-of-towner, and even if they got an entire body shot of him from one of the tapes, he'd more than likely be long gone by now. They thanked me for the lead and were going to secure the video tapes from the news services. Other than saying they'd get in touch with me if anything developed, nothing of any importance was said. I didn't feel it was the right time to bring up the license plate thing. By the way, the commentator on the news stated Mr. Haller worked for... Bonn Industries, right?"

"I believe so, in market research."

"That's right. Vice President of market research. That's something."

"What's something?"

"At the scene, the officer I questioned about the registration on the car said it was registered to Swiss Technologies. The news said Haller worked for Bonn Industries."

"Nooo, Brad, that's not quite what happened with the officer at the scene. You suggested *to him*, it was Swiss Technologies. Remember me asking you about it?"

"Oh, I remember, but, that's not what I was getting at."

"What then?"

"Only that Abe, remember, the desk sergeant at the 47th Precinct?"

"Yes."

"He told me that cars he knew of with this kind of plate, were registered to Bern Industries, a subsidiary of Swiss Technologies."

"So?"

"So, nothing, I guess it's just coincidence. Two divisions of the parent company would be named after European Capitals."

"Coincidence or not. I don't see anything out of the ordinary. What would you have a European Company name its divisions after, the planets, maybe ahh...different varieties of roses, or maybe, cat breeds?"

"Sam, I guess you're right," Brad said beginning to laugh. "I suppose, I'm just a little more than curious about these subsidiaries. I was hoping for something a little more definitive in their names. Something which would help me determine the kind of business they're in."

"Brad, my sweet, I hate to burst your bubble."

"What?"

"I know the capital of Switzerland is Bern, even though most people assume it's Zurich. For which country are you claiming Bonn is the capital?"

"Germany," Brad responded defiantly.

"Wrong. That's what I thought. Berlin is the capital."

"Right, and wrong."

"What?"

"You'd be right if the commies never built the Berlin wall during the cold war. Berlin hasn't been the capital *for all of Germany* for 45 years. It's been the capital of East Germany forever. The capital of West Germany was Bonn, until about 1990 when the two Germanys were re-united. If Swiss Technologies uses capitals to name their subsidiaries, Bonn Industries has been around at least five or six years."

"I knew you were right about the capital," said Sam teasingly. I was just testing you."

"You little con artist. I may not know much, but, when it comes to European cities, I'm pretty familiar with 'em. I'm a world traveler you know, having been with the US Ski Team. Speaking of bursting bubbles, there're some in dire need of being burst," Brad informed her as he pulled her by her hands up and against him.

"What possibly could you be referring to, mister?"

"The bubbles, we're going to make in the over-sized sunken bath tub in the other room, my love. Donald Trump thinks of everything."

"Oohh," cooed Sam, snickering.

"Something amusing about the idea. I thought it was a good one, personally."

"Noooo, Brad," Sam said, now laughing aloud. "I thought you were talking about having some champagne, you know, bubbly."

"Well, my sweet, we could do that first, or last, or shit, at the same time if you want."

Being quite serious and fully under control of herself, Sam looked into Brad's eyes and said, "Brad, I don't care when or where we do anything as long as it's together. Especially after the events of this afternoon. Let's just get naked and do something, anything crazy."

"Sounds like a wonderful idea to me. Sam... don't rip the shirt. I didn't bring that many with me."

"I'll be gentle."

"I didn't ask you to be gentle, just don't rip the shirt."

"Hush up and kiss me."

While Brad turned the gold plated handles and allowed the water to begin filling the small pond, referred to as a tub, Sam went to the windows of the suite and secured the drapes. As Brad then returned to the room, a smiling Sam came to him, placed her hands on his shoulders and directed him to sit on the sofa as she began her rendition of Blaze Starr. Brad had never seen the famed entertainer perform, or any strip-teaser, but, he'd never told Sam that little piece of information. Sam's slow, rhythmic moves to some unheard music, would make any woman professing to be a strip-tease artist, jealous with envy. Her undulations in slow motion and text book movements of her hands sliding sexily over her body emphasized her well-proportioned figure.

Both hands pressed firmly against her legs and below her hips, she moved them slowly upwards and over her breasts to behind her head. She pulled her short skirt higher up as she spread her legs further apart and with her back arched, she ran her slender fingers through the auburn hair as it dangled towards the floor. Her massaging hands then returned to her breasts and, as she bent forward, finally to her shapely ass, where their circular motion hiked the skirt above her waist. She was sexually torturing him, and, this woman... his wife-to-be, had yet to discard one stitch of clothing. His lap was about to explode.

With the gyrations of a seasoned dancer, Sam methodically peeled off her clothes, revealing inch by inch the firmness of her body. After what seemed like an eternity to Brad, she stood in front of him completely nude, looking better than anything he could have ever wished for. The champagne she poured over herself, trickled slowly down from her shoulders, its bubbles invading every crevice of her body. Her continuously moving hands and slender fingers spread the champagne over her ample breasts and flat stomach, across her tight inner thighs and firm ass, giving a sheen to her silken skin.

Brad stood as she took his hand and gently led him to her imaginary stage where she slowly danced around him in a most enticing manner. Then, she began taking off his clothes while caressing him provocatively. Now, both on the bed, her hands massaged his body with the foaming wine and made certain nothing remained dry. Nearly out of their minds with desire and both drenched in frothy bubbles of champagne, they made love, wild passionate love. It was the kind of love-making romance writers try to describe in words but never really succeed. It was, in a word, indescribable!

Afterwards, they both knew there'd be a phone call about the champagne soaked mattress and the overflowing sunken bath tub. Completely exhausted, they fell to sleep using the other king size bed in their suite. Trump *did* think of everything.

*****

Sam hadn't enjoyed one minute of the five thousand foot altitude flight from JFK International to Lake Placid and they'd arrived late to boot which had extended her agony by almost twenty minutes. Brad had smiled, recalling the small aircraft, a puddle-jumper, used only for short distances which held a maximum of fifty passengers. The air currents from the Adirondacks had bounced the small plane around pretty good on several occasions which caused Sam to get nauseous. Her upset stomach getting the better of her, she'd commented with an appropriate groan, "it was the first time she'd flown at an altitude reserved for take-off and landings and would never do it again".

Reluctantly, Brad had reassured her, "the return trip would be the last one". A simple "ohh" was the only reply Sam could muster as the aircraft had dipped into yet another air pocket. Although seated in the rear of the cabin, Sam had been the first to bolt off the plane, not even waiting for Brad.

They picked up their reserved rental car at Avis and settled back to enjoy the picturesque ride to the resort. "Look at those snow drifts over there," Samantha said, breaking into Brad's thoughts. "They must be ten feet high."

"Feeling better with your feet back on the ground?" Brad responded driving slowly so Sam could fully appreciate the scenery.

"Much."

"Sam, do you ever think back over things we've done together?"

"All the time. Nothing but good memories. There's just not enough of them." As an after thought, she added, "Yet." Then, she turned to look out the window of the four wheel drive. "Brad, this area is beautiful. It's so quaint."

"I know. I loved spending time here training. The village of Lake Placid only has about 2500 permanent residents. Hard to believe the 1980 Winter Olympics were held here. That's the year the US Hockey Team won the Gold. Exciting times around here then. That win probably did more for the sport of hockey in this country than the Boston Bruins."

"I'll bet. Who're they?"

"Who?"

"The Boston... Bruins?"

"See what I mean. I..."

Sam broke in. "I know who they are, Mr. Gullible. I'm only teasing you."

"I'll bet. Know a lot about the Bruins, do you?"

"Yep. Test me."

"Okay. Who's one of the team's *all* time famous players?" Brad drilled as if she were a hostile witness in a four-count, first degree murder case.

Sam thought long and hard. "Umm... Larry Bird," she innocently replied.

"Enough said," came the simple reply. "I rest my case, counselor. Sam, is this trip to California really necessary? I mean... you've already been offered a lucrative position with Colefield, Bailey and Nash, the most prominent law firm in DC."

"Brad, we've been over this before. I really don't want to go but, I feel... almost obligated. The firm in San Francisco and the three in LA have been in contact with me since last spring and I owe them at *least* a *visit*. And besides, they're giving me a pretty darn good offer considering I haven't even sat for the bar exam yet."

"Sam, everyone, including me who doesn't know a damn thing about it, realizes you're a cinch to pass it, so, why wouldn't they give you a good offer. The point is, what magical happens after you pass it."

"Brad, you say that like it's some kinda mid-term exam or something. It's a three day exam and damn hard to pass on the first go-around. That's why, once I know where I'm going to be, I'll get enrolled in a review course that helps you get in the right frame of mind for the test. As I understand it, most people fail it because they're not prepared and don't know what to expect. Half the battle is not being shocked when you open the first set of questions. Expect the unexpected, you know."

"I know what you're saying, Sam, but, the next exam isn't until June. You've got plenty of time to get prepared."

"Brad, most people graduate in the spring and then run down and take the test without any preparation. I've scheduled myself specifically so as not to fall into that trap. I want to pass it the first time."

"As usual, your logic is above reproach, but, why... California?"

"I want to be in international law, you know that. It's just a question of whether I want to represent Far Eastern or European clients. Besides, by making the trip, I'll have more leverage with the DC firm in negotiating position and salary. Heck, the partners in the firm are aware I'm going on this trip and it's making them a little nervous, especially Nash. And, for your information, it doesn't really matter where I pass the Bar. Most all the states, after a period of time, have reciprocity so, I could practice wherever I wanted to anyway. One state I know doesn't offer it is Florida, but, I don't have any lingering desires to move to Florida anyway."

"Thank you for sharing that with me. I know it's best for your career but, I don't know what I'm going to do without you for five whole days. We've been together every day since I woke up in the hospital."

"You're wrong. We've been together every day since the explosion at your townhouse. You just weren't very talkative the first couple of weeks. Believe me, Brad, the thought of being away from you for five days, even one day, doesn't set real well with me either. I love you so much, I don't know how I'm going to react," she concluded as she gave his leg a loving squeeze.

"I love you too Samantha, very much."

"You're really upset aren't you?"

"Yeah, I am. How can you tell?"

"You called me Samantha and I don't remember the last time you did that. We're just going to have to get through it, that's all, Brad. Bury ourselves in our work for five days."

"I suppose you're right."

Knowing Brad was in a down mood, Sam tried to change the subject and lift his spirits. "Is that the lodge over there?"

"That be it."

"It's beautiful. And, in such a gorgeous setting," she remarked as Brad swung into the circular drive in front.

The lodge was one of the older structures in the area and reached a five story height. Natural stone, used to face the building, provided an appealing contrast to the color of the snow-covered spruce trees. The lodge was architecturally laid out so most rooms would have a view of the crystalline blue waters of Lake Placid itself during warmer months.

Standing beside the rented Nissan Pathfinder and unloading the luggage, Brad heard Tony's familiar voice as he descended the steps in front of the lodge. "It's about time you two showed up. Congratulations on your engagement. Sorry I didn't mention it last night when we talked. When I heard you were in the middle of the shooting fiasco down there, I completely forgot. How close are you to tying the knot?"

"Late spring in Charleston. You'll be there, right coach?"

"Wouldn't miss it. Samantha, I'm glad someone finally slowed this nut down a little," Tony said, as he gave her a hug, lifting her slightly off her feet.

"Thanks, Tony. And you'd *better* be there in Charleston. We're not going to start without you."

"You two ready to get some skiing in? Take your mind off yesterday afternoon?"

"We *certainly* are," Brad responded and jokingly continued, "we didn't come all this way just to see your ugly face."

Tony was by no means bad looking. To the contrary, he was quite a handsome figure and one could tell from his stature, he was in remarkable shape. Considering the years of outside freezing temperatures he'd endured skiing and coaching, he looked great for a man in his mid-forties. He was a fit, six footer, his dark hair only showing a hint of tell-tale gray at the temples.

"I figured you'd be getting in about this time, too late to hit the slopes. They close around 4 PM. It's dark by 5. I've arranged for the Bob Sled run for you though Sam, if you're sure you want to."

"Terrific!" Sam gleefully said, jumping up and down excitedly.

"I guess that's a yes," Tony said.

"I'm afraid it is, Tony," said Brad. "*Shit*, she even wants to try the luge!"

"Are you nuts, Sam?" questioned Tony.

"You hit the nail right on the head. Crazy... nuts... insane..., and all those other words that mean the same thing and describe her to a tee." Brad said, not giving Sam a chance to answer the question directed to her.

"Excuuuuuuuse me, gentlemen. I've been on a sled before."

"Not one, only slightly larger than your ass though," Brad added in jest. "Tony, I told her that the only way she could go would be paired with me doing the steering."

"Have *you ever* been on a luge before?"

"No, but, how difficult can it be coach, if you don't let the speed get too high." Brad replied.

"Precisely my point, sweety. Besides, it can't be more dangerous than the flight we just got off. Can we take the bus back?" Sam chimed in, hoping for a reprieve.

"No, it'd take us forever," Brad said. "Case closed."

"This... this I have to see," Tony broke in. "I'll see what I can round up. In the mean time, let's grab a bite to eat before we head over to the runs."

*****

"All the damn rain at La Guardia last night must have been snow here. It's deep as shit. And it's colder than a well digger's ass."

"Probably lake-effect snows. Did the two of them show up?"

"Yeah, they're in the restaurant now getting somethin' to eat. I overheard them talkin' about the Bob Sled run. I think the fuckin' idiots are going to try the luge later under the lights. Christ, give the dumb fucks a little time and they'll kill 'emselves."

"Any ideas on doing a hit?"

"Not anything yet. I checked out the black trails earlier today. That's the ones they'll be skiin' for sure. It doesn't look like there's any place to fake an accident."

"Still like to snow ski?" I thought you turned into just a warm weather freak."

"I love to fuckin' ski. You know that. Have for years. I'd rather travel to the snow, though. I don't like living in the cold weather worth a shit. Let me get my runs in and go back to the fuckin' beach, you know?"

"Back to the brilliant blue skies, sandy white beaches with palms billowing in the tradewinds, and the turquoise waters of the Caribbean."

"Couldn't have fuckin' put it better myself."

"I know," came the reply with a hint of disgust implied.

"What?"

"Nothing. I agree with you though. I've skied Colorado a lot, but, wouldn't want to live there in the winter."

"The damn wind chill of forty below doesn't hack it."

"Any chance of something happening at the Bob Sled run?"

“Don't think so. Probably be too many people around. Besides, I want the next attempt to be the last one. This lucky bastard has really put a fuckin' cramp in my lifestyle.”

“We'll probably wait until their trip to Colorado later in the month. Maybe, we should just lay low 'til then.”

“That's your decision. I'm beginning to believe Haller had the right idea. Just blow 'em away like he told me he'd like to do at the Mall in DC. Make it look like a robbery.”

“Don't start thinking like Haller. You see where it got him. Besides, we have four to worry about now. Two separate muggings involving such close friends would raise suspicion.”

“It's just wishful thinkin', that's all. I know it's got to look like an accident. All this shit, because the asshole was late gettin' back from his mornin' jog.”

“It's been determined the other two, at least the guy, Sipel, would have to go anyway. He's too devoted to what they're doing to drop it, even if Claxton disappeared. Hang as close as you can. Try to find out whatever you can about the planned trip to Colorado. And, try to enjoy some skiing while you're there. You'd better tune yourself up for Colorado.”

“Did you know, you can't even smoke in the fuckin' restaurant here. Got to go outside and freeze your ass off everytime you want to light up. That really sucks.”

“That's the way it is everywhere now-a-days. Talk to you later.”

“You got it,” he said, moving towards the revolving door, a fired-up cigarette already in his mouth and his new muffler crossed in front, protecting his neck from the chill of the brisk, twenty mile-per-hour wind.

*****

“Brad, honey, you've got to try that. It was the most exhilarating ride I've ever had. That's more fun than the roller coaster at Six Flags.”

“Sweetheart, that's the first time I ever, *ever* saw the front person on a two man Bob Sled, go the entire distance with their head up. You're supposed to put your head down, inside the sled, so it goes faster.”

“What fun would that be? You wouldn't be able to see anything.”

"You're not supposed to. The guy in the back does all of the steering and braking. He's the one looking at the course on the way down."

"Then, I'll sit in the back."

"I'm afraid not. Sam, there isn't a person on the planet that'd ride up front with you behind steering and breaking."

"You've told me you'd do anything for me," Sam said sheepishly, her lower lip beginning to curl outward.

"There're limits, my love."

"I know, I'm just kidding with you. Can I go again, this time with my head down to see, or rather, feel the difference," she said excitedly.

On the second run, Brad told the driver not to use the brake as much so she could feel some of the G-forces. After the run, the sled came to a stop as the brakes caused ice to fly from beneath its runners. Brad hoped it would scare the shit of her so much she'd graciously wave her opportunity to try the luge. No such luck.

She scrambled out of the sled, virtually ripping off her goggles and protective helmet. With her long hair swaying from side to side, she yelled, "Fantastic!"

"My God. I've created a monster here. You liked it?" Brad questioned in disbelief.

"Liked it? Hell, I *loved* it. I'm still vibrating from all of the shaking and bouncing around. I could tell we were going faster, could you? We went up on those walls. I wanna go again. Can I?"

"Don't ask me, ask your driver."

"Can I?" she quickly turned and asked the driver.

Holding up one finger as if to say, sure, one more time, he and Sam departed for the top of the run.

*****

Sam and Brad stood at the top of the run, watching as a small piece of plastic-like material with runners was placed in front of them on the ice. Sam had completed five runs in the Bob Sled, and, *now*, it was time for a whole new ballgame.

"What's that?" she asked somewhat startled, but, already knowing the answer.

"That, my dear young lady, is the luge you wanted to ride." said Tony laughing.

"It's so..."

"Small?" Brad broke in helping Sam with her loss for the proper word and not believing the size himself.

"Tiny is more descriptive," Sam blurted out. "How am I going down the hill on that?"

"That's not the question, Sam. The question is, how are... we... going on that?"

"That's for two people?"

"That it is," replied Tony. "You sure you still want to attempt this?"

Before Brad could say a word, Sam responded, "Why not?" With her thumbs inside her pants, she hitched them higher, as if preparing to ride an irate Brahman Bull for the mandatory eight-second count on the professional rodeo circuit somewhere in Wyoming. She took a deep breath, each camel hump taking on additional water, and stated. "Let's *go for it*."

Brad realized the camel was now set for a three-month journey in the Sahara and replied laughing. "Let's do it. It isn't anything like the first Red Runner sled my dad bought me when I was four years old, but, what the hell?"

Brad was seated as far back as possible on the sled with Sam situated in front of him, her back tightly against his chest. Seemed nice enough to Brad. His legs straddled Sam's hips, who was sitting in an upright position. Seemed more than nice to Brad. They were instructed that, as the sled got underway, Sam was to inch carefully backwards. Seemed wonderful to Brad. They were to lean backwards into a prone position and with Sam on top of Brad and both on their backs, proceed down the course. Seemed like life couldn't get any better to Brad.

This maneuver took fifteen minutes of practice before it was accomplished without Sam rolling off. On their first attempt, Brad grabbed hold of Sam's camel humps to help her hold her position which caused a loud shriek. His desperate clinging had worked; however, they'd begun laughing so hard, they'd both rolled off. A small crowd was forming and very much enjoying the antics of their failed attempts. Sam said that getting on the damn sled was probably the hardest part of the entire run, not going down the hill.

Brad commented that they'd never be able to have children due to Sam's scrambling to get on his lap. He whispered to her, if she didn't stop all the squirming while they were getting prone, she wouldn't have to worry about falling off. They'd be stuck together and Tony would have to throw water on 'em to get them separated.

They pushed off with their gloved hands slipping on the icy surface and proceeded slowly down the run for about 50 or 60 feet where Brad steered them into a wall, knocking them off. "That was a whole, *hell* of a lot of fun," said Brad laughing. "At least it's over."

"Over?" questioned Sam. "No way, fella! I'm getting back on this thing. And this time, don't steer us into a wall," she instructed.

"I love your determination, Sam, but, I'm not so sure though, about your desire to finish this."

Getting on board at the top of the run, by no means compared to accomplishing the same feat on the icy incline of the run. The crowd proceeded down the side of the run to watch the procedure in anticipation of its consequences. In the next five minutes, Brad and Sam endured more humility than one should in a year. Barely able to stand on the ice, one would fall and pull the other down. On one fall, Brad lost hold of the luge which allowed it to begin sliding further down the course. Sam, without hesitation and to the applause of the crowd, dived to grab it by one of the runners and wound up thirty feet away from Brad. He proceeded slowly, sliding on his ass until they were together again. Finally, after five more miscues, they slid across the finish line at the bottom to a cheering audience.

"That was some display you two put on there." quipped Tony. "I don't think you're a threat though to beat out any of the US team members"

"Don't give me any shit, Tony." Brad said jokingly. "You must admit though, it wasn't so bad for the first time ever."

"Yes it was. The idea, Brad is to cross the finish line, on the sled, not in front of it."

"The next run we will," broke in Sam.

"The next run?" questioned Brad. "You're sure a glutton for punishment."

"Sure, we can do better than that," she said in an attempt to get Brad to agree with her.

“Of course we can, my love. As John would say, let's go for it.”

They'd spent the next two and a half hours to complete the “perfect” run. With the ease of a veteran lugers, they'd even climbed the banked wall a little, coming out of the turn dead on course. To a screaming crowd, they got up from the sled, hugged each other, and threw their arms in the air, acknowledging the victory to their many fans.

Tony approached and handed them their trophy, a video cassette tape of the entire evening. Brad and Sam laughed and thanked him, knowing it was a prize they'd cherish forever as they watched it over and over.

Later in the room they retired early due to their exhaustion. They slept well that night, falling to sleep, stark naked, having practiced the luge position until they were convinced they had it right.

---- Chapter Eight ----

Brad placed the half empty cup of coffee on his office desk, wondering if it was half empty or, half full. He eyed it closely. It *was* possible that it was both, but highly unlikely. It was midmorning and he was taking his first break since arriving at six o'clock. He'd arrived early and made the coffee himself, a task normally accomplished by Susan. She made great coffee; his was good. When Brad took a break, he did so completely, relaxing as much as possible. That's what a break's for. In his mind, there were only two choices; you either work or relax. He wasn't one to drink coffee while he worked, having tried it before only to have the steaming brew become lukewarm. He enjoyed his hot, not the ambient temperature dialed on the office thermostat on the far wall. He shuddered slightly at the thought of people actually enjoying coffee flavored ice cream.

He sipped the cup of coffee, cloud-like vapors still rising from its ebony surface. John's voice over the intercom interrupted his few moments of tranquility. "Can I see you for a couple of minutes, buddy?"

"Sure, what about?"

"A new hacker."

"Be right there."

As Brad entered John's office with his coffee cup in hand, he noticed the puzzled look on his face. "What's up?"

"I'm not really sure... yet."

"You look a little concerned. Did someone get entry into the system files?"

"No... but, they... seemingly got further along than anyone else trying it."

"Then your safeguards prevented access?"

"Not completely."

"What do you mean by that?"

"They were given only what my security system wanted them to have."

"Meaning, they received the virus program, right?"

"Right, unless they've got their own safeguards, it's eating the shit out of their data base right now."

"How's that work?"

"The program propagates copies of itself in their computer's memory. The duplication of itself continues until it damages or destroys enough information to cause their system to crash."

"So, whoever this is, their system is now in the process of being destroyed?"

"That be right, buddy."

"Serves their ass right. Did you get any feedback from your modem identifier program?"

"Yeah, that's what I'm concerned about."

"How so?"

"Look at this shit," John said, spreading some printouts across his desk. "The telephone number ID says the entry came from a pay telephone, a *pay* phone, Brad! Located outside of Chicago."

"I don't understand," he replied after he drained his cup. "Why's it such a big deal?"

"Nobody hooks up a modem in a God damn telephone booth."

"How do you explain the number then?"

"They must've hooked a remote dialer to the pay phone and transferred their activity through it. Then, they used their modem telephone to call the pay phone, which dialed us." What John said was more for his own benefit than Brad's, in an attempt to understand what actually was taking place.

"Is that possible?"

"Sure it is. The most disturbing thing to me is that whoever this is, he's not some damn guy sitting in a dorm at the University of Colorado. This guy's pretty damn good... pretty damn sophisticated. The technology I installed on our system for security, could never be breached by some novice. This guy knows what he's doin'... he's a pro, Brad."

"As I recall, you were a pretty damn good dorm hacker in Colorado."

"Not *this* good. Besides, I've learned a few things since being with the National Security Agency. I can identify top notch talent in this arena when I come across it."

"Have you ever had any other attempts from the same number?"

"No... and we probably won't have any more. He'll just change the pay phone locations he's using. Boy, he's gonna be pissed when he finds out he retrieved a virus program. But, his system would have back-ups and safeguards just like ours," John said to himself more than Brad. "He'll be back up and running in no time."

"He'd try it again after getting the virus?"

"Bet on it. Guys like this don't sleep 'til they've accomplished what they've set out to do. He wants out data base in the worst way, more now than before. Believe me! He merely has a bigger challenge on his hands than he originally thought. He'll thrive on it. I know, I've been there."

"What can we do?"

"I think it's a race against time. He's going to keep trying to gain access. In the mean time, I've got to modify my Modem Identifier Program to pass through the pay phone, to the modem source phone. Same thing he's doing... only in reverse. He now knows we have a pretty sophisticated system ourselves and you can bet he realizes what I'll be working on. Like I said, it's a damn race."

Showing concern in his voice, Brad asked. "That's all you can do to protect us right now?"

"Unless you want me to take us off line while I work on the Modem Identifier. It'll piss off our legitimate subscribers though."

"How long would it take to get the modifications in place."

"Somehow, I *knew* you were going to ask that. Shit, Brad, I don't really know. How big a shit does a bear take in the woods? Could be a day, could be a month. Remember, I'll have to set up something, duplicating what this guy already has. I need something to test the program against."

"Take us off line. I'll have Susan send out some E-Mail to our subscribers saying we're off line for a while, up-grading our system capabilities to better serve 'em. We've never been down before in our history. It'll pacify them."

"Probably would. You got it boss. In less than fifteen minutes, the only people with access will be located in this building. You're dead certain... you want to do this?"

"John, I can't see any other way from what you've been telling me. This bastard, according to you, is a computer pro,a fanatic, that'll continue his efforts. We *have to protect* all of the input we've received from our subscribers. If they found out our system had been breached, they'd be down on us like green flies on dog shit. By shutting down access 'til this is resolved, we're doing what we're contractually obligated to do. We're protecting them, the best way we know how, at the present time. Otherwise, the integrity of the system, shit, the integrity of the Center and all we've worked for, would go down the infamous drain. How long would subscribers remain with us? And, what would our chances of getting new ones be, once the word got out?"

"I *do* see your point. We're only doing what they'd want us to do. Protecting their interests, without actually admitting there's a potential problem. I'll get us off line."

"Great. And get started as soon as possible on that identifier program. If you need anything to help speed it up, let me know."

"Roger that, captain."

"By the way, have they ever found out anything about who side swiped you and Abbey on Thanksgiving?"

"Nothing yet. I think they've even stopped looking. They're saying it was probably a car from out of state. To me, that's saying the investigation is over."

"That would be normal, I suppose. The easy way out."

"When does Sam get back from Los Angeles?"

"Not 'til late Sunday for Christ's sake."

"I thought she was going to take the position with Colefield, Bailey and ahhh... Numbnuts downtown. What's that last guy's name anyway? It's a hell of a big outfit."

"Try Nash, John. The third partner's name is Nash."

"Oh yeah, but, like I said, I thought she was goin' with them. What happened?"

"I guess she felt obligated to go on these interviews. She's been in constant touch with them for some time. Besides, she's interested in international law and some of these firms in LA are on retainer for corporations that do business with the Chinese. That's what really interested her about them. No one knows how well the Chinese are going to contracturally perform, especially with Hong Kong being returned into the mainland China fold."

"I wouldn't trust their asses."

"I don't think you'll be laying wide awake at night concerning yourself with the issue, John."

"You got that right. Brad, it's already Thursday right?"

"You amaze the hell out of me with your knowledge, buddy. So, it's Thursday. So what?"

"That's ahh... *only* three more days 'til Samantha gets back."

"*Only*! That's easy for you to say. She's *only* been gone for *one* day and it seems like a damn year. I miss the hell out of that girl."

"Miss her huh?"

"You've *no* idea," Brad answered as he turned to leave John's office.

"Brad?"

"What?"

"Take your coffee cup with you this time. I'm tired of you coming in here and trashing my office," he said joking.

"Eat me," Brad replied as he picked up his Denver Broncos cup from John's desk and left.

*****

Abe and Ben Butterfield sat at a table near the stage. It was situated perfectly, too far away to concern themselves with sliding dollar bills into the G-strings of the dancers performing in front of them, but, still close enough to have an unrestricted view. Looking around the smoke-filled room, Brad spotted them peering at the stage, not the entrance of the club. Earlier in the day, he'd called the precinct to set up this clandestine meeting with Abe, through his interpreter Sergeant Butterfield, who'd also agreed to attend. It was Butterfield who suggested the "Crazy Sailor", as the place to meet.

The decor of the club, as the name suggested, was unmistakably nautical. The tables surrounding the stage resembled life rings thrown from the Titanic and the stage was a replica of the front half of a high masted sailing yacht. The mast was being used as a prop to help the dancer, currently on stage, perform her routine. The dancers entered and left the stage, through the likeness of the yacht's cabin. The bartender was dressed as a pirate and all the skimpily clad waitresses were his mates. *Damn lucky man.*

The bar, full of patrons seated on nautical bar stools, appeared to be an old dock and was a good 30 feet long, maybe 40. Along one wall was a large sandbox, fabricated to look like a beach. The clapboard tables were surrounded with logs placed on end for seating. As Brad swaggered by the beach, he noticed three or four old trunks, spotted here and there, open, with jewels spilling out. As he got closer, he realized the beach area had real sand as the floor. Passing by a reproduction of an old dingy being used as a table with seating for four, he felt the atmosphere growing on him.

As he approached the table, Butterfield said, “Mr. Claxton, good to see you again. How's the cell phone working?”

“It's doing fine. Remember I told you on the phone to call me Brad.”

“Forgot. Brad it is. Call me Ben.”

“That's a deal. Abe, how are you doin'?”

“Fine, Brad,” Abe said in a friendly manner and, at the same time, trying to add clarity to his response.

“How do you like this place?” asked Ben.

“Different than any place I've been before,” replied Brad.

“It kinda grows on you. I come here for the food. They've got great seafood. Do you want to order something?”

“Not me. I ate before I came,” Brad lied. “Go ahead and order something if you want. I think I'm just going to have a beer.”

“Gud choice... Brad,” said Abe, struggling to articulate his choice of words. “I cum here fer deh babes.”

“The what?” asked Brad.

“Deh babes, ye know... deh gurls,” he said, turning and pointing to the stage.”

“You foxy old devil you. At least, there's one honest person at this table, Honest Abe,” Brad said laughing and giving him a slap on his shoulder. “You two are probably wondering why I asked for this meeting.” Noticing them both shaking their heads in agreement, Brad continued. “From the get-go let me say, I don't want, or expect, either of you to commit to anything if you don't want to. Secondly, I don't want either of you to do anything that'd put your current position with the police department in jeopardy. Your work, I insist, comes first, and my request, second, if you decide to help me. Thirdly, and most importantly, what I'm about to tell you must, because of my position at the Center which I head up, remain confidential. I prefer this, for the time being at least, to be more of a ahhh... private investigation. More than likely, we'll find out, the entire situation doesn't even warrant an investigation. I don't want the embarrassment of having to answer a lot of stupid questions about my unfounded concerns. I hope we find out I've been merely over concerned about some events which have happened recently. Those are the ground rules. Anyone want to bail out now?”

Both agreed to stay and listen with Ben adding, "You're serious as hell about this, aren't you?"

"You got that right. All I'm asking you for is some relief from the anxiety my fiancee and I are presently undergoing. Hopefully, the relief will come from negative reports. If compensation, is necessary for your efforts..."

"Not necessary Brad," said Ben with Abe nodding his head in agreement.

"I just felt, after what you told me about Abe's investigative abilities and the access you have... shit, I didn't even know where to turn. I didn't want to go to some gumshoe private detective, if you two were willing."

"Christ, man. You're beginning to make this sound like something out of a damn novel about the CIA or something."

"In a worst case scenario, I'm sure it'll never approach something that dramatic. Like I said, I'm probably overreacting."

"Ye got me intrust... Brad, go hed." said Abe, straining for the right words so Brad could understand.

"Thanks Abe. And by the way, I don't mean to offend you when I don't understand what you're saying."

"Nun ticken."

Brad gave them an accounting of all of the events starting with his jogging episode, prior to the explosion. The two listened intently, Abe taking some notes throughout the discussion. Brad knew he had Abe's attention because he hadn't turned toward the stage one time. Brad's story took nearly an hour to recount, ending with the computer hacker as recently as that morning.

The two asked questions during the session, some personal. When Brad was asked how well he knew Sam, as if she were a suspect worth checking out, he'd become very defensive. He realized, anything less and he would have been disappointed. They were merely doing the job he asked of them. He told them, "It's not how long you know someone, but rather, how *well* you know someone that's important." They agreed.

"That's it?" questioned Ben.

"Pretty much the extent of it to date. Tell me I'm nuts, and I'll be satisfied. We could end this right here, if you say so, and I'll go home relaxed."

"It's kind of a weird story Brad. Seems as if every time something goes haywire, these damn license plates show up. Quite a coincidence. You agree Abe?"

"I sir do."

"Brad, I don't think you or your fiancee are in any immediate danger. Just to be sure though, I'd suggest you become very observant... almost suspicious of everything and everyone... until Abe and I have a chance to look into it deeper. Anything... anything at all, that might help us, give us a call. Don't call the precinct, call us at home."

"I wouldn't think of calling you at work. Like I said, I don't want to jeopardize your positions there. You think what I've said is something to look into then?"

"If only for your own peace of mind. But hell, I'd want some answers myself after what you've told us."

"Where will you start?"

"Probably getting some information on Swiss Technologies."

"Sounds like a good start point to me. I'd really like to know what they do. Also, if possible, how big they are."

"If there's any information available, Abe will find it. He has a friend that works for Interpol. He's got some other sources you don't even want to know about."

"What's Interpol?"

"Short for International Police."

"Oh," said Brad, noticing Abe beginning to laugh.

"Don't wurry, Brad. We find sumpton out. We beddah be goin Buddahfingah, early tomarrah."

"You're right Abe. Early shift tomorrow. We best hit the road."

The three men left the "Crazy Sailor" as Abe took one last look back to the stage to watch a shapely girl slide down the mast from the crow's nest. "Thanks for your help you guys."

"Save your thanks 'til we've done something. All right?"

"Sounds good, Ben. See ya," Brad said as he climbed into the Mustang for the short trip home.

Home? Hell, it wasn't home without Sam there. Hell, it was her house. Her vitality and zest for life invaded his body and without her, he was incomplete. Yawning, he felt tired. It was approaching midnight. He relaxed during the drive, knowing someone with some muscle would soon be getting answers. He'd tell Sam about the meeting when she called from LA tonight.

*****

Five days and counting 'til Sam would wear the gown purchased in New York City. Brad was looking forward to the gala being over so they'd return home and he then could give the gown the same treatment she'd given to a couple of his shirts. The event would more than likely take place on the dining room table he presumed or maybe on the soft-carpeted floor of the living room for a change. He really missed her!

It was Friday the thirteenth; but that didn't particularly worry Brad. His mind, as he sat behind his desk at the Center, was filled with thoughts of Samantha's absence from his life. During her cross country excursion to interview the San Francisco and LA law firms, Brad had renewed his regimented jogging routine in the mornings. His route took him past his townhouse in the process of being repaired where he stopped briefly and marveled at the distance the explosion had thrown him. Walking it off, he'd discovered it was closer to seventy than fifty feet to the tree where he'd hit his head. One of the workers couldn't believe Brad was still alive after hearing of the incident and informed him that if the weather held out, the job would be completed by late January. Throwing his head back, he'd let go one hell of a belly laugh when Brad asked him to double check the gas connections.

His Broncos cup was now empty, drained of the steaming brew, and the Joey's Deli bag was laying on the floor a good two feet away from the waste basket in the corner. He'd still be a failure in the NBA; it was the second day in a row he'd missed that shot. However, the bagels he'd picked up during his morning run were right on target. Brad was preparing to dig into the countless stack of computer print outs in front of him when he heard a quick three knocks on the door at the back of his office which led to the hallway connecting the other offices of the Center. At the same instance, it began to open and, from past experience, Brad realized who was entering. "Come on in Doc, door's open," Brad said, accustomed to his procedure after one and a half years.

One thing about Doc, he never bothered Brad unless he felt it was very important. Some would think that Doc was barging in, but, Brad never minded and if he did, he could always lock the door. Brad made certain there was teamwork at the Center and everyone was treated equally. They each knew the other's area of expertise and heavily relied upon it to achieve the Center's goals.

"Something I think you should take a gander at."

"Did you bring it with you?"

"No. I made it available on your computer screen."

Brad rolled his desk chair over to the computer, while Doc slid one from in front of the desk beside him. Doc brought the information up on Brad's screen.

"Exactly, what the hell am I looking at here, Doc?"

"I'd asked John to come up with a way to compare biological make-ups of compounds, agents, or anything with a matching chemical content. He installed it last week and what you're looking at is a listing of exact matches for antibodies from five different research labs. Their names are different because each lab has its own methods for identification, but, the structures are identical."

"Doc, isn't that one reason we're here, to stop this futile duplication of effort all over the world?"

"That's right boss, but, I can't find a thing to place this data in a futile category. I've found nothing, that would justify stopping the research and there's only one lab still working on it."

"Who'd that be?"

"The Colorado Springs Laboratory for Cancer Research."

"Phil's old man is Director of that lab."

"I know. Abbey just loaded their latest input into the computer. I used their antibody structures to test John's program. You're looking at the results. From all of the data available, each lab theorizes the antibody has an effect on cancer cells."

"The splitter that Malcomb was talking about on Thanksgiving Day."

"The what?"

"Malcomb, Phil's father. He was talking about a splitter theory as he called it. Something to break down the resistance of only cancer cells, allowing their invasion by an enzyme."

"I've never heard that term before, but, the theory's been pretty popular, so it appears according to this retrieval I've just made."

Proceeding up the list with his finger on the screen, Brad asked, "Doc, which lab is this one?"

Pressing a button on the computer and bringing up a second screen, Doc said, "that would be the Institute for Cancer Studies located in Ontario, Canada. Let's see here. They ahh... stopped research in March of 1991."

Going back to the first screen, Brad asked, "and this one," again pointing.

"That's the Center of Biological Studies in London. They terminated research on the antibody in the fall of 1989."

"The next one?"

"That one's the Yokohama Institute for Advanced Research Studies from Japan. Research was halted there in 1985."

"And who's this one at the top of the list?"

"That's the National Biological Research Center of New Zealand, located in Invercargill. They stopped their project in 1978."

"When'd they start the research?"

"From the data we have, probably the mid-seventies."

"You're telling me, an antibody, theoretically having an impact only on a cancerous cell, has been around since the mid-seventies?"

"I'm not certain. There's nothing in any of the data from these subscribers which actually proves the link between the two. All I'm saying is, according to what we have, there's no rational decision making process to *assume there wasn't* a link. Again, according to our information, studies of the antibody looked good, but, research *was* terminated."

"Any information why the research efforts came to a halt?"

"None what-so-ever. In all honesty, though, I've found occurrences where a subscriber, reaching a dead-end, merely stopped without properly documenting the reasons why. Scrupulous notes while the research shows promise, none when it fails. Might be the case here."

"Four times!?"

"Possible, I guess."

"Not likely."

"Probably not."

"Doc, could you have someone on your staff find out the reasons why these centers stopped?"

"I'll get someone on it. It's going to be pretty damn difficult with us being off line now. By the way, why are we off line?"

"John's working on something new for the system. Upgrade or something. Hell, it's the first time we have been off line since we opened. Do the best you can with this."

"Is it a priority?"

"Consider it so, although for what reason I'm not really sure. I'd like to take this information with me to the conference next month, if it proves to be of any value."

"You got it boss," Doc said as he exited Brad's office through the still open doorway. Smiling at the continuing ritual with Doc, Brad got up from his chair, walked to the door and closed it.

Alone now, Brad tried to comprehend what Doc told him. There were many possible reasons for ending a project or a study. Consolidations of labs, funding, dead-ends, even death of the researcher involved. All Brad wanted at this time, was *one* valid reason for each of the four labs dating back to the mid-seventies. He didn't care what the rationale was, only that it existed.

Brad spent the remainder of the day, until about 8:00 PM, putting into some semblance of order the large amount of data he'd been pouring through. Oddly, he noticed a pattern. The stack of data concerning the treatment and cures of diseases was roughly twenty times the size of data concerning prevention and contraction of the diseases in the first place. Although the two are related, he felt it odd that so much time and effort was placed into finding a cure and so little into the prevention or eradication.

His eyes were bloodshot as hell from all of the data he'd read and were getting scratchy and a little sore. Tired from the long day, he rationalized his concern about the lack of effort on prevention. *Shit,* he thought, *researchers can't provide prevention for something they don't know even exists. Once they're aware a disease exists, the most important thing to consider is the cure, not the prevention.*

Not his normal practice of being neat, Brad, left the papers where they were on his desk. He'd be back at it tomorrow, bright and early. With Sam out of town for a few days, he didn't really feel like doing anything else over the weekend anyway. He missed her terribly, even though they'd talked daily on the phone. At least, he was accomplishing something while she was gone, things which had to be done anyway and would be finished when she returned. Thinking of the quality time he'd spend with her when she returned, he left through the plush carpeted lobby and the large glass doors of the Center. He checked out the alarm system John demanded be on at all times when the building was locked up for the night. It was on.

*****

Brad stood at the gate waiting for Sam's flight from LA to deplane. He was tired, but, excited about her return home to him. He'd spent fifteen hours at the Center on Saturday and until two hours ago today getting things accomplished and out of the way so as to be able to spend more time with Sam over the next couple of days but, the toilsome task had taken its toll and he was worn out. Sam was always so vibrant, so full of energy, and, the thought of their age difference came into his mind. *Six years, so what? When you really thought about it, it wasn't so much.*

Brad rose unconsciously on the tips of his toes, straining for a better view as the passengers came up the corridor. There she was, walking briskly up the ramp, dressed in a black, tight fitting, short-skirted, "outfit" as she would call it. Brad no longer felt tired. His fiancee had that kind of effect on him and he noticed she was having an effect on others around her as they sneaked their looks. She proceeded towards him and smiled as only she could. Shit, you'd have to be dead not to notice this good lookin' woman, and Brad didn't see any corpses lying around.

"Brad, sweetheart," she said as they embraced tightly and kissed each other. It wasn't the kind of kiss normally seen at an airport. It was a kiss, lasting nearly a minute, a type reserved for two people who love each other with no inhibitions. Separating, to the grins and applause of those who had stopped to watch, they never acknowledged they were embarrassed.

"*Don't ever let me go somewhere without you again*!" Sam ordered.

"Never!" Brad promised.

Neither asked if the other missed them. They both knew the answer. They simply turned and, arm in arm, proceeded to the baggage claim area. "Have you eaten anything?" Brad asked, starving.

"Yes, I ate before I left and nibbled a little on the plane so we wouldn't waste any time when I got here. How about you?"

"Me too," fibbed Brad, his stomach growling at his words.

"Let's get right home."

"Precisely what I had in mind, my love. So, you've decided on the position with Colefield, Bailey, and Nash downtown?"

"It's a little less money than the offer I got yesterday, but, I believe I'll be moved into the area I want sooner with the DC firm. Besides, I've taken some German, French and Spanish. I can't speak them fluently, but I can at least understand the written language. With Chinese, I don't have a prayer and, I don't want to go back to school to learn it."

"Being in LA, you'd probably be given divorce cases for the Rich and Famous until you learned the language."

"How terrible could it be? Sam questioned with her hand stroking her jaw as if in deep thought. "Representing a Hollywood starlet against the iron disciplined will of her estranged husband. Um hum... definitely has possibilities."

"Did you say starlet or harlot?"

"Probably the later," she concluded.

After getting Sam's baggage off the carousel and stowing it in the trunk of the Mustang, they proceeded on the forty-five minute drive home. Come hell or high water, Brad was going to make it in thirty. Finally on the beltway after leaving the congestive airport traffic, Sam asked, "What *was that* noise?"

"What noise?" Brad returned the question.

Sam held up her hand indicating she wanted him to be quiet so she could hear better. "There. That noise. *It's your stomach growling*, isn't it?"

"Must've been something I ate."

"Or, maybe, something you didn't eat?"

"What do you mean by that?"

"You haven't eaten a thing have you? You're hungry," she concluded.

"Only for you, sweetheart of my life."

"Brad, be serious now. Have you eaten anything all day?"

"A couple of Joey's bagels this morning is all. You caught me, lady. I was busy at the Center trying to get a lot of things done before you returned so we could spend more time together. That's the truth."

"Oh Brad, that's sweet of you, but I don't want you getting sick or something because you didn't eat."

"Don't worry. I'll be fine." he replied as his stomach let out another defiant growl.

"I insist you stop and put something *in that animal* you call a stomach."

"No way. Besides, I had some time and stocked up the refrigerator with food. I can grab something there after we get home."

"What did you buy, some beer nuts and a few Budweisers?" she asked beginning to laugh.

"That, and a case of beef jerky as well," he responded. "I do know how to grocery shop, you know. Shit, I even used a coupon good for twenty-five cents off on a dozen jars of orange marmalade."

"Very thrifty and economical, Brad, but I don't like marmalade."

"I don't either. Was hoping you did. Seemed like a hell of a deal to me at the time and I couldn't, with a clear conscience, pass up such a bargain. Besides, the coupon was about to expire."

During the drive home, Brad showed the his enthusiasm for Sam's return in a number of ways... all of them appreciated by her. Things were back to normal. Sam was at his side, finally, after a five or six day absence depending on how you counted.

As Brad slid the Mustang to a stop in front of Sam's house, a practice becoming commonplace, Sam bolted from the car and ran towards the front door. Brad opened the driver's door, raced after her in wild anticipation of their love making and grabbed her on the front porch as she was fumbling with the key.

*****

"She's back," he said, sitting on the bed. "And, boy, do they look happy to see each other. They're playin' grab-ass on the front porch." From past experience, he knew there was no reason to be looking out the window because they'd not be going anywhere for a long time. "Where the hell's she been?"

"Interviewing with a law firm in LA."

"She do anything out there besides interviewing?"

"Not from what our people in LA said. They stuck to her like glue. I think you can relax. They're probably going to be there the rest of the night."

"You're not telling me something I don't already fuckin' know. Maybe they'll fuck 'emselves to death and we can move on to the other two."

"That's a good one. Find anything in the house?"

"Yeah, I found the reservations for his trip to Colorado."

"Good. When are they leaving?"

"Monday, the twenty-third."

"That's great to know. We can do some serious planning now."

"There might be a bigger fuckin' problem than you think."

"How so?"

"The reservations are for eight people."

"*Eight*?"

"I didn't fuckin' stutter."

"*Damn it.* That changes things a little. Who are the other four?"

"His sister and brother-in-law, the Bowers. I don't know the other two."

"What're their names?"

He pulled a crumpled piece of paper from his pocket, the pack of Camels falling to the floor. "Damn it!"

"What's wrong?"

"Dropped my fuckin' cigarettes on the God damn floor."

"Those things will kill you, man."

"I've heard all that shit before. It's a hell of a waste to die healthy, you know?"

"You'd know more about that than I would. Find the names yet?"

"Yeah. Evan McCardy and a Terri Westcomb. Who the hell are they?"

"Don't know. I've never heard the name McCardy before. The only Westcomb I've ever heard of is the New Zealand Ambassador to the United States. Might be his wife or daughter."

"How'd you come up with that?"

"Claxton's going to the Embassy for that gala thing in a couple of days. Remember?"

"I forgot about that. You're probably right."

"This could turn into an international thing if we hit 'em all. That's not good. This is becoming a hell of a problem."

"I've been thinkin' about this."

"That's a switch."

"What?"

"Nothing. What've you been thinking about."

"I can solve your problem in one fell swoop."

"How so?"

"Blow up the fuckin' plane. One big God damn accident."

"Shit! You just might have something there. It's nothing we haven't done before."

"I'm well aware of that. I built the fuckin' bomb for the one over the Atlantic. They never found out shit about that."

"Problem is, this one's over land the entire flight."

"That damn plane will be at an altitude of at least 30,000 feet. The wreckage will be spread over miles. They'd never find a damn thing. Even if they did, we could place the blame on some fuckin' raghead terrorists if we had to."

"Do you have enough time to come up with a package?"

"If the package is for Claxton, I'll make it a point to. I'll even gift wrap the fuckin' thing."

"I'll discuss it on my next conference call and get back to you."

"I can have it ready. The only problem, as I see it, is gettin' the damn thing on the plane. We had someone working on the tarmac at Madrid, but I don't know if you have anyone at Dulles. Let me know."

"I will, and soon. Talk to you later."

He reached to the floor of the darkened room and, fumbling around, picked up a cigarette separated from the pack by the fall. He struck the butane lighter, the flint magically igniting the gas. Slowly, the end of the Camel began to glow in the darkness as he inhaled. Smiling, he lay back on the bed and said softly, "Claxton, you're mine. This fuckin' job's almost over."

---- Chapter Nine ----

The telephone was ringing, but, Brad decided to let Sam's answering machine handle the call. It didn't matter who it was, if what they wanted was that important, they'd leave a message. Nothing was putting a damper on the time he'd been looking forward to for the past three or four weeks. Looking into the small foyer mirror, Brad straightened the tie of his tuxedo.

Samantha, after slipping into the magenta gown, was in the bedroom applying a minimal amount of makeup and was nearly ready. She'd selected a simple, double strand of pearls, choker length, to be worn high around her neck, and matching pearl earrings. She'd decided to wear her long auburn hair up to give the gown the heir of sophistication it demanded. Brad loved her hair down, but, with her hair up, she looked as if she came from southern royalty.

Brad heard the answering machine inform the caller of the day and date, "Wednesday, December 18th," and then give the familiar beep. "Brad, if you're there, pick up. This is Ben Butterfield. I have some information for you concerning our discussion. You can reach me at..."

Not really wanting to answer, Brad stopped the recording by lifting the receiver and cutting into Ben's statement in mid-sentence. "Ben. This is Brad. What you got for me buddy?"

"Nothing of any real importance. Am I catching you at a bad time?"

"On my way out the door to a party." Brad fibbed a little not wanting the discussion to last a long time.

"Won't take but a second. Abe and I started asking some questions but really haven't had any feedback yet. We did run across something coincidental about Swiss Technologies."

"What's that?"

"It seems they reported one of their cars, registered to Bonn Industries, stolen on Thanksgiving Day. The car was found yesterday abandoned in a remote, wooded area of Virginia. A couple of deer hunters found it. It appears it was stolen in Baltimore, had an accident along the way and was ditched in Virginia."

Quickly thinking, Brad asked, "Damage to the passenger side, with blue paint scrapings on it?"

"I believe that's what the report said. *How the hell did you know that*?"

"Would you believe, it was a lucky guess?"

"No way, Brad."

"If you would've... I'd be very disappointed."

"Seriously, how did you know that?"

"My best friend was involved in a hit and run accident Thanksgiving Day... night... or however the hell you'd say it. He and his, wife now, were sideswiped near one of the Laurel exits on the Baltimore Washington Expressway that night. The police haven't made any connection yet?"

"Not that I'm aware of. Did he report it?"

"Of course he did! Christ, he was almost killed, to hear him tell it."

"Damn. These coincidences just keep piling up. Coming in one after the other. What's your friend's name? I'll cross check and have them look into it."

"John Sipel. Do you need anything else?"

"No. I'll get what else I need off the accident report. Where does Mr. Sipel work?"

"With me at the Center."

"What's he do there?"

"He's the Director of Data Base Operations and Facility Security."

"Wears two hats, huh?"

"It does sound like it, but in reality, they're interrelated. Why are you asking?"

"Just doing what you asked me to do, Brad. He's pretty high up then, regarding his position at the Center?"

"He's basically my right hand guy. In my absence, he virtually takes over and runs the place."

"Why didn't you mention Mr. Sipel's accident to Abe and I the other evening at the Crazy Sailor?"

"Ben, I was relating to you things that happened to Sam and I, personally. Shit, *I just found out* one of their cars was involved in an accident with John on Thanksgiving. You think there's a connection?"

"Still too early to say... but, it appears Bonn Industries may... ooh, forget it. It's just too early on in the question and answer game to even assume anything, let alone suspect anything. To date, everything that's happened can be explained away with credibility. We need one thing, one item of information, to unquestionably raise a genuine concern. So far, we just don't have it."

"Look, Ben. John's going to be at this party I'm going to tonight. I'll ask him a couple of questions to see if he's noticed anything out of the ordinary. I'll let you know, sometime in the next few days, what I've found out."

"Sounds good to me, Brad. I'll let you get on your way now. Talk to you later and have a good time."

"Thanks, friend. Bye."

"Hello," a voice said in a very sexy, southern accent behind him.

Turning, Brad saw Sam leaning against the door frame of the bedroom, portraying the posture of a hooker using the support of a dimly lit lamp post. It was the kind of suggestive posture, used over and over again by ladies of the night. Sam was so breathtakingly beautiful he simply stood there, dumbfounded, not uttering a word. He'd not seen her in the magenta gown for over two weeks and forgotten how magnificent she looked. His trudging along to the various shops and boutiques was well rewarded.

"Hellooooo," Sam repeated, bending her head slightly and giving a small, inconspicuous wave in an attempt to get Brad's attention.

"What?" said Brad, breaking out of the trance she'd placed him in.

"Something wrong?"

"Ahh, no. Why do you ask?"

"You're staring at me."

"No *shit*, woman," said Brad, regaining his composure. "Who in the hell, in their right mind, wouldn't?"

"I'll take that as a compliment."

"That's the only way it was meant. Sam, I don't know what to say. Each time I see you, you somehow manage, and believe me I don't really understand how it's possible, to surpass the best you've ever looked to me. You are... I don't even know the right word to use. Remarkable in every sense of the word," he stammered. "The old saying that what's on the inside is more important, is true and there is nothing I'd want to change, believe me, but... if there were, and again, there isn't... Shit, I don't even know what I'm trying to say."

"You're saying, as I approach 80 years old, you're going to start telling me about all my internal quirks."

"*No, of course not.* First of all, you don't have any internal quirks worthy of mention. Second, I'm just trying to say, you're the most beautiful woman I've ever seen, physically or mentally and I love you more than life."

"Thank you for that Brad," she said walking, one foot in front of the other, over to him. "You *are* aware, of course, I feel the same way," she said with a warm smile.

"I am, my love," he said, embracing her and kissing her lightly, trying not to mess up her lipstick. "It's just your physical attributes... tend to get a little more of a rise out of me," he concluded, humorously.

Pushing him slightly away, Sam said, "You *are* terrible, you know that? I must concede though, that I'm getting a little excited myself."

He groaned. "Sam, I'm not really feeling too good. Maybe we shouldn't go to the gala," Brad said trying to convince her of his demise and giving a slight tug to the back of her gown.

"That, *as you would say Brad*, is pure bullshit. We're going to the party. I must say though, I'm looking forward to ahh... possibly an early departure."

"Well, I suppose I'll just have to suffer through it. As long as you've made the final decision, you may as well wear this."

"What?"

"This," Brad said retrieving a small jewelry box from the table near the front door. "I put it by the front door so I wouldn't forget to give it to you before we left."

"Brad, how nice. What's this?"

"Open it and see."

Fumbling nervously in her anticipation, Sam opened the small box and began laughing. "How precious, I love it." She pulled the magenta-colored ribbon slowly from the box until the mistletoe pendant dangled from its length. Laughing, she continued, "I think I'll wait to wear this until we get home, okay?"

"Shit. Wrong damn box."

"What?"

"I meant to give you this one," Brad said reaching into his pocket and extracting a second box and handing it to Sam.

"What's this? The set of holly ear rings?" she said in jest. Opening the box, the contents had the same effect on Sam as her appearance leaning against the door frame had had on Brad. She was totally speechless, her mouth gaping open. A total look of shock replaced her gleeful expression in an instant. The large, very large, emerald cut diamond engagement ring in the box had affected Sam exactly the way Brad hoped for. She, for once, was at a loss for words!

"You aren't saying anything."

"I don't... *it's beautiful*. Where? *Look at it sparkle* in the light. When did you?... *It's so big*!... You think it's *too* big?" Sam stammered, not taking her eyes off the ring.

"You like it then?"

"Do Azaleas bloom in the spring?" she asked innocently with her chin tilted just enough to give her the look of a jeweler in deep study. "*I love it.* What can I say? Whatever possessed you to get..."

"Sam, settle down a little. I..."

Sam impulsively threw her arms around him and planted one of her best kisses on him. To hell with the lipstick, she could re-apply it. Breaking reluctantly apart, Sam said, "Brad, *I love you so much...* it hurts. Thank you, sweetheart, for the most gorgeous ring. *When did* you get this?" she continued looking at the ring again with her arms still around his neck and her hand held high for the diamond to capture as much light as possible. "Why'd you choose tonight to give it to me?"

"Sam," Brad began, "I don't believe you know how... really lonely I was when you were gone to California on those damn interviews. It forced me to realize what my life would be without you. Other than wanting to spend every second with you when you returned, the main reason I spent so much time working was, I couldn't sleep anyway. I've become used to having you next to me, not just in bed but, next to me every minute of the day. You know, the entire, "we're going to get married thing" was forced on us by circumstances. Your parents catching us over there," he said, nodding with his head towards the dining room table. "I, at the time, felt it was the most wonderful idea I'd heard, and still do. I just... call me old fashioned if you want to... wanted to make a more formal proposal. I love you very much."

"You're asking me to marry you?"

"Formally... yes."

"That's sweet of you Brad. Of course I'll marry you. Because I love you back the same way. Ditto, ditto, ditto! Ask me a thousand times. My answer will never change. Brad," she questioned suspiciously, "you weren't concerned about my answer, were you?"

"Not really. But now, the traditionally proper dialogue has been followed."

"Kiss me, you idiot."

Brad held her very tight. He'd never let her go. The embrace lasted five minutes, both swaying in unison as if dancing to a silent song. Not wanting the moment to end, Brad looked into her eyes. "I adore you Samantha Sawyer. Very, very much."

"Brad, I'm not feeling so well myself. Maybe we should skip the party."

Laughing, Brad said, "Now Sam, you *know* that's pure bullshit."

"Why, is it bullshit for me and not for you?"

"You don't have the techniques to pull it off when you're bullshitting someone and, if you're going to be an effective lawyer, you'd better practice."

"I suspect we're going to go. I better re-do my lipstick. By the way, big guy, who was on the telephone?"

"Oh, that was Ben Butterfield. I'll tell you about the conversation on the way to the embassy."

*****

He slipped on the dark blue coat to his dress uniform, stepped back slightly from the mirror and rotated his shoulders to assure the best fit. Checking his appearance, he adjusted the various medals and ribbons he'd accumulated over the years until they were in perfect alignment. The insignia on the shoulder of the jacket identified him as a full bird Colonel. So far, all the medals and ribbons hadn't helped him achieve the rank of Brigadier General and he wasn't certain if they ever would. The salt and pepper hair was cut short and didn't need any attendance. The tanned face showed the lines of stress, a result, he was convinced, of recent pressures. All in all, he was in remarkable shape for a man fifty-five years old and who proudly wore the same size uniform as he did in the mid '70's.

She entered the bedroom from the suite's dressing area, her 34 year old body proudly filling out the azure gown. The brown, bedroom eyes, high-lighted with liner, would make anyone snap to attention and take notice, even full bird Colonels. She was of a Spanish lineage and her make-up was perfect, her expertise in applying it stemming from the numerous beauty pageants she'd entered. She'd won most and rumor had it that she was one vote, one judge, and one blow job away from winning the big one, Miss America. The lips were full and inviting and her dark brown, nearly black hair, was done high on her head. Naturally tanned, silky smooth skin swept from her neck and shoulders downward to the cleavage buried in the gown.

She moved slowly around the canopied bed and stood beside him gazing in the dresser mirror. The age difference of over twenty years wasn't that noticeable, a real credit to him, considering his Spanish wife looked young for her age. USAF Colonel Harold Dickey and his wife of two years, Carmen, short for Carmelita, made a striking couple.

They'd met on the French Riviera while Colonel Dickey was on a side trip to the Cannes Film Festival from TDY business in Zurich. Carmen had completed her tour of Spain, a fact-finding trip about her heritage, and decided to spend a few days in Cannes prior to returning to the States. She was taking full advantage of the beach, the sun and the local laws, basking in the raw.

Harold had lost his first wife less than a year prior when she'd telescoped her Nissan Pathfinder into the back of a fully stopped cement truck. He wasn't on the prowl, but also, wasn't passing up the chance to build some sand castles with the woman he'd been staring at for over an hour. One thing led to another, and they'd been married in a small, private ceremony in Bethesda, Maryland a few months later.

"What time's our driver picking us up?" she asked, turning sideways to look at the flatness of her stomach in the clinging fabric.

"He should be here any minute. The motorpool didn't have a car appropriate for the occasion. Unless you wanted to go in a four-door, Air Force blue wagon with USAF motorpool stenciled on the side. He's picking up a Lexus at the Congressional Garage for the occasion."

"That'll do. I love 'em."

"I'll say. I think it even has the dignitary flags on the front. It's one of the perks you get. Damn, you look good in that color. Reminds me of the water down in the tropics."

"I wish we didn't have to go to this thing. I'd rather just stay here and relax."

"Lady, you never relax. You're a damn nymphomaniac."

"That's never been a problem before. Are you complaining, sweetie?"

"No I'm not but see, you're not even denying it."

"I like sex. A lot, especially with you."

"You're goin' to kill me one of these days."

"I don't think so. You're in better shape than men half your age and, you're the best lover I've ever had."

"How many twenty-seven year olds have you been with lately?"

"Not near enough. You know, I am a nymph," she teased.

"Seriously, honey, we have to go to this thing tonight. I've had some pressure lately and must have a talk with this guy that's going to be there. We'll leave right after I talk to him if you want. I was ordered to put in an appearance by General Nuisance."

"Why do you call him that?"

"Because it's exactly what the hell Brubaker is. A general nuisance."

"Okay, we'll go. But, I'm tired and want to get to bed early."

"That's a good one. Somehow, the words "tired" and "bed" don't work well for you in the same sentence. I do love you though."

"More than your first wife?"

"I've told you before. Honestly, when I first married her, it was probably the same. But, over the years, as she began boozing it and finally the drugs... there's no way. When she slammed into the back of that truck, she was so drugged up it was unbelievable. Had a hell of a time covering that up to save my security clearances. When she died, I don't think I even loved her anymore. I *know* I didn't respect her."

"Why'd she start the drinking in the first place?"

"A number of reasons. I don't know how, but, she found out some of the things I was involved in. We moved around a lot. The topper was when she discovered she couldn't have kids. That's what really did her in."

"What'd she find out you did that upset her so much?"

"Classified stuff. I can't really get into it with you. Like I said, I don't know how the hell she found out. Most of it wasn't true anyway," he lied, straightening his tie.

They were interrupted by the sound of the intercom from the lobby of the swank high rise. Colonel Dickey answered and found their driver to be in the lobby waiting. He moved to the living room sliding glass doors of the tenth floor balcony and drew the drapes closed, hiding the view of the city.

Carmen watched him perform the normal ritual as they left the rented three bedroom apartment. Colonel Dickey, in his entire life, had never owned a home. He was permitted special housing allowances, not because of his rank, but, rather because of his position. On a moment's notice, he might be required to move to another city, or, even out of the country.

Carmen didn't mind. She enjoyed the excitement of not knowing what the next day would bring. She suspected him of being involved with the CIA or some other close-knit agency but, he never talked about it and she certainly wasn't going to rock the boat by asking.

"Who's the guy you have to see at the Embassy tonight?" she asked, watching him try the knob to make certain the door was locked."

"Name's Bradford Claxton. He's head of the biological clearing house, as I call it, located here in DC."

"What do you have to see him about?"

"Business," replied Harold.

*****

The Embassy's circular reception foyer was domed with a 2400 piece, hand-cut crystal chandelier imported from Austria hanging in its center and highlighting the mural laboriously painted on the ceiling. The hallways were lined with gallery art, proudly displayed against jewel-toned wallpaper. Stark white base and crown moldings along with the fluted door framings exaggerated the eighteen-foot ceilings and twelve-foot doorways. The floor was imported white marble excavated from the foothills of Italy with four foot high pedestals displaying pieces of art, sculptured in New Zealand. This was Sam's first visit to the Embassy and her photographic memory was being taxed to the limit. Her eyes were open wide and full of excitement and expectation.

The Wellington Room of the New Zealand Embassy was, in a single word, elegant. Previously in the room on a number of occasions, Brad felt it was at its best when decorated for Christmas, as it now was, in the traditional, down-under, Old World Style.

They checked in at the podium outside the entrance to the Wellington Room with a formally dressed young officer who wanted to make sure of the pronunciation of their names prior to their loud speaker introduction. Slowly, because of Sam's gown, they transcended the bright red runner of the cascading staircase to the ballroom floor.

As they were announced, a handful of people turned to acknowledge their entry and, with each step downward, more of the 800 guests turned to watch. Conversations came to a halt, the band stopped playing and dancing ceased. This didn't happen last year when he attended the gala, thought Brad, so he stole a quick glance over his shoulder. They weren't being followed by anyone, let alone someone of major importance, so he hadn't missed any announcement on the loud speaker.

Glancing to his left where Sam was at his side and holding his arm, Brad again was aware of her stunning beauty. The hair piled high on her head revealed the soft skin at the nap of her neck. Her perfect profile projected an air of confidence. The simple, yet somehow, elegant strands of pearls adorned her neck. That's when it struck him and it didn't bother him in the slightest. This prestigious crowd of attendees, full of their damned pomp and circumstance, was eyeing up with envy his fiancé of barely over an hour. He heard Sam whisper without moving her inviting lips, "Why'd it get so quiet and why's everyone turning around to look at us? Is this normal?"

"No, it's *not* normal and they're *not* looking at us and *not* at me, Sam," he returned quietly. "Everyone is looking at you and only you."

"I don't believe that for a minute."

"Okay, have it your way. This kind of reaction didn't happen last year, but, I suppose they could be enchanted with me, Sam, and not you. All of those guys frothing at their mouths you see down there and being poked in the ribs by their wives and girl friends are gay, Sam. They want my body so bad, it's unbelievable. Why would they possibly be looking at you?"

"I think I can live with your first story line the best."

"I suggest you do, sweetheart, it happens to be non-fiction. I warned you about wearing that gown in public," Brad responded as he proudly displayed her to the gawking crowd as they approached the ball room floor.

The band resumed playing where they thought they'd left off, no one really knew or cared, and Evan, with Terri on his arm, approached to greet them in their normal, vibrant fashion. "Quite an entrance Sam," said Evan in his down-under accent.

"*Notice* Evan said Sam, Sam. *Not* Brad. *Not* Sam and Brad. Just *Sam*, Sam. Fact or fiction, sweetheart."

"What *are* you two talking about?" questioned Terri excitedly, her long red hair bouncing off her bare shoulders as her ample breasts tried to escape the low bust line of her gown.

"Just a personal bet we had. That's all," replied Brad. "How's your father and mother, Terri?"

"They're fine. I don't know why they throw this thing every year. By the time the evening arrives, they're so worn to a frazzle, I don't think they enjoy it like everyone else." As she turned towards Sam, her hazel eyes, set deep in her family inherited English face, sparkled and highlighted the azure color of her gown. "Saaaaaammmmmmm, I love your gown. The color is so striking and the... the lines are fantastic. It ahhh... fits so well," she said taking full notice of Samantha's shapely figure. "Wherever *did* you find it? Probably not around the DC or Baltimore area I'll bet. And by the way, you both are devils getting engaged and all. Congratulations, I haven't seen you two together since a few days ago."

"Thanks, Terri. Brad and I found the gown in New York when we passed through a couple of weekends ago. I love yours too."

"Sam, with your body, you could get a gown at WalMart and make it look good," Terri said laughing.

"You don't think it's too tight?"

"Not at all, Samantha, it looks perfect. This top of mine... is the only downfall I have with mine. A little play on words," Terri said tugging slightly at her bust line.

Evan grabbed Sam's hand and gave it the customary welcome kiss. "Christ, what do we have on this little pinkie on the left hand," he said, noticing the engagement ring. "Damn Brad. Must have set you back a peso or two."

"Ohh, my God," shrieked Terri. "That's the most beautiful ring I've ever seen. Evan... take some notes son, and don't lose 'em," Terri said in jest. "I've made my Christmas list, and I'm certainly going to check it twice. Hell, I'm going to check it every day."

By this time, all were laughing at Terri's antics. As the laughter subsided Evan said, "Brad, you certainly have damn good taste. And, your choice of rings isn't half bad either."

"What's all the excitement about over here?" a familiar voice said.

Turning towards the source of the question, Brad said, "Sis, good to see you."

Chantal and Phil were picking their way through the crowd and John, with Abbey in tow, was close behind.

John said, "Last one to the party as usual, right buddy? You always have to make the grand entrance. And the one tonight, was indeed, grand. Sam, good to see you again and, of course, you look magnificent as usual."

"I asked what all the excitement was about," repeated Chantal, giving everyone a greeting kiss on the cheek.

"I suppose it was this that caused the commotion," said Sam, taking the opportunity to showcase the rock on her finger.

"Holy shit, pal. When you *finally* get serious, you get *real* serious don't you?" Phil chimed in.

"What's that Brad," John quipped, "a loaner until the big one gets in?"

Laughing at her husband, Abbey stood, stared and slowly shook her head from side to side. "Marvelous, simply marvelous choice, Brad. You're a lucky girl, Sam."

"Don't I know it," responded Sam, giving Brad a playful kiss on his cheek. "Who are all these people? They look so... important."

"Some are, most aren't," replied Brad.

"Some *think* they are... and aren't, but, would like very much to be," added John.

"That, my friend, probably fits most of them," concluded Brad. "Sam, now there's one over there that has a little influence. See the guy with the turban or whatever those rags piled on his head are called."

"How could I miss him?"

"He's in the news all the time. He works for the Kuwaiti government swinging deals for them."

"What kind of deals?"

"Kuwait's mostly sand and oil. It's more cost effective to buy whatever the country needs abroad than to bring in the raw materials for manufacturing. Besides, what technology the country has is pretty dated. It's easier to shop the world and make payments in barrels of oil rather than invading the treasury for cash. Hell, their oil *is* their treasury."

"That's probably why Hussein set fire to the oil fields during the Gulf War?"

"Part of the reason, I'm sure. One final blow for a lost cause before his armies returned to Iraq."

"Little brother, how'd we get on this morbid subject?" asked Chantal. "We *were* having a pretty good time until you brought up the sheik over there."

"I don't know. I'm sorry everyone."

"Nothing to prevent the good times from continuing," interjected John. "*Let's party.*"

"Let's," said Sam, smiling and dragging a reluctant Brad to the dance floor. "See you all in a couple of minutes," she said in her best southern accent, the engagement ring glittering in the soft lighting as she waved.

*****

The evening was proceeding wonderfully. Brad and Sam had danced a number of times, he being the envy of most men at the gala and even some gay women. Some of the diplomatic corps was known for its quirky choices in sexual preference. Every guy he'd noticed, no matter what his age, didn't steal quick glances at Sam. Rather, they'd stared at her, but, it no longer bothered Brad. *Eat your heart out* he'd think, turning Sam around so the engagement ring on her finger would blind them. *See that, you envious asshole.*

The band was on break so the girls went on an Embassy tour with Terri while Phil and Evan went to find some guy that wanted to meet Brad. He and John picked up scotch and waters from the bar, left the Wellington Room through the ten-foot high, French doors, and proceeded to the verandah and its view of the lighted Embassy gardens. In private and in the coolness of the evening air, Brad related all the information to him. Oddly, John didn't interject one word the entire time, but rather, rested one foot on a Grecian urn and his forearms on the verandah's sculptured concrete railing as he blankly stared out to the gardens and listened intently.

"That pretty well sums it up. You're pretty damn quiet John. Not your *normal*, go get 'em attitude."

Turning to face Brad, he said. "Brad, buddy, in all the years we've been friends, you've *never* wanted to talk to me in private... *never*. When you use the words "in private" and they're linked together with the expression you had on your face, it must be pretty damn important. So, I should be quiet and listen, right? Is there anything else?"

"That's it in a nutshell."

"Then, let me ask you a simple question."

"Shoot."

"Where the hell in my contract does it state, I have to put up with all this *damn cloak and dagger shit*?" John asked, beginning to laugh but looking at him rather seriously.

"You're crazier than hell, you know it? And, besides, you don't *have* a damn contract... and don't even ask for one," he added. "Buddy, as far as I'm concerned, you're a damn free agent, like an overpaid baseball player," Brad replied beginning to smile.

John allowed two couples getting a breath of fresh air to pass before continuing. "There you go again, insinuating cloak and dagger stuff by calling me an agent. Brad, those things you've just told me, I wish you'd have confided in me earlier. It might have helped with the anxiety you've been going through. That's what friends are for, buddy." He drained his scotch and water and rattled the ice cubes making sure Brad heard. "I need another drink after hearing all this. I see they have another watering hole set up outside at the other end."

As they made their way to the far end of the verandah, side-stepping other guests attending the gala, Brad continued in a soft voice. "I understand that, but, John, I don't like to burden my friends with my personal matters. All of this, whatever you want to call it, as Abe and Ben have pointed out, can logically be explained away. When I found my best friend in the world might be involved, I decided to tell you. Sam and I... we both thought it best. Your and Abbey's accident by itself, happens every day of the year to someone. The damn license plate thing doesn't though. Somehow, it may be a link. Without all the other things goin' on, the accident seemed meaningless. Sam and I thought you should know about everything. You know, so you could kinda stay on your toes a little."

"Having Abbey with me most of the time now, since our marriage, it's nice to have an idea before hand that something *might* be fishy. I appreciate the thought, buddy, but, I tend to agree with "Officer Friendly". I don't think there's anything to be that concerned about. What possible reason could there be for this type of... whatever you'd call it? You haven't pissed off someone have you... I mean *really* pissed off someone?" John questioned as they approached the bar.

"Nobody I'm aware of so, I guess I agree, but, just in case, be careful. Keep an eye out."

"You're suggesting I don't notice things. When I noticed Sam tonight, I realized what a lucky guy you are. She's a real beauty... and adorable. Hell of a combination."

"Much like Abbey, wouldn't you agree?"

"You've got that right, Brad. I love that little doll to death. I can't believe it took a near fatal accident to get us hitched."

"Freshen your drink sir?" asked the bartender.

"If you'd be so kind. You need one Brad?"

"Make it two scotch and waters," replied Brad holding up two fingers.

By the way Brad, before I forget, I've finished the Modem Identifier Program modifications and added a little surprise of my own. We can go back on-line Monday."

The bartender returned with their drinks and placed them on cocktail napkins. Brad rolled up a five dollar bill as a tip and stuck it between the branches of the small Christmas tree to his left, conspicuously placed there for such ornaments.

Turning to John he said, "That's great news. What's the surprise?"

"Remember my telling you the hacker was a pro?"

"How could I forget?"

Moving slowly from the bar and away from other guests on the verandah, John continued. "The changes allow me to bypass the pay telephone system and go directly to his computer's modem. It'll feed him a dummy data base that I've screened. The data looks valid as hell, but it's way outdated. He will, I guarantee you, have a virus program checker on his end to verify the same thing doesn't happen a second time. His computer will screen each incoming file as he extracts it and take a lot of time to check it out before he makes the add to his data base."

"So. What's the big deal? He's getting some bogus files without knowing it. Doesn't stop him from trying again in the future."

Once again at the railing overlooking the lighted gardens John explained. "The big deal is, while he's doing all this checking before adding, I gain entry to his computer and download all his files. Shit man. This asshole initiates the contact and we get all his data base files while he's receiving garbage."

"Will it work?" asked Brad enthusiastically.

"Need you ask? You're not talking to some novice here, you know. I'd never jeopardize the Center by going back on-line if it didn't. Of course it works. I've already tested it."

"Fantastic. By the way," said Brad as he took a sip of his drink and put it on the railing in front of him, "I've got some news for you. Doc made use of your new program that finds identical biological or chemical make-ups. He found an instance where the same structure was identified as far back as the mid-seventies. According to the information we have, research was stopped by a number of different labs on an antibody showing promise of breaking down cancer cells. He's assigned someone from the staff to find out the reason why the studies were halted."

"How many different labs were involved?" asked John, his interest being perked.

"Five."

"Five! Seems like a high number to me."

"I agree and they're from all around the world. It appears the research was never being conducted at the same time. In each case, development of the antibody occurred over a period of time up to a point and then activity just ceased."

"Brad, I know as much about that kind of shit as you know about computers. It does raise some eyebrows though, doesn't it?"

"And put some wrinkles in one's forehead. Probably nothing, but, it's damn sure interesting none the less. Historically, when labs run into a research-ending problem, they never document the reasons very well. Their protocol seems to fly right out the window along with any supporting documentation. We've made an effort at the Center to rectify this problem with our current subscribers. And by the way, smart ass, I do know how to use a computer."

"You know *how to use what I've put in* the damn thing. There is a *little* difference, dumbo," John joked back. He noticed Brad looking past him and turned to take a look of his own. Seeing nothing, he asked, "What're you looking at?"

"Only an asshole that just flipped a still-burning cigarette off the balcony and into the gardens down there."

"Which guy was it?"

"It wasn't a guy. It was the bimbo that's hanging all over the sheik down there. Where do some people get off? I hear the band starting up again."

After getting their drinks off the railing, Brad and John turned and walked towards the French doors and the Wellington Room. One door swung open and Phil came out into the night air accompanied by a man wearing a dress military uniform. He was, Brad estimated, in his late forties or early fifties with a thick head of salt and pepper hair. *He must continually work out,* Brad thought, because of the way his muscular frame filled the uniform. He was a handsome man for his years and a credit to the uniform. The man's expressive eyes were a deep brown and set very close together which made a person aware of the wisdom behind them.

"Brad, I'd like you to meet Colonel Harold Dickey, of the United States Air Force," Phil said putting his hand on the Colonel's shoulder.

Brad stuck out his hand for the typical greeting and said warmly, "Colonel Dickey, my pleasure, Bradford Claxton. Please, call me Brad."

"Call me Hank then, Brad. Good to meet you, finally, as well."

"Colonel, I always thought Hank was short for Henry, not Harold," Brad said smiling.

"It is, but the name caught on when I was about ten years old and somehow stayed with me all these years. Funny, most people don't catch that," he responded as he returned the smile.

Brad moved slightly closer to the Colonel. "Hank it is. You say that you've been trying to catch up with me for a while. By the way, Hank, this is John Sipel."

After their greeting and exchange of normal pleasantries, Phil broke in. "Brad, let me try to explain. Hank's been a long time family friend. He was in Colorado Springs attending the Air Force Academy when I was born. He's since been assigned all over the world with the Air Force but, has managed to keep in touch, off and on, with Dad and me. He's currently assigned to Bethesda Naval Hospital, as a liaison officer on staff. Hank, if you'd like to continue with what you need, go ahead."

"What was your major at the academy?" Brad interjected, now seemingly more interested.

"Chemistry and Biological Sciences."

"Biological Science?"

"I can tell by your reaction, you're as surprised as everyone else. You know, most people think all the academy turns out is pilots. The academy graduates a little more than fly-boys. The courses I took were designed to instill an interest in biological studies. Any student showing an interest in the field that could meet the stiff requirement standards of the academy, could transfer to other institutions, at Air Force expense, to do post graduate work in these areas. Actually, we've turned out quite a few damn good specialists in the field."

"You're right, Hank, I didn't realize. Continue, please, I didn't mean to interrupt."

"You didn't, Brad. The reason I wanted to catch up with you has nothing to do with the Bethesda Naval Hospital. I've been given the additional responsibility of coordinating governmental biological research efforts. The government's attempts to satisfy taxpayers' demands for a balanced budget and the resulting proposed cuts are really eroding the military's ability to conduct independent research. I've been given the task of combining the individual efforts of the branches of the armed forces into, shall I say, an all services organization located at one facility. The cost savings would be tremendous to the taxpayers, but, I'm having difficulty focusing on which projects should, or, could be merged. So Phil suggested I meet with you and discuss what your Center could do to help us out. You know, how best to combine efforts or maybe, which projects could be totally deleted. Mal, Phil's father, says the center in Colorado Springs is currently a member receiving your on-line data and has found it very useful."

"As always, we are eager to help, wherever and whenever we can, Colonel. This is the first direct inquiry we've received from the government. It's encouraging news, however, you've got to understand one thing. Our Center was established with its main objective being cancer cures. We've branched out substantially at the request of our subscribers, but, the bulk of our information, roughly two thirds of it, is cancer research oriented. Right John?"

"At least 60 percent, I would think." John responded to the question after he'd drained his scotch and water.

"So you see, Hank, the remaining 40 percent is divided up amongst numerous other efforts. Unless, we know specifics of your projects, we can't, at this time, even offer you an opinion whether the Center would be of any value in your consolidation efforts."

"How can we proceed to make that decision?"

"You'd have to become a subscriber, the same way any research facility does. We'd initiate the contractual obligations of both parties. Then, you'd forward your data bases of studies to us for review and validation. We'd make a determination, after massaging your data with what is available in our system, as to what information you'd be allowed access to."

"You mean to say, the subscribers to your system *don't* have access to *all* of its information."

"Most definitely not. If your doing research on cancer, you have no need to know how someone else might be progressing on... AIDS research, for example. That's a very important criteria under which we operate. Otherwise, someone could gain immediate expertise in an area at virtually no cost. That wouldn't sit very well with someone who'd endured years of study and associated expenses."

"I never thought about it in that light," the Colonel said with an inflection of disappointment in his voice.

Brad continued with his dissertation of the Center's SOP. "Protection of classified research data for each and every one of our subscribers is our keystone. It's why the Center's grown so large in such a short period of time."

"Without data protection, our network would be quite small, if existent at all," added John and continued. "Colonel, it's much the same as the protection the US Government affords its classified information. Dissemination is determined by a need to know."

"Exactly, I understand what you're saying. How long before we could get access to your information holdings?"

"Colonel," Brad said, reverting to the more formal military title, "I don't believe you fully understand what the Center does. We *aren't* a source for information at someone's whim. We, internally, look at the information at hand, and provide guidance to research facilities based solely on its content. We may tell a subscriber, discontinue that particular line of study, it's been previously tried, or, cancel that project, the same effort, several months ago, was found to be faulty. Things of that nature."

"They take your word for it and assume, without question, that you have the correct data upon which to make such decisions?"

"Hank, we *don't* provide decisions. The first thing we provide is integrity. We also, along with that integrity, provide suggestions and overall guidance for a specific program. Each subscriber makes his own decisions. Correct me if I'm wrong, but, I thought that's what you were asking me about in the first place. Guidance."

"Don't get me wrong. I apologize, Brad, if I've come off the wrong way. I certainly didn't mean to. I am *asking* for guidance. I guess I'm not really up to snuff on what your Center's capabilities are. You must have one hell of an operation down there."

"We'd certainly like to think so. As far as I know, Hank, there's not been one dissatisfied subscriber yet. And remember, these subscribers are more concerned with finding a cure, than any monetary rewards. It's strictly a non-profit scenario from the get-go. Much like the US Government."

"Is there anyway in the interim, the government could place a man at the Center to provide feedback to me until we're approved for access?"

"It's never been done before. Or even requested before, for that matter."

"It's just... I'm running a pretty tight ship on this consolidation effort and felt it might help speed up your recommendations for us. I'm getting some big time congressional pressure to get moving on this."

"John, what do you think?"

"What would this ahhh... man of yours be doing at the Center?" asked John as he drained his glass once again.

"Ohh, just helping with data entry and matching. Things of that nature."

"That ahh... really isn't necessary Colonel. We have a definite protocol we maintain and, I might add, have become quite proficient in doing so, especially in those areas. Thanks for your offer of help, but, your guy may be more of a hindrance than a help, with all of the procedures he wouldn't be privy to."

"Just a thought," Hank said with disappointment again in his voice.

"Hank," Brad said, "let's proceed on the basis that you're going to identity those areas you want us to look at. You have the data prepared for entry into our system and someone on John's staff will specify which formats to be used for transferal. In the meantime, within a couple of weeks, we'll formalize the contractual agreement, try to prioritize your requests and, hopefully, provide you with the information you want. That'd save a lot of time in getting the government up and running right there."

"Sounds like a good starting point, Brad. I'll be in touch the first part of the week. I better find Carmen, my wife, before she kills me. Thanks for your help and suggestions. It's been a pleasure."

"Good to meet you also, Hank. Enjoy the rest of the evening."

"Thanks, pal," Phil said to his brother- in- law, patting him approvingly on the back. "See you in a couple of minutes."

"Okay, buddy, no problem."

"Pleasure, my ass," said John when they'd both left.

"What do you mean by that?"

"I flat don't trust Colonel fuck-face worth a shit. I think I need another drink."

"You too, huh. Did you see that guy's eyes?"

"*Weird* looking dude, man. Looks like he'd be more involved with chemical warfare than finding cures. The gall of the sonuvabitch. Just because he's some government asshole, thinks he should have the right to flaunt our security for immediate access to our data base. *I hardly think so!!* Over my dead body, the rat bastard. NSA's full of those assholes. It they were *worth* a shit, they'd have made General years ago."

"Look, John. I know how you feel about the guy, that's obvious, but hold it down around Phil. Okay? He *has* known the guy all of his life."

"Agreed. I still don't trust him worth a shit."

"I think you've made that point clear to me. And, remember what we were talking about earlier."

"And what would that be?" John asked, still showing his dislike of Harold.

"You know. The cloak and dagger shit that's in your contract."

"Oh, that. I won't forget. We better round up the women folk before they have a shit-fit."

"Let's party."

"That's my line."

"I know. Let's do it anyway."

"Right on. Let's party."

The band was playing as Brad and John returned to the Wellington Room. The four couples, together again, were having a ball. Sam, in a thousand words or less at Brad's request, described how exquisite she found the Embassy to be on the tour with Terri and the other girls. She'd met Terri's parents and marveled at their charm. Brad had met her parents on a number of occasions and knew it wasn't a diplomatic front for his fiancee. They were genuinely very nice, sincere people, that would do anything for you and especially for their daughter, their only child.

The evening proved to be worthy of all its anticipated festivities. Sam was still being eye-balled by everyone, including the band members and the younger waiters carrying the trays throughout the room loaded with refills of bubbly champagne.

As Brad reached for a replacement drink for his empty glass, the band trumpeted every guest to attention and announced the last song of the evening. Staying this late wasn't exactly what Sam and Brad had planned, but, what the hell, when you're having a good time, it's hard to leave. After the dance, Samantha led Brad to where the elder Westcombs were standing and graciously thanked them for one of the most wonderful evenings she'd ever had. After saying their good-byes to everyone, they made their way to the line waiting for valet service.

Brad hurriedly drove home so he and Samantha could consummate their formal engagement. He was in such a rush that he'd even been pulled over by the flashing lights of one of DC's finest in his review mirror. Mention of Abe and Ben to the officer didn't sway him in the slightest from issuing Brad a ticket for failure to come to a complete stop at an intersection.

"What an evening," Sam said as the Mustang approached her house.

"What a day," said Brad.

"I'm very proud of you Brad."

"Not nearly as proud as I was showing you off. Do you have any idea how fantastic you looked tonight? All those envious guys, drooling their asses off."

"I noticed quite a few women drooling over you and wishing they were me. I'm a very lucky person Brad, to go home with you after an evening like this."

They pulled in front of the house, oddly enough, not to a screeching halt as usual, probably because of the citation Brad had received. As they walked hand-in-hand slowly towards the front door Brad said, "Do you notice anything funny?"

"No, not really."

"We aren't racing to get to the door and rip each others' clothes off."

"I didn't really notice, but, you're right."

"Do you suppose this is how a young, engaged couple is expected to act."

"Maybe, so. What do you think?"

"Race you," he challenged.

"You're on," she replied.

Slightly out of breath, they calmed down enough to reach an agreement about the magenta gown. Sam wanted to save it forever as a remembrance of the evening and Brad reluctantly agreed as he reminded her of his ripped shirts. For a change, they by-passed the dining room table and made it to the bedroom, where they slowly undressed each other. After a pause in front of the bedroom's dresser mirror, Sam turned to Brad with her hands held outward. The engagement ring glittered in the shadowed light filtering through the window.

"Sam, you put on the mistletoe pendant, didn't you?" questioned a anxious Brad in the near darkness.

"You *bet* I did."

---- Chapter Ten ----

It was Friday morning, nearly nine o'clock , as Brad placed his long distance coded message to "hell". With the time difference between EST and CST he hoped Ron Riddel would have time to call back before reporting to work at BioMed. Brad didn't have much information for him, actually none, but, wanted to contact Ron to see if he could relieve some of the anxieties surrounding his twin brother's death. And besides, Brad liked him quite a lot, even though they'd met only briefly. With the message placed on Ron's beeper, Brad leaned back in his leather-tufted chair and assumed a Samantha-like position with his feet on his desk.

The week so far had been in a word, fantastic, he remembered as he yawned widely. Nothing would ever top last Wednesday evening with his formal engagement to Sam and the gala and the time spent under the mistletoe all packed into one day. Hell, even the Skins stood a chance of winning Sunday's game at RFK Stadium and, thanks to Gus, he and Sam would be at the sidelines. Things were going right and he felt good about his life.

With the thought still in his mind, he heard Doc's familiar knock and acknowledged immediate entry into his office. Knowing without looking up that he was approaching his desk Brad asked, "What's up Doc?"

"Christ, Brad, you sound like God damn Bugs Bunny."

Jokingly, Brad frowned, "You'd better stop sneaking up on people... shit, I might just sick Yosemite Sam on your ass."

"I wasn't sneaking. It's this damn plush carpet you have. It cushions every step so you can't hear a thing. If your office had a tile floor, like you make the majority of us peons work on, you wouldn't have this problem. That reminds me, I've been wanting to talk to you about my back pains because of the working conditions around here."

"Yeah, yeah, yeah. The only pain around here is the one you give me in the ass," Brad laughed. "What's on your mind?"

"Besides the ration of shit I get for doing my job, only the information you wanted from last week."

"I didn't realize you were on rations. Hell, Doc, you can have all the shit you want. I assume you're talking about the stoppage of research on the antibody?"

"You assume right," he replied, brushing the snow-white hair from his forehead.

"That was quick. What were the findings?"

"The normal things, as far as we can tell. Looks on the up and up to me."

"Let's go over 'em one by one."

"Here's the scoop, boss. The Institute for Cancer Studies in Ontario stopped research on the project in March of 1991. Their lab was being contaminated from an unknown source so all projects were shut down and moved to another building. All projects, with the exception of the antibody study, were resumed in the new location. The contaminant didn't surface again so they felt strongly the antibody research was the culprit. They couldn't afford another shut down, so never resumed it."

"Was there any mention of contamination created by the antibody research from any of the other research centers."

"None from what we could find."

"That's interesting. Who's next."

"That would be, let me see, here it is, The Center of Biological Studies in London. Terminated the project in October of '89. They were bought out by a new company entering the research arena. They didn't want to wait until a building with labs and such could be built. They bought the company for its facilities only. All ongoing projects were canceled by the new ownership so they could begin their own studies but in different areas of research."

"All projects were canceled and never resumed?"

"That's right."

"Did the selling company build new facilities so they could at least continue the studies already started?"

"As far as we can tell, they never re-entered the biological research area again. It was a complete buy-out, facilities and technology. It included ongoing research, but, the new ownership never continued any of the research currently underway. They entered a completely new area of nutritional research. Research and development of vitamin supplements and natural health aids appears to be their forte, not biological studies. At the time of the purchase, they had a couple of health food projects underway."

"Doc, they must have paid top dollar for the facilities and technology. Why pay for all that technology if you weren't going to continue with its associated projects?"

"Who knows? Maybe, the seller demanded they buy all or nothing. You know, kind of like purchasing someone's reputation or goodwill. The buy-out didn't change the name of the research center. It remained the same, so, what I just said, kinda fits."

"I suppose that's possible, if the seller wanted to get out of the field all together. Even with that, the buyer may want to enter the field at some later date. By the way. Who was the buyer?"

"Says here, purchased by umm... Stockholm Technologies. That fits."

"What fits?"

"A Swedish Company. The Swedes are really involved in all this vitamin, natural cure and health food shit. Isn't that natural cough drop advertised on TV with the big God damn horn, a Swedish product?"

"Hell, I'm not sure. I think it's Swiss though. Another European capital," thought Brad aloud.

"What?" asked Doc, not hearing Brad's last remark.

"Nothing, Doc. Just kinda thinking out loud. Who owns Stockholm Technologies?"

"Can't really say. You didn't ask for that stuff. You want me to find out?"

"Do it," instructed Brad in a stern voice.

"Shit, Brad, what's gotten into you this morning? You normally ask for things. Now, it's like you're giving orders and making demands. What the hell gives, boss?"

"Sorry, Doc. Really, I'm very sorry I came off that way. I guess I have too much on my mind. Please, no offense."

"None taken. Is what's on your mind something I can help with? You know me, always eager to help."

"Basically, that's what I was trying to do when I asked... rather ordered you to find out the parent company, if there was one. Again, I'm sorry for that. Just let me know if you find out anything."

"Sounds pretty important."

"Could be. Which center's next on the list?"

"Let's see." Doc continued. "That's the Yokohama Institute for Advanced Research Studies in Japan. They stopped working on the antibody in early '85. That was *definitely* a funding problem. With the Japanese economy fucked up the way it was back then, the center resorted to find the big bucks wherever it was available. They got hooked up with some

Japanese billionaire and received an open-ended grant. He'd made his money in the electronics industry and was approaching his mid-forties when he discovered he had cancer. He was privately funding the antibody research to find a cure for his own cancer. He died and the funding stopped almost immediately. Project kaput."

"God damn cancer won the fight, huh?"

"It probably would've but, really didn't. The cancer was getting pretty bad and had progressed to the point where he'd less than a year to live. A lot like me, come to think of it. He actually died in an accident. His home caught on fire and he died in the blaze. Something crossed my mind as pretty ironic when I read it in the report."

"What's that?" asked Brad.

"Only that, here was a guy who made a small... no, make that a big fortune in the electronics industry and didn't even have a smoke or fire alarm to warn him."

"That *is* puzzling. You *sure* he didn't have one?"

"The report didn't really say if he did or didn't. I just thought how ironic it was. Even if he had one, it didn't work worth a shit. *He's deader than hell.* You want the scoop on the last center?"

"Yeah, that would be the one in Invercargill, New Zealand, right?"

"Right. The research stopped in the summer of 1978."

"January or July?"

"What do you mean by that?"

"Their summer or ours? They are way, way south of the equator. Our summer is their winter."

"Their winter. I mean our summer. Shit, I don't know. Who gives a shit. January it says."

"Then it's their summer and our winter."

"Who's cares anyway? You love to do that shit to people don't ya? Especially those that've never been anywhere in their lives, let alone, south of the equator."

"Just teasing with you, Doc. Go ahead. Any reason for the termination?"

"The data on the project is pretty antiquated. No actual reason for stopping the research was available. There is something that's interesting though."

"What's that?"

"As sporadic as the records are, it appears there was no research leading up to finding the chemical and biological makeup of the antibody. It just kind of appeared as part of the project... out of the blue, so to speak. Not there one day, there the next. Maybe not that quickly but you get my drift."

"Yeah, I do. Luck?"

"Luck wouldn't be the proper word. This antibody has a very complex makeup. You don't get results like that from pouring shit together and analyzing it after the fact. To come up with this on a first try would be like Jonas Salk coming up with the Polio Vaccine on his first shot."

"That complex?"

"You got it partner."

"Where *did* it come from?"

"Shit, I don't know. There was mention in some of the early-on documentation about a Tuatura."

"A what?"

"Tuatura. It's some sort of God damn lizard that lives off other lizards, flies, and that kinda shit."

"The damn thing flies?"

"Nooooo, Brad, it eats flies and other insects. Anyway, this damn lizard has been around since pre-historic times. A real life Jurassic Park thing, you know."

"It's actually pre-historic?"

"That's what I read when I looked it up. And get this. There is only one place in the world these little bastards are found. Guess where it is?"

"Ahhhh... in your mind?"

"You smart ass. No, they can only be found on a few small islands off the coast of New Zealand. How do you like that shit?"

"Christ. I spent all of those years, off and on, in New Zealand and never even heard of them. You said... they're mentioned in the data you have?"

"Yeah, they were. Not much. Just mentioned."

"Ya know something, Doc. Maybe, just maybe, this Tuatara Lizard thing, was the source for the antibody that just miraculously showed up in the project notes."

"Hell, nothing would surprise me. Maybe the theory was, here's this ugly God damn lizard that's survived for millions of years. Maybe the little son-of-a-bitch knows something we don't about survival. Maybe, just maybe, to steal your phrase, Brad, he's got some disease preventing antibody."

"That would mean, assuming it came from this lizard thing, it exists in a natural state. No development would be necessary."

"And; therefore, no notes in the project concerning any research efforts," Doc concluded.

"Right! Wouldn't that be the cat's meow?"

"No matter," said Doc, bringing Brad's excitement down about five levels. "There is no evidence from any of these labs suggesting there *was ever* a use for the antibody."

"None the less, Doc, it's very interesting, to say the least. Thanks for the information. And please, try to find out the parent company of Stockholm Technologies. And, while you're at it, check out a company called Swiss Technologies if you would."

"They related in some way?"

"Maybe, but I hope not."

"What the hell does that mean?"

"I'll let you know in due course. Okay?"

"Fine by me. See you as soon as I know something," Doc said as he left the room, leaving the door wide open.

"Shut the... never mind, I'll get it." Brad said, shaking his head and smiling at Doc's persistent, one-track mindedness.

Returning to his desk after closing his office door, Brad began pondering the implications of what he'd just heard. In deep thought, Susan's voice on his intercom startled him. "Brad, Ron Riddel on line three."

"Thanks Susan," Brad said lifting his phone off the hook and pushing the blinking light. "Ron, how we doing out there in God's country?"

"God's country? If it is, he's chosen to freeze everything and everyone in it. It's cold as hell here."

"I know what you mean, Ron. I've been in Chicago a couple of times during the winter. That damn wind coming off the lake makes it even worse. Drives the wind chill factor down and out of sight."

"At least, in this phone booth, I'm out of the wind. It's still cold as hell though."

"You're in a phone booth?"

"Yeah. Didn't want to call from my home phone. You may think I'm paranoid or something, but, I don't want anyone knowing about our contact. I've been trying to keep a low profile, but, at the same time, keeping my eyes and ears open. I'm not going to throw caution to the wind, even though it is blowing like hell outside this booth."

"Don't blame you for being careful," Brad said, not knowing why he was agreeing to what Ron had just said and continued. "You think your phone may be tapped?"

"Can't really say for sure. Just not taking any chances. Have you found out anything?"

"No, not really. Just wanted to touch base with you to let you know I haven't forgotten about our meeting in Crystal City. I have a couple of people working on some things, but, nothing's surfaced yet."

"What're they working on?"

"Ohh... we had a computer hacker trying to gain áccess to our data bank a few days ago. We've had a couple of occurrences in the past few weeks but, they proved, the way John would say it, to be nothing other than people surfing the net."

"Doing what? I'm sorry Brad, this wind is howling pretty good and it's hard to hear you."

A little louder Brad said, "Surfing the net. Hackers scanning the internet and trying to break into secure systems. According to John, people can become addicted to making these attempts. It's almost like a game with them. They really aren't after anything in particular; but, they've got a relentless desire to know everything that's out there. Even things they're not supposed to. You know what I mean?"

"I suppose so. I've never really got hooked on the computer revolution, but, I know some people who have. Personally, I never have time for all that kind of nonsense. I'm too damn busy. Who's John?"

"John Sipel. He's the Center's head honcho in security. John has responsibility for protecting the integrity of the data base from crazies like these."

"Is John more concerned about the latest incident than the previous ones?"

"No, I don't think so. I only brought it up because the latest attempt stemmed from the Chicago area." Brad said, not telling the whole truth. "Ron, let me ask you a question."

"Shoot."

"Has there been a change in ownership at BioMed?"

"Ya know what? I'm not sure, now that you mention it. But, I don't believe there's been any since I've been here. Before that, I wouldn't really know."

"Who owns BioMed currently?"

"Geeez Brad, I don't really know who actually owns it."

"What corporate name is on your paycheck?"

"Everyone's required to use direct deposit so we don't receive paychecks."

"Christ," said Brad disappointed. He thought for a moment and then continued. "Who sends you your W-2 statement at the end of the year for the IRS?"

"Let me think a minute. It's been almost a year since I filed. I believe it was a Norwegian name."

"Oslo something?"

"That's it. Oslo Enterprises. I'm certain of it. Why? And how did you know?"

Brads mind nearly went blank as he realized he was four for four and batting a thousand. "It was just a guess, Ron. We have a couple of other companies we're working with that use European country capitals as their names. Nothing out of the ordinary. You haven't noticed any cars that have license plates with a black oval and white lettering have you?"

"Yeah. There are some. Not many, but some. I see them mostly at work in the parking lot."

"I thought so," replied Brad as casually as possible and abruptly rose to his feet as Ron's last answer registered. "All these companies I was talking about that we do business with have the same plates. No big deal Ron. Just curious," Brad lied. "Look buddy, I have to run. If anything comes up, give me a ring. Keep that low profile for a while until we know something for certain," Brad said, this time meaning every word.

"Sure will Brad. Talk to you later."

About thirty seconds later, Brad called his brother-in-law, Dr. Phillip Bowers, on his private line.

"Phil?"

"Brad?"

"Yeah. Can you meet me at Joey's for lunch? We've *got* to talk. It's important!"

"What for?"

"Just be there," Brad insisted.

"It must be serious. You got it pal. See you at 12:30"

"Thanks."

*****

Joey's Delicatessen was full of patrons; however, Brad was more familiar with the breakfast crowd and only recognized a few people, none by name. The smell of warm pastrami and corned beef was in the air, favorites of those who knew the menu best. Joey was there laboring in the kitchen as they'd chatted briefly. He made certain Brad was using the passes to the Skins game or else the next time, he'd give them to real fans. Gus's name was now inscribed on the last stool at the counter in the form of a permanent reservation.

"This doesn't sound real good for the home front." Phil mused over an untouched corned beef sandwich and side order of cole slaw brought to him by Karen, the shapely, African-American waitress. He'd been listening to Brad's description of events.

"I'm sorry to drag you into this, Phil, whatever the hell it is. But, when I found a possible connection between the antibody Doc was referring to and the lab your father is associated with, I almost felt obligated. Your father might be smack in the middle of something and not even realize it. It just seemed too damn coincidental. Every time a research facility developed this particular antibody, something happens to squelch the project. Again, everything I've told you can be explained away rationally. Shit, who knows?"

"I tend to agree with you pal... it's a mystery. In all of the studies, except for the first one at Invercargill, the research showed a progression up to the point of its discovery. Right?"

"Right," Brad assured him.

"Brad, it seems to me, all of these incidents could be tied into this Swiss Technologies Company, whoever they are. Christ Brad, do you realize, in a lot of these incidents, a biological research center, or someone closely associated with one, has been directly involved. And, maybe not innocently. John and Abbey's accident on Thanksgiving, this guy Ron, or whatever you said his name was, from Chicago and even your townhouse explosion. Hell, we had doubts about its being an accident from the first day."

"I'm fully aware of all that. Tie in the professional hacker trying to get our data base holdings and the buy-out of the facility in London by a possible subsidiary and what do you have?"

"One hell of a widespread effort from a company with worldwide resources backing 'em up. What the hell would they be trying to accomplish? That's the question."

"If we're right about this, obviously something to do with biological research, possibly cancer research," Brad said taking a small sip of his now warm beer.

"Doesn't fit."

"What?"

"Narrowing it down to cancer research alone. If the incident in Chicago is related, you said they were involved the Ebola virus."

"So that means it would be biological research in general."

"Right."

"One thing, Phil, I have no idea in hell how that New York City incident would be involved in any of this. Sam and I were merely shopping for her gown when all that funny business went down."

"Hell of a gown, pal."

"Hell of a woman."

"You got that right, pal. Brad, maybe *that* was the only coincidental thing that's happened. It's possible, it had nothing to do with any of the other events at all. I'm going to the pay phone over there and call pop in Colorado Springs and tell him some of this shit. Just as a precautionary measure... and, get some of his thoughts. He's been around the business world quite a while and is wise like an owl."

"Might be a good idea, Phil. While your gone I'm going to get another cold beer and try to eat some of this pastrami and slaw."

"Back in a couple of minutes."

Brad took one bite of the hot pastrami, but, found it unappealing. It was now cold pastrami. The French fries were also cold and beginning to harden a little, but, Brad found them tolerable to munch on. The only thing warm on the table was the God damn beer! He quickly rectified the situation with a new draft from Karen.

He shouldn't really eat much anyway. Sam had decided to prove to him she was worth something other than good sex, as Brad had playfully put it one evening, and was preparing for him his favorite, a southern fried chicken dinner. Brad knew if she cooked as well as she made love, he was in for a gourmet's delight. The irony was, she was planning on using the dining room table for dinner, rather than for the purpose to which Brad had become accustomed. Life's full of new experiences!

"What the hell are you smiling about?" Phil said returning to the table.

"Nothing really. Sam's cooking me dinner tonight and I was just visualizing her in the kitchen up to her ass in pots and pans. That place is gonna be one big disaster when I get home. What did Malcomb have to say?"

"Not much really. He felt we, meaning you and I, had more important things to do than getting involved in some fictitious tale of espionage or whatever we're thinking it is."

"You told him everything?"

"Most everything. He thanked me, of course, for being considerate enough to call him when I told him I was worried about his safety. He simply said for us to drop it and leave it alone."

"That's it?"

"Yeah."

"He actually said drop it and leave it alone?"

"Yeah. He didn't think it was worth all the worry and bother."

"He's not sitting where I have been for the past six or seven weeks."

"He may be right, Brad. Most things can be explained innocently away."

"Possible, I suppose, but, if one more thing goes hay-wire, I'm not taking any chances on this one. Business as usual will come to a screeching halt. I'll be contacting someone for some major league help with this shit. At least, he's aware of our concerns and should notice anything out of the ordinary at the Colorado Springs Research Center."

"That's true. At least he has this stuff in the back of his mind. I feel much better having called. Brad, look, all of us are leaving on Monday for Denver and this adventure you've planned, whatever the hell it is. Maybe the clear Rocky Mountain air will allow us to sit back and analyze this a little more. Clear our heads so to speak. Hell, knowing you, whatever you've planned will probably take our minds off it completely. Maybe, we'll be able to look at it from a new perspective after our trip. Besides, if this is some sorta problem, it'll *never* follow us to Colorado. Let's put this out of our minds for right now. Kinda put it on hold until we get back. Christmas is only... shit, this is the twentieth, it's only five days away. Isn't that right?"

"Afraid so, buddy. This coming Wednesday. I hope this trip does clear our minds for a while. I can't deal with this bullshit. Besides, mom... well hell, Phil, you know how she enjoys the holidays. I don't want anything to get in the way of her having a wonderful time over Christmas. She still misses dad so much, she really looks forward to fussing over the family on these occasions."

"You're right. I've been there the past couple of years, you know. I'm married to your sister, remember. Your mother is a wonderful lady, Brad. Let's really try to put this stuff on the back burner until after the holidays. Okay, pal?"

"I'd like to put it on the back burner forever. If nothing else ever happened, I wouldn't be one little bit disappointed. I agree, Phil. Let's put this on hold for a couple of weeks anyhow. Who knows what the New Year will bring."

"Christ, it's late. I have to get back to the hospital. I'll see you at the airport along with everyone else, if I don't see you before." Phil said rising to leave. "Shit, I go to lunch with you and leave hungry."

"Sorry for the short notice. I thought it was necessary."

"Don't apologize. I appreciate the information. Thanks for insisting. See ya later, pal."

"See ya," Brad said, himself still feeling a tad hungry. He paid Karen and gave her a five spot for putting up with them over lunch. On his way out, he stuck his head through the double doors and said good bye to Joey.

Returning to the office, the words, *"drop it, leave it alone,"* wouldn't stay out of his mind. *I wonder what the word, "it," Mal referred to means,* he thought to himself. Only two choices Brad could determine. Either Mal felt the story Phil related to him was totally unfounded or... maybe, Phil's father knew more than he was willing to tell his son. Brad opted for the first choice and forced the implications of the second from his mind. He returned to his office to take care of a couple of things before going home to the dinner Sam was preparing.

*****

"Yeah. You have something to report?"

"*God damn it! Don't talk so damn loud*!"

"Do you still have the listening device in," he said, nearly whispering into the phone.

Reaching to his ear, he removed the high tech apparatus from his ear. "*Shit yes*. I forgot to take it out. *Loud* little bastard."

"Latest technology."

"I don't know how this thing works but it's damn good. I was sittin' two tables away and had to turn the volume down. And, they weren't exactly yelling. Matter of fact, they were trying to be very quiet about their fuckin' discussion."

"No problems then?"

"I heard it all. You know, with all this new fangled shit, this surveillance crap is a fuckin' piece of cake."

"Growing to like it?"

"Not really. The hours sure as hell suck. I prefer to be responsible for the end product. It pays better and the hours don't fuckin' kill you."

"What'd you find out?"

"They're *on* to you guys. The contract's definitely grown in size now."

"What do you mean?"

"They've tied five different labs together. They uncovered the antibody at Claxton's place this morning."

"*Damn it*. Anything else."

"Yeah. Bowers called to warn some other guy."

"Who?"

"Couldn't tell. The God damn little black whore of a waitress kept buggin' me about smokin' inside the place. She was goin' to get the owner or someone to make me stop. Didn't hear the fuckin' guy's name. They talked about the damn trip to Denver a little bit. Maybe, it was that McCardy character he called. Ever figure out who he is?"

"Yeah. He's the boyfriend of the Ambassador's daughter, Terri Westcomb. That's probably who he called to warn. For right now, we'll assume so. That means the contract is now at least six."

"Include the girls and it's eight. By the way. I overheard them talking about the explosion last month. They were suspicious right after he came out of his coma?"

"Why?"

"Have no idea. The arson squad wasn't even called in. Sounded as if Bowers was the first one to be fuckin' suspicious."

"Probably a good thing Claxton didn't die."

"How so?"

"There might have been an investigation going on and we wouldn't have known about it."

"I see what you mean. Any word on the package for the flight?"

"They're considering it."

"Seems like an easy fix to me."

"Would be but, we don't have anyone in place on the ground crew for American Airlines like we did in baggage handling in Madrid the last time. It's a little easier planting personnel overseas than in the States. We're still working on it. It may be a last minute thing. You have it ready?"

"It's set to go. According to the flight plans for their flight, they fly at an altitude of 39,000 feet until they're over Iowa. The Denver Control Center picks them up and vectors them on a new heading and drops their altitude to 33,000 feet. It arms at 33 on the way up and blows at 35 on the way down. Those fuckin' cornfields in Iowa are gonna be full of shit if we can get it on board."

"Time will tell."

"*Shit.*"

"What?"

"Ohh, the fuckin' little waitress bitch is bringin' her boss or someone over here. I'd better be goin'."

"Talk to you later. Keep in touch."

As Joey approached, he hung up the phone and crushed out his second cigarette on the checkerboard marble floor.

"Sir, I'm afraid City Ordinances don't allow smoking inside the deli. I'm going to have to ask you to leave."

"You the owner?"

"That's right," replied Joey. "You know, you've upset Karen here," he said, motioning towards the waitress. "She's only trying to do her job."

"Never mind. I'm on my way out anyway." He flipped down the coin return for the pay phone and found it empty. "Karen, is it?"

"Yes sir," came the quiet reply.

"I'm afraid the coin return's empty." He pushed past Joey and Karen on his way to the front door of the deli. "That's the only fuckin' chance you had for a tip," he said as a parting shot.

As he left the deli, he heard Joey and other customers consoling Karen. "Stupid bitch," he muttered as he rounded the corner and eyed the Cadillac parked half a block down the street.

*****

"Sam, I know you probably think I'd say this regardless of how I really feel about your cooking. It's important that you believe me, however; for all sorts of reasons." He laughed at his own words.

"Brad, just say how you feel. Don't make a federal court case out of it. If you didn't like it, I can't win them all."

"How I feel?" he repeated. "I... feel... full."

"Full? Is that it? After all the time I spent preparing this for you and you feel... *full*?"

"You didn't let me finish."

"Finish? Brad, you ate *everything* in sight including the *parsley garnish*."

"Not, *finish eating*, Sam. You didn't let me *finish* talking."

"I know, but, why so serious? I'm just playing around with you, sweetheart. What'd you think?"

"Honestly, Sam, I thought I was marrying a very, *very* sexy woman, not a cook. That was, until this dinner. I thought my mother's fried chicken was the best. This was just as good, believe me, if not better. By the way, I would appreciate it if we could kinda keep this our own little secret. Don't tell mom when we see her Wednesday. She takes a lot of pride in her chicken dinners."

"You liked it *that* much? Boy, hon, I had no idea you were *this* easy. I guess the saying, the way to a man's heart is through his stomach, is true.

In your case though, I think it should be changed to, over your stomach. I've never known anyone who could eat as much as you at one sitting."

"When food is this good, I just can't seem to stop. I am full, though."

"I promise not to mention to your mother you liked my chicken as much as hers. Ready for some dessert?"

"Noooo way. I couldn't eat another thing."

"Not even home made southern-style pecan pie?"

"Are you trying to entice me with my favorite pie? *How the hell'd you know?*"

"You really want to know?"

"What's that supposed to mean? Now you have my curiosity up. What're you talking about, little woman?"

"It's a long story."

"It can't be that long, Sam."

"Okay. When I said I'd make you dinner, I suggested my southern fried chicken."

"So?"

"I kinda found out from your mother on Thanksgiving it was your favorite, along with the pecan pie."

"A lot of people who've known me for some time are aware of that. What's the big deal?"

"Well, I've never really made fried chicken before."

"*This is your first time*? *No way*! Mom can *never* find out how much I liked it. For real, it's *really* your first time?" Brad repeated.

"Ahhh, Brad. I ahh... don't really cook... much."

"Saaaaaam, now I know you're joshing me. That's impossible."

"Not... really."

"All right. Let's put all the cards on the table. Maybe you can explain to me how someone who doesn't cook much can prepare a feast like this."

"Maybe, with a wee bit of help from a tutor." Sam replied, using her southern accent to the hilt and shamefully lowering her head.

"A tutor?"

"Okay, I'll come clean. My ahh...telephone bill is going to be huge. I spent over five hours, probably closer to six, on the phone, with... your mother. She, ahh... sorta coached me through this whole.... cooking thing. *Hell, Brad, you mother cooked it long distance*," she said quickly, being totally honest with him. "I just wanted to impress you. You're not disappointed are you?"

After a pause which seemed an eternity to Sam, Brad said. "Sam, I'm overwhelmed. Speechless. I don't know *what* to say about this."

"I'm sorry. I won't ever deceive you again."

"Come here, you silly nut. I'm not mad. You didn't deceive me at all. Sam, honey, you impress me in ways you don't even realize. For you to go to all that trouble for me is gratifying. Just continue being yourself, your honest self. I love you," he said, as he pulled Sam onto his lap. "I thought that chicken tasted awfully familiar. It was very good. And besides, you Sam, not my mother, cooked this dinner. I don't care what she told you on the phone. You did it including the actual seasoning and cooking and, it was wonderful. Incidently, do you think you could repeat this gourmet's delight without the telephone company declaring dividends."

"Honestly, probably not. I didn't write a thing down."

"Hell, you should've recorded the phone call."

"There was some woman talk during that five or six hours that I'd rather not be on tape."

"What'd you and mom talk about?"

"That's going to remain, forever, our little secret. We took the opportunity to get to know each other pretty well. She's a wonderful lady, Brad and I already love her."

"She is wonderful, Sam. I've known that for thirty years. Let me clear the table for you."

"Why, you ready for some of... your mom's pie?"

"Noooo, still too full. When I said clear the table, I meant clear it completely, including that dumb ass center piece."

"Whoa. You do have an appetite, don't you, fella?"

Kissing passionately, they retired to the bedroom. The hell with the dishes, they could wait. Sam and Brad couldn't. The dishes waited the same length of time it took Sam to complete a telephone conversation with Brad's mother about preparing a dinner. Brad and Sam had their own style of communication and were determined to perfect it.

---- Chapter Eleven ----

The eight of them had congregated on Monday at Dulles International early in the morning for the 12:34 PM flight to the new Denver International Airport. The Redskins had lost, but, what the hell, the four couples were heading west for better times in Colorado. They'd planned to meet about one and a half hours before departure, enjoy a leisurely breakfast and discuss the upcoming trip to Colorado. Their flight was delayed due to mechanical problems and the actual departure was postponed for nearly two hours. Now the four of them had moved to the American Airlines Admiral's Club.

"Hell, we could've slept in and still made the damn flight," claimed Brad, grabbing a Stuart Wood's paperback from his carryon bag "It's approaching two hours late getting off the ground."

"You wouldn't have been sleeping anyway, pal," teased Phil as he winked at Samantha.

"It's not late anyway," Evan informed everyone. "With the difference in time zones, it's right on time. Frankly, I could really care if the damn plane was ever ready for take-off. I hate flying with a passion."

"You're that nervous about it?" questioned Sam.

"Sam, you should've seen this panty-waste on the trip back from Australia," John said. "He didn't relax until he passed out from the scotch and waters."

"I wasn't *that* bad. It's just that I prefer wheels that stay on the ground. Like on a bus."

"You're the John Madden of New Zealand," stated Brad.

"I don't know who he is, but, if he hates flying as much as I do then, he's a friend of mine."

"With this time zone calculation of yours, I see your imagination is on the rampage again, Evan," Terri said shaking her head in mock disbelief.

"Evan's logic with the time zones is probably how the airlines maintain such a high on-time rating," Samantha added.

"I wonder if they have internet access on this flight. Some are providing it nowadays," informed John.

"I sure as hell hope not," chimed in Abbey. "If they do, we won't hear a peep out of you the entire flight. You'll be playing with the damn computer the entire time."

"Not really. I would just like to see how the response time is. Just kinda check it out."

"John, you've never *just* checked out a computer in your life," Brad said. "I remember how you kept me awake all damn night in the dorm."

Chantal broke into the conversation. "I think I should have eaten something when the rest of you did earlier," she said. "But I assumed we'd be in the air by now and close to lunch time. I'm getting a little hungry."

"Now, the airline food is some cuisine to be looking forward to," said Phil. "You'd better get a bite here before our flight is called."

"And what's wrong with the airline food?" questioned Brad.

"Coming from a man that could eat rusty nails, absolutely nothing."

"Your'e right about that, Phil," stated Samantha jokingly.

"At least the airlines put something into the food your Georgetown Medical Center hasn't been able to find during the past eight months."

"And what might that be, Brad?" asked Phil knowing he was setting himself up.

"Taste," stated Brad which caused a roar of laughter.

Samantha held up her hands for silence as she said, "I think they just called our flight."

"Damn it," said Evan. "My prayers are never answered."

Hearing the speaker announce a flight, Abbey said, "That's the one. Sounds like they changed the gate number back to the original one."

"Must have," said John. "I wonder what's going on with all the changing. We'd better get moving."

Once the flight had left the DC area and achieved its designated flying altitude of 39,000 feet, the couples had adjourned to the upper level of the Boeing 747 and the comfort of its lounge where Evan quickly ordered two rounds of scotch and waters for himself. Later, somewhere over the ploughed under cornfields of Iowa, as the flight was being vectored to a new heading and was adjusting to a cruising altitude of 33,000 feet, Brad mentioned Sam was giving his mother a cook book for Christmas. That tidbit, after the story about the "southern fried" chicken dinner, brought a few laughs from all listeners. Everyone was enjoying the flight, even Evan who was now dozing.

*****

"I've hung around the damn airport lounge for hours waitin' for a CNN news flash about the crash. What the hell went haywire this fuckin' time. The damn thing did get on the flight, right... or did it?" he questioned.

"Yes and no."

"What the hell does, yes and no, mean?"

"It was impossible to put it on the aircraft designated for the flight so our guy placed it on a standby 747 in the hangar. Then, he faked massive hydraulic problems on the original flight knowing the one in the hangar would be brought into service as a replacement. Everything was going according to plan until some young, smart-ass mechanic discovered there really wasn't any hydraulic problem. They decided to leave the original aircraft in service."

"That's *just* fuckin' beautiful. Where's the package I built?"

"Still on the second 747 in the God damned hangar at Dulles."

"*Jesus*. He's goin' to get the damn thing off isn't he?"

"No, we don't want him to take the chance and get caught removing it. We're just going to leave it there and whatever happens, happens."

"You're fuckin' kiddin', right? You're just goin' to leave it there for some unknowns to cope with at 33,000 feet."

"Since when did you develop a conscience? What the hell difference does it make to you?"

"My character's got nothin' to do with it. The difference is, you're probably goin' to want me to go to Denver now and there's a fuckin' 747 floatin' around out there that I don't want any part of."

"You've *definitely* got a point. Just hang tight. Not that I want to, but, I've been given an ultimatum to get personally involved with further negotiations on this contract. I'll be going to Denver with you."

"What about the fuckin' plane?"

"American Airlines isn't the only airline that goes to Denver. We'll make other arrangements."

"What if someone finds the device before the plane's put into service?"

"They won't. Besides, even if they did, you always use surgical gloves when you build this stuff so your prints won't be on it anyway, right?"

"Right. What about the guy that planted it?"

"He's never going to make it home from work tonight. Unfortunate, but, that's business."

"Damn it!"

"You have a problem with that now?"

"No, of course not. They just called my flight."

"Your flight?" he questioned a bit confused.

"Yeah. My fuckin' flight to Miami to connect with the short hop to Barbados. Shit."

"That's right. I forgot. Well, you better be packing some warmer clothes for Colorado. I'll be in touch."

"Let's just get the damn thing over with. I thought I was being hired by a first class outfit."

"It'll be over soon. Hang in there."

"Okay. See you later," he said, eyeing a passing young stewardess and noticing her long legs disappear into her short skirt. *She'd look good on the beach* he thought as his mind returned to the current situation. Under his breath he said, "Claxton, you're one lucky fuck. Under different circumstances, I'd pay your way to the roulette tables in Vegas. You've got nine damn lives just like that fuckin' cat I missed on the road a couple of weeks ago."

*****

As the four couples left the baggage claim area and went through the automatic doors, two Ford Broncos were parked with headlights on, idling at curbside. It was cold, probably twenty five degrees, proof of which was the billowing clouds of white smoke from the exhausts of the 4-wheel drive rentals. Brad knew they'd be more comfortable with two and not having to cram eight people, luggage and ski equipment into a minivan during the two hour trek to his mother's estate. He wanted this to be a great trip for everyone and, as part of his planning, he'd thought of everything for their comfort down to the smallest detail.

Brad, with Sam, Evan and Terri, was driving in the lead while Phil drove the second Bronco, with Chantal at his side and John and Abbey nestled in the rear. It was 8 PM local Colorado time, dark as hell, and snowing, not heavy, but just enough that relaxing while driving was out of the question. Brad's eyes, from the wearisome day and driving in the swirling snow-fall, were beginning to become irritated.

"How much longer?"

"Five minutes less than the last time you asked." Brad informed Sam with a dimpled smile that always made her feel so special.

"Does it ever *not snow* here in the winter?"

"Of course. Why do you ask that?"

"It's hard to see but it looks like the snow is piled up along side the road about six feet deep. That's quite a bit. Why's it only on one side of the road?"

"It might be because there's only one side to the road. You can't see it on your side because its dark, but... well, it just drops off, like a deep gorge."

"Drops off?" Sam questioned with anxiety in her voice. "How far?"

"Couple of thousand feet in some places I'd expect."

"You're shitting us, right Brad?" Evan asked from the back seat leaning in towards Brad with concern in his voice. "I was wondering why I couldn't see any trees or, anything for that matter, out this side of the car."

"Terri, calm him down would you. I've driven this road thousands of times people, there's nothing to worry about, except, maybe an occasional avalanche. It'd come from up the mountain on the left side of the car."

"Brad, that's not real calming for the nerves you know; talking about avalanches and deep gorges. That doesn't really happen around here does it?"

"Not often, but it can."

"I don't know what the concern is," Terri chimed in supporting Brad. "If an avalanche happened, there isn't a damn thing you could do about it, Evan. So, why worry? It'd be all over in a matter seconds," she continued with a low chortle, " you wouldn't feel a thing, I promise."

"That's kind of a defeatist attitude isn't it Terri," asked Evan reprovingly.

"Not really. If 50 tons of snow came crashing down on us right now, Evan, what would you suggest we do?"

"Before or after I shit in my pants? I do see your point Terri, but, I'm just not too keen on the idea of being crushed on this road by your 50 tons of snow so I can fall into a gorge 2000 feet to my death inside this steel coffin. That's all."

"I see your point sweetie."

"How the heck did we get on this morbid subject anyway?" Sam asked. "Can't we find something more enjoyable to talk about?"

"Won't have to, my love," interjected Brad. "We're getting close to mom's now."

"How can you tell? With all the snow coming down and these turns you can't see ahead more than five feet?"

"You see that light shining up against the clouds up ahead?"

"I see a glow in the sky that looks like it's coming from a small community. Is that what you mean?" Sam asked. "Is that area close to where we're going?"

"You might say so. That's Mom's estate... all decorated for Christmas."

"You're kidding me," said Sam nearly in a whisper.

"All of those lights are from your Mom's house?" questioned Terri incredulously from the back.

"I told you before, you'd have to see it to believe it. Mom does Christmas in a big way and I don't think I exaggerated one bit." Brad said now turning into a private road to the house.

"Not in the slightest," responded Sam. "This is remarkable. When you said she liked to put up a lot of lights, I had no idea. I've never seen anything like this. This is breathtaking."

The estate was nestled in a valley between two mountains. The road meandered its way down to the valley floor and allowed a total view from above. The walled-in area was nearly 25 acres in size and gave the impression of approaching the huge mountain lodge of a five star resort. Each tree, of which there were many, was illuminated with strands of clear white lights and the house, or mansion as Sam would later describe it, was outlined with the same type of lighting.

As Brad turned into the private drive they approached the estates's triple wide wrought iron gate which was spotlighted to reveal the most enormous pine wreaths Sam had ever seen. They were draped in bright red ribbon to accent the natural red holly berries. The wall was over ten feet high and had areas of freshly fallen snow clinging to its rough natural rock surface. A sweeping garland of fur branches began at the entrance and proceeded as far to the right and left as one could see, adorned with thousands of white lights.

Brad punched in the security code for the gate and the two Ford Broncos pulled onto the driveway leading to the house. With the heavy gate closing slowly behind them, they entered the main portion of the property. Neither Sam, Evan or Terri had said a word since first viewing the estate from higher up the mountain. It was simply magnificent and left one speechless.

Descending to the main gate, one didn't get a full appreciation as to the size of the trees on the property. Some poked majestically skyward over 100 feet towards the glittering snow fall and were completely covered with a mass of white lights. The breadth of the nearly 100 year old Pines lining the driveway created a spectacle that grabbed the attention of visitors as soon as they came into view.

The fresh snow made a squeaking sound as the snow tires of the Bronco packed it into newly formed tracks on the circular drive. Brad halted the Bronco at the base of the eight steps which led up to the massive, pillared porch area and the leaded-glass, double door entry. Although there was a large brass door knocker and a dimly lit doorbell button, they were seldom used at this house because Natasha Claxton always prided herself on meeting people outside and escorting them into her home.

"God Brad." said an astonished Sam. "Am I gonna meet Robin Leech doing his show here tonight?"

"Who?"

"Robin Leech. You know, the guy that has that show, *Lifestyles of the Rich and Famous*."

"Oh him. No, not tonight, Sam. He's already been here."

"*Really*?"

"No, just kidding."

"Your mother lives here alone?" Samantha continued

"Except for the help, who are like family to her. She also has lots of friends in the area. Heck, she has friends all over the world who spend time here. Terri's parent's spent a couple of weeks here last year, right Terri?"

"Yeah they did, but they never told me how... gorgeous it is," she answered quietly as she looked around taking it all in.

"Well, it's a pretty good size at that. I think, unless mom's changed things around, there are seven bedrooms, each with a private bath not counting the master suite."

"Only seven?" Quipped Evan. "Where in the hell are you going to sleep Brad? There's eight of us."

"There's four more in the guest house around the side if we need 'em, but I think we'll be doubling up anyway." Oddly, there wasn't any response from Sam. He looked over and found her completely mesmerized by the sheer size and grandeur of the home she was about to enter. He didn't bother to say anything else.

As Phil pulled up behind them, the four couples got out of their rental cars, carefully proceeded up the stairs through four inches of newly fallen snow and met Brad's mother on the front porch. After all of the welcome hugs took place, they decided to go into the house before Natasha froze.

"Samantha, let me see that ring I've heard so much about," Natasha said. She was dressed in her favorite Christmas sweater, the one Brad's father had bought for her when they had vacationed one winter in Augsburg, Germany. "Brad, I keep telling you, anything you set your mind to is possible. You did a good job. And Sam, I saw some pictures of you in that gown. Simply gorgeous my dear. Wish I could have been there."

"Thank you. I wish you could have been with us too. Actually, I wish we lived closer so we could see each other more often."

"Not to mention saving on the long distance calls, right." Brad's mom quipped with good humor.

"That's for sure."

"Here we go again," said Brad. "Taking advantage of me. Mom, how could you try to deceive me like that? Cooking that dinner for me long distance."

"I didn't cook it. Just gave her a few pointers, that's all. Son, if you're at all gullible, people are going to take advantage. And, Brad... you make a fairly good target." Natasha's last remark nearly brought down the crystal chandelier hanging from the foyer ceiling with laughter.

"Thanks mom, I needed that." Brad said giving her a second kiss on the cheek. "What a sense of timing. Not trying to change the subject. I think us guys should get the baggage out of the cars while we still feel like it. I know I won't later."

"I don't feel like it now," John playfully said. "That trip down that last road with the drop-offs and avalanches wore me out."

"I don't believe it," exclaimed Brad.

"What?"

"You had drop-offs and avalanches in your car too?"

"Phil brought it up."

"Phil, how could you scare 'em that way?"

"It appears I didn't do anything you didn't do," Phil replied laughing. "Let's get the baggage before we get into more trouble."

"So, all this avalanche stuff is... just a big joke, right?" asked Evan hopefully.

"It *wouldn't* be a big joke if they didn't create them on purpose." Brad's mother interjected.

"What's this on purpose stuff?" asked Evan.

"When there's been an uncommonly large amount of snowfall and they determine that there is indeed danger of an avalanche occurring, they block off the roads and cause one. They feel it's better to have one controlled than uncontrolled. It's really quite a sight to see," Natasha informed Evan. "They did it just last week and, on that very same road."

"I'd rather not see it, thanks. Film clips of one is as close as I ever want to be. I'm really not used to this country living you know. Even in New Zealand, except to go skiing, I didn't spend much time out of the big city."

"I remember, Evan," said Natasha.

"Okay you wilderness freak, let's go," broke in John.

"You boys go ahead. We girls will get the snack trays of sandwiches ready. I hope it's okay. I thought you might be a little hungry when you arrived. Brad, you're always hungry."

"Right, mom, I *am* hungry... as usual." Brad replied as he and the other three men went out to the Broncos to get the luggage.

"Does he always eat so much?" questioned Sam. "He has a stomach that's a bottomless pit when he's around me. It's like he has a hollow leg!"

"Always has eaten a lot. I don't know where he could possibly be putting it sometimes."

"We used to call him chipmunk." said Chantal.

"What?"

"Chipmunk. We have them all over the place out here in the summer months. They fill their cheeks with nuts and carry them off to a storage place for the winter. We thought he was doing the same thing with all the food he'd put away at the table each meal."

"Really. Oh my God, that's funny. Chipmunk." Sam repeated. "I'm going to remember that one."

"With Brad, any edge you have is well worth it."

It had taken about thirty minutes to stow away all the luggage in the appropriate rooms and they were seated together and conversing.

"Have you heard the news?" asked Brad's mother.

"News about what, mom?" asked Chantal.

"Just before you arrived, CNN had a breaking story about an airline crash."

"Didn't hear a thing about it, mom," replied Brad. "We didn't have the radios on during the drive up here from Denver. Where was the crash?"

"The plane went down someplace over Iowa."

"Any survivors?" questioned a concerned Phil.

"They'd just arrived at the scene and they claim everyone aboard was killed. The wreckage was scattered over miles out in the middle of nowhere."

"Damn, almost makes you not want to fly anymore. Where was the flight heading, mom?" asked Brad.

"According to the news, it originated at Dulles where your flight left from. It was going to Salt Lake City, and then on to Seattle."

"Damn shame," said John. "Do they know what the cause was?"

"No. And, according to the news, they will probably never know. Pieces of the wreckage are so small, it's doubtful they'll be able to reconstruct anything. The airline suspects a bomb. Maybe even terrorists!"

"Just like the airline. Don't blame it on mechanical problems or pilot error. Jump right to the conclusion that a terrorist bomb's at fault," John said almost derisively.

The rest of the evening was spent snacking on sandwiches and catching up on events which had happened since they'd last seen Brad's mother in New Market. She and Chantal had taken Terri, Abbey, Sam, Evan and John on a tour of the house, which was magnificently decorated. The round foyer, reaching over thirty feet in height, had a circular stair case on each side hugging the wall as it ascended to the second floor. The twenty foot high, live Noble Fir Christmas tree in its center, was decorated in a Victorian theme with countless silver icicles and lighted candles. The tree would be the newest addition to the grounds outside after the season. The garland, with its symmetrical loops, adorned both staircases and had wreaths spaced appropriately along its graceful lines. Sam was astonished to find there was also a circular staircase from the second floor of "this castle" to the third floor, where the master bedroom suite was privately tucked away. The staircase was normally used only as a last resort when the elevator was "on the blink".

Phil and Brad had retreated to the gardens of the atrium, situated next to the indoor heated pool, for a quiet drink while everyone else was on the tour. As if taboo to do so, neither brought up the events they'd promised to forget until after the first of the year. Rather, they chatted about their forthcoming holiday adventure which Brad said would involve a lot of skiing over a three day period. Shortly thereafter everyone, tired from the day of travel, retired for the evening.

*****

The climax of nine months of diligent planning was about to unfold in two days and the excitement wouldn't allow Brad to fall to sleep. He'd spent the past thirty minutes watching Sam as she slept and lightly kissing the skin on the nap of her neck. With his left arm around her, he began to lightly touch her with the fingertips of his right hand. He moved a wisp of hair away from her eyes and tenderly rubbed her cheek. His fingers slowly traced the outline of her chin and explored her neck. Barely touching her, his hand moved further to her breasts, gently moving in a circular motion. After a short time, her nipples began to harden so he knew she was becoming aroused. She rolled to her side and pressed them against his chest. "Brad, you horny devil," she said slowly. "What time is it?"

"I'm sorry, Sam. It's around 4:30."

"Don't be sorry, Brad. You have trouble getting to sleep too?"

"Yes, I guess I'm too excited about the next few days. And, with you laying here beside me, I couldn't keep my hands off you."

"Quite alright, big guy. I don't mind being woken up like this." She said, hugging him tightly and pressing her entire body against his.

"Sam?"

"What sweetheart?"

"Want to go swimming?"

"Swimming? Tell me your kidding?"

"Forget I brought it up," he said, clasping her firm, round buttocks in his hands and pulling her tight against his erection.

"Might be fun."

"What, Sam?"

"Swimming," she said becoming more aroused.

"Probably would be."

"Won't the water be too cold?"

"I checked it earlier when Phil and I were out there. It's 90 degrees. It's like bath water."

"I don't have a suit."

"Well, if you're going to let a little thing like that stop you, what can I say?"

"You want me to go nude?"

"I wouldn't have it any other way. Besides, I am."

"They'll hear us."

"No they won't. The pool is in a completely separate wing of the house. Just slip on your robe and I'll get a couple of towels."

"Okay, but I think you like to live too dangerously."

"Exciting, isn't it?"

The two tiptoed down the cascading staircase to the main level of the house moving as quietly as they could and trying not to giggle. The tile of the atrium was cold on their feet but, as they entered the sauna like atmosphere of the glass enclosed pool, they quickly forgot the cool floor. They peered through the clear roof of the structure surrounding the pool and noticed the snow had stopped and it had cleared. A near full moon cascaded its light all over them and created shadows at their feet off the panes supporting the glass panels. Most of the snow had long since blown off the roof and the moonlight provided all the brightness they'd need.

Sam quickly got in the mood of their romantic adventure, disrobed and revealed her tantalizing figure. She climbed onto the diving board and took three or four practice bounces to check its springiness. What the bouncing did to those 37's was something Brad would never forget. After removing the towel hanging from his lap, Brad entered the 90-degree water from the side of the pool until he was neck deep, and whispered, "The water's great."

Sam made a seemingly silent dive into the water and beneath its surface, swam to Brad, grabbed his erection and began massaging it. She then, in a slithering fashion, slid up his body, her wet, slippery breasts held tightly against him until her head broke the surface. Smiling in anticipation with water beading on her face, she said, "What's on your mind, mister?"

"I think you have a fairly good clue don't you?" he said, his hardness pressed against her.

"I certainly do," she responded, playfully beginning to swim away.

"Get back here," he said, grabbing her by her tiny waist and pulling her to his body. The lovemaking lasted only a few minutes, the warmth of the water adding to each of their desires. Afterwards, and although exhausted, they each decided to actually swim for awhile. They floated on their backs, looking through the glass enclosure towards the moon in the clear Colorado sky, with its reflected sunlight showering them with sparkling diamonds.

"Hard to believe that someone actually walked on that. And, before I was even born."

"July of 1969." Brad added. "Almost thirty years ago. And, still no God damn cure for cancer."

"Don't take it so personal, honey."

"I'm sorry sweetheart. Every time I think of that, I... can't believe it's possible. Walk on the moon thirty years ago and still can't solve the mystery of diseases that kill people by the hundreds of thousands. Somehow, it just doesn't seem right. Where is the justification in it. The main reason we went to the moon was political. Kennedy said we would do it by the end of the decade and, damn it, come hell or high water... we did. We beat the Russians to the moon. So what? All we proved was that we had the technology to do it. Nearly killed three astronauts on Apollo 13 going back. And what for, to pick up some more God damn rocks? Did they think that if they turned out to be valuable we were going to begin mining operations or something? All that money spent. Just to build the reputation of the United States in the global community."

"Brad, there were probably other reasons for the flights that you don't know about. Don't you think?"

"Probably so. It's just that I have my own thoughts about it. Probably prejudiced ones. I believe in fixing things on this planet first before going somewhere else to screw up another one. There is a lot to be fixed right here."

"I know. Think of all the poverty. What would the cost of one moon mission do for destitute people in this country? Quite a bit I'd imagine."

"You're right Sam. Quite a bit. And, you know the government has been overspending for years, not only in the space program but in other areas as well. The National debt is tremendous. They've mortgaged our futures... and our kids' futures too."

"Our kids? That's the first time you brought up kids. Do you realize, we've *never* discussed children or even a family?" Sam was no longer floating on her back. She was now standing in the shallow end of the pool with water dripping off her firm breasts.

"No, I didn't realize it, but you're right, we haven't," said Brad, now standing himself.

"How many children do you want?"

"Ahh... minimum of two. One boy and one girl. How about you?"

"That sounds like a good start point. We'll have those two first and then discuss more later on. Bradford Junior. J.R. sounds sorta nice, doesn't it?"

"I don't think so, Sam. Let's give the kids an identity all their own. Personally, I think that's important."

"I'll go along with that. Sounds reasonable enough to me," proclaimed Sam as the two hugged tightly, skin against skin.

They continued to lull around in the pool for a few more minutes talking quietly and finally decided to retire for the rest of the night. It was approaching six o'clock as they returned to the room. It took Sam a good half hour to dry her hair before sliding into bed beside her husband-to-be and his welcoming arms.

*****

Glancing at his solid, gold Rolex, he noticed it was 6:00 AM as the United Airlines flight lifted off from the Dulles runway in route to Denver. They were seated in the empty first class section of the L1011. People who could afford first class, didn't normally have to make flights at 6:00 AM. At least, they had some privacy. "This is a real pisser. What'd you tell your wife about where you were headin'?"

"Told her the truth. I'm going to Denver on business. Kind of makes me mad though, day before Christmas and all that. She wasn't very damn pleased about it either."

"You think she's pissed. Try hangin' around a fuckin' airport for about twenty-four hours and see how it effects your attitude. At least I don't have a damn wife makin' matters worse."

"I can see this is going to be one pleasant flight. How the heck are you going to make it through a non-smoking flight of over four hours?"

"Bought some of that damn nicotine gum shit. That's what I'm chewin' the hell out of right now. Also wearing a couple of patches on my arm."

"Christ. I thought that stuff was to help people quit, not pacify them until they could legally put another Cancer stick in their mouth."

"Whatever it's for, it's not workin' worth a plugged nickle for me. Damn it, I hate to fuckin' fly unless it's short hops. Shit, the flight I was supposed to be on to Barbados right now allows smokin'. I checked before I made the reservation."

"You would. I've got some more bad news for you."

"What?"

"You can't smoke in the terminal at Denver either."

"Like I really needed to hear that bullshit right now as jumpy as I am. I'm goin' to kill that son-of-bitch, Claxton."

"Hasn't that been the damn idea all along?"

"You fuckin' smart ass."

"Hey, I call 'em like I see 'em. As it turns out, according to the news, we could have flown American Airlines. The fireworks thing you built seemed to work okay."

"Was there ever any doubt? Let me out of here for a minute. I gotta take a leak."

"If you're thinking of grabbing a smoke in there, forget it. They've got alarms in the lavatories now."

"Shit!" he said, returning to his seat. "I'll kill the fucker!"

*****

The following morning, Sam and Brad woke to a soft medley of Christmas music being played over the intercom system. Realizing it was about ten o'clock, they hastily dressed and made a late appearance in the breakfast room to a round of applause. Somehow their skinny dipping episode had become common knowledge. How that particular cat was let out of the bag, neither Sam nor Brad pursued.

Later, in a one-on-one discussion, Phil informed him that Chantal couldn't sleep and around 4:30 woke and asked him to go swimming with her. They thought it would be kind of fun and decided to ask the other three couples to join them. The only problem was getting a response from Brad and Sam's room. Thinking they were too exhausted, the others proceeded to the pool, only to find it occupied by Brad and Sam, enjoying themselves in a manner which hadn't even entered their minds.

The new arrivals to the pool, "not dressed" for the activities that were taking place, decided it best to return to their respective rooms for the night. When Brad questioned what the other girls were wearing to go swimming, Phil said bras and bikini panties. Brad informed a laughing Phil that Sam didn't even own a bra.

Later in the afternoon, the eight of them had piled into the roominess of Natasha's Lincoln Town Car and taken a scenic drive throughout the surrounding area. They'd spent about three hours between shopping and getting a quick snack. Evan had approached near hysteria when, in daylight, he found Brad hadn't been kidding about the drop-offs. The views of the Rockies were simply astounding but at the same time a little harrowing. The seemingly endless, snow covered mountains set against the deep blue horizon presented a picturesque, almost serene feeling. They returned home shortly after dark, purposely waiting for the spectacular view of the Christmas lights to come on at dusk.

As they entered the house, Brad's mother told him that he'd received a phone call from Doc. It was so important, Doc was waiting at the Center for his return call. Dialing the unlisted number from memory, Brad waited for the answer.

"Brad." Doc's familiar voice questioned.

"How'd you know it was me?"

"Who else uses your private number boss?"

"No one... I hope. You're there kinda late aren't you? And, on Christmas Eve, yet. Must be pretty important. Whatcha got for me?"

"Two things. First, it turns out that Stockholm Tech *is* in fact owned by Swiss Tech. Stockholm Tech is strictly involved in vitamin research, natural cures, studies and the sort. The odd thing though, is that their *main* emphasis appears to be in marketing research. They're pretty widespread around the world, apparently on numerous contracts with a large number of facilities. They offer marketing strategy for products developed at all of these various locations on a consultant basis. Pretty much a top notch player from what I can tell. Is that what you wanted to know?"

"Yeah Doc, it is. Did you find out anything further on Swiss Technologies?"

"Only that they are a very large conglomerate, with divisions, as they're called, around the globe. Again, it appears that the main product is marketing research, not scientific research. Something strange though."

"What's that Doc?"

"As large as they are, it's very difficult to find any detailed information on them. Everything seems to be very general as if you're looking at a P. R. release on the company. Kinda strange, don't ya think?"

"Some companies want to do their research in private and don't want a lot of publicity. So they become very secretive."

"I understand that, Brad, but, if you were involved in marketing primarily and not research, wouldn't you want to market yourself first?"

"Point well taken, Doc. You mentioned that you had two things. Have we covered them both or not?"

"No. The second one I should probably talk to John about. The Chicago hacker is back."

"Shit! Let me put him on an extension." Covering the mouth piece of the phone, he yelled into the adjacent room, "John, pick up the extension in there. It's Doc."

After a few seconds, John said, "Doc, que pasa, mi hombre?"

"Only that the Chicago guy gained access this afternoon."

"Oh, is that all for Christ's sake! How'd the modem tracker do?"

"Worked like a charm. Unlisted number was retrieved. Passed right through the pay phone set-up like you said it would."

"So he down loaded a bunch of meaningless files?"

"Right."

"Did we receive anything as a result?

"Tons of shit."

"Yes!" said John yelling with excitement. "What's it look like?"

"Garbage."

"Probably coded. No problem, mon," replied John in his best Jamaican accent. Unless, it's a really sophisticated system."

"What do I do with this shit?"

"Get a hold of Joanna and tell her to run the data streams against program D1, D2 and D3 in that order. Tell her I'm sorry, I know it's the day before Christmas, but, I really need this done as soon as possible. I promise I'll make it up to her later."

"D1, D2, and D3 in order. Got it. What the hell are those programs?"

"Just something I put in the system in case we ran across enciphered data at some point. Tell her to dump the results into the H1 file. I can access that file from anyplace. Okay?"

"Roger, dodger. Dump to H1. Is that it?"

"As far as I'm concerned, Doc. You have anything else Brad?"

"Nothing. See you when you get back to DC, guys. Have a good Christmas. Bye."

"You have a good one too, Doc. See, ya," John said as he hung up.

As John entered the room, Brad asked, "what's this D1, D2 and D3 thing?"

"They're programs installed in the system to decrypt encoded data streams. No one even knows they exist except you and I and now Doc and Joanna. I didn't know if we would ever have a need for them, but, it appears we obviously do."

"Will they work?"

"Should. The three work simultaneously against the data. The design is there in the programs to break any cipher I've ever heard of, even random generated shit."

"Where'd they come from... or should I ask, seeing as how you did a stint with NSA?"

"These programs are of my own design since leaving NSA. They have a new technology base, completely different than anything used by the government. I should really copyright the damn things."

"Or, at least tell the government about them. Why would you think such a program was necessary or, that we would ever make use of it?"

"Have you forgotten that we've encrypted our own data base. Remember, we discussed it. We agreed that it was the thing to do with the way computer technology has advanced. *There's really an "information highway" out there*. Remember?"

"Yeah, I do."

"Brad, I only installed these programs to make certain the damn highway wasn't a one way road."

"Sounds fair to me. Not sure about how legal it is though. How long will it take to break it down?"

"Depends. If they've used a random, computer generated cipher system, our poor machine is going to work its ass off for quite some time. I'll know if it's completed when I access the H1."

"What's that?"

"The holding file the results are stored in. I can access it from any where in the world if I want. Even my lap top. If there's data there, it'll let me in, if not, it won't. That simple."

"Easy for you to say."

"That's what your paying me for."

"I guess so. It's certainly beyond my comprehension. This stuff, when and if you get into H1, will it be ahh... readable?"

"Should be in plaintext as they call it."

"Who is they?"

"Don't ask."

"Deal."

The two entered the dining room where dinner was just beginning to be served. From the aroma, Brad could surmise that it was fried chicken. He knew that both his mom and Sam would expect him to make a comparison for them after dinner. He'd already rehearsed his answer. Mom's cooking and Sam's were going to turn out to be identical in taste and appeal. That would satisfy both of them, somewhat but not completely.

The remainder of Christmas Eve was spent chatting and such. Brad's mother had pulled out the family album to show Sam some of Brad's earlier pictures. She particularly enjoyed the candid shot of him, at six months old, laying nude on a bed and remarked there hadn't been much change. The reference to his male appendage is what brought about the roar of laughter. To her shock, he said, "You didn't mention a problem in the pool last night." The laughter became even louder, with Sam hysterically exclaiming, "Touché".

The following day, Christmas, was one of those family days. Short strolls around the grounds of the estate. Looking for and finding wild deer in the surrounding area. Feeding the birds that remained to weather out the Colorado winter. Watching some football. Playing some cards. Eating dinner. Doing the dishes. And all of the time, remaining in the festive spirit with the sounds of Christmas being piped throughout the house from the complex sound system originally installed by Brad's father.

Conversations were spirited and all eight of them had taken a daily swim. Laughter prevailed. Gift giving. Attempts at singing Christmas Carols. Phone calls to relatives and friends. All of these things combined, made for a very tiring day, but the kind that one wished would never end.

As a group, they retired around midnight as Brad reminded them that they'd need a lot of rest because the next day the adventure would begin. Not wanting to alarm anyone, he never mentioned the helicopter which was picking them up at eleven AM.

He and Sam, both exhausted from a full day of activity, slowly undressed, not hugging until they were beneath the warmth of the bed covers. As if reborn, they each found the strength to fully satisfy one another once again. “Merry Christmas, Sam. I love you.”

“Merry Christmas, Chipmunk. I love you too.”

So tired, he could barely utter a sound, Brad said, “Ohhh noooo.”

At this point, they were both so fatigued, neither responded any further. They simply fell to sleep in each other's arms with smiles on their faces.

---- Chapter Twelve ----

"Mom, you didn't have to go to all this trouble," said Brad as he took a sip of steaming coffee. "This is a breakfast befitting a king. Pancakes, sausage patties, bacon, hash browns, eggs to order, toast and muffins. It's kinda like a Claxton family, Denny's Grand Slam."

"It isn't really that much work, considering all the help I'm getting from Samantha," replied Natasha.

Sam had helped with the preparation of the various items and decided she liked being in the kitchen. As he watched Sam work around the kitchen, she appeared very much at ease, and only one small problem had surfaced. Her eggs over easy had ended in disaster the first couple of attempts. She'd broken the yolks and overcooked them by several minutes. While Heinz waited anxiously by Sam's feet with his short, scrubby tail wagging furiously in anticipation of her failures, she'd placed them in his dish. With one look at the pancake-like eggs and a disappointed look on his multi-colored face, he'd slowly walked off and laid down near the fireplace, his favorite spot in the winter months.

"He must have ordered eggs benedict," said John as everyone tried to hold back their laughter.

"Heinz will never chase another *Frisbee* in his life," added Brad as he eyed the small, yellowish saucers in the bowl.

Sam took all the razzing in style as she broke the shell on yet another egg. She had finally realized, the order of, "eggs over easy," had a hidden, very important meaning. The egg was to be flipped easy, not like a bricklayer slinging mortar from his trowel.

"How are those my darling?" she asked as she slid them from the pan onto Brad's plate in front of him.

"Perfect, my sweet. I think your getting the hang of this cooking stuff and are going to make someone a wonderful wife one day."

They were all sitting, chatting, and taking their final sips of coffee which Brad made a point of keeping hot for the group. He was acting like a mother hen watching over her chicks. They were dressed in their skiing garb and each had packed appropriate changes of clothing in their backpacks keeping the weight to a minimum. Phil seized the opportunity and informed the others that Brad and Sam had a big advantage in holding the weight down because Sam didn't own a bra and wouldn't be packing one. Sam was laughing at the quip, so Brad felt she must have told Chantal at some point in time... he hoped.

All now heard the sound which was causing Heinz to bark. As the helicopter touched down in the fenced-in area, Brad looked at his watch and said, "Amazing, he's right on time." Peering out the back window to the source of the loud commotion they noticed a high wind causing the dry snow to blow furiously from the surface of the tandem set of tennis courts located a short distance from the house.

"Who is he and what the hell is that?" Evan questioned in shock.

"He's the pilot, and that's our ride."

"Our ride! You mean," Evan said and, after swallowing hard, continued, "we're going up in that thing?"

"Evan, where we're going... well, let me put it this way. I certainly wouldn't want to try to walk there. A chopper's the only way to go."

"I'm a little afraid of heights, you know."

"No, I didn't know. That's right, I remember now that you *weren't* with us two years ago for that bungee cord trip were you?"

"No, thank God."

"Hold on a damn minute, Evan. It was your idea for the Acapulco trip with the sky diving and parasailing."

"I know. I ahh... it scared the shit out of me. I think that's where this thing I.have with heights was really brought into focus."

"Christ man, you never said anything. It's too late now, buddy. You're going!"

"Maybe, I'll just stay here with Heinz. He likes me. Come here boy," Evan pleaded with the still barking dog. "Get the Frisbee out of your dish."

"No way. You're going even if we have to blindfold you. The flight's only about 30 minutes, maybe 35 tops. You can put up with that, can't you?"

"I guess I'll try it. I better go take a whiz before we leave," Evan said, trying to force a smile.

"Okay then. That's settled. Grab your ski equipment and your packs, people. As John would say, let's go for it."

*****

Natasha had just finished cleaning up from the breakfast and was near the telephone in the kitchen. She answered before the third ring. "Merry Christmas, Claxton Residence."

"Mrs. Claxton?"

"Yes."

"I'm sorry to bother you. Would Brad be there, please?"

"No, I'm sorry, he's not available. He left about a half hour ago."

"When will he return?"

"Not for three of four days."

"Oh, really. I thought he was spending the week with you."

"Well, he is and he isn't."

"How so?"

"He and his friends just left on a skiing trip."

"Everyone go?"

"All eight. They seemed pretty excited."

"Did they go to Aspen or Vail? I'd like to catch up with him if I could."

"They didn't go to a resort. They went wilderness skiing."

"Wilderness skiing? What's that? I've never heard the term before."

"I may be wrong but, I think that's what he called it. A helicopter drops them off and then over a period of three days, they make their way to a pick-up point."

"Cross country?"

"As I understand it, it's cross country, but not on cross country skis."

"How's that possible?"

"I have no idea. My son spent a lot of time planning this thing though."

"Where'd they get dropped off?"

"Like I said, I don't know that much about it. From what I overheard this morning, its somewhere about 30 or 35 minutes from here. I don't even know where they're being picked up. Bradford made all the plans. May I say who called?" Hearing a sound like she'd been disconnected, Natasha asked, "Hello, are you there? Hello?" With no response, she hung up the wall mounted phone. If he wanted more information, he'd call back.

*****

"You heard it all over the speaker phone, right?"

"I heard it. Think she's tellin' the truth?"

"Why wouldn't she be?"

"Maybe, he told her not to say anything even if she knew."

"Why would he tell her not to say anything. He left all his suspicions in DC. What do you want to do, send someone out to her place and beat the shit out of her to make sure?"

"No, you're right. She's got no reason to be lyin'.

So, they went out in the middle of nowhere skiing for three days. All eight of them. This may be perfect. Lots of things can happen in the middle of nowhere."

Looking at his Rolex, he said. "She said they left about a half hour ago. That means wherever they headin', they should just about be there. How do we find out where they fuckin' went?"

"I'll get hold of Lambert," he said, dialing the number.

"Who?"

"Robert Lambert. He's the head pilot out here. Been flying in this area for years. I talked to him earlier and told him to be on standby."

"Hello. Lambert here," came the response.

"Bob?"

"Yeah. Need a ride?"

"Afraid so. Got a little hunting trip to go on. The quicker you can pick us up out front the better? They've got a half hour head start."

"Where we heading?"

"Not really sure, but a thirty minute flight from the Claxton estate. You know the area a hell of a lot better than I do. They're doing some kinda cross country skiing over the next three days. You have any ideas?"

"That cocky little bastard will want a virgin."

"What the hell are you talking about?"

"A virgin, man. A mountain that's never been touched before. You know, never been skied. That leaves only one area within range of a thirty minute flight time. I think I have his ass already pegged for you."

"Great! Let's get hopping on this."

"Gotcha. Give me fifteen minutes and I'll see you out front. How many going?"

"Only two on this end."

"Any skis this time out? Don't have 'em with us right now. With luck, we won't need any."

"See ya in fifteen."

"I thought he'd know where they might be. Let's get our stuff together."

"I'm a tad fuckin' confused here about something. How are we goin' to do any fuckin' thing without our skis."

"Hopefully, we'll catch them above the tree line or out in the open. It's worth a chance, and besides, the most important thing right now is to find their asses. According to his mother, we've got three days to come up with a way to handle it once we do. We might just get lucky today."

"I was kind of hopin' to see that asshole Claxton face to face. He's the one that's caused all this shit. I wanted him to *know* it was comin' and *see* from who."

"Christ, George. What the hell's with you? He's become a damn obsession with you now."

"It has become kinda fuckin' personal. The bastard's lucked out three damn times and, what really pisses me off is, that the dumb fuck doesn't even know how lucky he's been."

"Don't let it get to you so much. You'll make a mistake."

"Don't worry about that shit. He's the problem and I'm the solution. I know what I'm doin'. He won't even know what the hell hit him if I get the chance."

*****

As the pilot lifted off, they turned their backs and ducked their heads to escape the blast of icy-cold wind and snow. Then in silence, they watched the chopper fly off in the distance and out of sight. With the exception of Brad, an uncomfortable thought entered their minds. They were alone out in the Rockies and, at least seven of them, didn't have the foggiest notion where they might be.

During the flight, Brad had outfitted each with light-weight outer wear for additional protection from the elements. The pull-over tops were loose fitting and slid over the backpacks of clothing and essentials that the guys were toting. The collars of the tops unzipped and held a hood which could be tightened with draw strings. The pants had a number of zippered pockets in which to place items for easy access.

When asked why everyone was now dressed completely in white making it difficult for them to be seen in case of a problem, Brad had given them the simple answer. It was the only color available when he'd called to place the order for the gear. John had jokingly said that they looked like a camouflaged, winter patrol from the Norwegian army.

Opening one pocket of his white pants, Brad pulled out a map and explained, as a precaution, there was one in each of the other suits. With the others making a circle around him, Brad pointed to the map and stated, "That's where we are." Moving his finger and stopping, he added, "and, that's where we're going. That's where we're going to be picked up in three days."

"That's at least 50 miles from here," exclaimed Chantal. "It's pretty rugged terrain, Brad!"

"Sis, it's closer to 75 miles. *Don't* worry folks. I've spent nine months planning the route, and it's really, quite simple. Everything's been arranged. You're all going to enjoy the hell out of this. Trust me."

Abbey did a quick 360 looking out towards the horizon. "Brad, I don't see anything, anywhere. It's so... so remote," she said groping for the right word. "We're going to be out here for three days and cross all that?" she stammered as she pointed.

"Abbey, whose idea was it to insist the girls accompany the guys on these yearly trips? You didn't have anything to do with all that did you?" he asked showing signs of a smile.

"Believe me, Brad, it was all Chantal's idea."

"Abbey, *you* can't blame me completely for that. I handled Phil. I didn't do the pressure work on John. You said *you'd* handle him. Well, you did and here we are, right where we *thought* we wanted to be. Looking around, I'm not so sure."

"It's real nice to know I've been handled," said Phil.

"Likewise," commented John.

Laughing and trying to set their minds at ease, Brad said, "Settle down everyone. Everything's under control. Believe me."

"Brad," Phil said slowly and continued. "You know, it isn't all downhill for seventy-five miles. How do we...?"

Interrupting, Brad said, "People, people, people! Let's not get over concerned here. You think I'd put any of you in danger. Let me explain everything first. Then ask the questions, if there are any when I'm through. Phil, in answer to your unfinished question. Transportation has been provided. Look here on the map," he said pointing again. "The first day, you ski from point S1A, where we are, to location T1B. The letter "T" designates transportation. From T1B, you go to S1C. From S1C, you ski to T1DF, and so forth, throughout the route."

"What kind of transportation?" asked Evan, a little concern in his voice.

"Not helicopters Evan," replied Brad seeing the relief in Evan's face. "Snowmobiles."

"Ohh," shouted Sam. "I've always wanted to do that. What does the "F" mean there beside the T1DF?"

"Food at the location." Brad responded and continued. "Let me explain the four characters. The first character is always an S, meaning ski from, or T meaning transport from. The second character is either a 1, a 2, or a 3, depicting the day. The third character, is an alphabetical progression by day, showing the order in which things are done, A, then B, then C and so forth The last character is always either blank, F, or C. The letter F equates to food, and the letter C equates to camp for the night which has food also."

"Christ Brad, you really did put a lot of thought into this thing didn't you?" said John. "I should have brought my lap top along to store all this shit."

"It's really not *that* difficult to follow, John. I don't think I've left anything out. We're going to enjoy the best three days of skiing anyone could hope for."

"I have another question, Brad," said Sam with her arm in the air. "Where are all the trees?"

"Sam, they're down there," he said laughing. "We're above the tree line here, probably 14,000 feet. I told you that you hadn't seen any real mountains in North Carolina."

"Evan's buddy, Heinz, would go nuts up here looking for something to lift his leg on." John said, laughing.

Terri was turning slowly and looking off in the distance with her hand held above her eyes to shield the bright sun. "It's kind of eerie. We seem so small and insignificant when you take in the whole picture from here."

"You can say that again. I don't see a damn thing except a lot of mountains and a hell of a lot of snow," said Abbey, turning in a slow circle and taking a long hard look. "I hope you're accurate on your maps, Brad."

"Don't worry, they're very accurate."

"I don't know about everyone else, but I, personally, am looking forward to this," Phil said. Brad, you've outdone yourself on this one, pal. I can see why it took you nine months to put this trip together."

With her eyes hidden behind tinted goggles and beginning to tear, Samantha said, "Think how close I came to not even being on this trip or knowing you all. I can't believe I've only known you guys for about two months. Somehow, it feels longer than that."

"Honey, good things do happen to people. I know, because, *you* happened to me," Brad said, bending to give her a quick kiss.

"Enough of this mushy shit," said John. "I'm ready. Let's go for it," he yelled, his echo repeating his call to the wild. "Which way?"

"Thataway," replied Brad, pointing to the rim of the summit. "It appears that all of you are more at ease with this adventure I've planned. There are a few surprises along the way, if we have the time, that I'm sure you will enjoy."

All eight, now in a row at the edge, peered down and across the enormity of the treeless bowl. They agreed on a point 350 yards away, maybe even 400, where they would meet. Each pair of skiers entered the bowl, selected their own route and began cutting paths diagonally across the virgin snow. As Brad and Sam began their decent, he realized how difficult it was to see the other three couples. Their white outerwear blended in with the powder snow and in the brightness of the overhead sun, even the fresh trails of their skies were nearly invisible. If John had not been yelling the entire time with his excited style of skiing, it felt almost as if he and Sam were alone, on top of the world.

With Sam following, they gained speed and stayed away from the areas where prevailing winds would dump the most snow. They coasted as high onto the sides of the bowl as their speed would allow and then, renewed the procedure. After their last run through the bowl, they approached the other six who were waiting.

"You guys learn anything about bowl skiing?" Brad asked as he and Sam came to a sliding stop.

"Yeah. I sure did after seeing you and Sam. Basically, stay away from the waist deep stuff, if you can. It slows you down too much. You two got a lot more skiing in back there than we did," said Evan.

"Right," replied Brad. "Anyone want to try it again?"

"Love to," said Abbey, "but, how are we going to get back up that?" she said pointing up to the summit.

"I'm sure not going to try and walk it carrying these skies," added Chantal. "I don't think I could make it."

"Me either," said Sam looking back up the mountain.

"Don't worry," replied Brad, "we don't have to climb it. See that red flag over to your right?"

"What the hell's that?" asked Phil.

"That's extra transportation not on the maps. It's one of the surprises I was talking about in case we had time to make second runs and, I think we have the time. Don't you?"

"All right," shouted John in his normal fashion, "let's go for it."

Sliding slowly up to the flag, Brad grabbed hold of it and pulled back the attached tarpaulin covering the four snow mobiles. "There's enough time to play on these awhile before we return to the summit. Only if you want to, that is!"

That's all the four girls had to hear and demanded to be the drivers. "That's fine." Evan said, holding up both hands in defeat. "You girls get used to 'em, while we laugh our asses off. I'm not getting on the back of the damn thing until I know Terri can handle it."

"Me either," the other three men said in unison.

"Stay away from the deep snow. You'll get stuck if you don't." Brad shouted over the roar of the engines as the girls departed. Nodding that they'd heard him, the four took off on their playful excursion like they were trying to win the pole position at the Daytona 500. They actually, did quite well. No one fell off, got stuck or, more importantly, ran into anyone. After about 15 or 20 minutes, when the four guys felt they would have at least a fifty-fifty chance of survival as passengers, Brad grabbed the red flag and waved it. The girls returned 15 minutes later, all with large smiles and claiming they didn't see him waving the flag at first.

The four couples made their way back to the summit with their skis strapped to the sides of the snowmobiles and parked the sporty vehicles to one side for pickup the following morning. The couples then proceeded to make their final runs through the enormous bowl with Sam and Brad providing the lead. Hooping and hollering, they were trail-blazing into an area that quite possibly had never been skied before. Robert Lambert was right. It *was* a virgin.

At the completion of the second run, nearly two hours into their adventure of a life time, it became overcast due to the arrival of a weather front from the west. With a light snow falling and no longer above the tree line, they made their way further down the mountain towards T1B, the first transportation location. All had stopped to take a final glance back up the mountain from which they had zig-zagged their ways downward.

"That's quite a sight," said Phil, "the only tracks in all of that snow are ours."

"Even that real wide one up there on the left, where you fell and slid about 50 yards." John said, laughing.

"Your turn *will* come smart ass," shot back Phil. "Brad, *this* is going to be a trip to remember. How the hell did you *come up* with this idea?"

"When I was in high school... eons ago, my friends and I used to come up to this area in the summer months. We used to camp out all over this area. Of course my parents never knew. I don't even think Chantal knew, did you?"

"No, and, if Daddy had ever found out, he'd have kicked your you know what, every-which-way but sideways. This *is* pretty remote out here Brad. He wouldn't have been too pleased."

"I know he wouldn't have been, sis. Anyway, I've always dreamed of seeing this area in the winter and skiing it. I must say, covered in five or six feet of snow, it certainly looks different. It's more beautiful, though, somehow. I decided over a year ago to merge my dream, somehow, into my choice for the trip this year."

"I can't speak for all the girls, Brad, but this being the first year women got to come along with all of you macho men, your choice has certainly made an impression on me." Terri said, rearranging her red hair under the knit ski cap. "I'm having a terrific time. Looks like you've left nothing to chance so far."

"I was about to say what Terri just did, but, at least, I can second it." Abbey said.

"Me to." Echoed Sam and Chantal.

"Thanks girls." Brad responded. "By the way. Do all of you see that smear in the snow up there on the right side?" With all agreeing, he continued. "That, happens to be exactly where John fell on his ass and thought no one saw him."

"Thanks for that, Brad, I owe you one," said John, the only one of the eight not laughing.

"Everyone, listen for a minute," instructed Evan holding up his hand for quiet.

After a short pause, Chantal said, "I don't hear anything. Wait a minute. Yes I do. What is that?"

"I can't really tell, but it sounds like it's getting closer," Sam responded.

Recognizing the now unmistakable noise of a helicopter, Evan exclaimed, "I think it's that damn chopper coming back."

"Sounds like one but, he wasn't supposed to come back 'til tomorrow to pick up the snowmobiles. Must've changed his mind."

Before Brad could continue, the helicopter passed them at tree-top height, about 100 yards to their left. It proceeded up to the summit and hovered, blowing the loose powder snow into wisps of white clouds. Although traveling quite fast, Brad knew it wasn't the one that had brought them to their destination a little over two hours ago. It was the wrong color and much smaller.

"Brad, did you say you had some binoculars with you?" Sam asked.

"Yeah, honey, they're in my back pack." Brad said, mesmerized by the hovering craft. "Why?"

"Let me have them for a second. I want to take a closer look up there. I think I noticed something but, I want to take another look."

"Okay, but you're going to have to get them out."

Lifting Brad's white jacket in the back, she unzipped the backpack and pulled out the binoculars from one side. On her first attempt to look up the mountain, she found she hadn't removed the lens covers. "Shoot," she said, hurrying to take them off. She slowly brought the hovering craft into focus and finally saw what she'd thought she did as it had sped by them at tree-top level. "Brad, take a look through these," she insisted.

Taking the binoculars Sam was holding out to him, he noticed concern on her face. "What's wrong?"

"Look," she repeated, almost ordering him.

Scanning the activity on the summit, Brad saw the chopper hovering and facing down the mountain, as if looking at him. Slowly, the craft drifted to its right nearly 90 degrees, until the unmistakable, large black oval with white lettering, was entirely visible. "Ohhhhh shit." Brad said softly. "You saw that when it zoomed by?"

"I thought so, but wanted to be sure."

"Saw what?" questioned nearly everyone else.

"I'm not sure yet, but, there's a good chance we might be in some kinda deep shit." Still looking up the slope, Brad continued. "Phil. John. I think our friends are back."

As he continued to watch, the chopper landed and two men, each wearing ski masks and toting what looked like weapons slung over their shoulders jumped from its side door. They ran, as best they could in the deep snow, to the rim of the bowl and looked down the mountain at the various trails the four couples had created. Finally, the larger of the two men pointed in the direction of the location where Brad and his friends were standing. The two men then turned and ran quickly back towards the chopper.

"People, do me and yourself a hell of a big favor! Do exactly what I say and don't waste time asking a lot of questions. Put your hoods over your heads. Take your skies and boots off and put them on the ground in front of you."

"Brad, what the hell is..."

"Evan, do it! We've only got a few seconds! I think that chopper is going to come looking for us and I don't really think we want to be found."

"Evan, he's right, do what he says!" instructed Phil.

Brad hurriedly continued shouting instructions. "Pull your pant's legs down far enough to cover your feet. I don't want any color visible from the air." Looking over his shoulder, he saw the chopper airborne and moving down the route they'd taken. "Here they come! Quickly! Lay face down on your skies and boots. It the tips of your skis are showing, sweep snow over them. Guys, check out the girls. Sam, honey, you okay?" Brad asked excitedly with concern growing in his voice.

"I'm fine so far, Brad. You'd better get your stuff covered."

Taking a final look over his shoulder and before turning his face towards the cold snow, Brad noticed the chopper was moving slowly because of density of the trees. Brad hoped the foliage the trees provided above their heads would hide them from the searching eyes. "Bury your gloved hands in the snow!" Brad shouted to all, "and no movement. These guys are going to have binoculars too."

The engine noise grew louder as the rotors began to softly blow the loose snow around him. Brad guessed it was no further than fifty yards to his right but, that's what he'd hoped for. If their tracks were visible from above the trees, the chopper would've been directly overhead and not fifty or sixty yards away. The pilot was searching for signs of people that he couldn't see, thanks to Brad's quick thinking. The sound from the engine was abating now as the chopper moving slowly down the mountain and away from the four couples.

As Brad lifted his head slightly for a better view, the unforgettable sound of automatic weapons fire rang out. He'd been holding Sam's gloved hand beneath the snow and noticed her grip tighten at the sound, a grim reminder of the New York City incident in front of the boutique.

Straining his eyes, he looked for any movement from the vicinity of where the shots had been fired. "They can't see us now," he said, noticing the others slowly beginning to look up. In the same breath, Brad yelled, "Look out!"

No sooner had Brad mustered the warning than a group of deer, two bucks and eight or nine doe, came crashing though the underbrush. Ears pinned back, they ran at full speed, jumped directly over the four couples and disappeared into the trees. "Christ, they scared me more than the damn helicopter," shouted John.

Beginning to laugh, Evan said. "Brad, you're really something, man. Planning shit like this to scare the hell out of us. One of your surprises along the way. What a guy! How the hell you got the deer to cooperate, I'll never know, but, it sure had a damn good effect. I know, they just kinda happened along, weren't part of the plan, right?"

"*Look*," said Brad, his goggles raised.

Now in a kneeling position, everyone turned to look where Brad was pointing. The tracks of the frightened deer revealed that at least two, maybe as many as four, were wounded and trailing blood.

Evan continued as his smiles and laughter abruptly faded. "Tell me this is really part of your planned three-day adventure. Jokes on us, right?"

"I wish I *could* say it was a joke. Unfortunately... I can't. Sorry, Evan."

"*Christ, you're not kidding, are you*? Is *everyone* else here as much in the dark about what the hell's going on as I am?"

"Well... Sam, Phil and John know about as much as I do. I don't know how much Abbey and Chantal have been told."

"Nothing," they answered in unison.

"Brad, if this is something the four of you have planned to scare the hell out of the rest of us, it's worked. Now, though, is the time to come clean and admit to the little prank you've dreamed up," said Chantal.

"Amen to that," chimed in Abbey. "John, this kind of stuff isn't funny. I hope you realize..."

"Abbey, I hate to say it, but, this little event *wasn't* planned."

"This *crap* is for real," exclaimed Terri, her face showing her immediate concern. "Ohh my God. What are we going to do?" she asked, inching towards Evan and his outspread arms.

"Brad, if all this is for real, Terri has a very good question," said Chantal. "What *are* we going to do?"

Dropping the binoculars from his eyes and letting them dangle from the strap around his neck, Brad rose to his feet. With the snow falling much harder now, the others stood beside him and silently waited for an answer. "Chantal, I'm going to say this once and *only* once. This was *not* some devious plan of mine to scare anyone. You honestly believe, I would have someone either kill or wound wild deer to make some stupid plan of mine look good? You know I'm not that kind of person, sis."

"I know, Brad. I'm sorry. I'd completely forgotten about the deer. I know you wouldn't."

"Sis... all of us for that matter. I think the best thing we can do right now is get the hell out of this area as quickly as possible. I don't think they'll be coming back soon because the weather is changing but, you never know for sure. Shit, I didn't expect anyone to show up in the first place. The chopper pilot, unless he's completely nuts, won't want to hang around with the weather deteriorating this quickly. I couldn't really tell for certain, how many got out up on the summit. If they're equipped with skies, they're more than likely waiting for word to start down the mountain."

"For what?" asked Evan.

"To ahh... find and get rid of us."

"*Get rid of us*! For what reason? And, by the way, *who* the hell are they?"

"I have absolutely no idea as to the reason, but, I've got a pretty damn good idea of who they're associated with. Evan, we *have* to get moving. I'll explain everything that Phil, John, Sam and I know later when we're safe and have more time, I promise."

"Sounds like one hell of a good idea to me. Let's hit it," John said, not yelling as he normally would.

"Good, let me lead," said Brad. "I want to get to the transportation waiting for us as fast as possible and begin to climb the next mountain. Anyone following us on skies won't be able to once we're on the snowmobiles and going up hill. Be as quiet as possible so we can listen for that damn chopper. We'll stay in pretty dense stuff for cover so let's do the rest of the descent in single file."

"At least one thing worked out pretty well."

"What's that Phil?" Brad questioned.

"This outerwear you provided us with, thank God they only had white. They probably would have spotted any other color from the air. Where'd you get the idea to lay on top of the skies to hide them?"

"I really don't know. It was the only thing I could think of to hide everything we had."

"Pretty quick thinker, Brad. I'm glad you did," Phil concluded, the other six nodding in agreement.

"Brad, before we leave, one thing. You realize, no one is blaming you for any of this, don't you buddy?" John asked, the others concurring with his words by shaking their heads.

"I think so and I appreciate the words. Somehow though, I can't help but feel responsible."

"One other thing. I want to trail everyone else."

"Why?"

"I want to tie some pine boughs around my ski boots and drag them behind me to help cover our tracks."

"Good idea, John. Another quick thinker. Let's get you set up with the branches."

After putting their ski boots on and snapping them into the bindings of the skis, they continued on down the mountain. They said very little on the descent as their skies glided silently over the snow. They stopped about 300 yards from where the snowmobiles were parked and Brad, indicating for all to be quiet, whispered, "On the way here, I had some thoughts. I kept asking myself, how'd they know where we'd be? They couldn't have found out from our pilot because he doesn't even know our plans. A different guy is picking us up. Regardless, they found us and, for right now, we have to assume they might know our entire route for this three-day adventure or whatever you'd prefer to call it now."

"Try three days of fear and agonizing torture," interjected Evan, also whispering.

"I agree, Evan, I'm sorry. The only thing we can do is use everything each of us has to offer to get through this. I honestly believe the only information they were cognizant of was a general area. They weren't certain where we'd be and were searching for us. Of course, that damn red flag we put alongside of the snowmobiles on the summit probably helped them a tad in their search. You know, we're a pretty damn smart group of people. Collectively, if we put our minds to it, we'll be okay. I feel strongly about that."

"You got it El Capitan," said John, his thumb raised in an upward direction. The other six gave the same sign, a quick, Siskell and Ebert two thumbs up, and a nod of their heads in approval. Brad even thought he noticed a smile and some color returning to Terri's face.

Inwardly smiling at the response, Brad continued. "In that case listen, I've thought a lot about all this shit as we were skiing down to this point. They flew to the summit and tried to track us from above rather than tracking us on skis because they, simply, don't have skis with them. If they knew our route, they wouldn't have gone to the summit at all unless they were trying to speed up our descent to a location planned for an ambush and the best place for that would be the first transportation spot, about 300 yards further down. I'm going to circle around and approach the parking area from behind to check it out."

"By yourself," whispered Samantha.

"I'll be okay, hon. It'll go quicker if I'm alone. If they're there, I'll return and we'll figure something else out. I'm *damn* sure not going to take 'em on. While I'm gone, one of you pull out your map and be working on some options. If the snowmobile area is okay, I'll start one and that'll be your signal to ski on down towards the sound. It's going to take me some time to accomplish this, especially if I have to return so, give me quite a while. It's snowing like hell now so, the tracks we left behind are pretty much covered, especially with John dragging those branches. Any questions?"

"Don't we need some kinda signal that it's safe to go down other than engine noise. What if the engine noise is one of the other guys startin' one?" questioned Abbey.

"John, you have a pretty smart wife there, you know?"

"Shit, I guess I do. That's why I married her ya know, not for the sex, for her brains. I never thought of that. What if you were to... give the old Morse Code, SOS, Brad. You could rev the engine, you know. Three longs, three shorts, and three more longs."

"Sounds like a good idea. After it starts, I'll let the engine warm a bit, then do the code. Any other questions?"

"Only one," Sam broke in, "you're going to be careful aren't you?"

"You already know the answer to that. Of course I'm going to be careful." Brad said hugging her tightly. "I'm looking forward to spring in Charleston too much not to be." He hugged her again, gave her a quick departing kiss, and skied off in a direction that would skirt the parking area.

It had taken Brad nearly 35 minutes to position himself on the other side of the snowmobiles and begin his quiet descent. His mind kept drifting back to Sam and what a woman she was. Even with the loose-fitting, white outerwear, it was evident she had a figure any woman would kill for. Funny choice of words thought Brad considering the present circumstances.

Sam had said, "Be careful." Shit, he was being so careful, he could hardly believe it himself. He took off his skies, lay flat on his stomach and slithered, snake-like, down the final 100 yards as the slickness of the outerwear against the dry snow made the chore almost easy. He took quick glances, left and right, for any signs of activity and was so quiet he'd even scared the shit out of a rabbit scourging for something to eat. It wasn't a one way street, Brad discovered, because the rabbit's sudden darting from the underbrush had caused his heart to pound in his chest.

The only movement was falling snow, a slight swaying of snow laden tree branches in the soft breeze, a God damn rabbit, and finally, the flutter of a red flag. Everything looked positive and untouched. He cautiously approached the flag in full awareness of everything around him and removed the tarp. What a sight he thought, eight snowmobiles in tact, no one around, and visions of Sam skiing into his waiting arms.

Turning the ignition key, the engine roared to life and, sounding like a Honda 250 motorcross bike, beckoned the others to join him. After turning the hand grip throttle to mimic the agreed on signal, Brad sat down on the snowmobile in exhaustion. The strain of taking the round-a-bout route and the anxiety of not knowing what was waiting for him had taken its toll.

Less than ten minutes had passed when, only a short distance away, maybe twenty yards, Brad noticed movement coming towards him. Looking between the trees he saw seven skiers in single file entering the small clearing where he was resting. Phil was in the lead, followed by Chantal, Abbey, Terri, and Sam. Evan and John brought up the rear, a short distance behind. They slid to a stop and formed a semi-circle around Brad, who was just standing. He walked the couple of steps to a smiling Sam and gave her a very tight hug.

"It's amazing, in those white suits, I didn't even see you guys until you were right there by that split tree," Brad said pointing.

"That close?" asked Phil in disbelief. "That's less than thirty yards, closer to twenty, and virtually out in the open. I guess with the snow fall, we blended in pretty good."

"You sure did. If your face was covered, you'd be near invisible." Motioning with his hands, Brad continued. "Everything around here has been untouched. I think we're safe but I want to get moving to the next ski out point. We'll start up the way I came down so I can pick up my skies. Let's get these other machines started so we can move out."

"Where are you going, Brad?" Sam asked.

"To get the God damn red flag and bury it with the tarp. No sense in helping those bastards any more than we have to."

"I agree with that. Let me help you."

They covered the evidence and swept the area with branches to cover foot prints and began the climb, each aboard one-man snowmobiles. After picking up his skies and proceeding over half way up the next mountain, Brad was waved to a stop by those in single file behind him.

After shutting down the engines so they could talk in peace and quiet, Phil said, "Brad, while you were checking out the last location for us, we tried to come up with some ideas of how we could shorten this ahh... adventure."

"With the situation we've just gone through I, for one, am for ending this thing as soon as possible. I'm open for any suggestions."

"Why don't we simply take the snowmobiles from one transportation location to the next, and so forth, until we reach the pick up point. They'd have the range for that wouldn't they?"

"Good thinking," replied Brad. "But unfortunately, there are some problems in doing that which aren't shown on the maps you have. The only way to get from one side of these mountains to the other is up and over the top because the terrain on the sides is virtually impassable by snowmobile or, even skis."

"Shit. An insurmountable mountain you might say."

"You might say so. At least from two directions."

Evan, then added an additional thought. "And, come to think of it, so what if we arrive early at the pick up point. Our ride would never know we were there."

"I hadn't thought of that Evan. Good point." said Phil.

Continuing, Brad said, "and on top of that, we'd be waiting for about the next two days with no cover and nothing to eat since this morning."

"My eggs are sounding better and better," quipped Sam still seated on the snowmobile behind Brad's.

"At least some humor seems to be returning to the party," replied Brad. "Let's get moving. I want to be at the camp site well before dark. And besides, I *am* getting a little hungry, I don't know about anyone else."

*****

The rotor blades hadn't stopped turning before he was catching all kinds of hell. They walked quickly through the heavy snowfall and into the hangar's office.

"God *damn* it. Why would you start shooting at a bunch of deer?" Lambert asked grabbing him by the shirt.

"I didn't know they were deer. I saw the fuckin' movement and fired. I thought it was them. We tracked 'em right into the same area until the trees got so fuckin' thick you couldn't see shit. I saw the movement and fired. That simple!"

"Stupid damn move."

"Lambert, if you've got a fuckin' problem with the way I do things, we can discuss it later, alone if you want. For right now, stay outta my face, asshole." After firing up a cigarette, he continued. "And, don't ever grab me again, unless you've got a fuckin' death wish."

Separating the two men who were holding each other's shirts he shouted, "*Knock it off*! Both of you. Lambert, you're right, he *shouldn't* have fired, but, hell, I *almost* did the same thing. You have no idea how long we've been trying to settle up the score with this guy Claxton. Just over anxious, that's all."

"Over anxious? Shit! We don't even know if they were still in that area. They could've been out of there for a coupla hours."

"They weren't. They were damn close."

"How do you know that for sure?"

"You're the one that said Claxton would want virgin snow. How long do you think it would take eight people to make all the snowmobile and ski tracks we saw? There damn sure wasn't anyone else out there helping them. They screwed around in that bowl for well over an hour."

"I hadn't thought of that. You're right, they probably were close by. That makes it worse?"

"How so?"

"They probably heard the shots and realize that it's damn sure not deer-hunting season. Especially from a helicopter with automatic weapons."

He coughed up a bunch of phlegm and spit it into a stained napkin he pulled out from under an empty coffee cup on the desk and crushed his cigarette out on the floor. "Even if they heard it, I don't think they'd ever tie the fuckin' two together, or think anyone was tryin' to put their lights out. They'll think it was a bunch of fuckin' weekend warriors that get their rocks off by shootin' deer from a helicopter. Illegal as hell but, there aren't many cops in the area to enforce it. There *are* some *real crazy* bastards out there, you know?"

"I hadn't noticed," disgustingly replied Lambert.

"What you gettin' at Lambert?" he said reaching for his lighter and getting the drift of Lambert's last remark.

"I'm not telling you two again. *Knock it off*! We have to assume they've been alerted to something and proceed accordingly. They aren't stupid. Lambert, I want you to get out your maps again and see if you can determine which way they might be headed. Hand me that phone number we took off the snowmobile on top of the mountain. I'm going to give that rental place a call and see what they have to say. And you," he said, watching him light his second cigarette in less than ten minutes, "better cut that shit out and prepare yourself for some heavy skiing tomorrow."

"You ever tried to out-ski a nine millimeter?"

"That cough you have doesn't sound real good. Those damn cancer sticks are going to be the death of you yet. You'd better be up to it tomorrow."

"What the fuck are they goin' to do, have a God damn snowball fight with us? I'm ready."

*****

He stood up from the table and began to pace back and forth on the pine plank flooring while draining his wine glass. He slowly proceeded to the half empty decanter, scratched the back of his head, refilled his glass, as much puzzled about the situation as anyone else, maybe more so, and returned to where the others were seated. "Damn Brad, what the hell did you do to piss off those guys so much?" questioned Evan. "In the past hour or so, you've brought us up to date and I think we *all* believe we're in a bit of a pickle, but, why would anyone want to knock us off? Did you butt-in line in the supermarket or something?" questioned Evan jokingly but still with a somber expression as took his seat next to Terri.

"In answer to your first question, Evan, I don't know of anything I did to anyone even associated with Swiss Technologies. Hell, until this shit began hitting the fan, I didn't even know they existed. I have absolutely no idea why they'd be after me. They are probably after the rest of you guys because of your association with me. To answer your second question, things could be better, but, if we proceed with the same kind of caution as we did getting here, we should be okay," replied Brad.

The eight were finally feeling a little more at ease and were trying to relax in the comfort of an old hunter's cabin while they mulled over what was going on and what to do about it. Earlier, they'd quickly and carefully proceeded up and over two additional mountains of Brad's planned route and to prevent being caught out in the open, they'd lined up just below tree line and made mad dashes up and over the treeless summits. Each time, they'd ridden the snowmobiles as far down the other sides as possible and hidden them from sight among the cover of dense trees. Finally they'd skied swiftly to the base of their third mountain of the day and entered the cover of the cabin.

The weather, with the sun falling to the horizon behind the cloud cover and mountains to the west, was becoming much colder. They'd left on their ski apparel and delayed lighting a fire for warmth until after dark when the tell tale trails of smoke wouldn't be visible. When safe, they'd built the fire and lighted the antique, wood-burning stove to cook the provisions with which the location had been stocked.

The cabin was constructed of a combination of rough sawed lumber and logs harvested from the dense woods nearby. Its interior consisted basically of one large room with the kitchen area at one end and the natural rock fireplace at the other. There was a make-shift ladder rising to a loft area for additional sleeping space. It wasn't designed for comfort but, rather as a shelter from the elements for those using it during the various hunting seasons. The furniture, of which there was little, was worn and not very comfortable, but, the people who frequented the cabin didn't expect plush-cushioned sofas or LazyBoys.

Thick Porterhouse steaks, potatoes, other vegetables, foot-long loaves of sour dough bread and a choice red wine or Coors, the beer of the Rockies, was the cuisine for the evening. All had seated themselves on the floor in front of the roaring fire to eat instead of on the wobbly benches placed around the uneven, bare wooden table. The warmth of the fire, somehow, made them feel more secure.

"I'm confident they don't know the route we'll be taking," Brad continued, "so, if we continue being careful, we *should* be able to proceed point to point like we've been doing."

"All we've seem to have accomplished here is to bring up a million unanswerable questions," stated Phil. "We don't even have enough answers to form any theories."

"I'll go along with that," remarked Chantal and added. "Brad, we don't even know *who* these people *are* or *what they want*. Maybe, they *are* just a bunch of crazies shooting deer from the air. Way out here in the middle of nowhere, who's going to tell them they can't?"

"Sis, I hope you're right but, this black oval with white lettering logo, or whatever it is, has surfaced too many times recently to suit me. For right now, I'm going to assume it's Swiss Technologies. Damn, I wish the hell I knew what that company was into. Sis, I don't think it's coincidence."

"Me either," interjected Sam. "We've been seeing that thing everywhere. After today, I'll probably see it in my sleep."

Abnormally quiet for some time, John said, "the first thing we should do when we get out of here is find me a computer and a modem. I think all the answers we *don't* have are in that H1 file back at the Center in DC."

"Maybe, we should contact the authorities too," suggested Abbey. "They should be able to help us out with this."

"I don't know hon, if that's a good idea," said John with this hand rubbing his chin and slowly shaking his head.

"Why not?"

"Who do we contact and what proof do we have about anything. We saw... no, let me change that. We heard someone shooting automatic weapons. We saw a helicopter fly over and we saw some wounded deer run by."

"I think you're right, John," added Samantha. "We can't prove they even shot the deer, let alone that they thought the deer were us."

"Personally," said Brad, "I'm for *not* contacting the authorities right now at all. They may not believe us and even if they did, like Sam said, what would they be able to do. There's no proof. Besides, what authorities do we contact? The police forces don't have any jurisdiction out here so it would have to be the County Sheriff of the State Troopers. I wouldn't give you two cents for their investigative proficiency. Frankly, the only two guys in a position of authority I'd consider trusting right now would be Abe Cannelli and Ben Butterfield back in DC."

"I think I have to go along with Brad on this one," said Phil. "The authorities aren't going to be able to do anything so, the only thing we'll accomplish is letting these nut cases know that we're on to them and where we are."

"I'll second that," said Evan. "I don't think we want them knowing our exact where-abouts. As long as they don't know where we are, they can't put any real muscle on us."

Continuing, Phil said, "I think we should concentrate on getting the heck out of these mountains in one piece and finding a computer for John to do his thing. Until then, we should lay low. Not even contact anyone after we get out. They may have access to our phone lines, who the hell can tell with today's technology?"

"Phil, mom's going to be pretty upset if we don't contact her," said Chantal.

"Sis, she probably will be. But, I think Phil's got a point. The less these guys know about where we are the better, for now anyway. She'll realize there must be a good reason for us not calling. Besides, I don't think its gonna take more than an additional day to find some answers. How about you, John?"

"One day should be plenty of time to get the file and take a look at it," he assured everyone.

"It looks like we're all in agreement then. Remember, we don't do anything unless all of us agree." Brad reinforced his words as he counted eight raised thumbs. "Good, I think we should hit the sack. We want to be up and done with the fireplace and stove before dawn. Besides, I want to be on top of the next peak as early as possible. I want to see if there's any activity on the peaks where we dropped the snowmobiles for pickup."

"That'll give us some time to take a good look at how we want to approach the locations for tomorrow. We don't want to leave anything to chance," John concluded.

"Amen to that," added Evan with Terri's concurrence. "You've been awfully quiet, Terri," he concluded.

"It's just... I don't know how to deal with stuff like this. I guess my approach is to just to sit back and listen until I hear something that I *really* don't agree with and nothing's come up so far," she said lowering her thumb and taking Evan's hand in hers. "If you don't mind, Evan and I will take the first watch. I don't think I'd be able to get any sleep right now, anyways."

The other six drained their wine glasses or took their final sips of Coors before climbing into the dual sleeping bags the cabin had been outfitted with for their one night stay. Falling asleep, they watched the flickering light of the fire reflect against the cabin's corrugated tin ceiling and wondered what the morning would bring.

---- Chapter Thirteen ----

The following morning Brad woke with a little stiffness in his muscles and wasn't certain as to the source of his discomfort, but, it was probably due to holding Sam unusually tight throughout the night in their sleeping bag. Under different circumstances, it would have been a great time.

Not knowing what the day might bring, the girls had prepared a large breakfast. At Chantal's suggestion, they'd sorted through the extra clothing from the four back-packs and combined only the necessities into one. In one of the three remaining packs, Chantal had stored any left-over provisions that were edible and wouldn't spoil. The other two packs had been used to store other essentials confiscated from the cabin such as candles, matches, small segments of rope, some tools and flashlights. The dual sleeping bags had been rolled as tightly as possible and rigged so they could be carried while skiing or side saddle on snowmobiles.

As they stepped outside into the early morning darkness and frigid temperatures they noticed the weather had cleared and there was only a slight wind from the west. The fires in the cabin had long been extinguished so, there wasn't any smoke drifting easterly. *The change in the weather was bad news,* thought Brad. *Flying would now be possible.*

"What the hell are those?" asked Evan pointing to some tracks in the fresh snowfall.

"Looks like we've had a visitor during the night. I didn't notice 'em yesterday," replied Phil.

"Me either," said Brad. "Looks like mountain lion tracks to me. What do you think Phil?"

"Probably, and a pretty good-sized one from the looks of the prints."

"Mountain lion! What the heck is he doing around here this time of year?" questioned a very much concerned Evan. "I thought those damn things slept all winter. Look, those tracks lead right up to the damn door of the cabin!"

"Bears do sleep in the winter, but mountain lions don't, Evan," said Brad beginning to smile.

"Can you imagine opening up the door and seeing that big cat staring back at you?"

"Evan, you'd probably give the poor thing a heart attack," Terri said trying to calm him down. "Besides, he's probably just investigating the activity at the cabin because, until we got here, it's probably been pretty quiet around here."

"Or, looking for something to eat," added John.

"John, the only reason you said that was to get under Evan's skin," piped in Abbey. "Stop it."

"Okay. Terri's probably right, Evan. Remember, we're invading his domain, not the reverse. He's probably just curious."

"Damn. Helicopters, automatic weapons, people chasing us, and *now*, mountain lions. Brad, is this adventure of yours going to have any more surprises?" asked Evan.

"I don't know, but, I sure hope not."

"Look at it this way, Evan," said Sam. "You could be back in DC, bored to death. Poor choice of words. Sorry."

"I think that's enough chitchat folks. It's beginning to get light so we'd best be moving it out," said Brad. "We want to be on top of the next mountain as soon as possible."

"Lead the way," said John, "I, for one, am anxious to get this over with as soon as possible."

"I think we all are," added Samantha as she gave Brad a quick kiss, moved to her snowmobile and cranked it into operation.

Brad made sure all the machines were started and then began to lead the single-file train of machines up to the summit.

*****

"I know two thirds of this country speaks German, but, you know what? I don't give a rat's ass if the entire country speaks it. Speak English damn it!" The majority in this room, *now*, understands English best, so speak it!" He rose quickly from his chair, violently grabbed the easel holding the latest corporate profit and loss figures and threw it into one corner of the spacious conference room nearly knocking over the half full pot of steaming coffee. Then, he proceeded to one of the windows, spread the blinds for a better view and looked outside. He noticed that the waters of the Aare River were hidden from view by the snow covered ice. In the distance, the vista of the surrounding Alpine scenery was broken by the steeple of the Bern Cathedral.

Roof tops were heavily snow-covered from the storm that passed through the area during the night. It was, now, mid-afternoon and people were milling around on the streets below. He glanced at his watch and said, "It must be close to dawn in Colorado."

Another well dressed man with a full head of gray and white hair who had remained seated replied, "Probably is. Wonder how soon we'll hear something?"

"I hope it's better news than yesterday or I'd rather not hear anything," replied a third man as he stood up and stretched.

He turned from the window and looked at the five men still seated at the conference table and the lone man standing and stretching. "Fred, have a seat!" He cleared his throat and continued. "Gentlemen, it had better be good news or, I promise you as CEO of Swiss Technologies, heads are going to roll. And, quite frankly, I don't give a shit whose heads they are. If it has to be a board member sitting at this table, then so fucking be it. You six guys *each* have been given certain responsibilities that you're well aware of and I'm not talking about the *bullshit* we fed to that bunch of wimps who just left the corporate meeting a half an hour ago. Those assholes are so much in the dark they need a flashlight to find their dicks. I'm tired of excuses! All I want to see are some God damned positive results. Enough said about the Colorado thing. Fred, what's going on with the Capital Hill thing in DC?"

"Only one thing to report since the last meeting. Our guy was nominated Chairman of the War on Cancer sub-committee, as it's been so named."

"He was actually voted in?"

"Yeah, but only after the Senator from Montana was killed in a hunting accident."

"An accident hunting?"

"Yeah, well ahh... call it creative politics."

"Now that's what I like, some progress. Someone's thinking for a change. Then, everything is under control with our man providing the necessary steering currents to make sure the committee stays on *our* course?"

"Very much so. And, our lobby effort is ready and in full force if and when we need it."

"If they need some more cash, let us know through the normal channels."

"You got it."

"Let's move on," the CEO said as he paused to collect his thoughts. "How about the shit that's hitting the fan at the World Bank."

Another man, completely bald and looking much older than his 49 years, proudly grabbed a sheet of paper from his brief case and waved it slowly. "What I have hear, sir, is a copy of the denial letter that our guy had the bank issue to the Jakarta Lab. What is says is that additional loans at this time are impossible."

"Without funding, this lab has to shut down, right?"

"Within a month is the best estimate."

"Those damn Indonesians. If they can't borrow money, they don't have any of their own, which is fortunate for us. See gentlemen," the CEO boasted, "progress is possible. Any new business on the horizon?"

Another man, in his mid-fifties and dressed in a dashing wool tweed suit, began his report. "The only thing on the table right now is the company in Edinburgh, Scotland. We've already booked the flight to New Zealand to pick up what we need for the presentation. We leave in a couple of days and will be in Scotland the following day."

"They didn't buy the taped presentation?"

"I'm afraid not. They actually want to see it work in a lab. It doesn't present a big problem though. We've done it before and, to see it in a lab is very persuasive. They should be in the fold as a client the first or second week of January at the latest."

"Again, progress gentlemen. It appears the only area where we're lacking is this *damn* fiasco taking place in the states. Who's heading up the team in Colorado?"

"Our guy in the Virginia office, the one in the CIA, has personally taken responsibility for the outcome and flew out there. He's going to handle it from here on out."

"Was he a party to yesterday's screw up?"

"I can't really say, but he's assured me that the problems *will* be taken care of. He's given me his word."

"His *word* is good enough for you?"

"Has been in the past."

"For your sake, Albert, it *better* be! Meeting adjourned!"

*****

As he approached the hangar, he watched his breath hanging in the air and noticed that the cloudless sky to the east was beginning to reveal the orange glow of the rising sun. It was cold, damn cold. *Sixteen below zero,* the radio had said on his short drive to the airfield and the sun wasn't expected to add more than ten degrees of warmth during the day. As he entered the building, the thoughts of Barbados, the beach, ninety degree weather and palm trees blowing in the tradewinds returned to his mind. "I don't need this fuckin' shit," he muttered. "Today's the day Claxton, you son of a bitch."

Considering the constant blasts of cold air from the door opening and closing, the small space heater, laboring overtime in the office, had raised the interior temperature to a respectable fifty-five degrees. "It's about time you showed up. I was hoping to be airborne already," said Lambert.

"Damn car wouldn't start right away. Can't say as I fuckin' blame it though. Had a hard time gettin' started myself this morning. People shouldn't have to go out in below zero weather. This shit really sucks, man."

"Lambert, you'd better go out and get the chopper cranked up. The guy at the rental place said the snowmobiles were being picked up this morning for an afternoon rental. That means they're going to be picked up early and I want to talk to the guy getting 'em."

"Give me a couple minutes to get it warmed up. I've already got your skis loaded."

"How many are going with us on this venture?"

"Two others, both top-notch skiers and marksmen."

"I doubt we'll need them, but it's good to have some backup," he said as he watched Lambert slip on a replica of a World War II leather bomber jacket and his Ray Ban sunglasses.

After coughing violently, clearing his throat and hocking the result into a nearby wastebasket, he asked. "That's all the rental place said? Nothin' about any other fuckin' equipment they'd dropped off for this asshole's party?"

"Nada, not a damn word. That's why it's important we don't miss this character."

*****

Somewhat at ease because he felt the people from yesterday's fiasco didn't know the route he and his friends would be taking, Brad still approached the apex of S2A alone as a precaution. He was standing and doing a very slow 360 degree turn with the binoculars buried in his eyes. After carefully surveying the surrounding terrain and finding no apparent problems, he drove to the edge and motioned for his waiting companions to join him. Then, he returned to where he had been standing and began looking, towards the peak where they'd been dropped the day before.

With the sound of the approaching snowmobiles in his ears, he noticed a helicopter approaching the peak and appeared to be the correct chopper that was to pick up the snowmobiles. At least, this one had no black oval insignia on its side. With a watchful eye, Brad continued to view the other peak as everyone pulled up.

“Anything going on over there, pal?” Phil asked.

“Nothing unusual. The chopper is there to retrieve the snowmobiles we left on the summit. Everything looks cool to me. Kind of a relief.”

“I'll say,” said Terri in agreement. “I don't know if I could put up with more tension like we went through yesterday.”

“You know something, Brad?” questioned Evan. “If it weren't for all this... extra-curricular activity, a person could really enjoy a trip like this.”

“I agree,” said Abbey. “Without all this... unasked for crap... I'd be really enjoying this. Maybe, they decided to leave us the hell alone.”

“Yeah, maybe she's right,” suggested Sam. “They, like we were saying last night, might realize there's nothing to prove any of what happened yesterday. They could just leave us alone and... deny everything if it ever came up.”

“I hope you're right, but, I think... that might be a lot to hope for, Sam,” replied Brad. “If they were willing to do that today... why did they start this shit yesterday at all. Why not just leave us alone to begin with?”

“That makes sense to me Brad.” John said. “I don't think we should let our guard down for a second.”

“I agree,” said Chantal. “I don't want to take any chances with guys that shoot from a moving helicopter. I think we should proceed, very carefully, the entire way... until we are totally out of this mess.”

“My big concern, right this second, is to get somewhere that has a computer. I really do want a chance to retrieve that H1 file,” John said.

"These bastards have really perked my interest. I'll bet we are going to find a bunch of shit to shed some light on the question of "why". Hopefully we will also find out more about the question of "who" as well."

Pulling out a second pair of binoculars borrowed from the hunter's shack, Phil began to peer towards the other peak. Brad had only seconds before dropped his to his side to turn and talk to everyone. "Brad," Phil said, trying to get his attention. "Brad," Phil repeated much louder.

"What?" he responded turning towards his brother-in-law.

"Something's going on. There is a second chopper setting down."

Raising his binoculars to his eyes, the two stood watching the activity, playing out in front of them. The second chopper was nearly the same size as far as they could tell. Maybe, they needed two to transport all the snowmobiles. Brad was not sure how many were used to deliver them or if possibly more than one trip had been made by a single chopper.

"What's going on you two? Don't just watch... say something. We... do have a slight interest in the activity also."

"Sorry Sis. It's not the same helicopter that gave us all the trouble yesterday, if that's any relief. I can't see its side for any logo because its facing me but it's larger and a different color."

"Of course it's a relief Brad. I was... merely wondering if we were... going to have to start running for our lives again. That's all."

"Ohhh, I know what's going on. It's probably another chopper to pick up the machines we hid on the other side of the second mountain. He probably can't find them and flew over to find out what the hell was going on. That could be good for us folks. At least, someone friendly is aware that something strange is going on."

"You're probably right, Brad. The second one is airborne again and looks like it's heading to the second peak. Wait. Now it's hovering a distance away and... what the hell is that?" questioned Phil, seeing a trail of smoke from the second chopper quickly approaching the craft remaining on the summit.

"Shit!" yelled Brad, seconds before the sound of the explosion reached their ears. "The bastards just blew the other one up."

"What?" was the general outburst from the listeners.

"The second chopper fired something at the one on the ground and blew the damn thing up! A missile or something. Look, you can see the smoke rising from the peak... even without binoculars."

"Christ All Mighty, pal. I don't think these guys are going to give up. They're damn serious. We better be moving out of here."

"Go ahead, Phil. Get everyone off this peak and to the tree line on the other side. I'm going to hang out here for a couple of seconds and see where they head. That'll help us know if they've found out our route."

"Let me stay this time."

"I appreciate the offer, Phil, but it has to be me. Whether they fly directly here or perform a search and end up here, I want to be able to lead them on a wild goose chase. I'm the only one that knows these mountains at all and how to get from one place to the other without taking a direct route. You get everyone out of here, hide the snowmobiles and proceed to the next point on the map, T2B. Remember, approach it with caution."

"Gotcha, pal. Good luck. See ya down the hill."

Walking over to Sam, who was still sitting on her snowmobile, Brad said with a smile, "Don't say it, I already know. Be careful. And, again, I promise. I will... because I wouldn't miss Charleston for anything. Love you Sam," Brad said giving her a parting kiss.

"Love you back... you crazy fool," replied Sam.

Brad turned away from the single file progression of his wife to be, his sister, his brother-in-law and his friends and began his watchful vigilance of the now departing second helicopter. He had made the decision that if it flew directly at him he was going to proceed directly towards it in full visibility. Seeing him, he hoped, would divert attention from the other seven, giving them more time for an escape. As it turned out, the chopper proceeded down through the bowl over the tree line, in the direction they'd taken yesterday. Good news so far. They probably did not know the route or they would have flown directly to this peak, or at least directly to the point at the bottom where he was to meet everyone later.

Continuing to view its activity, Brad noticed the chopper flying to another peak, one not even on their route. *Fantastic news,* he thought. He then realized, they were probably checking above tree line for any signs of activity from which they could pick up the actual pursuit. Because of yesterday's snowfall, the one he was on would be the only one which had any tell-tale signs. Not good news! Eventually, given enough time, they were going to get to this one. That was worse news. What the hell to do? Too late to try and cover the tracks of the snowmobiles. What could he do?

Brad kept watch for the helicopter as he criss-crossed the crown of the mountain in numerous directions, making certain that each crossing made an entry into the tree line. They were going to know there had been activity here, but, at least, they wouldn't know which way it had come from or was headed, he thought smiling. How many passes Brad had made up and over the apex of the mountain he wasn't sure. He had lost count at fifteen and on his final one, he realized the mess he had created for anyone trying to follow.

Returning to his vantage point on the top, Brad once again raised the binoculars to his eyes and began to scan the distant peaks. There it was, just lifting off and proceeding in his direction. It was time to get to the tree line and set up the false trail. Brad selected a route to the side of the mountain somewhat familiar to him from his high school camping days. Further down, this side was not passable on a snowmobile and would be barely so on skis. Brad figured with all the years of skiing he had under his belt, he had a better than average chance to navigate the rocky decline.

He took up position on the edge of the tree line, his skis now securely clamped to his boots. He'd left the snowmobile where it would be visible to draw their attention away from the route the others had taken. The chopper was setting down and furiously blowing the dry snow into clouds. Two men wearing ski masks, jumped out, began to survey the numerous tracks Brad had left in the snow's surface and threw up their arms in confusion. The plan was working. They had automatic weapons draped over their shoulders and, from the way they walked, Brad knew they were wearing ski boots. Brad's heart pounded in his chest as he realized a chase was imminent and he had no weapon. They spotted the snowmobile, turned and ran hurriedly towards the chopper waving their arms and were handed their skis through the chopper's open door. Brad quickly departed the area purposely leaving the keys in the snowmobile's ignition.

If one of the men were lazy, Brad felt they'd crank up the snowmobile for the pursuit. Besides, it would prevent them from having to climb back to the summit on foot. If Brad was right in his thinking, it would also reduce them to one person following him on skis, rather than two. The skier would be first, being able to maneuver much easier as he tracked Brad through the dense trees. The one riding, would be further behind, having to go slower.

*****

"There's only one fuckin' machine here and only one skier leavin' the area. Look at the tracks," he stated in disbelief.

"I'm not blind, I see the tracks! The others must have taken a different route. I wonder who this loner is."

"Two fuckin' guesses and the first one doesn't count. Messin' up the top with all those tracks and leavin' this machine in plain site. Shit, this is *Claxton's* work and that's whose tracks were lookin' at," he concluded as he threw the Camel to the ground and watched it sink slowly out of sight as it melted the snow.

"I think you're right. Let's head over to the other side and take a look for more tracks."

"The only tracks I'm interested in are starin' me right in the face. They're the ones I'm gonna follow."

"George, you're not using common sense. It's obvious he's leading us away from the others. I think we should head the other way."

"Without Claxton dead, you might as well forget the other seven. He's got a knack for survival, like a cat with nine lives, and our chances of pickin' up his trail later will be impossible. I say we get rid of his ass before we lose him and can't find him again. The other seven, without him taggin' along, won't be that hard to find. To me, lookin' for seven is easier than lookin' for one. Especially when the one is. luckier than a fuckin' two time Lotto winner."

"You may have a point."

"Damn right I have a point. Look, I think the dumb fuck's luck has just about run out. He left the damn keys in the ignition."

"Don't count on it. He's not stupid. He left the keys there for a reason," he replied trying to comprehend Brad's actions.

"I don't agree with you. He's runnin' scared now and just plain fuckin' forgot 'em. He knows we're goin' to be after his ass. By the way, an ass that's mine, remember? You crank up this thing and follow me down the mountain. It'll save us a walk back up after I blow his ass away," he said patting his nine millimeter automatic.

"You forgetting something? He skied for the US Team you know. You're never going to be able to catch up with him."

"Don't worry, I'll catch him. He has to pick his way through that shit down there," he said pointing to the dense trees and underbrush. All I have to do is follow the route he picks. I'll be movin' faster than he is. Besides, I'm five years younger than you and have always been the better skier. Just bring this machine down as far as you can so I don't have to walk back up this fuckin' mountain."

"Have it your way George. Just be careful. You never know what that guy might be up to."

"Like I said in the hangar. What the hell is he going to do, throw snowballs. The next time you see me, Claxton will be fuckin' history."

*****

Brad had proceeded a couple hundred yards when he heard the snowmobile being started. *Dumb ass,* he thought smiling, they fell for it. Now he had to find a way to get rid of the skier. Picking up speed, he began looking for a site along his route that would serve the purpose. After about five minutes, Brad made a small jump off a rocky ledge to a soft landing in a clearing, disappeared into the foliage about thirty feet and came to an abrupt halt. This was the perfect set-up he thought as he took off his skis. He back tracked around the perimeter of the clearing so no tracks would be evident and took up a position under the lip of the ledge.

Brad heard the sound of the snowmobile off in the distance so glanced over the edge back up the mountain. There was the man on skis dressed in bright blue, moving rapidly through the trees and following his tracks. Brad positioned his back towards the lip of the ledge for leverage and placed one of his skis between his legs pointing skyward. Brad listened intently for the approaching skier with his eyes staring at the lip of the ledge. Then, he heard the groans of the man making the sharp turns Brad had left for him to follow and knew the man was approaching the jump. With his heart racing, Brad prepared himself, not even blinking, as he looked for the man's ski tips coming off the jump.

Seeing them, Brad quickly thrust the ski he was holding upward and heartily rammed it into the airborne skier's mid-section. It wasn't a strong blow that Brad delivered, but certainly one that had caught him directly in the solar plexus and had thrown the jumper off balance. As a result, the man had made a head first fall into the landing area and slid to a stop in a heap against a tree on the far side of the small clearing. Brad took full advantage of the situation as he moved quickly down the incline towards the man before he'd even stopped sliding. As he approached, he noticed the man wasn't moving. Closer examination revealed his unblinking eyes peering blankly through the ski mask in a horrified manner. His head was at a peculiar angle and he wasn't breathing. He'd obviously broken his neck in the fall. Feeling sick, Brad turned away and began to vomit and gasp for air.

Regaining his composure and realizing he was in a tenuous situation, Brad removed the man's ski mask and closed his staring eyes. To deaf ears, Brad said, "Tough shit, asshole. You shouldn't have blown up that helicopter on the other peak." As he continued to search the man's body, Brad recovered some clips of ammunition for the automatic weapon now slung over his own shoulder and quickly put them in his pocket. In another pocket, he found a half empty pack of Camels and an unused airline ticket to Barbados which he hurriedly threw to one side. Finding no identification and hearing the engine of the approaching snowmobile, Brad refitted his skis to his boots and proceeded further down the slope.

Brad had a good view of ledge as the second man on the snowmobile came to a slow stop. Peering down, he noticed his companion lying there and in a rage began to pound the hood of the vehicle. As the engine died, Brad could hear him screaming. He then put on his skis, made the jump effortlessly, slid further down the slope to the dead man and pulled something out from his own red ski jacket. Brad pulled out the binoculars for a better look. The man was talking into something and probably in contact with the chopper. The man then turned and looked further down the slope towards Brad's position viewing the tracks he had left.

As Brad adjusted the focus, the man's eyes peering in a hateful fashion through the ski mask, became very clear. *Weird*, thought Brad. Replacing the communication device back in his jacket, the man began to slowly pick up Brad's trail. *Well, he's not giving up,* thought Brad, *but why though, was he proceeding so slowly?* He'd probably noticed the weapon missing and was in no hurry to ski into an ambush. He was merely going to continue tracking me and keep the chopper informed so he could increase his odds. Brad's mind was racing. *This shit has to stop. I can't continue to dodge this guy forever so somehow, I have to stop him. Shit, I don't even know how to fire this weapon.* Brad formulated another plan in his mind and quickly skied away down the mountain to find another ideal spot.

*****

“It's final, Chantal,” said a determined Phil. “I'm heading back to see if I can help your brother. I didn't like the idea of his being out there alone to begin with.”

“But, he said he'd catch up with us later and you don't even know where he is. You'll probably get lost out there.”

“I'm not going to get lost Chantal. I'm going to follow the clearing for these power lines for awhile and see what I can come up with. Besides, if I go away from the clearing I can always follow my own tracks back to this point.”

“Someone else could follow your tracks back here also,” she said in a last ditch effort to convince her husband.

“Chantal, Phil's right,” interjected Evan. “Brad may be in trouble. They know we've separated and he's on his own. They're obviously not following us for the moment so Brad's plan to lead them away is working. They wouldn't be expecting anyone else to show up. They think they're following one person so if Phil could meet up with Brad, it might give him an advantage he needs.”

“You're probably right,” replied Chantal as she reluctantly gave in.

“We've agreed that I am the logical choice for this excursion. Evan, we've decided, isn't exactly a wilderness freak and is of more use here; and, John has to stay out of trouble so he can do his thing with the computer and the H1 file when he ever gets the chance. You have the maps to show you the route for the rest of the day. We'll leave Brad's snowmobile here and pick it up later when he and I get back. We shouldn't leave the key in the ignition though, we should hide it in case the wrong people show up. I don't want them getting a free ride up this mountain.”

“Good idea,” said Samantha. “I know the perfect place. And, Phil, when you find Brad, tell him how much I love him.”

“Samantha, he already knows, besides, you can tell him tonight.”

“Be careful and don't take any unnecessary chances,” said Terri.

“Same goes for me,” echoed John.

“Thanks everyone. And John, stay alive buddy so you can do your thing when you get the chance.”

"I"m planning on it. See you tonight."

Phil slowly maneuvered his snowmobile into position and proceeded down one side of the clearing for the erector-set-structures supporting the high voltage wires. The other six watched until he was out of sight and with John's order to "Saddle up," they proceeded to climb the next mountain.

*****

With the weapon draped over his shoulder, Brad was nearly finished with his preparation. He looked at the automatic carefully and hoped he would never have to rely on his expertise with it. He hated guns and all the death they represented. He felt confident he could fire it if necessary, but, whether he could hit anything was totally another question.

Brad had already secured some branches and larger rocks to his pair of skis. The purpose was two-fold. First, they had to remain parallel and second, there had to be enough weight to make them continue on course further down the slope. The setting was perfect. There had been a small, man-made clearing across the mountain. The area, about thirty yards wide, had been cleared for structures which supported the high voltage lines strung high overhead. There was about a 45 degree incline at this point which would allow the unattended skis to slide across effortlessly, leaving the tell-tale tracks. They hopefully would enter the trees on the other side far enough to be out of sight before getting hung up. As he watched them slide out of sight, Brad let out a sigh of relief.

He then, used branches to sweep the area making certain only the tracks of the skis remained visible. Behind some cover provided by the remnants of trees discarded by the clearing operation Brad dug an area in the snow about two or three feet deep and scattered the snow removed around the area to cover his activity. With his white hood pulled over his head and ready to pull some covering branches over him, he waited for the tracker, remembering the hateful, leering eyes. He had decided, if possible, to get some answers from this bastard.

About ten minutes passed when he saw the red jacket moving silently along. He was being very cautious to make certain that he was not ambushed. About ten yards from where Brad was kneeling, the man stopped as he noticed the clearing. Thinking he was safe, he continued to follow the tracks of Brad's weighted skis to the edge of the clearing and focused his eyes on the far side for any movement.

Brad slowly, holding his breath the entire time in fear, got to his feet from his hiding position. The snow he had pulled over him fell harmlessly to the ground without noise. As he approached the tracker from the rear, Brad yelled, "Hey, Hank!!"

As the man turned, the weird eyes reflected his surprise. Brad swung the automatic and caught him in the stomach causing him to bend over in pain. The second blow from Brad to the back of his head, put him out of his pain, an enthusiastic Brad realized. Brad rolled him over, removed the ski mask and realized his yell had been correct. "He would never forget those eyes," is what he had told John, and apparently, he hadn't. It was the infamous Colonel Harold Dickey who Phil had introduced him to at the New Zealand Embassy gala. *When this asshole comes around, he's going to have some questions put to him,* thought Brad.

Brad, was wondering though, after the question and answer session, what the hell was he going to do with Hank. Still pondering this question, Brad heard a slight moan, making him aware that this disgrace to the US Air Force uniform was finally regaining consciousness. He had taken his weapon as well and had it pointed at the man when his eyes opened.

"Who the hell are you?" questioned a bewildered Colonel Dickey.

"Short memory, blurred vision or just a hell of a headache?" shot back Brad in a loud voice as he removed the hood from his head.

"Brad Claxton. Jesus Christ. I can't believe the two of us have been taken out by the likes of you... a God damn Boy Scout... at best. Where the hell did you come up with all this savvy?"

"Let's just say that... when your life is in danger, you come up with something. Let's also get one thing straight from the beginning. I'm the one holding the weapon and therefore, I'm the one that's going to be asking the questions from now on. While you were taking your cat nap, I thought of a list longer than your God damn leg that I need answers to. By the way, Hank... how are you enjoying your ski trip so far. Havin' any fun yet?"

"Mister tough guy. And what if I choose not to answer?"

"That's another question, dip shit." Brad informed him, striking the Colonel across his mouth. "Can't say I didn't warn you. You have, Hank, kind of... caught me in a foul mood so to speak. Don't take it personal."

Wiping the blood from his lip, Hank said. "You know Brad, you're starting to piss me off a little. Playing Mr. Tough Guy and all this shit. You have no idea what you... and your pals are involved in. There's no use in trying to avoid... what's going to happen to all of you. You'll never get out of these mountains alive, you smart ass little bastard."

"Let's put it this way... Hank. Right now it appears my chances, as remote as you might think them to be, are a whole lot better than yours, you dumb ass... wouldn't you agree or haven't you noticed?" Brad responded shoving the barrel of the automatic into his mouth. "And besides, what do you suggest we do... just lie down and let you and your buddies at the top of the hill knock us off?"

After the gun was removed from his mouth, Hank responded, "Kill me... if you can do it, Brad. I don't think you have the damn guts for this kind of stuff. I saw the spot where you puked up the mountain next to my brother."

"That was your brother up there that took the nasty fall?" asked Brad with the surprise evident on his face.

"It sure as hell was and for that, Claxton, you're going to pay. I can promise you that. There's a hell of a lot more where he came from. His whole green beret unit is on our payroll."

"Somehow, the fact that he was your brother doesn't seem to bother me in the slightest. And, I don't see any other members from his unit around. Now, back to the questions I want answered."

I'm dead anyway, if I answer your questions. Go ahead and shoot, you little prick. You're never getting out of this alive. We know where you are going to be picked up and there are only so many routes you can take from here to there. They'll find your butt and blow you away."

"If I'm the *little* prick, what the hell does that make you, the *big* one? You're the one on the ground with the God damn head-ache, stupid. If I'm going to die anyway, why wouldn't I finish your ass off? Why me? Why any of us for that matter? What the hell is Phil going to say when he finds out you're involved in all this killing shit. At the gala he even said you were there when he was born. What kind of a nut case would put the life of someone you care about, in jeopardy, let alone, killing him on purpose?"

"Phil is the only one I give a rat's ass about, but... all things have a price."

"The price being murdering a life-long friend to achieve some goals you have?"

"As always, people like you don't have the foggiest idea of what reality is."

"Enlighten me."

"For example, when I told you I was there when he was born. It's true. I was. I was also there when he was conceived. He's my son. How's that for a shot of reality, Brad?"

"Your son! Phil is your son? You sick bastard. That's bullshit."

"Not really. Although, it's still considered to be a rumor. Sybil, his mother, did have an affair with a cadet from the Air Force Academy. Me."

"You're lying. Shut your God damn mouth." Brad yelled in rage, striking him across the face again. "You're trying to get me to lose my concentration here and it's not going to work. You want me to believe you would kill your own son to better your own position."

"Others have done far worse than that to promote their well being. Believe me or not. I don't really give a shit. I'm just trying to tell you the type of thinking you're up against. You don't have a snowball's chance in hell, you idiot. I think you're in trouble now because I hear a snowmobile. That'll be my friends. What the hell are you going to do now, hot shot?"

"I'll think of something, I always have up to this point. For beginners, how about if I put your ass back to sleep for a while?" he said, striking Hank again, this time with a clenched fist and knocking him unconscious. *God damn that hurt my hand*, Brad thought as he scrambled for cover. *I should have used the damn gun.* As he released the safety on the automatic, he thought as he waited, *how in the hell could the word "safety" be associated with something as deadly as an automatic weapon?*

Once again hidden, Brad began to peer in the direction of the approaching engine noise. Odd, the noise seemed to be coming from his left and out in the clearing. There it was, slowly making its way along the edge of the clearing towards him. With his hood pulled back over his head and staying hidden as much as possible, Brad made his way to the edge of the clearing. When the snowmobile was within twenty feet, Brad darted into its path with the automatic in a ready to fire position. The rider made a quick dive off the machine, to his left and yelled, "Brad, it's me, pal."

"Phil, for Christ's sake man. I could have shot you. What the hell are you doing here?"

"Trying to see if I could help you in any way. We were crossing this clearing higher up around the other side of the mountain and we decided someone should follow it down to see if you were around anywhere."

"You mean this clearing goes around the mountain?"

"Yeah. It winds around and reaches pretty high up the mountain on the other side. It was a pretty easy jaunt down to here."

"These things weren't even here when I was in high school. You really shouldn't have come. I've had a pretty rough day and... am a little on edge right now. I could have blown you away by mistake, buddy."

"Speaking of blowing someone away. Where the hell did you get those things," he said referring to the two automatics. "Let me see one of them for a minute."

Brad handed the deep blue-gray automatic he had been aiming at Phil to him. "Couple of things I picked up along the way. I don't have a clue what kind it is."

Examining the gun, Phil said, "Looks like it holds about twenty rounds. I don't know what kind it is either but it's probably European manufactured. Man, this thing's *light* as hell" he said waving it around. "Pretty nasty little thing, isn't it. By the way, you couldn't have shot me. You don't have the safety off."

"Christ. Lucky for you. You know me. I don't know a whole hell of a lot about guns. I hate the damn things. You mean it has to be turned the other way?"

"Right, like this," said Phil showing him. "Where the hell did you get them?"

"One is from a guy who definitely had no further use for it. He's dead."

"You killed him?"

"Let's just say he took a nasty fall and leave it at that. The other one belongs to someone I want you to meet over here. Come on," Brad instructed, "follow me."

Upon entering the woods again, the two friends made their way back to where Hank was lying in the snow unconscious. As they approached him, Brad turned towards Phil and said with one hand held outward towards the Colonel, "Phil, I would like to introduce, Colonel Harold..."

"Look out," yelled Phil, shoving Brad to one side and raising the automatic. Brad heard a single shot as he felt a stinging sensation along his side. It was followed by a rapid succession of firing from the automatic Phil was holding. Turning again towards Phil, he noticed him standing there with the smoking barrel of the automatic still pointed at the Colonel. A quick glance towards Hank, revealed some holes in his red jacket and one in his throat. Phil moved cautiously towards him and felt for a pulse. "Sorry dad," he said softly, "but you really gave me no choice." He kicked the gun out of Dickey's hand.

"You knew then?" questioned Brad, walking slowly over and holding his side where the whiteness of his jacket was now blood stained.

"That he was my... my biological father?"

"Yeah."

"Yeah, I knew."

"Damn. He just told me a few minutes before you arrived. I thought he was lying. Phil, I'm sorry. I... had to... kind of put him out. I didn't know it was you coming and didn't really know what else to do."

"Brad, you did what you had to do. Just like I did. Don't feel a damn bit guilty about it. Mom told me years ago. She wanted me to know in case of hereditary diseases and such things with getting married to Chantal. Malcomb... my *real* dad... doesn't know though. She wanted me to know so that I would be nice to him if he were ever around," he said pointing to the man he'd just killed. "Their affair broke off right after she found out she was pregnant with me. He left the area on another assignment with the Air Force, but kept showing up in our lives for some damn reason."

"God damn, buddy. I'm sorry. What a damn rotten thing to have happen. Even under the circumstances, killing..."

"I appreciate your concern, Brad. But, my father, the only one that means a damn thing to me, is still very much alive in Colorado Springs. This guy... for some reason, I never found it easy to be around him. He didn't know that I knew the truth, but, still... he knew and was never much more than... someone I put up with because of mom. He never... really tried to get to know me... at all."

"His loss, buddy."

"I'd appreciate it if we kept this between ourselves."

"I'd like to Phil, but, the others have a right to know he was involved in this shit up to his ass."

"I realize that, Brad. I meant the fact that he was my biological father. I don't think Chantal could take news like that very well."

"Nor Sam for that matter. Consider it between us buddy. By the way, did the Colonel have a brother?"

"Yeah, as a matter of fact, he did have a younger brother. I think his name was George Dickey. Why do you ask?"

"I believe your biological uncle is back up the mountain with a broken neck."

"Is *that* who you got the first weapon from?" asked a startled Phil.

"Yeah, why?"

"Jesus, Brad. You don't have any idea who you were dealing with do you?"

"Your talking like I should've been concerned."

"That, my friend, is one *hell* of an understatement."

"You've perked my interest. Who the hell is... or rather was George Dickey?"

"He was only an ex-Green Beret. And, a damn good one according to Harold."

"If he was so good, Phil, how come he's an ex? Seems to me that he'd still be in the service."

"Brad, pal. The only reason he left the service was because there wasn't enough action to suit him. He loved to blow up shit and kill people so he became a mercenary contracting himself out to the highest bidder. He supposedly was an embarrassment to the Colonel, because it didn't matter what the job was, legal or not."

"Damn," said a shaky Brad. "I guess I was pretty lucky up there, Phil It appears though, that the Colonel wasn't as upset with his brother's activities as he let on to you. They were both trying to put some serious hurt on us not to mention the chopper on the other peak that they blew up. Well buddy, I'm sorry this has turned out like it has for you."

"Thanks Brad. How are you doing there?" said Phil, noticing Brad's side.

"Just a small nick. Looks worse than it is. By the way, thanks for saving my life."

"The least I could do after what you've been through the last hour or so."

"What are we... umm... going to do with him."

"Brad, I know you feel... uneasy," Phil said, searching for the correct word, "about what just happened, but, try not to. He, along with the people he worked for created the problem. I don't think it's our responsibility to make a decision of... what to do with his body. We have other things to worry about... like making sure we don't end up like him. Speaking of choppers, there is still one left for us to be concerned about. We have to... just leave him here."

"You're probably right. He was talking to someone with a communication device of some sort. Shit, maybe we could use it to call for some help."

Phil draped the nearby ski mask over the face of his father and began to search through his clothing. From one pocket, he pulled a communicator which had been riddled by one of the bullets entering his body. Holding it up for Brad to see, he said, "Won't be able to use this damn thing."

"See if he has any refills."

"What?"

"Refills or whatever they are called. You know, more bullets."

"Christ, pal, you really don't know much about guns do you. They're called clips. Here's four of them," he said extracting them from another pocket of the blood soaked jacket.

"I got four of them off the other guy also. Must be standard issue for these bastards," said Brad. Thinking of what he had just called Phil's late father, he continued, "Sorry, Phil. Didn't really mean to call him a bastard."

"Brad, as long as I've known you, you've always called them like you see them. I don't think just because he was my father that you should change. Quite frankly... he was a bastard... a ruthless rat bastard. Shit, man, he did try to kill us you know."

"I just kind of feel weird about this whole damn thing."

"Don't, pal," ordered Phil. "We'd better be headin' out of here to join up with the rest. Someone's waiting for you. I think we both can fit on the snowmobile.

"Sure is going to beat the hell out of walking like I was going to have to do until you showed your ugly face. We better get moving before that damn chopper on the top comes down to check on things."

The two moved back into the clearing and boarded the snowmobile. Phil was slowly following the tracks of the route he'd taken while Brad was maintaining a watchful eye for any signs of the helicopter.

"Shit," yelled Brad into Phil's ear. "Those bastards don't give up. The chopper just came out above the clearing about two hundred yards back. Right where we were."

Phil steered the machine slightly into the woods on his left trying to get under cover. "If they look hard enough, they'll see our tracks. What do we do? Christ, the clearing is so wide here, they could possibly land that damn chopper."

"Let me think a minute." Holding the automatic so Phil could see it, Brad asked, "Is this stupid safety off now?"

"Yeah, why?"

"How the hell do you put refills... ahh new clips in this contraption?"

Showing Brad how to reload the automatic, he said, "You still haven't told me why."

"Look, Phil. When that chopper goes back over the trees, I'm going to go out in the clearing and lay face down. When I signal to you, I want you to ride out into the clearing so they spot you and then haul butt up the slope. Go about a hundred yards or so and then duck into the trees again and find some cover."

"Brad, what the hell are you going to be doing pal?"

"With any luck... blowing them away."

"Give me a break pal, I don't think..."

Cutting him off, Brad said, "Phil, their eyes are going to be on you. They won't even see me lying out there. They're going to get a one *hell* of a surprise. You have the hard part. If I miss, you're in deep trouble, not me. You have a better idea?"

"Yeah, let me lay out in the clearing and you be the bait. I think I'm a little better shot than you are. Christ, have you even fired a weapon in you life?"

"Yes."

"Where?"

"At the arcade at the State Fair."

"This is... a little different, pal."

"Phil, I *know* I can do this. Trust me!! If I miss, your going to get your chance anyway. Let's stop arguing and get this plan moving."

Brad waited until the chopper was out of sight and moved into the clearing. With the white hood in place, he laid face down with his head towards the upslope so when he rolled over and sat upright, he'd be facing the on-coming chopper. As he waited for the signal to move out, Phil found it hard to see Brad from the edge of the clearing, a distance of only twenty or so feet, so the element of surprise should work.

Then, there it was with the black oval insignia on its side cut in half by an open door and the legs of someone searching dangling below. Brad gave Phil a motion with his arm. With that, Phil sped into the clearing and pointed the machine up the slope. Brad could tell from the sound of the chopper's engine that it must have seen him and was in pursuit.

When the snow began to blow up around Brad from the rotors, he, rolled over, sat up, aimed, and fired. The RayBans flew off the pilot's head as holes appeared in the Plexiglas and the helicopter began to gyrate out of control. It first gained some altitude but quickly headed downward, spinning quickly in circles until its tail eventually hit one of the supporting towers for the high voltage lines. Then, it swerved sharply to the right into the tall pines on the far side of the clearing, crashed and exploded in a ball of flames.

Brad glanced up the clearing to see Phil coming towards him on the snowmobile with arms waving in excitement. As he pulled up beside Brad, he yelled, "Jesus Christ, Brad, you're a God damn "*Rambo*" or something. That was beautiful, pal."

"The damn pilot sure as hell didn't think so. I couldn't see his eyes because of his sunglasses but, I could tell from his actions that he knew his number was up. I don't think there's any reason to check the wreckage, do you?" he asked as the two of them surveyed what was left of the smoldering helicopter across the clearing and watched the billowing black smoke trail up in to the bright blue Colorado sky.

"Nooooo, I don't think so. They bought it pal. The farm's all theirs. That was fantastic. You must have scored pretty high at the arcade."

"Actually, I don't believe I hit a damn thing there."

"Now you tell me."

"For some reason I... just felt I could do this. Must've been the adrenaline or something. Probably, I was just pissed as hell and determined to do something about it, ya know?"

"Whatever it was, it sure worked. Maybe we can proceed in peace and quiet for a while and join the others."

"Yeah, we should. I'm kind of anxious to see Sam. You know something, Phil, through all of this shit since I left you guys on the top of the mountain, as occupied as I've been, I can't get that woman out of my mind."

"That's called love, man. I miss Chantal all the time when we aren't together."

"Where're the others?"

"I told them to continue along the route and get as far away from this mountain as possible. John's leading and Evan is trailing the four girls. I told them to go slowly in the most direct route possible. The two guys," began Phil, thought for a split second and then continued, "shit, all six of them are capable of finding the different stops along the route. We've got a lot of catching up to do. They're probably eating right now at the second transportation point of the day."

"I hope they're that far along. We better get moving if we're going to catch up before the end of the day. Those bastards over there cost us a lot of time," Brad said, pointing to the wreckage. "Shit, I have to go back down there."

"Why?"

"I forgot about my skis. I have to pick them up. They're on the other side of the clearing."

"How the hell did they get over there?"

"Part of my "Rambo" instincts. Let's pick them up and get the hell out of here."

"You got it pal."

The two picked up the skis and packed some snow in a piece of cloth to use as a cold compress for the wound in Brad's side. On the snowmobile designed for one, they slowly made their way to the point where Phil and the others had separated. There, they found the other snowmobile waiting for them. "Christ, there's no key in the damn thing!" Phil exclaimed looking around the snow-covered machine.

"You're shitting me?" shouted Brad. "That's just great. Are you sure?"

"I sure as hell don't see any. I can't envision walking up this mountain carrying skis," said Phil in a disgusted tone. "They must have hidden the key in case someone other than us showed up. Good thought, but, where the hell would they hide it?"

After a short pause and still searching the vehicle, Brad said, "Phil, look for three rocks in a row." Quickly scanning the surrounding area, he further directed, "Over there. Behind you... pick up the third rock on the right."

Phil bent down and moved the rock, stood up and turned around with the key dangling from his hand. "Here it is, pal."

"Sam, Sam, Sam. I love you." said Brad.

"She said you'd remember, I just didn't believe her."

"What?"

"I knew where it was all the time. Before I left them to go and find you, she said we should hide the key for the snowmobile they'd be leaving behind, just in case. Damn smart girl, Brad. She suggested the third rock thing because she knew you'd remember where the extra key to her place back in Georgetown was hidden because of parents. I was just testing you pal."

"Thanks for putting my heart in my throat again, buddy."

"What's this thing about her parents?"

"Ahh, it's kinda private."

"Well, at any rate, you two sure are on the same page, aren't you?"

"Same book also. And, if I have anything to do with it, the God damn book is going to have one hell of a lot of chapters."

"Sorry, for the scare. I never thought for one minute, the book, as you call it, was destined to be any short story."

"Let's get this thing cranked up and be on our way. I want to catch up with them and start the next page."

"You got it."

*****

"Which direction do we take from here John? asked Terri.

"Evan and I agree, we go thataway," he said pointing up the ensuing mountain.

"Samantha, did you hide the keys for Phil and Brad?" asked Chantal.

"They're under the third rock like the two times before," replied Sam. "I wish we knew what that black smoke was we saw earlier. I'm really worried about them."

"I know you are but, don't worry girls, we'll know something before long. Right now, we have to continue on," urged Evan.

"These machines are two seaters so, Sam and Chantal, you two team up," instructed John.

"That won't be necessary," shouted a gleeful Chantal. "They're here. Look!!"

The others turned and saw Brad and Phil skiing towards them out of the woods. Sam and Chantal ran to greet them, giving them each big hugs and kisses. The guys shook hands and hugged each other as well.

"I didn't expect to see you two until the camping location tonight. How'd you catch up so fast?" asked Evan.

"We're not in any real danger right now, or for that matter the rest of the day," replied Phil. "We were able to proceed at a faster pace than all of you and besides, all we had to do was follow your tracks, not blaze the trail."

"Speaking of blazes Brad, we saw smoke curling up off in the distance. You know anything about that?" asked John curiously.

"Let's just say the score is one to one on choppers."

"Bradford," Sam said, "I want you to tell the truth. Where did you get those things," referring to the weapons they each had slung over their shoulders, "and what happened to your side?"

"Ohh... these things," Brad said realizing it was the first time Sam had ever called him by his full first name. Holding one of the automatics up, he continued, "a couple of guys we ran into... didn't need them anymore."

"And, as for his side," Phil added, trying to make light question, "he tried to stop a bullet, but missed. You know him... he can't do anything right."

"A bullet?" shrieked Sam and echoed by a concerned Chantal.

Phil's attempt to down-play the incident hadn't worked thought Brad, but he appreciated the effort none the less. "Honey, for right now, let it be enough that Phil and I are fine... really. I just, wasn't as careful as I should have been. That's all."

"Who the hell shot you, buddy?" John asked.

Before Brad could respond, Phil interjected, "Ahhhhh... my father shot him."

"Malcomb shot him! What the hell is he doing out here?" asked a confused Chantal.

"No, no, no... not Dad, my... biological father. Brad, I learned something from you back there. Call 'em like you see 'em, right? Might as well get it out in the open." Seeing Brad nod in approval, he continued, "Dad, Malcomb is the only real father I acknowledge. I've known for a long time, Chantal honey, that... he wasn't my biological father."

"Who is then?"

"Colonel Harold Dickey was."

"Colonel Dickey is your biological father?"

"Was."

"What do you mean was?"

"He's ahhhh... dead."

"Ohhh, God Phil. I'm so sorry," said Chantal in a soothing voice. "How did it happen?"

"I shot him with this," Phil said slowly holding up the automatic slung over his shoulder and continued, "before he killed us. That's when Brad got wounded."

"What a bummer," said Evan, his arm draped over the five foot tall Terri, "having to kill your own father to save your life. Sorry, man."

"It is, kind of a bummer, Evan, but... I'm okay with it. I never really liked the man, even after I found out our true relationship. I've discussed this with Brad and he knows my feelings. It's just... something that happened, something I'm going to have to live with. I wasn't going to mention it but, on the way here I remembered the pact we all made last night. You remember, the all for one and one for all bullshit." He laughed slightly and continued. "I felt obligated to let you all know."

"If Phil hadn't done what he did... well, neither of us would be here now, that's for sure," Brad said. "We wouldn't have been around to find those keys under the third rock to the right," he said in jest, giving Sam a playful poke in the ribs. Trying to change the subject, he continued, "that was ingenious, Sam. I'm proud of you."

"Thanks, Brad. Honey, you sure you're okay?"

"I'm fine, Sam. Really, I am. Phil and I will give all of you a complete account later. I still want to get moving up and over the last mountain to the camp site for tonight. We'll discuss this later over some hot food and try to figure out how the Colonel's tied into this crap."

"Sorry about your father, Phil," said John.

"John, don't worry about it. I'm really okay with it. I never really trusted the guy, as long as I knew him."

"Okay, man," John said, not mentioning that he hadn't trusted him either. "Let me ask everyone something then."

"What?"

"Is anyone having any fun yet?" he yelled, trying his best to put some humor back into the solemn crowd.

"Not really," replied Phil, "but we can certainly work on it."

"At least," interjected Brad, "we're not bored." *Thank God,* he thought, they'd caught up to the others. Not that he had anything against Phil, but Sam would be more comforting on the ride with her inviting breasts nestled against his back. “Sam, honey, climb aboard and let's get this show on the road.”

*****

As they stopped outside the A-frame dwelling Chantal remarked, “This is pretty nice, Brad. Whose is it?”

“I really don't know, Sis. It belongs to some guy from New Mexico that's an author and uses it as a retreat from the craziness of the civilized city life,” he replied knowingly.

“How would he ever get here? This is in the middle of nowhere. There can't be any roads around here, are there?” she asked hopefully.

“No, there aren't. The owner is also a pilot so he can fly in here whenever he wants to get away by himself. See the clearing in front? You can't tell now because it's frozen and covered with ice and snow, but it's really a lake. He's got a small, single-engine plane with pontoons and actually lands on the lake.”

“Must be nice,” remarked John.

“We could sure as hell give him a story to write about,” added Evan.

“There isn't any electric power out here but, around the side there's supposed to be a generator. You all go on in, the key is under the mat,” Brad said and then, added as an after-thought, “not the third rock to the right, Sam. I'm going to go crank up the generator. The starter is battery operated and was recently checked out so there shouldn't be any problems.”

The other seven had barely made their way inside when they heard the generator kick into operation and noticed a couple of lights come on, dimly at first, but growing in brightness as the generator built up the power level. As Brad came through the front door, he noticed someone had already turned on the two space heaters provided to help warm the inside more quickly. The water was ready to turn on. The pipes were wrapped with a low voltage warming tape, wired to the battery of the generator, to keep them from freezing in the frigid temperatures of the Colorado winter. Hot water was nearly instantaneous, being provided on demand by an instant heating system. *Pretty ingenuous,* thought Brad. *Why pay to keep all the water heated, when you don't need any.*

Peering through the large A-frame window, at least 25 feet at the peak, Chantal said, “Phil, this kind of reminds me of back home in New Market. The view is wonderful... so wide open with the lake out front.”

“You're right honey, it does. Kind of wish we were all looking out our windows right now.”

“I still wish I'd stayed with Heinz,” joked Evan. “I bet he still hasn't touched those eggs, Sam.”

“Come on now, Evan. You have to give me a little slack. I finally got the hang of it. By the way, I didn't see anything left on your plate that morning and you're still alive,” Sam responded.

“This is great,” yelled out John from the loft area of the dwelling.

“What's great, John,” Brad yelled back.

“This guy has one hell of a computer system up here. I should be able to retrieve the H1 file from the center on this thing. It probably has a modem, but I don't see any telephones.”

Taking the stairs two at a time, Brad entered the loft. “There wouldn't be any phone service available way out here. How the hell would he be able to use a modem?”

“You're right, buddy. I don't see any phone jacks around anywhere. How the hell would he do it?” asked John, more of himself than Brad. If he had a cell phone with an adapter, he could hook it up. That has to be how he uses it. This would be the battery pack charger for the cell phone, right here,” he said dragging it from a drawer and holding it up to show Brad.

“Brilliant, John. Only one problem.”

“And what, pray tell, might that be?”

“There's nothing on the end of the damn cord. There isn't any cell phone to use.”

“Shit! You're right but, that doesn't mean there isn't one around here some place,” he said as he began pulling the drawers of the desk open.

“I doubt you're going to find anything. People have cell phones to carry with them, not to leave behind. He probably took it home with him to New Mexico.”

“This really sucks! I thought we had something here. Wait a sec. What's this damn thing?”

Evan had just entered the landing and saw what John was pulling from the bottom drawer. “Looks like a transmitter/receiver of some sort,” he said.

"You got it, Evan. This little thing is battery-operated so it's portable." Looking at the back, John continued, "Yep. This little thing is used with a lap top computer to send and receive data. We might... just be in business."

"By the way, there is a dish on the roof," added Evan.

"Why didn't you say so before? The computer is probably hardwired right into the dish," said John in excitement as he placed the transmitter back in the drawer.

"When are you going to know?" asked Brad showing some excitement.

"What's going on up here?" asked Phil as he and the four girls came up the steps to the loft.

"John thinks there's a chance we can communicate with the Center," said Evan.

"Well Christ. Just call them up."

"It's not quite that simple, Phil. There isn't any phone. Unless this guy's bill is current, which I doubt, he won't have access to the internet, if he was a subscriber in the first place."

"You can't talk?"

"No, there's no way I can send any E-mail without the internet," he responded as the computer sprang to life. "Let me see if I can jury rig something that will at least allow me to retrieve the H1 file."

"Everyone, let's leave John alone so he can do his thing. Let's get something to eat while he performs his dormitory magic," Brad said as he herded everyone back downstairs.

*****

The sun had long since disappeared behind the mountains in the west and, with the exception of John, all were seated downstairs, trying to relax after the rigorous day. John had yet to eat, his only hunger now being to solve the problem with the computer up in the loft. The group consensus was that Phil's father, Colonel Dickey, was probably acting on his own as an employee for Swiss Technologies and that the USAF had no knowledge of his activities. And, they further agreed that even if Colonel Dickey had been lying about knowing where they were to be picked up, they couldn't take any chances. The question of the day then, had become, *if they couldn't proceed to the pickup point, where would they go?*

The only option left open to them was to change their route to a different mountain and proceed to the road on its far side that Brad and his school friends had used to reach the general area. The only stickler with the plan was that the snowmobiles wouldn't be able to reach the summit and they'd have to climb the last 2000 feet or so to reach the top. In the summer months, it had been relatively easy, but covered with ice and snow, it would definitely present a problem.

"Here it comes," John yelled out from above.

"What?" yelled Abbey in return.

"The H1 file! Boy, there's a ton of shit!!"

They raced up the staircase to the loft and watched John at the computer. Absolutely no one understood what was going on, but, as long a he did, that's all that was important.

"Shit." John said in disgust.

"What's happening? What's wrong?" asked Brad.

"Only that these bastards double-encrypted their files. The program I installed at the Center only made one pass through it and dumped the results into H1."

"How do you know it made even one pass? The data looks pretty screwed up to me," asked Abbey.

"Honey, if it didn't complete the deciphering, there wouldn't be anything at all in the H1 file to retrieve. It doesn't dump until it's finished."

"It's still unreadable though, I don't understand, John."

"The program I designed and installed, breaks the last encoding system used to encrypt the text. It then dumps the result into the H1. If it is still encrypted, you simply run the H1 file itself against the program which would break the next system used."

"Then what's the problem?" asked Phil. "Just run the H1 through your deciphering program again."

"The problem is, from here I can't. I can only retrieve files, not instruct the computer on what to do with them. It's a safeguard I installed to prevent this type of activity from an outside source. The thing works pretty damn good. Too good. I can't get around it."

"Damn. That means all this shit we have, we can't read it?"

"Looks that way, Brad. What really pisses me off is that the first system is usually something pretty easy to crack. It's normally used to prevent employees from bringing up a file and reading it. Kind of an "eyes only", in-house protection. If someone were to pull up the file by accident, or on purpose for that matter, they'd be looking at what we are. The only time it's necessary to double encrypt something is if it's going to be transmitted somewhere. When my system sucked all the files out of their computer memory, the transmission encoding system automatically kicked in to operation. No guarantees, of course, but the program I installed would probably decode what we are looking at in a matter of minutes."

"By simple, what do you mean? Something that could be done without a computer?"

"Possibly."

"Any way to tell if it's possible?"

"Let me think that one over for a minute." Paging the computer screen for some time, John said, "Brad, my boy, I think we might be onto something. Has anyone noticed anything missing in all of this data?"

"No," was the consensus.

"What we are looking at is text in the proper format. There appears to be no spillage of data from one data field into another. That suggests the data fits the intended fields so the possibility of it being a simple, substitution system is high."

"A what kind of system?" asked Brad.

"A substitution system. Letter for letter switching."

"That sounds good, but... you said something was missing."

"Right. Everything we have paged through so far has not had one digit in it. No numbers, man. All letters. What's the chances that there are no numbers anywhere in any of this shit. Very slight, I would think."

"Probably so," confirmed Chantal. "There isn't any punctuation either."

"Good point, honey," Phil said, "does that help any, John?"

"It sure might."

"John," said Terri softly, "the embassy has files that have a similar... look to what's on the screen now. They're personnel files."

"Damn, Terri, you may be right!! Anybody notice anything else?"

"Maybe, Sam said. Can you go back a couple of pages?" After a few seconds of scrolling she instructed. "There! Stop! Shoot, go the other way two or three. There!"

"What is it, Sam?" Brad asked.

"See that first group of letters right there?" she asked, pointing it out to everyone. The "JCKARQT" is the same thing that was inside the oval on that helicopter yesterday. I saw it when it flew by us."

"Sam, that thing was moving pretty fast. Are you sure?" asked John.

"She's sure, John," said Brad. "She has a photographic memory. I've tested it before and believe me... she's sure."

"Okay then. What is usually the first entry on a personnel record, Terri."

"Employee name."

"I guess... that would be last name first."

"Probably."

"Okay then. We possibly have somebody named "JCKARQT QMARQT B," important enough to possibly have his last name on the side of a helicopter. The last letter could be the middle initial. What's next on an employee record."

"I don't want to interrupt the train of thought here but aren't records usually sorted alphabetically? Wouldn't the first record start with the letter "A" for Adams or some such name?" asked Sam.

"Yeah, they probably would," said Terri. "What are you getting at?"

"John, try going towards the front, page by page, for me."

"Let's go for it."

After about twenty pages, Sam said, "hold it right there. Phil, wasn't your..." she paused, thought a second and continued, "wasn't Colonel Dickey's first name Harold?"

"Yes, it was."

"This record has an "E" for the first letter of the last name and also an "E" for the last letter of the first name. So does the name Harold Dickey, except they're "D's". John, wouldn't that mean that a "D" might be an "E"?"

"Jesus Christ, Sam. What the hell made you think of that?" asked Brad.

"Only that... well his is the only name we know to be associated with these creeps. I thought it would be a good place to start, that's all. I used to do those puzzles in the newspaper all the time."

"Honey, that's brilliant."

"I'll say it is. Could have used more like you at the agency," said John, grabbing some paper and a pencil. "If you're right, Sam, then this is what we have." John wrote the following on the piece of paper.

EGNIRY FCQMJE
DICKEY HAROLD

"That doesn't look like it works," said Abbey. Honey, if a "D" equals an "E" then wouldn't "C" in Dickey equal a "D"?"

"Not necessarily, my love. If they did a simple slide of one alphabet against another, it wouldn't. It appears that's what they might have done here. See the "Y" equals "Y"?" he said pointing with the pencil.

"Yeah... what's that mean, John?" asked Brad.

"It means there's a strong possibility there's a key word involved at the beginning of the alphabet."

"What the hell is a... key word?"

"If Sam's right, it'll become obvious. So Terri, what would the next entry be on a personnel file?"

"On ours, it's the address of the employee."

"That would be street address, city, state, and zip code, right."

"In the United States, yes. In New Zealand, it's a little different."

"Okay then... there we are... right... there," John said, pointing at the screen. "A two-character, abbreviated state field followed by a five character zip code field. That means the field in front of the state field would be the city field. I wish the damn field names were printed out, but, they're probably blanked out on purpose. They must have an access code for people allowed into the file which puts everything in plaintext and reveals the field names. I think we're moving along pretty good. Phil, what city did... Colonel Dickey live in?"

"Bethesda, Maryland," Phil responded. "I'm way ahead of you... I think it fits."

John wrote down the following on the piece of paper he was using.

BETHESDA MD
ARTFRSEC KE

"It does fit," exclaimed an excited Phil. "Look, the "D's" in Bethesda, Maryland, Dickey, and Harold, all equal the letter "E".

"Sam, you're fantastic. I can't believe we got this far without even having to do a frequency count. You saved us a hell of a lot of time, young lady."

“That's the 4.0 average coming through,” said Brad giving her a big hug. “What the hell's a... frequency count? Is that what you said, a frequency count?”

“Basically, the letter “E” is the most common used letter in the English language, “T” is next, followed by “N”, “O”, “R”, “I” and so forth. We would have had to count a bunch of these letters in this garbage to find out the most common letter and so forth to match against those in English.”

“You're saying then, that the letter R on the screen there, will appear more often than any other letter?”

“Damn, you people catch on pretty damn fast. That's exactly what I'm saying. An “R” is the encoded letter “E”. Let's see what we've got here so far.” John put the following on the piece of paper.

CANER--FG-IJ--M--QST----Y-

“Jesus Christ, folks, he continued. “We broke this system, keyword and all. Here's what we have. Alphabet on top, and keyword strip below.” So that all could see, John, on a blank piece of paper, wrote:

<u>ABCDEFGHIJKLMNOPQRSTUVWXYZ</u>
CANERBDFGHIJKLMOPQSTUVWXYZ

“So the word “caner” is the keyword?” asked Brad.

“Possibly, Brad, but, not necessarily. Once a letter has been used in the strip, it's never repeated. There are only 26 characters available and you have to represent each letter. The actual keyword for example could be...” Stopping in mid-sentence, John wrote down on the piece of paper in large letters what he felt the keyword was.

C A N C E R

“The keyword is cancer?” a shocked Brad inquired.

“Not definite... but it fits! Drop the second “C” and you have the word “caner”.

“Why would they use the word “cancer,” of all words,” asked a befuddled Abbey.

"Hey, guys," Evan broke in. "Four of us are kind of... late comers to all this. But, last night... I forget who was filling us in, but, someone was mentioning that there were four or five research centers around the world that shut down projects on an antibody or something. Wasn't there some involvement by these guys each time? If so, it's certainly clear to me that they're interested in something to do with Cancer."

"Hell of a point, my man," John said, now assured that he was correct.

"This... I don't even know if I should be saying."

"Go ahead, Sam," said Brad. "This is an open forum here. Speak what's on your mind."

"I'll say," added John. "If it wasn't for you, we'd all be counting letters right now."

"It's a pretty terrible thought. I don't know."

"Sam, we are dealing with some pretty rough people," added Terri. "What has you concerned?"

"Well, after hearing about all of this stuff... Brad, honey, didn't you say that from the information Doc uncovered, there wasn't any rationale for stopping research on that antibody?"

"Haven't found a reason so far."

"What if... no, it couldn't be."

"What?"

"Okay, this is going to sound stupid, but I'm going to get it off my chest".

"That's a hell of a task, sweetheart," Brad replied with everyone laughing at Sam's expense.

"Ohhh Brad, listen to me for a second," Sam said, smiling herself but holding in her own laugher.

"I'm sorry, honey. Go ahead."

"Okay. As terrible as this sounds Brad, you've enlightened me over the past few weeks about how self-serving some of the people in this world really are. Things like, false reporting to assure funding of projects would continue and patents on prescription drugs and so forth and so on. Remember?"

"Yes, I remember, honey."

"What if these people are involved in shutting down research projects on cancer because they knew ahead of time the results would be good?

Carrying it a little further, what if there is a cure and they're hiding it? There, I've said it. Now, everyone can say I'm crazy."

"My God! I can't imagine what you're saying... no offense Sam, could be true. Could people really be that terrible? You said last night that this research on the antibody began in the middle 70's, Brad. What possible reason could there be for hiding a cure to such a disease?" asked an astonished Terri.

"It was, like I said, a pretty sinister thought. I was stupid to mention it."

"Noooo, Sam. Don't be sorry for bringing it up." Phil said and continued. "With the situation we all find ourselves in, each of us has the right. No change that. Each of us has the obligation to bring up points that might be, however remote, pertinent. As you know, I'm not really that involved in the research arena; however, I am involved in treating patients who have it. I'm also very much aware as to how expensive treatment can be. Not just, my fees, mind you, but, also the expense of drugs, equipment and all of the other requirements necessary to cure it or prolong someone's life. Basically, there's a hell of a lot more money to be made by treatment of the disease than the actual curing of it or preventing it in the first place. If the disease could be prevented, somehow, all of the dollars spent on treatment would dry up and blow away."

"That's sick," said Chantal.

"So's blowing up a helicopter sitting on the ground, Sis, and trying to kill me and your husband. A little smaller scale than what Sam and Phil are talking about, but, not necessarily the actions of a sane person."

"The sick part of it is, people that are insane, still can have intricate planning to achieve their ultimate goals," Abbey added.

"Right on, honey. Look, all we have right now is a theory. There may be something else on this H1 file that can help," John said.

"That's going to take forever to go through all that letter by letter. We don't have that much time," said Brad. "I, personally, am leaning towards the theory, as you so eloquently put it, John, that Sam brought to light. Phil's expansion of it really, I guess, put me over the edge. We actually, know very little about this organization. I wish we could find out where their revenues come from. Basically, how would they profit from preventing a cure for cancer being found? That's the question."

"Buddy, now that I know the system, I can write a program here to decode this shit. Give me about an hour to draft it and get it installed. Again, maybe, some answers are in there just waiting to be found."

"Shit, why the hell didn't you say so earlier?"

"No one asked."

"Alright get started already, John," instructed Abbey.

"Yes ma'am," replied John, saluting his wife.

"Before you begin John, there is something you might want to know."

"What's that Sam?"

"There's two other names that should be on the computer screen somewhere. Names from license plates Brad and I've seen."

"You're kidding."

"No she's not," said Brad, reaffirming his trust in her photographic memory.

"Okay, what are they?"

"STRVRLS and HCKRS," she said, spelling them for him.

Decoding them, John said, "that would be Stevens and James and... there they are, right there. No wonder you graduated a year ahead of your class. That's remarkable, Sam."

"There is one other name."

"And what's that one?"

"It's not going to be on there."

"How do you know that, Sam?" asked Brad.

"It doesn't fit. The guy in New York who was killed on the street in front of the boutique, remember?"

"Yeah, how the hell could I forget something like that?"

"His name was Haller. The license plate was "DAYYIJ." Same number of letters, the two L's match the two Y's, but, it doesn't match the letters in the strip John has written down there," she said pointing.

"Shit, Brad, she's right."

"What the hell does that mean?"

"I'm afraid, buddy, it probably means another strip, with another keyword."

"And to carry it a step further, possibly another disease they're interested in?" asked Brad.

"Possible, friend," John replied.

"I was afraid of that," said Sam.

"We don't know that for sure, Sam, but, if that's true, this thing, like the Colonel said to me, is pretty big. John, let's see what happens when we scan this shit without having to decipher it first."

"I'm getting right to it. Can someone bring me a beer. I do my best work after one or two brews, they relax the hell outta me."

"I'll get you one," said Abbey.

*****

Brad was in a deep sleep and dreaming of more pleasant things, things involving he and Sam. He was exhausted from the day's activities and had dozed off in the midst of the group's discussion. He was awakened by a gentle kiss on the cheek and a soft voice, whispering his name.

"What time is it?" he asked her, groggy from just opening his eyes. "Time to leave?"

"No," she said. "I thought you might be more comfortable lying down than sitting in that chair breaking you neck," she said smiling.

Completely disoriented and thinking he was back in Georgetown he asked. "Where we going, Sam?"

"Brad, do you know where you are?"

He sat up straighter in the chair, rubbed his eyes, rotated his head to remove the kink in his neck and looked around. "Thanks a whole lot for reminding me, Sam," he said in a low growl. "I was dreaming of better times. I'm just tired, that's all. How's John doing on the program?"

"It's running now. He said it's going to take a while to go through all the different files, but it's working. He's taking a little nap, himself. Don't you want to lay down and be more comfortable."

"No. I'd rather go for a walk outside. Maybe, the cold air will help clear my head a little. Want to go?"

"Sure, but it's snowing."

"What time is it, anyway," he asked her for the second time as he stood and rubbed the back of his neck.

"About 2:30 in the morning. Is your neck sore?"

"Just a little stiff. Damn. I've been sleeping for a couple of hours. Did you get any rest?"

"Couldn't sleep. For some reason, I'm just not that tired."

"Honey, you have to get some rest. I don't want you getting sick on me or something."

"Don't worry, I won't."

Of all the others, only Chantal was awake, scurrying about the kitchen. She'd just poured herself a hot cup of coffee and turning around, noticed Brad awake. "Want some?" she asked raising the cup for him to see.

"No thanks, Sis. Maybe when we get back inside. We're going out for walk and some of that good old Colorado night air. I'm trying to get the cobwebs out of my brain. Want to come?"

"I'll take a rain check, better yet, a snow check. It's coming down pretty good out there."

"Suit yourself. See you in a while," Brad said as he and Sam closed the door behind them.

They walked slowly, arm in arm, towards the frozen lake. Neither said a word as they stepped onto the snow-covered dock. Standing at its end, they turned and looked back towards the lighted A-frame windows and then towards each other. They tightly hugged each other, quickly kissed, brushed the snow from the end of the dock and sat down with their legs dangling in the air. All either of them wanted was for this "adventure" to be over so they could continue their lives in peace.

"Brad, honey, I'm proud of you for what you did today. It was, as they say, above and beyond the call of duty."

"Thanks, Sam, but, I'm not proud to admit that I blew away someone. It's not something that... what was the decoded name on the side of the helicopter?"

"Robert F. Lambert."

"Right. I'll bet you that Mrs. Robert F. Lambert or any of his kids, if he had any, wouldn't be too proud of me."

"Brad, sweetheart, he deserved it because of what they were trying to do."

"I know that Sam. It's just that his wife or kids or mother and father doesn't deserve what they will be going through. It's just not fair. I know I did what I had to, but I still feel guilty as hell... I suppose because of all his family," he resolved after swallowing hard.

"When they find out the truth, there's no way they'll be able to blame you for protecting yourself. It was self defense, plain and simple. And,

Brad, they will know the truth because, however large this thing turns out... you and I, together with the other six up there," she said, turning and pointing to the A-frame, "are committed. Brad, honey, because of what you did we still, the eight of us together, have a chance to put an end to all this and put things right. Not just for us, but, for anyone else that has been wronged or might be in the future by these people. I love you for being who you are, a protector, a lover, a man who is caring, and the man I'm going to marry in the spring."

"Sam, you certainly have a way with words. You sound like you're in front of a jury giving a final argument. Thanks for the vote of confidence, Sam. I love you too, more than you will probably ever know."

"How about showing me then."

"Funny you should bring that up." Brad stood up on the creaky dock and helped her to her feet. "Come with me, I want to show you something."

Hand in hand, Brad led Sam through the heavy snowfall around to the side of the house to a large unlocked shed. Opening the door and pulling the string to the overhead light bulb, Brad said, "Welcome, my love, to my private abode."

Looking around, Sam noticed one of the dual sleeping bags lying invitingly on the floor and smiling, said, "You devil you. When did you have time to get this ready?"

"I make time for important things," Brad responded.

They embraced each other and sank slowly to their knees. Magically, their clothes were off in a matter of seconds, the two not even noticing the cold. The time they spent making love was brief, but, it still relaxed them both and put Brad in better spirits than when they'd first stepped out in the cold night air. The weather, as they made their way back to join the others, was getting worse, the snow now coming down under near blizzard-like conditions. Holding the door securely to prevent it blowing open, Sam and he entered. To his surprise, everyone was up and beginning to move about. Odd he thought, it was only 3:30 AM, but, on this trip, you should expect the unexpected.

"What's going on?" asked Brad. "Why's everyone up?"

"John's beginning to print out all the individual files from the... whatever he calls it," responded Terri.

"He says that the printer setup this guy has is pretty old fashioned compared to the computer system itself. It's going to be a while," Evan added.

"Looking at the weather out there, we have some time," said Brad. "If this keeps up, we won't have any visitors tomorrow."

"That's good news," said Phil. "That means we should be able to make the roadway you were talking about, without any damn interference from them."

"There is a problem with that, Phil. As I mentioned, changing direction to the other mountain is the smart thing to do. We all agreed on that earlier. Problem is, it's dangerous enough in good weather to climb to the top of that peak, but, in the middle of a snowfall like what's going on out there, I'm not so sure we should be trying it. We may be better off waiting this storm out like they're going to have to do."

"You're right. You know something though?"

"What?"

"There's still a slight advantage to us, even if we do wait for a change in the weather. They won't really know we decided to wait so, they may think we're all ready out of here... out of the mountains. Of course, if they can't fly, they'll know no one else could either and that we haven't been picked up yet."

"That's right, Phil, but, they'll be searching the hell out of the pick-up area, not the peak we decided to go over to the road. When day breaks, one of us has to keep an eye on the weather. If there's the slightest chance a chopper could fly in it, we have to be prepared to leave here immediately. That means everything packed on the snowmobiles and everyone inside ready to walk out the door and leave at a moment's notice."

"Let's get everything together we're taking and Terri and I will go out and get the snowmobiles ready. We should have that done before daylight," offered Evan.

"Good idea, Evan," said Chantal. "If anyone wants to clean up and change clothing, they should do it now in case this storm lets up by daybreak. And Evan, keep an eye out for mountain lions."

"Don't worry, Chantal, I'll make sure he leaves the big cats alone," Terri said amusingly.

"You people amaze me, at times," said Brad.

"Why do you say that?" asked Abbey.

"It's just that, with all this stuff going on, you all seem to stay in good humor and remain so focused."

"We're just trying to make the best of this adventure as you've so proudly proclaimed it ever since I've known you," Sam said, grinning.

The others joined in the laughter, and Evan added, "I still prefer to call it the three days of hell and agony."

"One thing, I do know. None of you are going to let me live this one down, even if I live to be 100 years old."

"We're never going to let you plan another trip for as well," added Phil.

"I think we should try to get some rest now but in shifts. To here you tell it Brad, that mountain is no easy task to climb," offered Abbey.

"We should! The others, if John ever gets his act together up there, can begin going over the information in those files to see what we can put together."

"I heard that, Brad. My act is together. The printer is beginning to output now."

"What took so long?"

"If we had to leave here in a hurry, we couldn't carry reams of paper with us. I probably wiped out this A-frame owner's next best seller but I used some of his discs to make copies... one for each of us. If only, God forbid, one of us gets out of here, at least there'll be something for someone to look at."

"You *are* thinking up there, aren't you? Good idea man. But, the idea we don't want to lose grips with is that each one of us is going to give someone a copy."

---- Chapter Fourteen ----

"Terri, what's the weather looking like out there?" Brad asked from the kitchen as he placed the final touches on his second sandwich of the afternoon.

"I don't know if this snow will ever let up, Brad," she replied as she stared out the window at the gloomy, gray-white scene. "I got a little concerned one time that we should leave. It lets up to the point where you think it might stop, but then, here comes more of the white stuff. It looks like it's getting pretty deep out there by the dock but you can't really tell with all the wind blowing it everywhere. I've never seen it snow like this in New Zealand. At least, not for this long."

"Can I fix you something to eat or get you a drink while I'm out here?"

"No, Brad. Thanks anyway."

"It's so late in the day now, we're almost to the point that we'll be spending another night here," he said walking over to the window to take a look. After a few seconds to devour the bite he'd taken from his sandwich he continued. "The way the cloud cover looks, I'd change that to we *are* at the point of spending another night. It may not be doing anything where they are, but they'll never be able to fly in this kinda stuff," he said trying to point with his finger and still hold onto a glass of Coke.

"I'm certainly not going to argue the point. Any breather we can get from being chased I'll welcome. Besides, I kind of like this place."

Looking around Brad responded, "It is kinda nice isn't it? Evan still upstairs with John?"

Terri only nodded as she stared blankly out the window with her thoughts far away on more tranquil memories. *Probably New Zealand,* thought Brad as he took another bite of his sandwich, turned away and headed towards the steps.

When not taking breaks or catching a few zzz's, the eight of them had meticulously gone through the reams of data that John had output on the printer. Even though both sides had been used, they'd run out of printer paper and now, were taking turns using the monitor to look at the remainder of the H1 file.

As Brad reached the loft, he noticed John stretching backwards in the chair and moving his head in a circular motion to remove the stiffness in his neck. Before taking the last bite of his sandwich, Brad commented, "It looks like we're going to be spending another night. How are we doin' up here?"

"Basically, here's what we have... so far," John replied holding up a sheet of paper and continued. "The corporate name, year founded, keyword and disease of interest are in each box. If something is in parenthesis, it's a best guess at the information." He then passed the sheet to Brad so that they all could take a look.

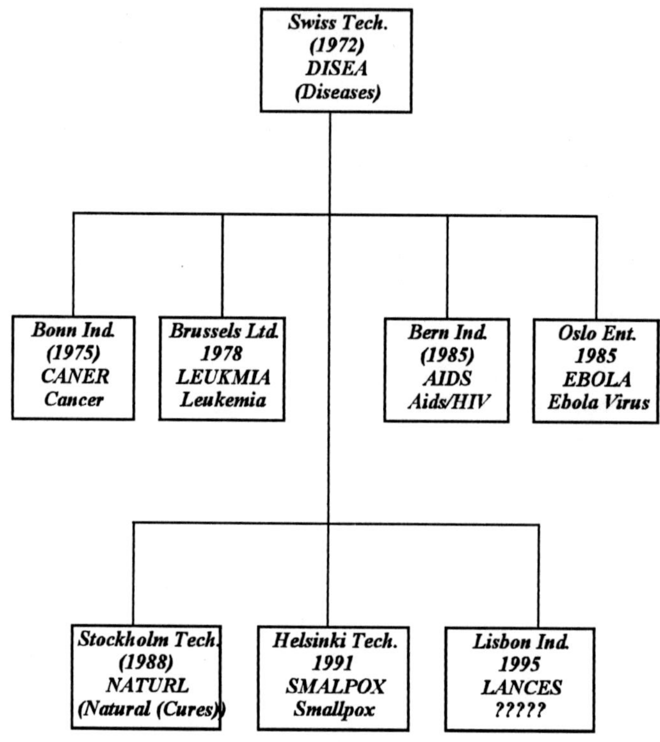

"Christ! Take a look at this," exclaimed Brad. "This is one big organization! How the hell did you come up with all this stuff, John?"

"Let's just say I learned a few things at NSA. When the intelligence analysts wanted programs written, I'd have to know all the intricacies involved to provide the output they required. Besides, I had a lot of help from all of you. Especially when Evan here," he said giving him a slap on the back, " discovered that the same message had been sent twice to the same address encrypted with two different encryption strips. The first message had been encrypted using a strip from another subordinate company of Swiss Technologies and had been sent to the "new guy on the block", Lisbon Industries, which was established earlier last year. Whoever was responsible for preparing the message for transmission had used the keyword strip for Helsinki Technologies. Mistakes such as this, are what make supposedly secure systems, not secure."

"What are the question marks under Lisbon Industries for?" asked Phil.

"I was hoping you could tell me. The keyword is LANCES but, I couldn't even venture a guess as to the disease this company is interested in," replied John. "We'd probably have to extract their data base to be able to tell for sure. Remember, we're only looking at the data base of the company involved with cancer research. The other keywords recovered are pretty obvious with the exception of Swiss Technologies and Stockholm Technologies. Those are guesses."

"Pretty good guesses, John," replied Brad. "Especially the one for Stockholm. That fits what Doc was saying back at the Center about the company when it bought out the research lab in London."

"Was that the one that never resumed any of the research studies after they were bought out?" questioned Sam.

"Right, honey. They bought the facilities only... supposedly to begin research studies on natural vitamins. Going along with what you said, Sam. Maybe that wasn't the reason for the buy out."

"What do you mean by that?" asked Terri as she made her way to the loft. "Brad, it's snowing harder if that's possible."

"Maybe this vitamin research was just a bunch of bullshit. Maybe the actual buy out was for the on-going research projects only. The hell with the facilities. They only kept them to make things look on the up and up."

"You mean they may have bought the company for the projects just to stop further development on them and not for their own studies?" asked Phil.

"Possible buddy."

"What better way to stop someone from pursuing an avenue of study than to buy them out and use the vitamin thing as a cover up for their true intentions," theorized Chantal.

"No suspicions would surface at all. Just one big company buying another. Happens every day of the year," stated the always matter-of-fact John.

"Sam, forgive me for not taking what you said before seriously enough. Now, I think I'm moving into your corner," said Terri. "These guys are really sick. I think they're making a big effort to keep the information about that antibody a secret. I think they know it's effective in some way against cancer and are hiding it from the public."

"They are certainly willing to spend a lot of dinero to do it," said Evan. "Can you imagine what they spent for that London facility?"

"That brings up the big question again. Where is all this damn money coming from?"

"Brad, certainly not from their marketing research contracts. I wouldn't think," added Phil, "there would be enough profit to afford outright purchases of companies the size of the one in London. Their revenues have to be coming from product generation and sales of something."

"But what, Phil?" Brad asked. In all of this documentation we've been through, there's no mention of revenues. We know that, at least the employees of Oslo Enterprises are paid by Oslo Enterprises."

"Refresh my memory. How is it we know that?" asked Evan.

"The conversation I had with Ron Riddel at BioMed in Chicago... God damn!"

"What's wrong?" asked a shaken Sam.

"That poor guy. That's the first call I have to make when I get to a phone. I have to call him and warn him about what's going on. You know something, Sam? I'm beginning to wonder if he wasn't right."

"About what?"

"His brother Richard's death. Maybe it *wasn't* suicide. Maybe, it was murder!"

"Ohhh my God, Brad. That's right. We've got to get a hold of him. Ever since I met him in Crystal City I really liked him. "

"Me too. He's definitely a guy on a mission. I just hope he holds down his curious nature until we reach him. Damn. Two bucks says he *was* murdered because he'd found out something about the Ebola virus studies they were conducting. Damn it! What an outfit we're dealing with! Those bastards!"

"Calm down, Brad. There's nothing we can do for Ron right now. You were saying something about the conversation you had with him," reminded Chantal.

"Yeah, damn it." Back on track, Brad continued. "His W-2 form has Oslo Enterprises on it. That means that this damn Oslo outfit actually owns BioMed but never renamed it after the purchase. They must be getting their funding from somewhere to operate and pay employees."

"I think you overlooked the most important point, Brad. That would be the second facility purchased by a subsidiary of Swiss Technologies," informed Abbey.

"You're right... I did. That means more money spent and without any idea of where the hell it's coming from."

"Precisely," concluded Abbey.

"How many people... on an average, would a place like BioMed or this London place, employ? Anyone have any ideas?" asked Terri.

"That's hard as hell to say. These facilities vary in size so much depending on what they're involved in. I think there are too many factors involved to really arrive at an average from the limited information we have. What are you getting at?" asked Brad.

"Don't we have an employee listing for Bonn Industries? I was just curious what the total payroll amount would be and how large this organization might be."

John began paging through the employee records file of Bonn Industries, making a rough estimate as he proceeded. "Jesus," he said, "they have over 800 employees. The average salary looks to be in the neighborhood of about $35,000, give or take. That would be a payroll of roughly ahhh... 30 million dollars a year. Shit, that can't be right... can it? I must've added an extra zero. No, damn it, it is right... about 28 million a year. That's a hell of a nut to crack for payroll. I wonder what kind of project funding they have."

"Better yet, who's doing the funding?" asked Abbey with a concerned frown.

"Damn... 28 million. And that's only one of seven company payrolls. Eight, if you include the payroll of Swiss Technologies," said Brad. "Bonn Industries is the oldest of the subordinate companies and may have the largest payroll. Even if we assume the others only have half the staff of the Bonn Industries, that would still mean an annual payroll of... shit, well over 100 million. Your nut's getting bigger and bigger, John."

"Basically," added Sam, it doesn't matter if the payroll is one or a hundred million dollars. We still don't have the slightest idea of where the funds are coming from to finance these operations. It seems to me that we have to get our hands on either the banking records for these companies or the files of Swiss Technologies. According to the sheet John's put together, they're the controlling organization in this whole mess and more than likely control the money distribution."

"I think you're right, Sam," said John. "Unfortunately, I can't do that from here. I have to be tied into a computer system that has access to ours."

"Where's the closest one?" she asked.

"At Brad's mother's estate. The system there's tied into the center. Problem is though, we can't go back there right now. They're going to be watching that place like a hawk and we wanted to stay out of sight for a while, remember?"

"If someone is a subscriber to the Center... is that what you mean by having access?" asked Phil.

"You bet. If I could get on a subscriber's computer system... don't tell anyone, but, there *are* ways to get around all the safeguards installed for security. Remember, I installed the damn things."

"I think we should head for Colorado Springs. The research center there is a subscriber. Hell, Pop even has a remote terminal at his house."

"Perfect. That'll work, Phil. I can't wait to get into that damn Swiss Technologies computer system."

"How are we going to stay out of sight, at your parents' place in Colorado Springs," asked Terri.

"Good point, Terri. How are we, Phil?" asked Brad.

"Today is the what, the 27th?"

With all the activity, the days had merged together in one big blur. Brad had to think for a moment before answering, "Actually, it's the 28th and tomorrow is the 29th. Why?"

"My parents are leaving on the morning of the 30th for San Francisco to spend New Year's Eve with friends. Right Chantal?"

"I think they did say the 30th," she replied after some thought.

"That means the house will be empty, right?"

"That's right, Brad."

"Then that's where we're heading."

"First thing, when we get there, is the call to Ron Riddel," reminded Sam.

"You bet it is, Sam. The second call is going to be to Ben Butterfield in DC. He and Abe are going to have to be a little careful in their investigation as well. I want them to be completely aware of what's going on."

"That's a relief," said Evan.

"What is?" asked Terri.

"Just that we finally have a plan of action against these guys. This outfit has had us on the run so much, we've only been able to play defense. Maybe, we should play some offense for a while."

"Certainly would be a welcome change," said Chantal.

"I think we may have gotten a little off track here," said John. "If we're going to be the one who's forcing the issue, then we'd better have all our homework done. There is something here," he said, holding up the piece of paper, "that I'm curious about. Brad, what were the termination dates for those centers working on the antibody?"

"I'm not sure I can remember them all. It is that important."

"I *think* so."

"Brad, honey," instructed Samantha, "close your eyes and get a mental picture of the conversation you had with Doc. It's really not that hard."

"Bullshit. Maybe not for you. Hell, everyone here knows about your photograhic mental capabilities."

"Trust me. Everyone has the ability to recall things. Just try it."

Closing his eyes and concentrating, after a short period of time Brad said, "the Ontario Canada project was canceled in 1991 because of contamination problems. The project in London, was stopped because of the buy out by Stockholm Technologies in 1989. The project in Japan was halted in ahhhhhh...1985, because of the sudden death of the man supplying the funding , and the New Zealand study was halted for an unknown reason in the winter of 1978, our winter, their summer," added Brad smiling as he recalled the confusion he had created with Doc. "I can't believe I remembered that shit. You were right, Sam. I actually, in my mind, saw Doc's face as he was telling me this stuff, right down to his expressions. That's amazing."

"What's amazing is the human mind," she corrected.

"I have something more amazing than any of that shit," said John.

"And what's that, lover?" asked Abbey trying to calm John down a little.

"Only that the Canadian project terminated the same year that Helsinki Technologies was founded. The London project terminated in 1989 and Stockholm Technologies, we tentatively agree, began in late 1988. The project on the antibody research in Japan ended in 1985 with at least Oslo Enterprises and possibly Bern Industries beginning operations in the same year. Lastly, the project down under stopped in 1978, the same damn year that Brussels Limited surfaced. With everything else, I don't think it's coincidental. Maybe, I'm just tired. How about the rest of you?"

"I think the rest of us are tired. Regarding your first question, it looks pretty damn suspicious to me," agreed Phil.

"You should be tired, John. You've spent hours and hours in front of the damn computer. I'm surprised you can still see," said a comforting Abbey.

"Yeah, but what do you think about what I said?"

"I don't know."

"I think you have hit on something there buddy," said Brad. It appears, every time there's progress made on that damn antibody, Swiss Technologies started a new company. The sole purpose of the new company might be to find a way to snuff out the research on the antibody."

"And, a new company... wouldn't have a historic association with Swiss Technologies if something didn't proceed according to plan," added Chantal.

"That's right, Sis."

"Is this really happening?" asked Sam. "I keep hoping I'll wake up from this nightmare. What I said about knowing the results and hiding information from the public, well, this just adds more to the credibility of the theory."

"That it does, honey. Sorry, but, it appears we're going to have to accept it and do something about it."

"I know. It's just frustrating being stuck out here and not being able to do anything."

"We all feel that way, Sam," said Terri, "but, we're finally beginning to go on the offense. Was that what you called it?" she asked turning towards Evan.

"That's right. We have the damn ball now and are going to put some damn points on the scoreboard before this is over," said Evan.

"Brad, do you know all the ramifications of what we're saying here. Besides a buy-out of the London facility to disguise the actual purpose of halting the antibody study, we're suggesting that the research lab in Canada was infiltrated and sabotaged with contamination."

"I realize the implications, Phil. Carry it a step farther. If what we suspect is true then, that Japanese financier didn't die so suddenly in an accidental fire. I'd suggest that he might have been dead before the fire."

"Murdered?" asked Chantal.

"Even though all the evidence we have is circumstantial, it certainly points in that direction," said Sam.

"That's your suspicious legal mind speaking now, and we should listen damn hard," said a smiling Brad.

"I think you missed the most important word, sweetheart. I said *circumstantial* evidence. We don't have one shred of hard evidence linking these people to anything."

"Sam, what about the events of yesterday. Two helicopters blown away and Colonel Dickey and the other guy that was chasing Brad?" asked Abbey.

"I'm sorry to say, but it's our word against no one's. Sure, we have a story to tell, but, can we prove why any of it happened? I don't think so. And, rest assured that a company that throws around money like Swiss Technologies will have a very good legal staff to protect themselves. They spend all kinds of money in cover-ups and insane activity. We know that, but, a court of law won't. The bottom line is, we'll never be able to prove it in court without hard evidence."

"What you're saying is, we have to get into the files of Swiss Technologies to find more concrete information like you suggested before?" asked John.

"Only as a means to point us in the right direction. I don't think everyone here understands something. All this paper we have spread out around here was obtained illegally. It's inadmissible in a court of law."

"None of this shit can be used in court?" questioned an astonished Brad.

"Oooh it could be used in court all right. The problem is, it could be used in a lawsuit against John. He's the only one there's a case against. Hard evidence. All the printouts, any programming recovered from the computer and to top it off, there *are* witnesses to his crime... us!"

"That sucks, Sam," said John. "We're here trying to get information to save our lives and put an end to this bullshit they're spreading around the globe and I'm the fall guy. I can't believe it."

"I didn't say it was right, John, just the way it is."

"It still sucks. We still have some things on the computer we couldn't printout. Who's got the next shift?"

"As it turns out, that would be Brad and I," replied Sam.

"Then girl, find us some hard evidence or at least a clue of where to get some," urged John.

"Before we start, there is one other thing on this sheet that might be of some importance," said Evan staring at the sheet.

"What's that Evan?" inquired John.

"If what we think is happening then... what antibody study is Lisbon Industries chartered to bring to a screeching halt? That company evolved earlier this year."

"Shit, Evan, you're right! We've equated only four of the seven subordinate companies with the antibody research cancellations," said Brad. Looking at the information on the sheet again, Brad continued, "if we assume that Bonn Industries was established as a legitimate expansion of Swiss Tech then, that would leave either Bern or Oslo and Lisbon with no apparent association."

"Brad, how complete is the center's data base?" asked Sam.

"I know what your getting at Sam, but, there isn't any way of telling. Labs sign up with us only if they want to. There's nothing in our agreement forcing the labs to provide us with that kind of information. There could be all kinds of data missing about other antibody studies."

"Shoot. You're right of course but, at least we know there was something else happening in the 1985 time frame."

"And something else in the 1994 or 1995 time frame as well," interjected Phil. "The only thing I'm aware of is Pop's center in Colorado Springs. They're currently involved in this same study. He told us Thanksgiving Day, remember Brad. Now we have three people we have to contact immediately."

Nodding in accord, Brad said, "That's right, Phil. That's the only one I'm aware of and if we're aware of it... they naturally would be also."

"Even though the Center isn't doing any research on the antibody, we certainly know of its existence. That would be why they're after us... right?" asked Abbey.

"That would be affirmative," said John with a slight nod of his head, and then with a serious expression on his face continued. "They don't want its existence known. But... why?"

"They must be profiting somehow by keeping it under wraps. Now, the question is how rather than why," added a bewildered Terri.

"When we find the answer to that question, we'll know where their revenues are coming from and how they can afford all of this subversive activity they're engaged in," said Sam. "That should prove to be very interesting because it's gotta be costing someone a real bundle."

"You said *prove*. Does that mean that they can be stopped when we find out?" asked Brad.

"Not necessarily, but, it would certainly add a lot of credence to our theory. That might just be enough to convince the authorities to do a full scale investigation and find the legitimate proof they need."

"We better get busy with the rest of those files still in the computer, Sam. While we're doing that, why don't the rest of you guys try to relax a little bit and try to round up something to eat."

"Brad, weren't you eating when you came up here?" asked Chantal.

"That he was," Terri informed her. "He also ate a sandwich earlier."

"Brad, where *do* you put it all?" asked John. "Jesus, pal, you ought to weigh a ton."

"Give me a break, you guys. Let me get to work here," said Brad trying to change the subject. "Sam, have a seat and let's get started. We'll see all of you in a coupla hours, or so."

*****

As Sam returned to the loft with Brad's iced tea to wash down his fourth sandwich of the afternoon, she noticed a drastic change in his demeanor. He had become very quiet, his color was rapidly fading and beads of perspiration were glimmering on his forehead. Very concerned she asked, "Are you feeling okay, honey?" He didn't answer so she continued, "What's wrong with you, Brad? You're beginning to worry me. What is it?" He nodded with his head towards the monitor's screen.

Displayed was a carefully worded message from Swiss Technologies passed through Bonn Industries to one of its divisional offices located in Denver as well as one in Alexandria, Virginia. It briefly discussed the previous failures to rectify two problems and further stated that because of the initial failures, the first in mid-November and the second, *an overtime negotiation on the holiday,* the problem areas had increased to a total of three by early December. The New York negotiations had fallen through on December 2nd and there had not been enough time to arrange another meeting on the 3rd or 4th. The company had decided to wait and analyze the current size of its growing concerns to make certain any further actions would encompass the entire situation and that any action taken would eliminate all snags in proceeding with the contract. The message had identified a total of eight areas which were now compromising the companies' position and needed to be taken care of immediately. The negotiating personnel of both the Alexandria, Virginia and Denver offices were to work out the details in a joint effort in Denver on or about the 26th of December. Further, no excuses would be acceptable for not completing the contract prior to year's end.

With one final "Oohh, my God," Sam reached over and grabbed Brad's hand and held it tightly. "Sweetheart, you okay? Where do we go from here?"

Shaking his head slowly from side to side, Brad said. "It really doesn't change anything. It only confirms what I suspected all along but refused to completely accept because of its outrageous implications. I'm fine, Sam, really. Just a shock to see in black and white that John and I have been targets since at least mid-November."

"I can't believe how innocent this message would appear to anyone other than us. Everything fits exactly right down to the overtime effort on the holiday, meaning Thanksgiving Day and the attempt on John and Abbey."

"What really has me upset is the reference to you being the third problem which occurred. It just isn't setting real well with me. I can't believe that just because of your association with me..."

Cutting him off by placing her hand gently over his mouth so he couldn't continue, Sam said. "Brad, you had no idea. You can't blame yourself for this. Besides, I wouldn't have it any other way. Your problems will always be mine and vice versa."

"You're going to be hard pressed to beat this one, Sam, but, I appreciate what you're saying. I do love you."

"Love you back, big guy. You're right, this message doesn't change anything and we do have a course of action now. Brad, do you understand what they're talking about when they make reference to the New York thing?"

"I really don't. Haller was killed at point blank range on the street in front of the boutique so, he was definitely a target. But, according to what we're looking at, the attempt was a failure. See," he said pointing to the screen and continuing, "where they say not enough time to schedule another meeting on the 3rd or 4th. If it *had* been successful, they wouldn't have needed another meeting. Unless," he stopped a moment thinking it over. "Unless you and I were the actual targets in New York and they couldn't arrange anything for the time we were going to be in Lake Placid visiting Al. That would fit."

"Why kill Haller then? You said you saw the entire confrontation with the tow truck driver and everything. Besides, only stray bullets came through the window of the boutique. The assailant walked directly up to Haller, almost as if he knew him, and began shooting. Heck, he had a ski mask on and could have come into the boutique to kill us, but didn't. Didn't you even say he took something out of the trunk of the car?"

"You're right, Sam. Sure looks like Haller was the target. Maybe, he was trying to break free from the organization or something. I don't believe, as ruthless as they are, they'd appreciate anyone leaving the organization or even attempting to."

"I just thought of something. The numbers don't add up. They identify eight problem areas. There are eight of us on this ski trip. If they didn't complete the job in New York, there'd be more than eight."

"Good point, honey. That means they knew our itinerary included going to Lake Placid. Damn! They know all our moves! Shit, what was the date of this damn message anyway?" Scrolling the screen back to the top of the message, Brad continued. "There it is, December 17th. Christ, that's the day before the gala at the embassy! They've known since the 17th the eight of us were going to be in Colorado on this ski trip. Those bastards! They have been making plans all of this time to get rid of us. They wouldn't have to be that careful out here in the middle of nowhere. Merely kill us and get rid of the evidence in some remote area. Shit, we're all ready in a remote area. Talk about making it easy for someone... Christ! And then, that son of a bitch, Colonel Dickey. He just *had* to meet me at the damn gala. Come to think of it, he met us all. Probably so the bastard could identify our bodies and confirm that all eight of his God damn problems in the contract had been handled."

"I'm afraid you're right. He probably works out of the Alexandria office of Bonn Industries."

"Not anymore. The bastard! And Sam, if there is one, Mrs. Robert F. Lambert is going to have to live with what her husband was. Now, after seeing all this, I don't feel one bit guilty about his death out there in the mountains. Mine was a reactive situation. His was planned!"

"I'm certainly glad you've finally realized that, sweetheart. I know it bothered you, but, you really didn't have a choice."

"I think we should show this to the others and let someone else handle the rest of the data in this H1 file. I'm exhausted."

They summoned the other six to the loft and showed them the message. After the shock wore off and a short discussion, Evan and Terri said they'd look over the remainder of the file for further information. The others would make final preparation for their departure at daylight the following morning. Phil's last check of the weather revealed the snowstorm was over and the stars were beginning to reveal themselves in the dark Colorado sky. The next day would be bright and sunny and another to remember.

*****

"Are you sure you know where you're heading?" asked Evan.

"It's becoming more and more familiar to me the farther we go. In answer to your question, Evan, up there," he said pointing towards the top.

"Shit, Brad. We're going to climb up that?" asked John in disbelief.

"You got it buddy. It looks harder than it really is," Brad lied.

"Somehow... I don't believe you," said John.

"Me either," agreed Evan.

"Evan, honey, where's your sense of adventure?" questioned Terri.

"I think I left it with my sense of humor. Back with Heinz at Brad's place."

After the laughter subsided, Brad pointed out the route they'd be taking to the top. "When you're climbing it, you realize it isn't as steep as it looks from down here," he lied again.

"Let me say it this time, John," said Sam.

"What's that, Sam?"

In the strongest and loudest southern accent any had heard in some time, Sam yelled out, "Lets go for it."

"Didn't quite sound the same to me," said John. "But I could tell you were sincere in your effort so, let's do it," he yelled.

The snowmobiles had carried them as far as possible and the eight were now trudging through snow, at times over knee deep. They were quickly becoming exhausted trying to carry the skis and maintain their balance. Without warning, the helicopter flew over their heads in the direction of the peak. *They were back!*

"Shit, I though we were in the damn clear," yelled Brad. "I don't think they saw us yet. Everyone, get your skis on," he said realizing they had all beat him to it. "We still have pretty good cover here but, if they search carefully, they'll see the snowmobiles where we left them." The helicopter was now returning at a lower altitude and moving much slower. "They must have landed on the lake by the summer retreat and seen the direction of the snowmobile tracks, flew to the peak and found nothing so are slowly back-tracking to find us."

"Any suggestions, Kimo Sabe?" asked John.

"Not at the moment," replied Brad in the deep simulated voice of the Lone Ranger. "Damn it! One thing is for sure though. They won't be able to land the damn thing up here. It's way to steep for that, and there's no clearing around big enough."

"At least," said Evan, showing some relief after what Brad had just said, "we won't have to climb to the top of this damn mountain."

"Better yet. They didn't catch us about half hour later. We would have been caught in the open and unable to ski."

"Should we all thank God, now or later. We're still in a hell of a mess," said John. "I think the damn chopper is getting closer again Brad. Think we should take off, buddy?"

"Hold tight for a minute," Brad said as the chopper flew quickly overhead again on its way back to the peak.

"What are they doing?" asked a frightened Sam.

"I'm not sure. They look like they are hovering about 200 yards off the peak."

"They already know we aren't up there, don't they?" asked a terrified Abbey.

"They should be able to tell that from where they are," said John trying to comfort her.

"They know we're somewhere between the snowmobiles and the top. Oooooh shit!" yelled Brad as everyone saw a trail of white smoke leave from the helicopter and slam into the side of the peak with a resounding explosion.

"What the hell are they shooting at?" questioned Phil.

"Whatever it is, I think they missed," said Terri.

"They didn't miss. They hit exactly where they intended," said Brad. "They hit the God damn mountain. Let's get the hell out of here."

"Why would they shoot at the mountain?" asked Evan.

"Of all people to ask that. Believe me, Evan, you don't want to know. Let's move it, now! Follow me, I just remembered something that just might save our lives," he concluded as he headed back down the mountain on a peculiar angle off to the left. This route would put them out in the open for a short while, but, Brad figured the end result would give them the best shot. With the sound of additional explosions ringing in their ears, they proceeded single file, following Brad.

"They saw us. Here they come," yelled John, bringing up the rear.

"What the hell is that noise?" yelled Evan.

"You don't want to know," yelled Brad. "Keep your eyes forward, we're entering the trees again."

A short distance inside the cover of the trees, with the deafening sound getting closer to them, Brad skied sharply to his left, around a huge, outcropping rock and came abruptly to a halt. "In... in... in here, everyone," he said pointing with his ski pole to the opening in the side of the mountain. Following his instructions, they quickly entered the abandoned mine. As Brad was following John into the mine, a cascade of snow, dirt and rocks began to slide over him. Reaching back, John grabbed his ski pole and pulled him further into the opening. Then, total darkness.

"Everybody okay?" asked Brad struggling to his feet and out of breath.

"I assume... *that* was a damn avalanche," said Evan in total darkness. "I can't see a damn thing."

"Well, Evan, at least I know you're fine. How about everyone else?"

One by one in the darkness of the mine entrance, they all sounded off.

"Shit, pal, that was close as hell. They fired those rockets to start the damn thing didn't they?" asked Phil.

"That, my friend, is why they were shooting at the peak," informed Brad.

"Why didn't you say something earlier?" asked John.

"I wasn't too sure how well the seven of you would ski, if you knew an avalanche was chasing your ass." Fumbling around in the dark in his back pack, Brad finally pulled out the flashlight and turned it on. Shining its light on all there faces, one at a time, Brad continued, "I think we're safe now. They're probably giving each other high fives, thinking we're buried under tons of snow. Idiots."

"Brad, I hate to bring this up, but, aren't we ahhh...kinda buried?" asked a concerned Chantal.

"Honey, you're right, but, we're all alive and kicking thanks to Brad," said her husband. "Pal, how'd you know this place was here?"

"Something had been bothering me about this mountain for some time... something I just couldn't remember. Looking back down the mountain after the first explosion, I regained my bearings. In high school, we used to camp in here. The large rock we passed on the way in here... I remembered the entrance was just on the other side of it. Thank God it wasn't blocked already."

"Speaking of being blocked, shouldn't we start clearing away the snow?" asked Terri.

"Don't bother Terri," said Brad, "that would probably take a month to clear all that out of the way."

"What do we do then, wait for the spring thaw?" asked Evan.

"This is perfect," said Brad laughing.

"Sweetheart, I don't think there is really much to laugh about. You just said we are stuck here for a month," reminded Sam.

"Nooo, I didn't Sam. I'm sorry guys, you just don't understand," Brad said still laughing.

"We nearly got wiped out in an avalanche and this guy's laughing his ass off. What's going on?" asked Evan. "Did something besides snow land on your head as John yanked you in?"

"No. And, by the way, John, thanks for the assist. If I'd remembered this mine earlier, we could've driven right to the entrance on the snowmobiles. We wouldn't have had to put up with any of the shit we just did."

"So what? Seems to me were worse off. Unless you know something we don't," said Phil.

"There's another entrance people. It's on the other side of the mountain. We simply walk through the mountain, not climb over it."

"You're kidding, Brad," said Chantal. "We went through all this and didn't have to?"

"I'm afraid so, Sis. Sorry."

"Don't be sorry. I'm just glad you remembered it when you did. This is one time I'm glad you did something that Dad wouldn't have been too pleased with."

"Is there anything we should be concerned about as far as getting to the other entrance?" asked Evan.

"There might be some animals in here. You know, bears hibernating or something."

"Are you shitting me? Christ!"

"Just hold the noise down, and they might not wake up. You wake one up from his winter nap and... well, they get pretty pissed, Evan. We certainly don't need that."

"You are shitting me," said Evan in relief and then asked. "Right?"

"Right," said Brad after a short pause and giving him a playful jab on the shoulder. Let's get the rest of the flashlights out and head to the other side."

"How far is it?" asked Sam.

"Quite a ways. From what I understand, they wanted to mine this area as quickly as possible so made another entrance. This one here is actually the second one. The original entrance is the one we're heading to. They mined from both sides, until they met somewhere in the middle of the damn mountain. I've made this trip through here, well, more times than Dad would have appreciated that's for sure, right Chantal?"

"That's for sure, Brad. If he had known you were up to this, you wouldn't have been able to sit down for a week."

"One thing *is* for sure," said Sam.

"What's that honey?"

"They must feel pretty confident that they've resolved all eight of their contractual problems," said Sam.

"Shit, man, that's right," exclaimed John. "They think we're dead. Now, *we* have the advantage. As long as we're careful, we can do pretty much what we want about them." They all agreed.

*****

"Hello," he replied in a groggy voice. "What is it?"

"Sir, this is the overseas operator. I have a call for you from Denver, Colorado," came the reply.

"The United States?" he asked with his excitement growing.

"Yes sir."

"Put it through operator," he instructed as he sat up in bed, rested his back against the gothic headboard and turned on the bedside lamp. Its brightness caused him to slightly squint.

"Hello?"

"This had *better* be good news. I told everyone concerned not to call me with bad news," he said rubbing the sleep from his eyes.

"It's good news sir. All eight areas of the contract have been worked out to your satisfaction. It's been signed, sealed and delivered."

"That's for certain... right?"

"Yes sir. For certain. By the way, you're probably going to hear about a disaster here in the Rocky Mountains on tomorrow's news."

"And what might that be?"

"Seems there was an avalanche which buried four couples."

"Sorry to hear that," he lied. "Pity."

"Real shame, sir. One never knows."

"You certainly have that right. About the contract. Congratulations. It was a job well done. I think there will be something in it for you."

"I appreciate the words and the thought. I've got to clean up a few things here so I'd best get moving."

"Do what you have to and then book yourself on a flight to Corporate Headquarters."

"Yes sir, I will. As soon as possible. Talk to you later. Bye."

"Bye," he said as he put the phone back on its cradle. Progress, gentlemen, progress he thought as he shut the light off, slid down in bed and pulled the goose down-filled comforter around his neck. Thinking of the coming morning with a smile on his face, he knew the conference room would be a happy place for a change. He'd inform the three board members who'd flown to Scotland on business about Claxton's fate from the secure line in his office. Buried in an avalanche. Hell of an accident!

*****

Climbing through the abandoned mine shaft proved to be relatively simple. Because the markings he and his high school buddies had placed had long since faded away, they'd made new markings along the way in the unending tunnels to retrace their route if necessary to find another direction. A couple of wrong turns happened, but generally by following the rails used by ore cars, it was relatively easy to find the daylight on the far side of the mountain.

With everyone believing they were buried alive and under the bright blue, sun-filled Colorado sky, they'd skied openly down the mountain and began their trek to the access road without further fear of being pursued. Finally at roadside, they'd changed from ski boots to footwear and stowed the white outer wear, skis and boots in a cache to be picked up later. Now standing on the road with a confused look, John asked, "What now?"

"Now that we're here, I'm not sure. If my memory serves me right, this road connects to another one about three miles that way," Brad said pointing. "There should be more traffic on it than on this one. From the tracks, it looks like only a couple of cars have come down this way since the snowfall. At least we can walk single file in the tracks instead of battling fifteen inches of snow every step of the way. We simply start walking and hope for the best. Maybe someone will come along and give us a lift."

"One thing's for sure. I'm damn sure going to check the license place before I accept the ride," said Evan.

"I'm glad to see a little humor returning. After what we have been through it's kinda nice for a change," said Brad.

"Brad, I'd like to take this opportunity to ahhh... personally thank you for one of the *best* ski vacations of my life. I *hate* to see it all end," said John as the others began to howl with laughter.

They'd proceeded less than a mile when they noticed a truck approaching from over a slight hill in front of them. Before they could determine how to handle the situation, Chantal noticed the yellow, unlit, emergency light on the roof of the cab. "I think it's a power company truck. Aren't they that color and don't they have a yellow emergency light on top?"

"In Maryland they are. I think you're right," replied Phil.

"That's what it is, Chantal," added Terri. "He should be able to give us a lift."

Flagging the truck to a stop, they approached the driver's window. "What the hell are all you people doing way out here?" he asked in a deep, raspy voice. Although seated and visible only through the door's window, it was evident the driver was a large muscular man. His neatly trimmed full beard couldn't hide the weathering of many Colorado winters nor the innocence apparent in the deep-set hazel eyes. It was obvious he was not a couch potato but rather, a man who enjoyed being outside in the elements, a hunter-fisherman type. He reminded Brad of Paul Bunyan, right down to the plaid, flannel shirt he was wearing.

"Long story," said Brad. "Could you give us a lift to the village?"

"Sure, but, I have to repair one of the feeder lines further up the road. You're welcome to ride with me or I can pick you up on the way back. What's your poison?"

"I think we'll ride with you," Brad said and continued. "It's getting pretty brisk out here."

"That, it is. Move whatever you have to back there to make more room for everyone," he instructed as he removed his cap, its logo revealing his choice of beer.

As the eight of them began to pile into the warm interior of the truck John asked. "How long will the repair take?"

"It's not really a repair, I just have to check the line. There was a voltage spike out here and reports say that there was another avalanche in the area. We're required to check the lines whenever it happens."

"No shit, an avalanche?"

"Yeah, most of them are small, but, I guess this one was pretty big. Tore the hell... sorry ladies," he apologized. "It tore the heck out of the trees on the other side of that mountain over there, so I hear," he said pointing through the windshield to the mountain covered with the recent heavy snowfall.

"What caused it?"

"Who knows? I've been doing this job for over eighteen years and no one ever knows. Way out here, they kinda just seem to happen. I sure as hell... sorry again ladies. I wouldn't want to be under one of those darn things," he concluded scratching the beard under his chin.

"Know what you mean," concluded Brad, not carrying the conversation any further.

"You never said what you were doing out here."

"Ohh... we've been winter camping and hiking. With that snowstorm that just passed through, we've had enough for a while. Damn snow is so deep, its hard as hell to hike through. We're exhausted."

"What some people do for exercise. Better you than me," the driver said.

"You don't know the half of it. Quite an experience, believe me."

"There it is," said the driver. "Probably take me longer to clear the snow out of the way than to read the voltage."

*****

The utility worker had been pleasant enough and had even gone out of his way to drop them at the one and only pay phone, outside the general store, in the small township nestled in the midst of the mountains. There, they'd made arrangements to rent a van for cash and have it delivered to them. According to John, if they were going to remain incognito, the last thing they wanted to do was leave an electronic trail so, credit cards were out.

The general store for the surrounding community looked as if it had come from the Hollywood set used to film *Gunfight At The OK Corral.* Actually, it was a combination of the old Assayer's Office, Western Union and hardware stores. *Ned's Supplies and Provisions* remained faintly visible on the faded red clapboard siding of the second story above the roof covering the 30 foot long pine floor porch. The hitching rail in front with two horses tied up, offered evidence that some of its customers preferred the old fashioned, not necessarily less sophisticated, way of travel or, because of the weather, they felt safer on horseback.

Next door was Wilson's Feed Store, an appropriate name for the only restaurant in the village. It was a new structure in comparison but was built to look old down to the white-washed siding which had grayed from the harsh winters, and the wood shingle roofing. On the far side of Wilson's was the actual blacksmith's stable from years past that housed horses and mules as their prospector owners visited Ned's Provisions. The stable was now stacked with fifty pound bags of various kinds of feed and fertilizer for local purchase. On the far side of the stable was the circa 1890, three-story Murphy's Hotel that had remained in operation to the present day under the same family ownership. In the mid forties, they had added the two Standard Oil gas pumps in front to service the influx of automobiles in the area. The word "Ethel" was still visible on the faded glass dome of one pump while the other had long since been smashed by an errant driver and was unlit and inoperable. A dark blue Ford was parked in front having its tank filled with super un-leaded, the only grade of gasoline now available.

Not exactly a thriving community, thought Brad, as he noticed the lone pedestrian cleaning his worn leather boots on a black wrought iron boot scrape before entering Warner's Western Wear on the other side of the general store. Brad's eyes followed a wire stretched from the second floor of the apparel store to a make-shift pole on the far side of the road. A blinking yellow caution light hung precariously over the narrow, poorly-paved road and served as the only traffic signal in the village. There were no buildings on the far side of the road because that area was reserved for a small ice-covered stream which became a torrent in early spring as the mountain snows melted and ran off.

Brad glanced at his watch. With the rented van's delivery to be anytime now, he placed a call to Ron Riddel's beeper and left the code word "hell" and the number of the pay phone from which he was calling. He then placed a call to the 47th Precinct, where hopefully, Ben Butterfield would be working the present shift. *His luck was changing*, thought Brad, as he waited for someone to inform Sergeant Butterfield of his call.

"Hello, this is Sergeant Butterfield. What can..."

"Ben?"

"Yeah, who's this?"

"It's Brad."

"Brad! Brad Claxton?"

"Yeah Ben, it's Brad. Try to hold it down... I don't want anyone to know it's me."

"Brad, we *have* to talk, but it can't be here. These lines are all recorded."

"Can't you turn the damn thing off?"

"No, I don't have any control over that."

"Then swipe the damn tape afterwards or erase it. This can't wait!"

"I'll do it. Listen, I'm glad as hell you called. You better be careful as hell Brad, someone is trying to blow your ass away."

"No shit, Sherlock!" Brad said disgustingly at the old news. "I've known that for the past three days. We've been having a grand time out here running for our lives. What the hell finally enlightened you?"

"Abe called an old friend of his in New York. They did some ballistic tests on the slugs they found. Brad, there were two shooters, both using nine millimeter weapons. All of the slugs they found in the boutique, were from a second gun. From the rifling, it looks like a silencer was used. The boutique was the only place they found evidence of the second gun. Looks like you at least, if not Sam also, were the intended targets. All the mayhem on the street was to draw attention away from the second shooter and to get you and Sam to the window."

"Those bastards. Kill all those people on the street; and, for what. Just as another cover-up for their true intentions."

"Brad, you sound as if you know who they are."

"I don't know them by individual names and...well, yes, I do, about 800 or so of them. I really can't prove anything right now but the main reason for my call was to let you know that I'm going to send you a computer disc in case anything happens. Pay particular attention to a December 17th message on the disc."

"Sounds like you've been a little busy."

"I don't have the time to explain now. Just keep it quiet that I contacted you."

"Okay, but why?"

"They think we're all dead and buried in an avalanche they started. For the time being, I want to leave it that way."

"Christ! Sounds pretty serious out there."

"Ben, you have no idea what the eight of us have been through on this ski trip. It hasn't been real pleasant, to say the least."

"Anything else I can do from this end to help out?"

"Didn't Abe say he had friends at Interpol?"

"Yeah, why?"

"We're going to need them."

"In what capacity?"

"Hell, I don't know. Maybe they could coordinate a joint search and seizure raid or whatever the legal term for it is."

"Against who?"

"Against eight," he responded and after thinking continued, "at least eight corporate headquarters located in Europe."

"God Damn! How big is this shit?"

"Enormous, Ben. Enormous. Look, I have to run, which lately seems like all I've been doing. Remember the December 17th message and take a look at the flowchart I'm sending you as well. And, Ben, for God's sake, you be careful. These people are ruthless and will stop at nothing to protect their interests."

"What are their interests?"

"I'm leaning towards... shit, I don't even know what to call it. They appear to profit somehow from preventing cures for diseases from evolving, if that makes sense. Keep that general idea in your head when you and Abe are going through the disc I'm sending."

"They stop cures for diseases? That's a horrible thought."

"No shit, man. They're horrible people. By the way, their ranks have been diminished by at least four. I'll explain what I mean by that later. Got to go, man. I'll get back to you later, I hope."

"Bye, Brad and, good luck."

"I could use a little; hell, I could use a lot. Bye."

As Brad was hanging up the receiver, the phone immediately began to ring, scaring the hell out of him. After a couple of rings and calming down, he lifted the receiver back to his ear. “Hello.”

“Brad?”

“Ron?”

“Yeah, what's up?”

“Ron, listen to me carefully. I don't have the time to repeat this. Where're you calling from?”

“The pay phone across the street from BioMed. They called me in for some damn reason on a Sunday for Christ's sake. Why?”

“Listen carefully. I'm going to throw some things at you pretty quickly and I want you to do exactly what I say, with no questions. Trust me because your life may depend on it.”

“Let me have it, pal. Short and dirty. Whatever it is I'll do it.”

“Without question?”

“You got it.”

“I believe your brother Rick's death wasn't any suicide. I think he was murdered. You can't tell anyone you've heard from me. I'm staying out of sight because of the circumstances I'm in. Certain folks think that I and my companions are dead and I want them to continue thinking it for a while. Next, I want you to leave immediately from BioMed go pick up your wife and blow the Chicago area until all this shit is cleared up. Don't, I repeat, don't even go back inside the facility to give them an excuse for your leaving. Just do it now. Get in your car, pick up your wife and leave. I know it's cold in Chicago, don't even go back inside to get your coat. Promise me that.”

“Do you have any idea what I paid for that damn overcoat? Just kidding. You have my word.”

“Good. Ron, there's a possibility the phone you're using might be bugged. Don't waste any time.”

“I doubt this one would be tapped. There's also one inside the lobby of BioMed which I could've used but decided against it. If they were going to do any wire tapping, that would be the one they'd more than likely tap.”

“Your probably right. Just pick up your wife and get the hell out of Chicago. I've got to go man. If you don't hear from me inside of a week, make contact with Sergeant Ben Butterfield at the 47th Precinct in Maryland, outside of DC. Not, I repeat, not sooner than a week. Tell him you are a friend of mine and know about the computer disc. That should verify to him that you are on the up and up."

"Butterfield at the 47th. Got it. Brad, it sounds pretty serious."

"It is. Now beat it, pal. Talk to you later. Bye."

"Bye, buddy; and, thanks for the call."

"What did they say about all this stuff going on?" asked an approaching Samantha.

Brad closed the glass-paned, bi-fold telephone booth door behind him and said. "Everyone's damned shocked at what's going on. Did you drop that extra disk in the mail?"

"I sure did. Right over there," she replied pointing to the bright blue box. "At least someone besides us will have a copy. Somehow, I think it's taken some of the pressure off us to prove everything."

"Are you going to make a quick call to your Dad in Colorado Springs?" Brad asked Phil as he arrived taking the final bite of a cold-cut sandwich.

"I've thought about that Brad and I don't think so. Not right now. That message you and Sam found dated the seventeenth didn't mention anything about Colorado Springs so I don't see any reason to call. Besides, if he were there, he may not appreciate the activity that John's got planned for his computer system. It's not exactly legal, you know? Also, he'd probably want to go directly to the authorities and let them handle all this crap, something we agreed wouldn't be in our best interest right now."

"Whatever you think's best. That sandwich any good?"

"It's definitely not from Joey's but it's not so bad. Kinda dry though," he commented as he drained his Pepsi can. "I wonder it that's the van we rented," he said as he nodded with his head towards the road and tossed the empty into a fifty-five gallon oil drum being used for trash.

"Looks like it," said Sam as the van pulled to a stop in front of the store. "I'll go in and get the others."

---- Chapter Fifteen ----

Phil pulled the van into the drive of his father's Georgian colonial home where he'd spent most of his youth. It was 1:00 PM and they'd decided this arrival time would assure that his father would have long since departed for San Francisco with his mother. Phil began to insert the key into the lock of the front door when it was quickly pushed open from the inside.

"Phil, what the hell are you guys trying to prove?" Mal's booming voice demanded.

"Pop!" an obviously startled Phil said. "I thought you and mom were going to San Francisco."

"Why, were you and your friends going to throw a party like you used to in high school when we were out of town?" Mal kidded in a stern voice.

"You decided not to go then?"

"Your mother left on time. I stayed behind to see *what the hell* all of you were up to. I'm flying the lear jet out after I find out. I *am* a pilot you know. Just, what are you guys up to? Where were all of you last night?"

"I know you're a pilot pop. We spent the night at a motel hoping... ahh, thinking you'd be gone by now. What do you mean though, where were we last night?" asked Phil, thinking his father's mood didn't fit that of a father who had just lost a son and his daughter-in-law in an avalanche.

"You haven't seen the news this morning?"

"No, we haven't. We've been kind of busy."

"Your mother and I... and your mother as well Brad and Chantal, were pretty upset at the news that you were buried in an avalanche. We've been up all night and didn't sleep a wink. We couldn't."

"Pop, you said you were upset. Does that mean you aren't anymore?" Phil hopefully asked as everyone was herded inside to the foyer and the door was closed behind them.

"I'm still upset that you made no effort to contact us yesterday when the electric company worker dropped you off. How could you not phone someone to let them know you were all right? That's not at all like you, son."

"How did you know about the power company truck driver, Mal?" asked Brad.

"He was on the news this morning. He had seen your pictures on a previous newscast where they had interviewed the helicopter pilot that saw you swallowed up in the avalanche and called the station. He positively, with no doubt in his mind, identified the three of you, actually, all of you, as being the ones he gave a ride. His claim was verified by someone else in the village that sold the bunch of you some sandwiches. And another person saw you leave in a van, probably the one out front, right?"

Phil, not answering his father's question, said, "Shit, it was on the news. That means everyone knows we are alive."

"And what we are driving," added John.

"That's... not... good," said Evan slowly shaking his head from side to side and placing his arm around Terri.

"Is there something wrong with the people that care about you knowing you're okay? I don't understand," stated a confused Mal.

"It's the ones that... don't care for us that have us concerned, Mal," stated Brad squeezing Sam's hand.

"Just what have the eight of you gotten yourselves involved in? Does this have anything to do with the phone call you made to me from DC, Phil."

Remembering the call he placed when he was having lunch with Brad, Phil replied, "I'm afraid it does, Pop. It has really mushroomed... kinda outta control."

"You bunch of amateurs. Damn it. Follow me into the other room. I didn't want to but, the hell with 'em. It's getting pretty personal now. I have to discuss something with all of you."

"Pop, you said the hell with them. Who are *them*?" asked Phil, following everyone into the recreation room.

"Phil, when you called me from DC, I told you to leave it alone, remember?"

"I remember you saying something like that but, I really didn't think you meant anything by it. I didn't even give it a second thought. Christ, Pop, I was calling to give you a warning, not to receive one. As a matter of fact, Pop, I still don't know what you're getting at."

"Brad, remember the three of us shooting pool on Thanksgiving Day. I said I had other interests to kinda occupy my time."

"Vaguely, I recall you saying something along those lines."

"I know, I'm going to get my ass in a lot of trouble, excuse my French," he said to the four girls and continued, "but, I'm fed up with the lack of progress they're making and you guys are getting too caught up in their bullshit."

"Pop, you keep referring to them, they and their. *Who* are you referring to?"

"Where to start? I shouldn't be making you aware of this, but I don't believe, at this point, there is anything else I can do. You are all in a position that... well, someone might not want you around because of what they *think* you might know."

"What you are trying to say is that someone might want to kill us?" asked Phil.

"Son, that's exactly what I'm trying to say. You've hit the nail right on the head."

"No shit, Pop! Do you *really* think that damn avalanche was an *accident*?"

"You mean it *wasn't*?"

"Of course not for Christ's sake! It was started on purpose to try to get rid of us and make it look like an accident; and, that's not the half of it."

"You mean there's more?"

"Try three days worth on for size and see how it fits," said Brad, growing a little irritated and as a result getting a squeeze from Sam's hand. Calmer, after the squeeze, Brad continued, "Mal, we've virtually been running for our lives for the past three days."

"Christ, I had no idea it had gone that far. But, from who?" Mal asked with legitimate concern in his voice.

"From these guys," Brad said handing Mal a copy of the flowchart they'd prepared showing the corporate structure of Swiss Technologies.

Looking at the sheet of paper, Mal said, "Holy shit! Where'd you get this from?"

"Something we came up with in our spare time when we didn't have anything better to do," quipped John. "Sounds like, you might be, shall we say, a little familiar with what's there."

"Well, Pop, do you know anything about it?"

"Only the one company... Bonn Industries. Where the hell did you get all this other stuff?"

"It doesn't really matter right this second," said Phil, "we can prove it is a viable corporate structure," he concluded, holding up his copy of the computer disc.

"Did I call you guys amateurs earlier?"

"I believe you did. Why, dad?" asked Chantal.

"Only that, it's obvious, they're approaching this in the wrong way."

"There you go again with the "they" thing, Pop. I think, if you know anything at all, you owe us some straight answers."

"Absolutely. You've accomplished more in three days than they have in nearly a year."

"*Who* the hell are they?"

"The God damn CIA, that's who."

"The CIA? The Central Intelligence Agency out of Langley, Virginia?" asked John incredulously.

"The same ones," replied Mal, his Texan accent all but history. "I've been working with them for about a year on special assignment. That's what I was talking about on Thanksgiving Day, something to keep me occupied."

You went to work for the CIA, Pop?" asked Phil.

"Not exactly, they recruited me for this. I didn't go to them. It's a task force set up to investigate suspected international sabotage."

"Sabotage against what?" asked Sam.

"It's only a theory and I don't even know from what information the theory was developed but, to answer your question Sam, sabotage against medical research facilities."

"Does it have anything to do with a particular antibody?" asked Brad.

"I don't know anything about any antibody, other than the one the CIA insisted we make a record of in my center's data base. They gave me all the data to enter and I did it. After about six months of no activity, they instructed me to make a report about it, as if our research efforts had uncovered it, and send it to your center, Brad."

"When did the first report go out, do you remember?"

"Probably around the first of November."

"Damn, two weeks before the explosion at the town house."

"You mean that it's related?"

"That and a ton of other shit."

"Are you serious?"

"Why do people always ask me that. Is it a particular look I have or what? Of course, I'm serious."

"Pop, I think, as hard as it might be for you to swallow, that the eight of us here know more about what's going on than, the so-called professionals you've become acquainted with. Do we know any of them that you're working with?"

"Probably the only you know is Colonel Dickey. Brad, you met him at the gala. I believe he told me that."

"Christ! Colonel Dickey was involved with this shit for the CIA?"

"Hell yes he is. He's heading up the task force that I'm a part of."

"No, he isn't, Pop."

"What's that supposed to mean?"

"He's dead, Pop."

"Dead! How the hell did that happen?"

"I ummm, shot and killed him out in the mountains two days ago."

"*You did what*?"

Seeing Phil was having difficulty, Brad took over. "Mal, Colonel Dickey was a, how do you say it, a double agent. He was actually working for the Swiss Technologies Company. Shit, he tried to kill me and Phil saved my life. He had to shoot him or Dickey would have gotten me first and then Phil next. It's that simple."

"What did you use to shoot him with? Hell, I thought the eight of you went skiing, not hunting."

"With this," said Phil, pulling the weapon from beneath his jacket.

"Where the hell did you get this damn thing?" asked Mal, taking the automatic from Phil to examine it.

"Brad got it from Colonel Dickey's brother. He didn't really have a use for it anymore," replied Phil.

"Sweet Jesus! You mean George, the Green Beret?"

"He's not a Green Beret any longer," added Brad.

"I know he's not now, but he used to be," replied Mal.

"He used to be a lot of things, including an assassin for Swiss Technologies, but no longer. He had a terrible fall and broke his neck."

"*George is dead also*? This is too much to believe. Harold would never have killed you Phil, he's your..." Mal stopped in mid-sentence not wanting to complete the thought.

"You were going to say that he was my real father, right Pop?"

"You knew then?"

"Yeah, mom told me when Chantal and I got married. I'm surprised you knew."

"I've known all along, son. You see, I can't have kids because I've always been sterile. I considered myself lucky because he gave me something I couldn't provide on my own, you son," he said, his eyes beginning to well up. "You've made me nothing other than proud. Your mother seemed happy enough. She was very young and immature then and realized she'd made a mistake. Without saying, I forgave her for her one night. *Hell,* I wasn't any angel myself. I do love you, you know."

"I know and I love you to," Phil said giving his father a hug.

"Are you okay, about Harold, I mean."

"I'm fine with it Dad, believe me. He got what he deserved, believe me. And, now this double agent thing yet."

"Double agent." Mal repeated. "No wonder there wasn't any progress being made by the damn task force. Phil, don't get me wrong, but, I never really liked or trusted that guy. Something about his eyes."

"Exactly," seconded Brad. "Look Mal, we've gotten involved in something here by accident. Something, it appears, bigger than you or this damn CIA task force you're a part of even dreamed of. The big problem is, as I see it, we don't know who we can trust. In the mean time, hit men from Swiss Technologies are on a relentless mission to wipe us out."

"He's right dad," said Chantal.

"Pop, raise the garage door for me. I want to get that damn van out front, inside and out of sight."

"Go through the garage and open it from the inside, Phil.

"Mr. Bowers, have you ever heard of Lisbon Industries before?" asked Abbey.

"I think they have some marketing people working at the lab. Why? You think they're connected in some way?"

"Look at the sheet you have," instructed Abbey. They're the newest division of Swiss Technologies. New divisions, at least we think so, are brought into being for no other purpose than to destroy research efforts on promising work such as the antibody the CIA wanted you to put into your data base."

"You mean that it's a valid antibody? It actually works as a splitter? Where did the CIA get a hold of it?"

"At this point, that doesn't really matter," informed Brad. "What matters is that your center, as well as mine back in DC, are targets because we know of its existence. Shit, there may have been a leak in the Swiss Technologies organization. Anything could have happened. At least, the CIA knows about the problem, one which Harold Dickey was trying to squelch by not making any progress. Looks as if they wanted to set up your center as bait and when it didn't work, they decided to use the Center back in DC as additional bait. Now, it's really working. These rats are coming out of the woodwork."

"Mal," interjected John, "while Phil is getting the car out of sight, we should brief you on what we know to date and how we went about finding it out. We were hoping you wouldn't be here so we could use your computer link up with the Center to continue finding out what we can about this outfit."

"You uncovered all this other stuff using a computer?"

"A computer and a lot of help from each and every one of us."

"Amazing. First, let's see how much you have and then, you can let me know what you think the next best step is."

"Fair enough," concluded John as the eight began to bring Mal up to date on all of the events that had happened.

*****

"My God," said Mal. "I can see why you're trying to stay out of sight. In barely over an hour, you've convinced me that these guys are willing to do anything to protect their interests. I'm shocked as hell all of you are still breathing."

"Well, Mal, we can still put steam on a mirror but, it hasn't been any picnic the last three days," said Evan and continued. "All I know is that the eight of us are pretty fed up with this stuff and are determined to put an end to it."

"I couldn't agree with you more, Evan. Brad, where do we go from here?"

"We have to get John's ass back on the computer terminal, if he's up to it."

"He's ready," said Abbey. "He's been anxious to get at the Swiss Technology data base for some time."

"John, you mean to tell me that you can get into their data base?"

"If I can't, it'll be the first one ever that I couldn't hack into. Besides, I'm more determined on this one than any other I can remember because they've pissed me off. I don't think there's any question, especially with the start we have from the Bonn Industries' data base. No doubt about it; I'll get in! It's just a matter of time."

"You've never seen him operate, Mal," said Brad. "He kept me up all damn night doing this kinda stuff when we roomed together in college."

"It's never going to happen if I don't get started. Where's your computer system anyway Mal?"

"In the office at the back of the house."

"I'll show him, dad," chimed in Chantal.

*****

Nearly two hours had passed since John entered Mal's office and, as ususal, he had yet to take a break. The others were gathered in the living room and in the midst of a hot discussion. As Mal learned more about the events since November, he would simply shake his head from side to side in disbelief, most of the time not saying a word.

"Mal, is there someone we can trust on this CIA task force, or anyone else for that matter, with some authority to do something?" asked Sam.

";After finding out about Harold Dickey, I couldn't venture a guess on who we could trust. I didn't really like the guy at all but at least I thought he could be trusted. Guess I was pretty stupid after all."

"Not really," assured Brad. "He's been fooling a lot of folks for a lot of years. There was no way you could have known. What I don't understand is how someone like him can get inside an organization like the CIA. I wonder how long he's been working as a double agent."

"As far as I know, he's been with the government, off and on, for at least 25 years probably using the Air Force assignments as a cover," Mal replied. "My guess is he was recruited by Swiss Technologies after being an agent for the CIA for a number of years. As I understand it, that's normally the way his type of scum surfaces because it would take too long to groom someone else for the position. And then, after all their efforts, the guy may not pass the security clearances required to gain employment with the agency or, even if he does, he may not be assigned to a section that directly benefits them. They probably target people for recruiting that are all ready in a position that can help them and then, pay them a ton of money for the classified information they want."

"Brad, how's that wound on your side doing? Do you need anything for it?"

"It's fine, Mal, thanks for asking. I've been in worse shape."

"Like right after your crash in the Olympics for example?" he asked with a smile in his deep Texan drawl.

Brad shook his head and returned a grin. "I'm never going to be allowed to live that one down. You know what though? Through all this crap over the past three days, my shoulder never popped its socket. I'd say that's pretty damn good."

"Brad, honey. We should change the dressing on it though. It may not be that bad, but you don't want it to get infected."

John entered the room, rubbing his eyes, and said, "We should be getting something soon... maybe in the next hour or so. I'm into their system and the decryption at the Center back in DC shouldn't take that long before the transmission of the data here. I've set the alarm on the system in your office, Mal. When it sounds, we will begin receiving the files. You have a hell of a system in there."

"Damn, John. You're really something on those things. Hell, I wouldn't know if it's a good system or a bad one. I rarely use it so couldn't really say what all it can do."

"One good thing, you've got a damn fine printer hooked to it. Not like that one we had to use the other day. It's a page printer, not a line printer; prints a whole damn page at once so, it'll save us a buncha time. By the way Brad, the Center's off line until this stuff is finished. I wanted to make sure nothing screwed up the process."

"No problem, John. I doubt if anyone will be trying to contact the Center until the day after tomorrow anyway."

"What's the day after tomorrow?"

"The second of January. You know, the day after New Year's Day."

"Darn, with all this going on, I completely forgot. *Tomorrow* is New Year's Eve. I don't suppose there's any chance we'll be back in DC for the party we were supposed to go to."

"Hardly. From what Mal's told us, most everyone is aware we're alive, but they still don't know where we are. We're certainly not strolling into a party as if nothing's happened."

“You all would probably be better off staying right here until this blows over,” said Mal.

“Pop, this isn't just going to blow over. We've found ourselves in somewhat of a dogfight here. As I see it, it's basically come down to us or them. The past three days have proven just how persistent they are. Actually, they've been determined to protect themselves ever since shortly before the explosion at Brad's. It's up to us to find a way to expose them and put them out of business.”

All nodded in agreement as Mal said, “Phil, I know you're right, but son, I'm worried that the eight of you may be a little out of your league. You're definitely going to have to come to grips with the fact that you're going to need some professional help. Help from someone with the authority, power, and resources to do something other than just talk.”

“You're absolutely right Mal,” said Brad. “The problem is, we don't know who the hell that might be. These bastards have already gotten into the CIA for Christ's sake. God only knows what other organizations they might have infiltrated by now. We simply don't know who to trust. And, until we do, we're going to continue to gather as much information to use against them as possible. The more stuff we have to sink their ship when the time comes, the more responsive the proper authorities will be.”

About to add to the discussion, Mal was cut off by the sound of the computer alarm from the back side of the house. “Here it comes,” said John excitedly, jumping up and hurrying back to the office. “This should give us some answers.”

“I hope it provides us with enough to take it to the authorities and get the responsibility off our backs,” said Abbey.

“It's got to provide more than conjecture and theories or, I'm afraid the authorities will be handcuffed from doing anything,” said Sam.

“If they can't do something with what we already have,” quipped Evan, “they should be handcuffed and led away.”

“That's for sure,” concluded Terri. “I'm not sure about the law, Sam, but I don't think the authorities in New Zealand would make light of the information we have.”

“Evan, maybe we *should* approach the authorities in New Zealand. After all, as far as we know, that's where all this stuff started. Maybe they'd spearhead an international investigation into the activities of Swiss Technologies.”

"I hadn't thought about that possibility before but we should probably discuss the matter with Terri's father. What do you think, Terri?"

"It just might work. At least the authorities at home would be hearing it from one of their Ambassadors and not his air-head daughter."

"But, would he do it?" questioned Brad.

"If he believes someone is trying to put the hurt on his daughter, he'll do it! Believe me," said Evan. "I know my future father-in-law well enough to know that."

"Ohhh really," said Terri.

"Of course he would," said Evan.

"I don't mean that. I'm talking about you calling him your future father-in-law. Do you know something I don't?"

"Ohhh that. I've been meaning to talk to you about it. I kind of assumed it was a given you know, that we were going to get married."

"A given? A given, you say? How come I'm unaware of this given? What time frame are you talking about?"

"As soon as possible. That is if your answer is yes," replied Evan, turning slightly red and noticing everyone smiling at the situation he had created for himself. "As soon as we get a break from all this stuff. The first time we get home to New Zealand, I think we should tie the knot as they say in the states."

Enjoying Evan's squirming, Terri paused before answering. "I've always wanted to get married, since the first time I met you at the embassy. And you know, I also always wanted to get married in New Zealand. Nothing against the United States everyone," she apologized to the group with a smile and continued. "I couldn't imagine a better home coming, Evan. Of course I will; and I hope everyone here can attend." She noticed the immediate relief on Evan's face, crinkled her nose in a girlish affectation and gave him a big kiss.

From the doorway to Mal's office, John asked. "Are any of you people the least bit interested in this stuff?"

"Sorry, honey, but Evan just proposed to Terri. They're going to get married," informed Abbey.

"That's great news you two," John said as they entered the office. He hugged them both and immediately began to pass some papers around as the printer continued to output the information. "Remember, the most important thing we're looking for is where the hell this organization gets its revenues. How the hell does it make its money?"

After scanning the computer output for nearly an hour, Chantal finally said excitedly, “I think this is what we've been looking for.”

“What do you have there, honey?” asked Phil.

“It looks like an accounts receivable file.”

“If that's what it is, it's exactly what we need,” said Brad.

“Call me stupid but I still don't understand what's so important about Swiss Technologies' revenue sources,” stated a befuddled Mal.

“Pop, we suspect the company of stopping medical cures from surfacing which falls in line with the CIA task force's belief that there's espionage against medical research facilities. They have to have a motive for doing it. Most companies are in existence to make profits. Now, how can someone profit from halting medical research studies?”

“I have no idea.”

“Well, we don't either. The answer might lie in who they are receiving their revenues from. That's why this accounts receivable file may be so important.”

“Well, let's get to it. What does it say Chantal?”

“Heck, I'm no accountant, but it appears to be a ledger of some sort which shows billing and payments. It lists companies and changes in their respective balances due. Now, that's odd.”

“What's odd?” asked Brad.

“It appears the balance due for each company is increased or decreased by the same amount each time there is an entry. I don't understand what's going on.”

“It looks pretty simple to me, Sis. These companies are being provided a service rather than a product. Chances of all the companies ordering the same exact dollar amount of products month after month are nil. They're receiving a service of some sort from Swiss Technologies.”

“You mean like at the Center back in DC, right Brad?” asked Abbey. “Our subscribers are charged the same flat fee for access to our data holdings.”

“Only one difference and, a hell of a big one,” stated John.

“How's it any different?” asked Brad.

“Take a quick look at what the monthly flat rate is.”

“My God!” exclaimed Brad. “That can't be right, can it? One million dollars a month. Hell of a nice round number, don't you think? For what service?”

"Each of the subsidiaries of Swiss Technologies, at least on the surface, has appeared to be involved in marketing research. Is it possible for a company to hire marketing help at the rate of twelve million per year?" asked Sam.

"Marketing or advertising. Pretty much the same thing the way I look at it. A lot of larger companies have budgets that would boggle your mind. I wonder what General Motors spends?" asked John. "Shit, what was the cost for 30 seconds of advertising during the Super Bowl. Probably a million for half a minute. Hell, Pepsi Cola does probably five or six spots during the course of the game. That's half a year of marketing support from Swiss Technologies. Pretty cheap when you look at the big picture."

"I think you may be overlooking something here."

"What are you getting at Brad?" asked Sam.

"I only glanced over the listing of companies here, but, I don't see any mention of companies or research facilities that we know they've been involved with. For example, BioMed isn't even on this list and according to Ron Riddel, that's why they were in Chicago. This listing isn't for marketing research. It reflects charges and payments for some other kind of service, whatever it might be."

"Can I interject something into the mix?" asked Mal.

"Feel free, dad," said Chantal.

"I don't know what each of these companies does but, I'm familiar with some of them. It appears, this is a listing of companies in the pharmaceutical and diagnostic fields or they are manufacturers of medical treatment equipment. This one here, for example," he said pointing, "manufactures the radioactive seeds for implanting in cancerous tumors. And, this one manufactures directional radiation therapy equipment."

"What are you saying, Mal," asked Evan.

"Only that," Mal said and continued after a short pause, "the ones I'm familiar with on this list are involved with drugs, equipment, or whatever, used to treat diseases. Even this one. It's the leading manufacturer of a drug to alleviate nausea in patients under going chemotherapy."

"How many companies are on that listing?" asked Terri.

"Looks like about 120 or so," said Chantal.

"One hundred and twenty companies times twelve million a year," said John, arriving at a total in his mind. "Christ, that's one point four billion dollars a year. We sure as hell know now, where their payroll money is coming from. That's unbelievable!"

"Unbelievable," echoed Brad. "And for what?"

"You youngsters are really kinda in the dark about the atrocities that can and do occur in the real world, aren't you?" asked Mal.

"What do you mean by that pop? In the past three days we've been involved in some pretty evil things and have been pretty much enlightened with regards to the real world."

"It's obvious to me, son, what's going on here. And, believe me, it really makes me sick."

"Don't keep us in limbo here, Mal. What are your thoughts?" asked Brad.

"It's obvious these companies are being blackmailed into subscribing to Swiss Technologies. There's no marketing or advertising being performed on their behalf that we know of so, the only thing Swiss Technologies has to offer them is protection."

"How so, blackmailed?" asked Evan. "I mean, what happens to them if they don't pay their monthly tab and what kind of protection could they offer them that would cost a million bucks a month."

"Maybe, protection was a bad choice of words. Let's call it assurance instead."

"Insurance against what?" asked Chantal.

"Not insurance, Chantal, assurance."

"Assurance of what?" questioned Phil.

"Sadly enough son, assurance that the products they produce will always be in demand."

"And just how would they be able to assure such a thing to these companies? Shit, never mind, Mal. I just realized how," said Brad.

"Well, I haven't realized it yet. How about informing me," said Sam.

"Honey," replied Brad, "you're the one that came up with the sinister idea as you called it, of what they were doing, remember? Stopping progress on research studies that were showing some promise."

"So what you're saying Mal, if I understand," said John, "is that for a million bucks a month, Swiss Technologies is making certain that cures, or whatever, are not allowed to surface that would make these companies' products obsolete. Correct?" asked John.

"In a nutshell, that's it," replied Mal. "For example, the company I spoke of earlier, the one that produces the nausea drug. If cancer was eradicated, the company would more than likely go out of business because that one drug is basically their claim to fame. It's the product that generates most of their revenues. Another one there," he said pointing to the listing, "makes parts for Catscans and MRIs. They don't manufacture them, but provide an awful lot of the components. Like General Motors has suppliers of motors and car bodies. These components are designed specifically for the equipment they're intended for and basically have no other use."

"Wouldn't these companies have been allocating money to research and development in case their products did become obsolete?" asked Terri. "Wouldn't that be just good business?"

"They probably do have research efforts underway. What their budgets are, who knows?" stated Brad. "But, you know, if they have guarantees that their existing product base is going to remain unchanged and their products are going to remain in demand, why would they care what the results of an in-house research effort might produce? They would simply sit back and continue to reap the rewards without much further effort. The stockholders of the companies are only interested in the bottom line figures, not how they were achieved. As long as they keep getting their dividend checks and the price of the shares they own doesn't fluctuate drastically in a negative way, they'd never be suspicious."

"Brad, we had a discussion about patents running for, I believe you said, seventeen years. Wouldn't other companies then begin to make generic products for consumption."

"You're absolutely right, honey. They would certainly have to control that situation as well, at least in some manner. Maybe, they are and we just aren't aware of it. Hell, we already know they're controlling the demand for the product. They have probably already developed a methodology for controlling the supply as well. Basic economics is that if you have control of both the supply and demand, you can name your own price. A pretty enviable position to be in."

"I might be stupid but, I don't understand how this scheme ever got started in the first place," said Evan. "If someone came to me and said that for a million bucks a month they'd guarantee my products would remain in demand and that I would remain as one of the primary suppliers, I, quite frankly, wouldn't know what to make of the offer. I would automatically smell a rat somewhere and be suspicious as hell as to the offer's legality. Swiss Technologies *has* to have some assurance of its own to go around making offers or demands such as this. They'd have to know the companies would accept with no questions asked. *How* in hell is that possible?"

"Hell of a point Evan," said Brad. "Getting back to Mal's choice of the word blackmail, how would they convince these people that they could put them out of business?"

"Simple, tell them you have a cure for the disease that would make their products obsolete."

"You're right, John, but, who would believe someone *telling* them there was a cure?"

"Then, Brad, prove it to them. Show 'em the damn cure!"

"Hold on a minute here! Do you have any idea what you just said?"

"Of course I do Brad, but, can you think of a better scenario to answer Evan's question?"

"Not off the top of my head, that's for sure," Brad replied slowly, obviously caught off guard.

"It certainly makes sense to me," said Evan.

"Me as well," interjected Mal. "They *must* have a cure for cancer for Christ's sake! And, whatever they have, it must be preventative as well."

"Why do you say that?" asked Phil.

"If it didn't prevent Cancer, they'd simply market the cure themselves and reap the rewards. And, very high ones for the next, ahhh was it seventeen years, Brad?"

"Only if they applied for the patent. As long as no one can duplicate it, they simply wouldn't bother. They'd produce it forever, capturing sole possession of the market place and setting their own price. It can either be duplicated or like you say, Mal, it's preventative as well. I tend to agree with you."

"Let's slow down here," said Terri. "Let me try to catch up with what's being suggested by you guys. We now feel that Swiss Technologies has a cure for Cancer and that they're using this knowledge to force companies into million dollar a month payments or they will run them out of business? Is that basically what I'm hearing?"

"I think you've got it, hon," said Evan.

"Okay. Well then, what's to prevent one of these companies from getting together and reversing the table on Swiss Technologies. They could blackmail them by saying they're going to inform the authorities of what they've been doing."

"They may not be aware of anyone else being extorted," said Phil. "Even if they were, how would they prove anything against Swiss Technologies. They've seen proof of the cure, but rest assured they don't have the cure in their possession. Besides, Swiss Technologies has provided these companies with a sure-fire method of showing enormous profits for years to come. A million a month is a small price to pay."

"The ends justify the means. I've always hated that saying," said Sam. "Where do people like this come from? People with no morals whatsoever."

"By the size of this organization and the number of companies under their control, from everywhere it appears," said Brad. "One thing that I don't want to lose sight of is, getting a hold of the cure they've been hiding for all these years. Can you imagine the ramifications? How much money is spent each year on Cancer treatment that could be better spent?"

"I think it's very important to all of us, Brad," said John, "you understandably even more than the rest of us. The question is, where is it and where is the documentation on the studies that developed the cure? What damn vault would Swiss Technologies be using to house that information. I doubt very seriously they'd maintain a file on their data base. That's too easy to get at. It would have to be in hardcopy someplace, on paper, but, where?"

"Maybe," said Abbey, "the rest of these files we're looking at will point us in the right direction. There might be some reference to the location of the documentation we're looking for."

"We're never going to know if we don't start looking through this stuff. At least we know what we are looking for," said Brad.

*****

After six or seven pots of coffee and a few bites of food they had barely put a dent in the reams of paper generated by John's intrusion into the Swiss Technologies' data base. The printer had bombarded them with seemingly an unending pile of information and with the exception of one item, they'd been able to verify all the information they'd prepared in the A-frame.

"Amazing," someone had said, "what can be accomplished under pressure." The only question remaining unanswered was the actual name of the disease being used as a keyword for Lisbon Industries. No one could venture a guess and they'd even gone to the extent of looking for an association in Mal's considerable medical library. "LANCES" simply didn't exist. It was very disturbing, especially considering that everything else on the flow chart fit perfectly.

Other recovered information proved beneficial in building a case against Swiss Technologies. It was revealed in one message file that a Doctor Peter M. Phillips, currently employed as an executive with the Center for Disease Control in Atlanta, was on the Oslo Enterprises payroll as well. In fact, he'd been instrumental in setting up Oslo Enterprises in 1985. That bit of information shed some light on how BioMed in Chicago might obtain some of the Ebola virus for research efforts, a fact that Rick Riddel, Ron's brother, could have discovered while working there. Put simply, it provided a possible motive for his murder. Throughout the evening, Mal just kept muttering the words "shocking and disgusting".

Another file, entitled *Divisional Disbursements*, provided a breakdown of funds allocated and electronically transmitted to the various divisions to later be passed to their key employees scattered around the world. The amount of money being transmitted was astronomical and was done on a monthly basis. The file further revealed three categories for which the funding was earmarked, Team Salaries, Team Expenses and Team Special Funding.

It was determined that the key employee of the respective division was actually a team leader for Swiss Technologies even though he was paid through the divisional level. This person would most likely be the only one employed by an unsuspecting facility and would have his own secretive staff of employees who he controlled and paid, hence the category *Team Salaries.*

The category of *Team Expenses* more than likely dealt with the normal expenses associated with employment such as travel expenses, lodging, transportation and the such. "God knows," someone had said, "these bastards certainly get around."

The third category, *Team Special Funding,* after lengthy discussion, was determined to mean special allocation of funds to be applied to specific projects, such as *contract negotiations and problems*, which Swiss

Technologies approved. There was absolutely no doubt about it now; Swiss Technologies was running the entire show.

Allocations had been made to a few key employees or team leaders which coincided perfectly with the events Sam and Brad, as well as the other six, had been undergoing since that fateful day in November. The final link in the operation of Swiss Technologies was the final allocation of special funding to the Team Leader, Harold Dickey, on December 24th, just prior to the events of the past three days.

"That's the final touch. I think we have enough now to bury them in any court," stated Sam in a litigious manner.

"It's not good enough to think it. We have to be damn certain," suggested a concerned Brad with a frown. "When the authorities make their move, it has to be swift and the indictment has to be strong enough for any judge to deny them bail."

"You're right, pal," said Phil. "If they get out on bail, you can bet your ass they have enough money stashed away to go into hiding forever. Once they have them in custody, the evidence has to be strong enough to keep them there."

"That brings up something that has been bothering me for a couple of years," said Evan.

"A couple of years? What are you talking about?" asked Terri.

"Only that... never mind, it's not pertinent."

"Shit, Evan, spit it out. What's on your mind?" asked John.

"Well, you know when you go into a Post Office here in the states and they have pictures of the... I guess your FBI calls them the Ten Most Wanted."

"Yeah, that's it Evan, you're right. So?"

Continuing, Evan asked in a serious manner with a totally straight face, "Well, why the hell didn't they hold on to these guys when they were taking their damn pictures?"

Evan's query brought a round of laughter from the group.

"Christ, Evan, that's a hell of a good point," stated John. "That's good man, food for thought. What made you bring it up a time like this?"

"I just thought, we might need a little humor before we take a break to get something to eat. I'm starved."

"That's Brad's line, Evan," said Sam. "But now that you mention it, I'm a little hungry myself."

"We've been at this for hours. I've been so wrapped up in it I didn't even realize what time it was or that my stomach is growling and saying feed me, feed me," said Brad. "To use a well known phrase, I am starved. Mal, have you anything to eat around here?"

"Hell, I don't really know. Sybil does all the shopping."

"Well, Dad," said Chantal, "how about the four girls go out and round something up and you guys try to relax and take a break for a while."

"Sounds good to me," replied Mal. "I'm kind of looking forward myself to putting something in here," he said grabbing his stomach with his hands. "Chantal, see if there's any chili out there."

"No way man," said Brad, "not after the story you told us on Thanksgiving Day! Sis, if you find any out there throw it out."

"Don't worry, Brad, you can bet on it. I don't care if it's the only thing in the house to eat," Chantal said over her shoulder as she and the other three girls left the office, "it's going in the trash."

"What the hell is wrong with chili?" asked Evan. "I've grown to like it since I've been in the states."

"Let's just say, it does funny things to Mal here," said Brad faking a punch to Mal's mid-section.

"I think I get your drift."

"If Pop had some chili," said Phil, "you'd be getting a drift you didn't bargain for. One that would gag a maggot."

"It's not that bad, son. You know, there's something that hasn't been discussed yet that could be very serious."

"What pop?"

"Only that, Colonel Dickey, as it turns out, was a team leader. How many were in his team for this special funding thing out here? Better question, how many people on the CIA task force were members of his team?"

"There isn't any "could be serious" about it. It is serious Mal. Now you know our concerns about who the hell to go to with all this shit," said Brad. "Christ, these guys are into the CIA, the Center for Disease Control and God only knows what else. They own or have infiltrated numerous facilities engaged in research and are in effect, blackmailing about 120 other companies and facilities. Their organization makes the Mafia look small in comparison and the activities they're involved in makes them look like Saints in comparison. They also have a data base of medical knowledge that makes our Center in DC look small."

"And to add to the data base thing, Brad," said John. "They're exactly 180 degrees out of sync with what we're doing. The Center's data base was established to find or promote research into finding cures. Theirs is designed to provide information so they can hide or prevent cures from being developed."

"Shit. You guys have really stepped into it," said Mal. According to the records we've gone through so far, it suggests to me that they were involved in the latest outbreak of Ebola in Africa. Christ, they had one of their Team Leaders on the expedition that went over to the Dark continent after the outbreak started. Shit, they could've started the damn thing with having their man Phillips in Atlanta. We know the same damn guy was in Africa about a month before the outbreak occurred. Probably wanted to test a treatment."

"What good would that do them?" asked Evan.

"If they've developed a cure for it and the formula proved out for them in Africa, they could charge a pretty penny for it."

"Providing there were outbreaks they could, of course."

"If they can start one in Africa, they could damn sure start one here," concluded Mal.

"You mean, you think these guys would start an outbreak just to sell... never mind, I already know the answer to that."

"Ruthless as hell, aren't they?" asked Phil. "I see what you mean, Brad, when you say they make the Mafia look like angels."

"What about all these other diseases that they're associated with; Leukemia, Ebola, AIDS, Small Pox and Lances, whatever that is?" asked Evan.

"Let's go through them one by one," suggested Brad. "Leukemia is a form of Cancer so more than likely, they have a cure for it."

"I'll give you that," said Phil.

"The next one, as far as we can tell, would be Ebola and Mal's given us a pretty viable scenario for it."

"I'll give you that one also," said Phil.

"Let's see, that brings us to the AIDS virus."

"How are you going to develop a theory about that one?" asked John.

"Mal, if you would, take a look at the listing of companies that Chantal found on that accounts receivable ledger. See if any of them are primarily involved with AIDS. While you're doing that, let's move on to the Natural Cures from Stockholm Technology. I believe, they're primarily involved in making certain that natural cures don't surface in the areas they're most concerned with."

"You mean things like eating a ton of broccoli a day?" joked Evan.

"Precisely to the point as usual, Evan," said Brad. "We can tell from the records we have that their Team Special Funding has been minimal recently. Probably not much of a threat to them in the natural environment. Shit, they haven't even had a Team Leader assigned to them in the past three years. The only thing we can prove about them is that they're the ones who bought out the facility in London."

"Okay, pal, what about Small Pox?" asked Phil.

"Hold it a minute!" said an excited Mal.

"What you got, Pop"?

"At least seven of these companies, I know are strictly associated with AIDS. This one here manufactures the blood test kits. They're the only ones that produce the kits. They supply the world. What a blow to them it would be if AIDS went away. And this one, another nausea drug manufacturer but for AIDS patients. It helps patients keep their food down during later stages of the disease so they don't have to be fed intravenously. It helps them maintain a higher body weight to battle the disease as long as possible. Brad, my boy, it appears there may be a cure for AIDS as well. Why else would these companies be on this list. They have nothing what-so-ever to do with Cancer. Ten bucks says they're being blackmailed in the same way."

"Shit, Brad. What the hell have we uncovered here?" asked Phil. "Okay, I'll give you the AIDS as well. Pop, are there any companies there, associated with Small Pox?"

"Don't see any but, I wouldn't really expect to either."

"Why is that?" asked John.

"In recent history, Small Pox hasn't been a real big issue in the medical world. It's nearly been eradicated so, there would be very few companies devoting much of their resources to it."

"That makes sense," said Evan. "But, as lousy as these bastards are, I wouldn't put it past them to bring it to the front of everyone's mind again. With some new strain or whatever you call them. A mutant or something?"

"Good point, Evan. Does that give you a theory to hang your hat on about Small Pox, Phil?"

"Sure does, but, this Lances thing, we have no idea what it even is. Shit, it may not even be a disease. It may have to do with something all together different, like the Natural Cures thing."

"Possibly, but I wouldn't count out the disease thing quite yet."

"I'm sorry to interrupt your train of thought but, look at this," said John pointing out a message form.

"Where did you get this from?" asked Brad.

"It was on top of the pile of stuff we haven't gotten to yet."

"What is it?" asked Mal.

"It's a memorandum between Swiss Technologies and the facility in Invercargill, New Zealand. Looks like an itinerary for some high-ranking individuals from Swiss Technologies that will be visiting their facility. It says the subject of the visit will be to return the Tuatura File. Brad, wasn't that damn lizard called a Tuatura and wasn't there some mention of it concerning the antibody?"

"Christ! You're exactly right, John! The damn cure must've been the result of a study done on the Tuatura lizard that lives off the coast of New Zealand. They've named the documentation for the cure after the damn lizard. That *has* to be it. What a better place to store the file than in New Zealand, way out of the way of the world's mainstream."

"I'll take exception to that," said Evan. "We may be at the ends of the world, but we are definitely laid back," he joked. "You're right, Brad. It *would* be a great storage location for information that, according to John, should remain only on paper. He's proved a computer file isn't safe."

"They must only bring it out when they have to convince someone to join their ranks at a million a month," said Mal. "And then, return it for safekeeping afterwards."

Brad's mind was racing. "We're going to have to go to Invercargill and get it before we pull the rug out from under them. Otherwise, we may never get another chance to recover it."

"Just pop in and say, "hey, by the way, could you run me off a copy of the Tuatura file?" Are you nuts, Brad?" asked Phil. "How do you propose we do this?"

"I don't know, Phil. All I know is, this file is to damn important to take a chance on losing it. Evan, maybe what Terri suggested could fit into our scheme of things some way, you know, having her father help in some manner."

"I feel certain after what we've uncovered here, he'd be more than willing to help in any way he could. I know the man pretty well and he's pretty straight forward. If we do go after this file, what's to assure us that it will still be there when we get there? They may use it to convince another prospective client of theirs to go with the program."

"I doubt that they'd allow all copies to be checked out at the same time. It's for their protection to have at least one copy that never leaves the storage site."

"Son of a bitch! Those bastards."

"What is it, Pop?"

"These three guys that are hand carrying the file back to Invercargill," he responded, pointing to the names.

"What about them?"

"Remember at your place in New Market on Thanksgiving, I mentioned the guys that ruined my practice here in Colorado Springs. I said I didn't know where they were other than some place in Europe."

"I remember, Mal," said Brad.

"These three guys here, the couriers, are the same three. I'm *really* glad to see they've come up in the world. *The dirty bastards*! *They're* the ones doing the blackmailing for Swiss Technologies."

"Small world, Pop. What goes around, comes around."

"I can't wait to put those mothers in their place," stated a raging Mal, his eyes narrowing to slits as he frowned.

"The idea that we may have the cure for cancer at our fingertips is just mind-boggling," said John.

Before anyone could respond to what John had just said, the front door bell of Mal's home sounded. It rang impatiently three times.

*****

After making certain everyone was out of sight, Mal peered through the peephole of the front door and recognized the man. Opening the door he said, "Stone, what the hell are you doing here this time of night? Christ, it's after midnight, almost one in the morning."

"I was ahhhh...driving by and saw all the lights on,"said the six foot sandy haired man still dressed in a business suit covered by an unbuttoned beige overcoat. "I heard you were going to San Francisco for New Years with Sybil and thought I better check it out," he continued, looking past Mal's shoulder into the foyer.

"I appreciate your concern but everything's fine. Sybil has already left for Frisco and I'm planning on flying the lear jet out in the morning," Mal cautiously lied.

"How come you didn't fly with her?"

"Oohhh, with all this shit going on with my son, I was kind of hoping to hear some good news from him to put my mind at ease. You know, he and his wife, along with three other couples, went skiing over the past few days and they were supposedly in that terrible avalanche; but the news said they were alive. Quite frankly, I don't know what the hell's going on. Just kind of hanging around in hopes that Phil will call."

"No contact from him then? Haven't heard anything or seen him huh?"

"Nada. Zip. Not a word. I sent Sybil on ahead once it was verified they were all seen alive after the avalanche. That's really all she needed to hear and besides, she'd probably be driving me nuts about now with all her questions that I don't have any answers to," replied Mal, trying to make a forced laugh sound genuine.

"Have you heard that Dickey is dead?" asked Stone.

"Dead? How the hell did that happen?" asked Mal showing legitimate shock on his face, not from the news of the death but rather from the fact that Stone had asked the question. "Accident of some sort?"

"Yeah, a nine millimeter accident."

"He was *shot*? By who?"

"You got a minute?" questioned Stone, obviously wanting very much to enter.

"Actually, no I don't. I was just getting ready to turn in."

"I tried to call you earlier a number of times but your line was always busy. Who were you talking with for over three hours?"

Remembering the phone had been tied up while John was doing his retrieval, Mal replied, "Sybil out in San Francisco. She kept asking questions, those questions I told you about that would drive me nuts."

"How would she expect you to find out anything if she had your phone tied up all the time?"

"Jesus Christ Stone, what's this third degree shit with you tonight. I feel like you're going to pull out the God damn rubber hose and bright lights any second."

"It's just that you're expected to tell the damn truth when you're working for the CIA, Mal, and unfortunately, you've been anything but honest with me. I had your line checked and you, or someone, was using a modem."

"Is that it," replied Mal. "You know, Stone, you're not as God damn smart as you think you are. Christ, I always suspected you were a real dumb-ass and therefore never cared for you very much."

"What?"

"I know where your nickname, Granite, came from. You're built like a God damn rock. The problem is, you have a brick for a brain.. Have you ever heard of the internet?"

"Yeah," replied Stone. "So what?"

"Do you know that you can connect to it through a local number and then talk to anyone in the world on the internet and not pay long distance rates? It saves you about 75% so I was using the internet to call Sybil in San Francisco you dumb bastard."

"Hell of a nice try you fat shit. I don't think San Francisco has an area code of 301. You were tied into a computer in Maryland you smart ass and you wouldn't know how to do the things that were being done with that computer unless you had help. Now, where the hell are they?"

"Who?"

"The missing eight, that's who?" replied Stone, pulling a weapon from beneath his jacket and in the same motion jamming it into Mal's mid-section. "I'm about to cause a leak here if I don't get some damn answers pretty quick," he continued, smacking Mal across the face with the back of his hand.

From behind him, Phil came into the foyer and said, "Okay, Stone or Granite or whatever your damn name is. This has gone far enough. For someone in the CIA, considering I pay your salary along with all the other good citizens of this country, you're not a real nice person. What the hell do you want?"

"Specifically, you and your seven friends, standing right here in front of me. Understand one thing, jerk. I'm paid by someone who pays a little better for my services than Uncle Sam and I'm going to do anything I have to for my next pay raise. Where are your buddies?"

"Well, you see," replied Phil. "That's where you're shit-out-of-luck. Come on out guys," Phil said over his shoulder. "There's only six of us here. The other two, don't know anything about this stuff. All they wanted was to be left alone and go back to DC. I suspect, they're arriving right about now," said Phil taking a casual glance at his watch.

"That would be the Ambassador's daughter and her boy friend?" asked Stone as the other five joined them in the foyer.

"What you see is what you get; just the six of us, actually seven now that Pop here has some knowledge of what's going on with your well-paying employer. Are you paid by Swiss Technologies directly or one of its divisional subsidiaries? Let me guess, you're probably on a team, the one headed by Dickey, and, the promotion you're talking about was taking his place as team leader, right?"

Obviously in shock about how much he knew, Stone began to stutter a little, "I, I, I don't un, un, understand..."

Interrupting him in mid-sentence, Brad said, "Hey, look man. Phil here, talks too *damn* much. To make a long story short, we want to put an end to this shit. We're as interested in big bucks as anyone but, no one has approached us about joining the team. Maybe a poor choice of words, but, hell, you know what I mean. Why didn't someone ever think of asking us if we were interested in some big bucks?"

"Your saying that you'd consider joining forces with us?"

"Of course," said John. "You only go around once in life. Why not do it with some style and a few bucks."

"A few bucks?" questioned Brad. "From what we've heard, it's a *lot* of money. You know something Stonie, if you recruit us into your effort, well then, you've solved all your company's problems. Helluva feather in your cap, man! I would think there'd be a certain promotion on the horizon."

"No doubt about it," confirmed Phil."

"We know you wouldn't come here by yourself to confront nine people," continued Brad. "Call your buddies inside here, out of the God damn cold, make any phone calls you want to and let's talk this thing out. Shit, we didn't ask for this stuff to happen. It just kinda did, ya know. All we want is the opportunity to take advantage of it, like your doing, Granite. That is your nickname, right?"

"Yeah," was the dumbfounded reply. "Okay, but don't be trying anything."

"Absolutely not," replied Mal, the automatic still held tightly against his stomach.

Pulling what looked like a pager from his pocket, Stone said, "Everyone, join us inside for some discussions. There are only a total of seven here. Two are back in DC. These guys are trying to negotiate for positions with our company for Christ's sake. Can you believe it?" Directing his attention to Mal, Granite continued. "If you were all so interested in changing allegiances, why'd you give me such a ration of shit before, Mal?"

Picking up on the scam being played out by the others, Mal responded. "Granite, think about it for a second man, we had to be *certain* where your loyalties lie before we could approach you. The only way I could make certain was to kinda piss you off a little. It seemed to work."

"I'll give you that much. You did piss me off and, not a little."

As they stood in the foyer, three men jogged to the front porch, their breaths showing heavy in the cold night air. Each was dressed in a similar fashion and more than likely carrying firearms of some nature under their top coats. There was no question that Stone was in charge and the resident heavyweight of the group.

The first man to cross the threshold into the foyer was definitely Italian, in his mid thirty's, and sported a well-trimmed, coal-black goatee. He could have been typecast for a part in the *Godfather* without a screen-test and a strong odor of garlic followed in his wake. The second man to enter was probably the same age, not quite six foot tall and had light brown hair with a neatly-trimmed pencil mustache. His nervous-like brown eyes danced around surveying the room as he entered. The third to enter was definitely the rookie of the squad. He was probably in his early twenties, but looked seventeen tops and had crew cut blond hair and saucer-like blue eyes. His scarred face provided evidence that he was fighting an apparent losing battle with acne; the latest zit was still oozing blood.

"Christ, man, you brought a God damn army didn't you?" asked John. "Is this everyone?"

"Sure did," responded Granite still holding the gun on Mal. He then ordered the newcomers to search the rooms for any other "live bodies", a term which made Brad feel very uncomfortable. He'd placed his arm around Sam as they entered the living room and gave her a reassuring squeeze as they sat on the sofa facing Granite. "Ya know something, Granite, you are making a pretty good coup de gras here."

"Whatcha gettin' at?"

"Only that, after you recruit us, you'll probably get a pretty hefty bonus along with a promotion. Mal here, well never mind, you know what Mal has to offer your organization. John, the guy over there," he said pointing to where John and Abbey were standing, " is probably the smartest computer whiz in the world. He's the one responsible for finding out all the stuff we did about your company. If it wasn't for him, we wouldn't have known we wanted to team-up with you. He's going to be a *hell* of an addition to Swiss Technologies computer efforts. Phil, well, you probably know about him, but, he has a lot of connections back in the DC area, right where future ventures of Swiss Technologies should be focused. And me, what the hell good would I be to your organization? Only that I have in a matter of less than two years, through all my contacts, put together a data base that your company would give an arm and a leg for. It's all theirs, providing the position I'm given with the company is commensurate with what I'm offering. You see Granite, you've stumbled onto something here, much the same way we have."

"Sounds like it."

"I only wish they would've tried to recruit us before all the shit hit the fan. There could've been a lot of lives saved, but, look at it this way, it did create an opening for you."

"You're a pretty hard little shit to knock off, you know it?" asked Granite.

"Believe me, it's been sheer luck. When guys are trying to wipe you out, you don't have much time for planning. Know what I mean? You been involved in any of the attempts against me or my friends?"

"Just the one in New York City."

"You the other shooter there?" questioned Brad.

"How the *hell* did you know that?"

"I told you before, John's our computer guru. We don't do anything without him. He recovered some data base stuff that pretty much spelled it all out. What *did* Haller ever do wrong?"

"He was expendable according to the upper brass."

"He must have pissed someone off who's fairly heavy in the organization."

"The only thing I know is that once you're in this organization, there's only one way to exit. Rumor has it that he was working two sides of the fence. He had ties to the Mafia and was trying to get them involved in our operations. It didn't work for him and won't for anyone else. This organization only lets in who it wants in and gets rid of anyone else that tries. Doesn't really matter who it is. The organization answers all five w's, who, what, where, when and why. Once they approach you about joining, well, you don't have much of a choice. They figure once someone knows about the organization, they either join or cease to exist."

"That's what these teams like yours are for?"

"Right. We're kinda like the police force for the organization."

"Well, buddy, I'll be the first to admit that you certainly are persistent. This is more than likely a first though, right?"

"How so?"

"Someone finding out about the operations first and then asking to join the organization."

"I wouldn't really know but, I suspect that it's not the normal procedure. Quite frankly, I don't know how it's going to sit with them."

"Do you really know what the organization does or are you just kind of on salary and taking assignments as they come up?"

"I know enough and am paid pretty damn well for what I do."

"I'll bet."

Granite's companions re-entered the room and informed him the house was clean. Brad knew they weren't talking about the job the maid had done. Evan and Terri, to Mal's astonishment, had vanished, but he knew something was brewing.

"Granite, for Christ's sake, do you have to keep that damn thing poked into me. It's making me a little nervous," Mal said, speaking of the gun still held tightly against his ribs.

"Why don't you make whatever phone calls you have to and let's get this thing resolved," said Chantal. "Maybe a little drink would taste good and help to relax everyone."

"May as well," said Granite who had taken off his coat and revealed why he'd been given the nickname.

This guy was some specimen of body-building. His large muscular frame, accentuated by his rather large rugged face and square jaw line, presented one mean looking individual that shouldn't be fooled with in a fight. The outcome would not be pleasant thought Brad. Better to continue letting him believe they all wanted to be on the same side. "Phone's over there on the table," said Brad pointing it out and not moving from the sofa where he was seated. "If they want to talk to me, whoever they are, I'd be more than happy if who you're calling is actually in a position to make a decision?"

"Not really, but, they can get a hold of who can and give me a ring back." Moving to the telephone and away from Mal, Granite picked up the receiver and roughly punched in the number. No sooner had he done so than the front door bell rang once again. Replacing the phone to its cradle, Granite motioned for Mal to go to the front door.

With Granite out of sight, Mal looked through the peephole of the front door and immediately recognized Terri. Opening the door Mal asked as the cold night air rushed past him, "What can I do for you young lady?"

"My car quit running up the street," was the reply, "and yours was the only house with the front porch light on."

"Just stalled huh? This cold weather can be rough on batteries. Do your lights still work?"

"They seem pretty dim and the car won't start at all. Would you mind if I used your phone to call my husband? If you have a portable, I'll wait right here if it's okay. I don't want to track all this snow into your beautiful home."

"Suit yourself. Step into the foyer here, out of the cold and I'll go get the portable for you."

"Thank you."

Mal retreated to the living room and picked up the phone Granite had just replaced in the cradle. All eyes in the room followed his every step. As he was leaving the room and all eyes were still on him, especially those of Granite's brigade, Brad carefully reached beneath the skirt of the sofa and pulled the automatic out from its hiding place. As Mal approached Terri in the foyer, he noticed Granite coming around the corner from the dining room with a shocked expression on his face. He was followed by Evan with the other automatic pressed firmly to the back of his head. Evan handed Mal Granite's weapon which he had confiscated.

"Here ya go, young lady. Hope your husband's at home," said Mal, still playing the part as he handed the phone to Terri.

"Shit, how the hell do you work this damn thing," said Terri in a louder than normal voice.

That was the cue Brad had been waiting for. When Terri uttered cuss words, something she never does, it meant that things were under control in the foyer. "Hey guys," Brad beckoned to Granite's three associates. "I believe that control of the situation has changed somewhat in the last few seconds."

Turning towards Brad and staring at the automatic he was holding, only the Italian was able to mutter a word. "Shit," he said in total disgust over the change in events.

"Hands out of your pockets and reach for the ceiling like your life depended on it, because it does," continued Brad.

Brad couldn't see the third man plainly and never realized his overcoat was beginning to rise up as he was preparing to aim and fire his own automatic hidden beneath. Luckily, as Evan entered the room, he noticed and quickly ran towards the man yelling something to draw his attention. Evan jumped in the air, turned a complete 360 degrees and caught the man in the side of the head with his foot. The force of the blow knocked the man across the room and sent him crashing through the glass top coffee table in front of Brad where he lay unconscious.

"Jesus Evan, what the hell was that?" asked a stunned Brad.

"That my man was a round kick and it felt really good. I always wanted to do that for real."

"Where the hell did you learn how to do that?" asked John.

"Remember the guy, Brad, what the hell was his name? Joe something. He used to pick on me when we were in school together in New Zealand. Oh hell, you used to protect me from him. Remember?"

"Yeah, what *was* his name? Joe ahhhh, no, it was Joey something. Joey Withers. That's it, Joey Withers. He was nicknamed Joey after what they call a baby kangaroo. He supposedly had a kick like a kangaroo."

"Well, after you moved back to the states, he used to kick the shit out of me on a regular basis. I finally did something about it and enrolled in some classes to learn how to kick box. I actually became fairly good at it."

"Evan, honey, you're being modest," said Terri. "Brad, there were some people who wanted him to become a professional. He was *that* good."

"From what I just saw, I believe it," replied Brad. "That was awesome. You were *that* good?"

"Let's just say Joey never bothered me again."

"Damn Evan," added Phil, "you're really pretty laid back. I'd never have dreamed you could pull off something like that. It's great!"

"Well, I suppose because I'm the way I am, it kind of gives me an advantage over people. They don't really expect me to be able to do much. I've never had to use it before, at least in a situation like this."

"I know one thing," said Mal. "Sybil is going to be pissed at you. You smashed the crap out of her antique table. By the way, how'd you overcome brick brain here?" he asked motioning towards Granite.

"We knew they'd be searching the house for us so when we heard him summon everyone inside, Terri and I slipped out the butler's pantry window next to the dining room. When we saw through the window that everyone had returned to the living room, we knew the search of the house was over. Terri gave me a couple of minutes to go back through the window and then she went to the front door and rang the bell. Actually, with his eyes and ears focused on the front door and knowing the house had been searched, he wasn't a big problem at all."

"Damn, did I call you guys novices before?" asked a befuddled Mal. "I sure understand now how you made it out of the mountains."

"I hate to bring this up but, what are we going to do with these guys?" asked Sam.

"That's a question I don't have an answer for, honey," replied Brad.

"We can't just turn them over to the police. What would we say happened?" asked Chantal.

"We're not even sure we can trust the damn police anyway," added John. "Looks like we're kind of stuck with this vermin."

"How about we lock them in the wine cellar in the basement. No one would ever know they're there," said Mal.

"Seems too good for them somehow but, you're right, we have to put them some place and keep them out of circulation until we get to the bottom of all this. They *now* know how much we know," said Brad.

"They're going to be charged for all they drink," said Mal. Turning his attention to Granite, he continued. "Hey brick brain, pick up your pal here and get his ass downstairs."

It took about ten minutes to get them all tightly bound and gagged in the wine cellar. They didn't want them talking to each other. Mal then removed some of his better vintages from the collection as a precaution. Together once again in the living room, Brad said, "Sam, honey, hand me the phone."

"Who're you calling?" she asked.

"I'm not sure. I just want to hit the re-dial button and see who good old Granite placed his call to. Terri, you didn't do any dialing out in the foyer did you?"

"Didn't touch it," she replied.

"Good. Let's see what we have here," he said as he hit the re-dial button.

"Who's going to answer this time of night?" asked Phil.

"Don't have the slightest idea. Granite thought someone would though. Someone he reports to or gives him orders."

After five or six rings, a male voice, obviously awakened by the ringing phone answered. "Yeah."

"Got them," stated Brad, trying to disguise his voice and sound like Granite.

"Where?"

"Doctor Bower's place."

"All of them?"

"Yeah."

"Contract completed?"

"Not yet."

"Why the hell not?"

"They want to re-negotiate it."

"What the hell are you talking about?"

"They want employment with us."

"What?"

"They want to join our organization. What do I do?"

"Complete the original contract like you're supposed to, you God damn idiot."

"I think it might be a good idea to check higher up."

"You're not paid to think, dumb-ass. You're paid to do as you're instructed. Now complete the God damn contract or you'll be the next one!"

"I'm not sure I like your tone. You know the price went up because of Doctor Bowers."

"Stone, what the hell are you trying to pull? You don't like my tone? What the hell are... wait a minute. Who the fuck is this?"

"Brad Claxton, you son-of-a-bitch. Who the hell are you?"

The resulting click didn't do much in answering his question but Brad had already resolved in his mind who was on the other end of the line. Turning around, Brad faced everyone with a sullen look on his face, obviously dispirited.

"Brad, sweetheart, I've never seen you look like this before. What's wrong? Who was on the phone?"

Dejectedly, Brad replied. "I hope to God I'm wrong but, I don't think so."

"What the hell has you down so much, pal?" asked Phil. "Do you know who it was?"

"I want to be sure before I answer. Mal, do you have a digital read out for this phone that shows the number just called. I know it was long distance but I'd like to check the number."

"Sure, Brad. We can get it from my office desk phone."

Not wanting to believe what he already suspected to be true, Brad took a hard, long look at the number. "That verifies it. It's his home telephone number. I've called it often enough to remember it."

"Whose number is it?" asked Evan.

"Doc's," replied Brad in a hushed tone.

"Doc! Doc from the Center? asked Abbey.

"The same. I can't believe it. I couldn't tell at first but, the more he woke up, his voice became clearer and then I could tell."

"My God," said Sam softly, "why would he be involved in this stuff? He appeared to be such a... a nice guy. They must have something on him for him to be involved."

"Isn't he the guy who's dying from cancer, Brad?" asked Phil. "And now he's in remission?"

"Right. That's him."

"Maybe, they didn't have anything on him. Maybe, they offered him something he couldn't refuse."

"Like what?"

"His life. He may not be in remission, he may be cured."

"Damn, Phil, you may be right. It's always puzzled me how he's lived so long. The kind of cancer he has, well, it rarely goes into remission."

"That's probably it then," added Mal. "He was their inside man at the Center in exchange for his life. He must've been with them long before joining your Center though, Brad. He's calling the shots on a pretty high level."

"Exactly, for someone to make the decision of who lives and dies, he must have put in some time with the organization," said Chantal.

"He was so... cold about it," Brad informed everyone. "Christ, I thought we were friends. Damn, he even helped figure out some of this shit with me. When I asked, he even came up with the answers."

"That's the point. You asked. He couldn't very well refuse you and draw suspicion. Besides, he wanted to remain in the middle of things to see how far you were going to take this and what to report to his boss," said Abbey. "I'm still shocked outta my mind. You really can't trust anyone these days."

"The question still remains, what do we do next?" asked Terri.

"Honey, I think it's time to place that call to your father. We, at least as far as I see it, still have the primary objective of getting a hold of that damn cure which we've discovered is in New Zealand. Do you agree Brad?"

"More than ever now that we suspect Doc was cured. Terri, would it be possible for your father to provide us with incognito travel arrangements to New Zealand?"

"I'll get on the phone now and ask him. After what I have to tell him, I'm sure he'll help us somehow."

During the nearly forty-five minutes Terri was in deep conversation with her father, with Brad adding information on a second phone, the others spent cleaning up the mess in the living room and destroying all paper documentation they'd recovered from Swiss Technologies. John had, once again, reduced the more important pieces to multiple copies on computer disks.

As Terri and Brad entered the room with smiles on their faces, a beaming Terri said. "He's going to help us with everything we might need."

"I *knew* your father would come through. I told you so," said Evan.

"What's the plan, pal?" asked Phil.

"Mal, the lear jet you're taking to San Francisco. Is there room for eight passengers?"

"Actually, it can carry up to twelve comfortably. Why?"

"We have to get to San Francisco - Oakland International to meet the New Zealand Embassy flight. It's going to report some mechanical difficulties and land there to check them out. That's where we're going to board it for the flight to New Zealand."

"Who is we?" asked Mal.

"All nine of us. Those that don't want to go don't have to, but, right about now I can't think of a safer place to be than out of the country. They'd never expect us to show up in New Zealand. Besides, I thought we were all kinda in this together."

Everyone confirmed that there was no way they were being left behind, including Mal. "I assumed that would be everyone's response," continued Brad. "Terri's father is going to have all the necessary paperwork ready for us when we board in San Francisco. We'll have the entire flight to Wellington to plan our course of action, and believe me, it's not gonna be easy."

"Shit man, it hasn't exactly been a cake-walk to this point. Why would we would we think it would get better?" asked John with a wide grin on his face and rubbing his hands together like in couldn't wait to get on with it.

"Terri's father gave us a contact in New Zealand that he'd trust with his life. I reminded him that he'd be trusting his daughter's life to this person as well and he said he was well aware of it. So, at least we have a potential friend over there willing to help us. He's been involved, as an agent of sorts, with the Ministry of Defense. Evan, two guesses who it is and the first one doesn't count."

"Honestly, Brad, I don't have a clue."

"Would you believe, one Mr. Joe Withers."

"Joey? Joey Withers? I wondered whatever happened to him. Small world. Actually, we did become pretty good friends... after I kicked his ass that is. I do know he can damn sure be trusted."

"Well, he's our source of help. We better get what we need together and be on our way."

"Do you think we should take this arsenal we've collected over the past couple of days?" questioned John.

"We better hold on to anything we can for our protection until we know exactly where we stand. And, someone better get rid of the car these assholes in the wine cellar were driving before it's spotted."

"I'll pull my car out of the garage and someone pull that one in to hide it," offered Mal.

"I'll get it, Pop," said Phil.

"Shit," said Evan and Terri, nearly at the same time.

"What's the problem?" asked Brad.

"The driver. The damn driver is still in it. In all the excitement, I completely forgot about him," said Evan.

"Christ, man, you seem kind nonchalant that one of these guys is still outside," said a concerned John.

"He's certainly not going anywhere," said Terry. "Evan gave him a pretty good pop with the butt of the automatic, after he was unconscious from the kick he received. He was standing beside the car and well, that's when I saw Evan use the round kick for the first time tonight. Besides, he's tied and gagged anyway."

"Evan... why would you hit someone with the butt of a gun after they were already knocked out?"

"Brad, you know when you're watching a movie and the good guy, or girl, knocks the bad guy out. Inevitably, he always wakes up and continues to wreak havoc on people. You always say to yourself, "I'd make damn sure that son of a bitch was out."

"Yeah, that always happens in the movies."

"I was just making damn sure it didn't happen here, that's all."

"Well, Evan, I can't say as I blame you. These guys deserve to have the shit beat out of them, even if they're unaware of it happening."

"We'll just throw him in with brick brain and the others downstairs," said Mal.

They carried the unconscious driver into the house and dumped him into the cellar, bound and gagged, with the others. Then, the car was hidden and the house locked up before leaving for the airport. The nine of them piled into Mal's Lincoln Town Car which was more than roomy enough for all of them; however, Sam and Terri had to sit on their men's laps. Brad gave Sam little playful pokes on her buns the entire 23 miles. She didn't seem to mind at all.

Mal had previously filed a flight plan for San Francisco, so there wasn't any delay in their departure. They'd been airborne for nearly an hour and Sam and Brad were just returning from the restroom at the back of the aircraft where they'd been "cleaning up." They'd heard about people making love in the restroom of an airplane and therefore making themselves eligible for immediate membership in the rather exclusive "Mile High" club but had never realized what a true accomplishment it was until they tried it themselves. Having to be more exceptionally quiet because of the proximity of the others to the door added to the excitement of their lovemaking. As they took their seats again with flushed faces and trying their best not to laugh, they realized that the others knew what was going on, but, it really didn't matter. With the exception of Mal, who was piloting the lear jet, everyone had decided to "clean up" in pairs.

---- Chapter Sixteen ----

"It's amazing how much room there is inside one of these planes when they don't load them up with 300 or so passenger seats," stated Sam.

Looking around the spacious interior of the DC-10 as he enjoyed the comfort of the over-stuffed lounge chair, Brad asked. "Terri, your father really travels in style. All this is for being an Ambassador?"

"It's not all just for him, Brad. New Zealand has two planes like this and they each travel around the world, but in different directions, making stops at the various Embassy locations. They have pretty much an on-going schedule. Those that have a need, such as couriers, or Ambassadors for that matter, can catch a ride.

"Then, there's a chance we might be picking up someone else?"

"No chance, Brad," Evan interjected. "Terri's father made certain of that. This flight's private."

"Pop would've liked to see the interior of this thing," stated Phil. "I hope he and mom are doing okay back in Frisco."

"Honey," said Chantal, "we agreed it was best for your mother's safety that everything appear as normal as possible. Remember, we agreed we don't know how extensive Swiss Technologies' surveillance is. They certainly haven't left much to chance so far."

"And, besides, Malcomb has a disk that he's personally going to get to Brad's police friends in DC," stated John. "We didn't have time to mail one and the sooner they get a copy, the sooner they'll be able to help straighten this mess out."

"As it turns out, it's probably for the best," added Brad. "We need someone in the states who knows what's going on and can ramrod a coordinated effort. By the way John, do you have all the things we confiscated from Granite and his pals."

"There in a bag right over there," John responded, pointing to a small table on the other side of the cabin. "Why?"

"This whole Doc thing isn't sitting right with me. I just want to check something. I can't comprehend how this supposed friend of mine could, so coldly and in a calculated fashion, order my death, along with all the rest of you."

"Call it a woman's intuition, but, I agree with you Brad," said a comforting Sam. "You told us Doc provided you with information and, as it turns out, correct information. It seems to me if he were involved in any way..." After pausing to search for the right words, she cleared her throat and continued. "Well, his actions just don't seem to be consistent. If he was involved, he'd be trying to throw you off the track," she concluded.

"I suppose he could have been having a guilt complex at the Center and since then did a complete turn around but, I honestly don't believe he's capable of something like this. I know him too well! He's the one that first mentioned the Tautura Lizard and joking around said something like *maybe they have a knack for survival that we don't know about.* He had no idea how *true* his statement was! No one can put on that kinda act. Those weren't the actions of a man trying to cover up something. They were the actions of a man trying to provide honest, straight-forward answers to a legitimate question."

"Here, Brad," said Abbey as she handed him the bag from the table.

After three or four minutes of looking through Granite's possessions, Brad said. "There's something fishy around here, people."

"Fishy in what way?" asked Chantal.

"Simply put sis, it stinks," replied Brad. Holding it up so all could see, he said, "here's the card Granite was looking at when he made the phone call to Doc. There's five numbers on this card and not one of them is Doc's home in Maryland! And, I couldn't find it anywhere else in this stuff," he concluded as he threw the bag back on the table. "I was wrong, but how? *His* number showed up on the digital read-out in Mal's office!"

"There's no way, Granite could have remembered that number. He probably has trouble remembering his own," said Sam. "I agree, sweetheart, something's not right."

"Does this fancy airplane have a telephone system and a computer?" questioned John. "It seems to have everything else."

"Sure it does. It's towards the front compartment, near the cockpit," responded Evan. "Why?"

"I want to check something out, that's why. Lead the way, my man."

Sitting at the sophisticated electronic console, John dialed the only number on the card with a Maryland area code, waited for one ring and immediately hung up. Pointing to the digital monitor he said. "Look, Brad, is that Doc's home number?"

"It sure as hell is," replied an astounded Brad.

"Son of a bitch," John said slowly. "These guys are amazing for Christ's sake. Somehow, the receiver changes the number dialed automatically. I've never seen anything like this before."

"But John, the voice was definitely Doc's," informed a now more confused than ever, Brad.

"That part of it is relatively easy to explain, Brad. They probably recorded Doc at sometime and then had it copied onto a computer-generated voice synthesizer. No matter who answers the phone, it sounds like Doc. Hell, a damn woman could answer and you'd still hear what you thought was Doc talking. This damn outfit has thought of everything. Pretty damn ingenuous. There's been call waiting for a number of years. There's call transferring, conferencing and the such. More recently," he continued, "there's call blocking and caller ID, which tells you the identity of the caller. Finally, thanks to Swiss Technologies, we have call framing. If you want to get someone in deep shit or just protect your own ass, for an additional charge from your local supplier of telephone service, you can now designate the caller ID you want to place the blame on. It can be either random or, for a slight additional charge, personally selected. It's your option and something every teenager wants under the Christmas tree this year."

"I wonder who the fall-guys are for the other four numbers on that card," said Abbey.

"Let's call them and see what numbers pop up," urged Samantha. Two had area codes for DC, and two had area codes for Virginia. They repeated the process performed to reinstate Doc's good standing, letting it ring one time only, and looking at the visual display. Each time, the visual display depicted a different number than the actual one called. All four of the numbers returned on the display were unlisted but, through the computer system on board, it was easy enough for John to hack into the needed telephone company files to recover the names and addresses.

The list of individuals who were destined to become Swiss Technologies scape-goats proved to be quite interesting. The first DC number proved to be the personal office phone of Senator Charles Detwiler, representing the state of Florida. He was responsible for funding criteria of certain health related projects and was a starch advocate of the Medicare system. His roughly eight years in the House of Representatives had been spent primarily focused on the aging population and making certain that his elder constituency was well taken care of.

The second DC number was the home number of Glynda Swanstone, the incumbent director of the National Institute of Health. Her position is chartered by Congress to oversee international health organizations with regards to medical crisis of a global nature. In her position, she'd have numerous contacts within organizations such as the World Health Organization at the top level and small, so-called, subordinate organizations like the Center for Disease Control in Atlanta.

The first Virginia area code number turned out to be the personal residence of the Governor of Virginia, an advocate of medical research and the growing health care concerns of the US citizenry. He'd been closely associated with attempts to develop a national health care system and was using it as a springboard to what some folks believed would be a bid for the presidency.

The second Virginia based number was that of the Director of the Central Intelligence Agency. His responsibilities and duties go without saying, but what better person to place blame on, if necessary, than this individual. The American public would believe the CIA capable of anything, even for the actions of Swiss Technologies.

The whole idea behind this innovative technology, was to throw up one hell of a smoke screen should anything go wrong. This would allow the actual people involved enough time to make their escapes to whatever pre-arranged rock they'd decided to slide under. Now, everyone was growing concerned about how many of these *card holders*, like Granite, were running around the world with different numbers on them. If the authorities didn't take the time to check into the situation like Brad and the others had done, there'd be chaos to pay as a price. Numerous false arrests and accusations would occur and innocent people's integrity would be placed in immediate jeopardy. The attendant unfavorable newspaper publicity would wreak devastation on the reputations of some very prominent individuals. Their influence on decision making during the crisis would be virtually nil because of the immediate lack of trust. Multiply that by the number of cards being carried and it could potentially mean the downfall of the global hierarchy of the medical research community. It would be a hell of a price to pay for bringing down Swiss Technologies, something its Corporate Board of Directors was relying on to cushion the blow and provide them with some sort of comfort level.

Brad and the others summarized the latest development and faxed a copy over the secure line to Terri's father at the Embassy. He was asked in turn to notify Malcomb because they wanted as many people as they could trust to recognize the imminent and dangerous situation before the, as John so eloquently put it, "shit hit the fan."

*****

Brad's ears were beginning to pop as the aircraft began descending for its approach to Wellington. While he'd made this flight numerous times, this particular trip seemed exceptionally long due his anxiety concerning the recovery of a Cancer cure. That it had been kept secret for fifteen or twenty years and covered up made him furious, but, the excitement of potentially ending the existence of the dreaded disease far outweighed his rage with Swiss Technologies. What Swiss Technologies had done was inexcusable, but, in his opinion, what the cure meant to the world would be unbelievably received by the medical profession. He forced a deep yawn to clear his eardrums, now quite uncomfortable. He and the others had to stay focused on the priorities which they'd set forth during the long flight from San Francisco. First and foremost was the recovery of the cure itself and second, was dealing with the money-mongers of Swiss Technologies to make sure their reign ended.

"What time is it?" asked a still-awakening John as he entered the lounge area of the converted DC-10.

"It's 1:00 AM, New Zealand time," replied Brad glancing at his watch. "We're beginning our descent into Wellington now."

"The flight didn't take as long as I thought it might."

"Eighteen or nineteen hours, the usual."

"That long?" asked a sleepy John.

"Yeah, it's January 2nd you know."

"Didn't we leave on the 31st, New Year's Eve?"

"Yeah, as a matter of fact we did."

"What the hell happened to January 1st, New Year's Day, for Christ's sake?"

"It's history, man. We crossed the International Date Line."

"Shit."

"What's the matter?"

"Only that, not only did I miss the party back in DC but I missed the entire first day of the New Year. Do you have any idea how pissed I am to miss all the damn Bowl Games this year. It's like the first day of the year didn't even exist."

"Shit, John. It's still January 1st in the states. You really didn't miss the day... you just weren't a part of it."

"Precisely my point. These damn guys really have me pissed now. Because of them, I've lost a holiday and all the football games."

"You'll get the day back when we cross the date line going the other way."

"You're saying that if we left here on the tenth of January, I'd arrive back in the States on the 1st?"

"You know better than that. It would be the 9th."

"Then what I said about losing the first is true. It's gone forever, right?"

"Right."

"Now you know why I'm so pissed off. They took a God damn day out of my life. I'll never see that first of January in my life-time. I'm pissed, buddy," stated John, trying not to laugh but finally breaking down and continuing. "If ever someone had a reason to get even, this is the only one I need for Swiss Technologies."

"Thank God you finally have a valid reason, after all that's happened, to direct your frustration and rage at their organization," replied Brad.

"Anyone else up?" asked a finally serious John.

"As far as I know, just Phil and Chantal. They're up front in the cockpit talking with the pilots. I left Sam in our stateroom. She's exhausted."

"After what Abbey and I heard through the wall of the adjoining room, I can certainly understand that. Hell man, after all of that activity, you ought to be dead," said John.

"Holy smokes, everyone knows every little thing that happens," said a disgusted Brad.

"I wouldn't go so far as to call what we heard a little thing. Christ, it sounded like a Wyoming rodeo or something, Brad. You two normally that loud? All the noise sure as hell turned on Abbey though. For that, I want to thank you. Because of you and Sam, we had a hell of a time."

"You're welcome you damn idiot. Let's round up the others so we can stay out of sight after we land."

As a precaution, they'd called and made arrangements to remain on board for about an hour after the flight landed. Then, they'd disembark and proceed to the designated area where Joey Withers was to rendezvous with them. He'd provide a couple of vehicles for their transportation to a smaller aircraft waiting at a nearby private air strip for the next leg of their itinerary.

*****

Brad shook Joey Wither's hand, noticing that the young boy had turned into a fine-looking man since his school days in New Zealand. "Joey, it's been a long time," said Brad as he gave him a warm smile. Joey had matured into a very big man, probably six foot four inches and a muscular 225 pounds. Brad thought he still looked like the Joey Withers he remembered, only about three times the size. Brad felt confident he would've recognized him if they'd passed on the street under different circumstances. "You're a little bigger than I remember but, you haven't really changed that much. Good to see you man. You should be playing football."

"It's good to see you to Brad. It has been a few years. By the way, I did play professionally for the Hamilton team until I blew out my knee."

"You weren't on the team when they won the championship in '87 were you?"

"Sure was. I got the injury the following season that ended my career."

"I'll be damned. That game was shown in the States but I missed it. I sure wanted to see it."

"It was the most exciting game I'd ever played in and incidently, I was watching the Olympics in '88 when your ski career came to an abrupt halt. That was one hell of a fall you took. They still show that from time to time down here."

"Here too, eh? Nice to know someone appreciates talent."

"We better be moving out before we're spotted by someone," said Joey after all the introductions were made. "We have a bunch of gear already loaded on the plane that's waiting for us. It's ready to go. We have about a 1700 mile flight to Invercargill ahead of us."

"Damn. It seems as if I've been on an airplane my entire life," said Evan.

"You still involved in that kick boxing stuff?" asked Joey. "You became... pretty good at it as I recall. So much so that I even took it up."

"I haven't done anything with it for years, but, just recently got back into it."

"How long you been at it this time?"

"Two or three days. It was kind of a necessity. I'll explain on the way."

"You know something, Evan? You really *are* something. All the girls in school always liked you best. Now, here you are, with the Ambassador's daughter. She's a hell of a good-looker, man. How serious is this thing with ahhh... I think her name is Terri, right? I've just met so many people, I can't remember all their names."

"That's right, Terri. We're getting married the first chance we get while we're here. I love her a lot. Never really tell her as often as I should, but, she knows."

"Certainly won't hurt your career any either. And Brad, that guy has really found a woman in Sam. What's Sam short for?"

"Samantha."

"Her name sure fits her accent. She seems pretty bright."

"That's not the right word. She's smart as hell. Photographic memory and everything. She graduated almost a year early from law school with a straight 4.00 average."

"Wow! Well let's get into the vans and head on out."

As Evan and Joey climbed into the van, John asked, "Why the hell is it so hot?"

"Because it's summer here, buddy," replied Brad smiling as he recalled his conversation with Doc about summer and winter. "Summers are warm. It's really not that hot John, you're just used to the Colorado winter. It's probably only about 70 degrees."

"I could never get used to this. January 1st... or 2nd... whatever it is and I'm hot." As Joey closed the back door of the van, John said, "Joey, hold it a minute. Open the door again."

"John, is it?" questioned Joey.

"Right."

"You may be warm, but we can't be driving around with the back door open. We do have air conditioning down here. It'll cool off soon enough."

"It's not that, Joey. I thought I saw something."

As Joey opened the door, Brad asked, "what did you see, buddy?"

"I was right. Over there next to that building. See that plane?"

"Yeah. What about... oh shit. It's got the black oval insignia on it."

"What are you guys talking about?" asked Joey.

"That plane belongs to Swiss Technologies," said Brad. "That black oval... well, let's just say we've seen too many of them lately."

"I don't understand."

"We'll fill you in completely on the flight to Invercargill, Joey. For right now, let's just leave. Actually, John, we knew they'd be here in some type of capacity. What we don't want is for them to find out *we're* here. We've gone to extremes to hide our whereabouts so we'd have an advantage on them."

The two unmarked vans sped off in the pre-dawn darkness and proceeded to the private airport. The driver had radioed ahead and as they pulled alongside of the airplane, the flight plan had been filed, the tanks had been fueled and the engines were ready to be fired up for takeoff. Again airborne, the weary travelers reiterated their story for the benefit of Joey and his team.

*****

The facility provided by the New Zealand government on the outskirts of Invercargill was a four story, refurbished hotel now used primarily as a recreational retreat for employees of the New Zealand government. Everyone currently at the facility had been asked to leave so "repairs could be made to the electrical system"; therefore, the plans and strategy could be formulated in complete privacy. There were complete facilities including swimming pool, tennis courts, and an eighteen-hole, championship golf course. The security-cleared staff of the facility remained for the newly-arrived guests including the chefs to prepare the various menu items offered by its restaurant.

Mid-afternoon of January 3rd found Brad and Sam sitting on the balcony and enjoying the stunning beauty and tranquillity of the view. From their balcony they could see the sprawling, lush-green golf course reaching downward to the river's edge and beyond. The only activity on the golf course was the groundskeepers mowing one of the fairways near the hotel and magically leaving patterned cuts in the grass. In the distance, near the horizon, they could enjoy the sunlight bouncing off the deep blue waters of the South Pacific Ocean.

Sam, her eyes scanning the magnificent view, asked, “Brad, is all of New Zealand this breath-taking? I've heard that Ireland is supposed to be so green and lush, but it's hard to believe any where else could be as beautiful as this.”

“Actually, it is. There are areas that make this place look bad in comparison. It's a beautiful damn country, Sam, no two ways about it.”

“I'd like to spend more time here after all this is over. Could we?”

“Well, I don't see why not. You know, we haven't decided where we're going on our honeymoon. Maybe we should seriously consider coming back here. We could spend a month or so touring the country so you could see what I've been talking about.”

“That's a great idea, sweetheart. I'd love that. Everything seems so relaxed as you look around. No one is in hurry and there doesn't seem to be hoards of tourists milling about cluttering the restaurants and shops.”

“New Zealand it is then. I'm really looking forward to it, honey,” Brad said as he leaned over and gave her a small kiss on her cheek. “New Zealand is very fortunate in a way, that it's off the beaten path so to speak. If this place was located closer to the States or Europe, a lot more people would be coming here. I personally think, any increased activity in the tourist industry would probably destroy the serenity of the countryside, the very thing that makes it so attractive.”

“You're right. I agree. I've seen it in *li'l ole Charleston*,” she said in her best southern accent. “It's not your usual tourist Mecca mind you, but, over the years as I grew up, with all of the historic restoration and all, more and more people visit there. I don't think all the increased activity has necessarily been for the best.”

“It's nearly three o'clock. We better be heading down to the restaurant to meet with Joey. He's due back any minute with the architectural plans of the research facility. He is also supposed to have what we need to get into the damn place.”

“I wish I were going with you guys. I'm worried.”

“We've been through all this Sam, and besides, it's really Joey's call. He's been involved in things like this before. Like he says, you formulate a plan, select the best people for each segment and leave everyone else out of it. I'm probably the only one here that can identify the Tautara file, the one we're looking for. I doubt that it's properly labeled so as to be easily identified. We're also trying to recover the actual antibody itself which is probably cross-referenced in some sort of code. That's why John's going so he can get into the in-house data base files. We're also, John, Evan and I, and remember, Joey doesn't know this, going to try to find some information on that Lances thing we could never figure out. Phil's responsibility is to coordinate the effort here in the hotel with Abe and Ben back in DC. You remember, we have Interpol ready to act as soon as we're finished with what we have to do. "

"He's probably right, but..."

Before she could continue with her argument, Brad stood pulling her up with him and then embraced her tightly. Her firm young breasts buried in his chest, he kissed her, his hands exploring the curvature of her buttocks at the same time. "I love you, Sam and I'm going to be fine. When you hear the complete plan, you'll agree. Trust me."

"Okay," she responded dejectedly. "I love you too. That's why I'm so worried."

"I understand, honey, but, really I'm going to be just fine," he assured her. "If I didn't think so, I wouldn't be making plans for our honeymoon with you," he said, smiling. "We have to get down there. They're probably waiting for us."

"Okay, I trust you," she said as they took one last look at the panorama in front of them and then turned to go through their room to the restaurant.

As they entered the room, Joey was spreading out the architectural drawings of the research facility on one of the banquet tables. He'd laid out a second set of plans as well. "We have a slight problem here, Brad," he said as he noticed them.

"What's the problem, Joey?"

"It appears, that not only is there the research facility here in Invercargill, but the company also owns a smaller storage site on one of the small islands off the coast. The problem I think is rather obvious. Which of the locations would have the file you're looking for?"

"Damn. Nothing's ever easy with these people. How big is the storage facility?"

"Actually, it looks fairly small according to these drawings, but they're pretty old. It butts up against some cliffs right near the coast. It's a pretty remote area and sparsely populated. The government has a meteorological station on the northern tip of the island where there's a small airfield. But other than the storage building, that's about it. There really isn't much else there."

Looking at the drawings and in particular the sizing of the rooms, Brad finally asked outloud, more to himself than anyone, "Why would they use this place as a storage facility when there has to be a number of places in Invercargill they could use for such a limited purpose? Why go to the bother of transporting records for storage all they way out in the middle of nowhere?"

"That's something I can't answer," replied Joey.

"It's just possible they could be using this site for something other than storage," mused Phil scratching his head.

"What are you getting at?" asked John.

"Hell, I don't know. Maybe the place is used for actual research as well."

"That's a hell of a thought," exclaimed Brad. "I'm not sure it's large enough after looking at these drawings. You should have a lot more room to house a lab and all the other things necessary like cold rooms, freezers, decontamination equipment and things that normally go along with a full lab set up."

"You're probably right. They'd also have to have living quarters for all the personnel involved in such research effort."

"Not to mention all the security personnel," reminded John.

"I guess that doesn't help us much as to which site to visit," stated Joey.

"Brad, if the place was used for storage of records, how much power would it use?" asked Sam.

"I would think minimal. The place wouldn't have to be lighted much, only when someone was dropping off or picking up some documentation. Why?"

"Well, if it were used for a lab, with all those things you and John just discussed as well as all the appliances for food preparation and storage, wouldn't the power consumption be pretty high?"

"Jesus Christ, Sam," said Joey. "You're smart as hell!"

"I don't understand what's going on," stated Brad.

"Your girl friend, here, has come up with the answer. All we have to do is call the utilities commission to see what the power consumption is for this place. If it's low, it's probably just a paper storage facility. But, if the consumption is higher than what's expected for a facility of this size, we have the answer. Shit, we have all the electrical drawings right here. Right Sam?"

"That's what I was suggesting," she said with a smile.

"Damn, honey, where *do* you come up with all this stuff? You're, without a doubt, amazing. Probably why I love you so much."

As Sam was explaining that she'd remembered studying a case at Georgetown University involving electrical consumption, Joey was placing the call to the appropriate utility center to check on the power usage. As he returned from the front counter of the restaurant, he had a large grin on his face.

"Look at this! With this amount of power usage, God only knows what the hell kind of activity they're engaged in. This is about 50 times the amount of power they should be using even if they left everything shown on these drawings turned on 24 hours a day."

"Christ, how can that be?" asked John. "This place is too damn small for all that stuff."

"The only way possible," stated Brad, "is if they've added onto the facility."

"They haven't, at least to all outward appearances," stated Joey. "I've already had some aerial photos taken this morning and here they are," he informed everyone as he laid them on the table. "They don't show anything more than what's already here on these drawings."

"What if the additions were done underground or into the cliff that it butts up against. They wouldn't show from the air," said Chantal looking at the photos.

"Good point, and they could've brought everything they needed in by boat, under the cover of darkness onto the beach in front, over a period of time. No one would realize anything," added Evan.

"This is the place we want to go," said John emphatically.

"How are you so certain?" asked BP.

"That perimeter fencing shown here in the photo. That's not the kind of fencing you normally see around a storage site, or medical research facility for that matter. This type is similar to what you expect around NSA or CIA sites. *Something's* inside they really want to protect against intruders. It looks like it's electrified and has motion detectors. Probably cameras as well. Dollars to donuts, this is where the Tautara File is located, along with a lot of other shit."

"Damn. How the hell do we get in there undetected?" asked Brad.

Joey's mind had already been working on the problem. "From above," was his simple answer.

"From above?" asked Evan, suspiciously.

"Yeah, from above," he repeated. "We rappel down the cliffs to the roof. Go to the ventilation system here," he said pointing to the roof of the photo in front of them, "and proceed into the facility."

"I was afraid of that," replied a now grim-looking Evan.

"Not very anxious to get involved in this situation, eh?" asked Joey, beginning to laugh.

"Don't slow me up, Joey. I'll be right on your ass," replied Evan in a flippant tone, trying not to show his concern and forcing his returned laughter.

"John, here's an enlargement photo of the roof. Do you see anything, that looks like it's designed to provide an alert to access from above?"

Scanning the photograph, John answered, "Unless the roof is pressure sensitive, I don't see anything."

"What do you mean ahhh... pressure sensitive?" asked Evan.

"Simply, if anything adds weight to it, it sets off an alarm."

"That's just great," said Brad. "How do we know if it is or isn't? We have to get inside undetected to recover the file before they have a chance to destroy it."

"No way of telling, except standing on it. With everything else they have, I'd be surprised if it wasn't rigged," John concluded.

"Jesus! How the hell do we get around that?" asked Evan.

"We don't put any weight on it," said Joey. "Like you said before, we go around it or bypass it. We go directly from overhead into the ventilation system."

"How's that possible?" asked Evan.

"Evan, let me and my guys worry about that," said Joey. "All the rest of you have to do is play follow the leader down the rappel lines. We've gotten into places more difficult than this one."

"Better you than me, pal," said Evan.

"We're going to have to delay this thing for a day or so. I need some time to get all the gear we need together. We're only going to get one shot at this, and also, I want to set up some contingency plan in case the file isn't there. We want another team ready to go into the research center here in

Invercargill, just in case. Phil, that entry should be coordinated with Interpol at all the other sites."

"Gotcha," replied Phil.

"As of right now, I'd estimate we'll be starting this action about 5:00 o'clock Sunday afternoon. We're going to have to land by boat on the opposite side of the island and go overland to the point above the facility. Looking at the map, the island is probably one and a half miles wide at that point, two at most. Don't bother asking why we don't just use the airstrip. If this group is as sophisticated as they appear to be, they know everything about everyone that lands at that airfield. We're close now and don't want anything to tip them off."

"I think we're all in agreement with that Joey," said Brad. "We haven't come this far just to blow it because we don't want to walk a mile of two."

"Don't get me wrong, Brad. It isn't any walk in the park. It's pretty rough terrain we're going to be crossing and, in the dark."

"I understand but, going along with what you said, we don't really have a choice, do we?"

"None if you don't want to be setting off alarms or be visually sighted."

"That's it then, barring any new information. Phil, you should work out the approximate timing for Interpol's operations and get a short message to Abe and Ben so they're on standby. As Joey has said, our first goal will be to knock out their communications then, we begin looking for the files and, hopefully, secure the site itself so we can really sift through their stuff."

"I'll tell you one thing," said Evan. "I've never looked forward to the end of a weekend more in my life."

"I think that goes for all of us," concluded Brad with a somber face.

--- Chapter Seventeen ----

Rowing was becoming much easier as the three rafts picked up speed approaching the shore line because the swells became more prominent and gave them more momentum. While the late evening air was cool; nevertheless, they were sweating profusely from their exertion. The eight men; Joey, Brad, Evan and John in one raft and Joey's team in the another, had been paddling for about an hour from their drop-off point near the island. It wasn't the distance or rough swells that had caused the exertion, but rather, the third raft they towed which was loaded with all the necessary equipment. The moon was partly hidden behind cloudy skies and on occasion caused a silver etching around passing clouds. The water was completely void of any color, not like the rich blue that Brad and Sam had viewed from their balcony two days prior. Rather, it appeared dark, almost murky, and totally uninviting. The sound of the surf crashing on the beach could now be heard as waves broke and ran ashore as if trying to grasp something and drag it back into the sea.

Sunday was proving to be a good day for their covert operation since the research complex was nearly vacant except for the security detail. As they had departed on their mission, Evan said he looked like a damn cat burglar in the garb he'd been given to wear but realized it was to be worn only until they made their entrance into the facility. Once inside, they wanted to "fit in" as much as possible, giving the appearance, at least initially, that they were employees of the company. This, Joey felt, might offer a slight advantage if confronted by an unknowing guard rather than a bunch of guys running around all darkly dressed with blackout all over their faces.

When the others prodded Joey about how he could operate under the auspices of the New Zealand Government in performance of an illegal operation, he'd told them this action fell within the special operations division of the Ministry of Defense. When they'd pressed him further, he'd told them that "It means we're kinda on our own according to the New Zealand Government but with their blessings... so long as we don't get caught. The same kind of thing goes on all over the world, government's funding of private, covert actions in the interest of national defense. In this case, let's just say, the ends justify the means. If what we're after is what it's cracked up to be then I, at least, feel justified in our actions. And, that's all

I need in my own mind to give it a 100% effort." Everyone, including the girls, agreed with Joey's rationale.

As they approached the shore, Joey and the four men from the other raft, jumped into the knee deep water and began pulling rafts. "Could use a little help here guys," he said in a tone which made Brad, John and Evan hurriedly proceed into the cold water to lend a hand. "Don't be afraid to get your feet wet, we have to get that third raft in here before it capsizes. You'll dry out on the trip across the island."

"Sorry," said Brad, "we weren't thinking."

"No problem. Let's get these things off the beach and hidden. I don't think anyone will be coming along, but why take the chance."

Within a half an hour, they were on their way to the other side of the island. Each had a back pack and had been paired with someone else to carry ten foot sections of expandable tubing to be used in avoiding any weight sensitive alarm system on the roof. How it was to work, Brad hadn't the foggiest, but, according to Joey, it was going to be quite simple. They'd proceeded for about 45 minutes when Joey, who was in the lead, stopped and placed the tubing he and Evan were carrying on the ground. The other three pair of men came along side and followed suit.

"It's all downhill from here, guys," Joey said. "There's the beacon from the airfield over there in the distance to the left," he said pointing. "Straight down that way," he continued moving his arm to the right, "is where we want to go. That'll bring us out right above the facility. It's quiet time now so, no talking, unless absolutely necessary. Any questions before we head out?"

"It's not really a question. Kind of a request I guess," said John.

"What is it?" asked Joey.

"I don't know how to put it."

"What the hell is it, buddy?" asked Brad. "You having second thoughts about this?"

"No, definitely not that."

"Then what?"

"All right. I... I have to take a shit."

"For Christ's sake, man, get over there and do it."

"All right... all right! Anyone got any paper on them?"

"Not for that, buddy. Use leaves or something."

"Brad?"

"What?"

"You got change for a twenty?"

"Get outta here!"

Again on the move, Joey reminded all of them they had no idea how well armed the security forces might be. If necessary, he further made it clear they had to fire their silenced weapons to kill and not, simply to wound. He'd seen or heard about too many people killed by persons, both men and women, who'd only been wounded. Also, on past missions, there was more definition as he called it, about the potential hazards involved and this was a unique experience for him, not knowing for sure what might be coming. With luck on their side and using the element of total surprise, they'd be able to secure the facility without any hostile action.

Now on the cliff above the storage site, they began putting together the tubing and other paraphernalia they'd lugged across the island. At completion is looked like a twenty foot, light-weight ladder, nearly 20 feet in length, that was extendable to thirty-five feet. Brad, with a little concern in his voice, questioned, "Joey, I assume we're going to climb out on this thing. It looks like it's built out of *Tinker Toys* or *Legos*, man. How much weight will this contraption support?"

"Actually Brad, I really don't know for sure. All I know is that it will support all of us at the same time if necessary but, total weight, I couldn't really say. I don't know what alloy this metal is, but, it's strong as hell."

"That's good enough for me. One other minor question. How the hell do we get that thing in position?"

"Pretty simple. You know what a drawbridge looks like in the up position?"

"I've noticed a few."

"Well, we lower the unit down in an up position and attach the adjustable base of each tube into one of these adjustable hinging brackets," he explained showing a bracket to Brad. "These brackets are held in place against the wall of the cliff by pitons driven through these holes. There's ample allowance for fitting because the hinged receivers of the tubing slide back and forth in the bracket," he said as Brad watched the receiver slide. "Once the two bases of the ladder are in place in the brackets, the unit is lowered like a draw bridge into a level position over the roof and tied off from above. This cable here," he said, showing it to Brad in the near total darkness, "is only about an eighth inch thick but, can support a ton if necessary. It's like a suspension bridge, supported on one end by the brackets housing the tubes and on the other end by the cable attached at the top of the cliff."

"Basically, what you're saying, Joey, is that this little cable," said Evan, looking at it with concern, "is the only thing preventing the bridge and us from falling onto the roof?"

"You got it, partner. Shit, you're only going to be about two feet off the roof."

"Did you hear that shit, John?" asked Evan.

"Sounds like a good plan to me, let's go for it," responded John in a soft voice.

"You're crazier than I thought. What the hell... Never mind, I'm game too," Evan said after a pause.

Peering over the edge to the roof top, roughly 300 feet below, Joey said to a member of his team, "Sniper, that light's got to go, man. The one in front of the building shining on the entrance. It's illuminating the area too much when we get down close to the roof."

The rationale for the man's nickname would become apparent to Brad and the others in the next few moments. Without saying a word, Sniper, began assembling his rifle, complete with silencer. After attaching the scope, he lay in a prone position, nearly overhanging the edge of the cliff, totally exhaled, took careful aim through the scope and slowly squeezed the trigger. Standing only a few yards away, Brad barely heard the sound of the weapon firing but, did notice the light was no longer a problem.

"Hell of a shot, man." Brad said softly to Joey standing next to him.

"Not actually. I've seen him drop a moving target five times that distance and, with a single shot," Joey whispered back. "He goes to Australia during some of his time off and hunts in the outback. I went with him one time and I couldn't believe the shots he was making. The man never, never misses."

"What if they notice the light out. Won't they be a little suspicious?"

"Probably not. They'll think it just burned out and besides, at nearly two o'clock in the morning on Monday, who the hell would even look at it. The guards at the entrance sure as hell don't know anything about maintenance on that kind of a lighting set up."

"I suppose you're right."

"As a precaution, Sniper's going to stay up here until we're all inside the building. If anyone goes to check on the light and gets overly excited about the small bullet hole... well, let's just say, they won't know what hit them."

"That seems like ahhhh kinda brutal treatment for someone just checking a light bulb."

"Brad, someone that just checks light bulbs wouldn't necessarily get excited about a small hole. On the other hand, if he does, Sniper will, without hesitation, do his thing. Simply put, a light bulb changer, as you choose to call him, wouldn't recognize it as a bullet hole, just a hole, unless he has other responsibilities with this organization to raise his suspicions. Hopefully, he doesn't. Besides, we're talking about something that probably won't happen. Remember, my first objective of this mission is to get you and your buddies into this place, come hell or high water, so you can do your thing. How that objective is accomplished, well, I've been given free license to do what's necessary."

"Sure you have, Joey, as long as those people giving you the license will never have to claim responsibility."

"Brad, I think your judgment is being clouded a tad here. When you're having trouble justifying what is about to go down here, stop and remember what's happened to you and your friends over the past six or eight weeks. Also, think about what the world has gone without for the past fifteen or twenty years because of this organization. Those folks down there," he said, nodding with his head to the edge of the cliff, "they work for those bastards and you can be certain, they don't think twice about what they've done or what they're going to do."

"When you put it in those terms, it's hard to disagree, Joey."

"Those aren't *my* terms, Brad. They are terms dictated by *them*, not us, and ones under which we have no choice but to operate."

"Of course, you're right. I suppose the problem is, I don't have the ability to keep focused on how terrible these guys are. Just keep reminding me in the future, if you have to."

"No problem, Brad. I don't expect you, or John and Evan for that matter, to be as seasoned as myself and my team. If it weren't for the fact that you've shown some ahhh... expertise in this type of activity, that being, running around the mountains of Colorado and evading these guys for a week or so, we wouldn't be here attempting this. I know, when push comes to shove, I can rely on the three of you to do the right thing."

"Joey, I appreciate the confidence builder. Let's get on with it then."

"You got it partner," Joey said in conclusion.

Joey and one of his team members outfitted themselves with ultra-sensitive microphones and ear attachments held in place by a strap around their necks. They'd remain in communication with each other as well as the man left on top taking instructions about passing items down the cliff when they were in position. Sniper was totally preoccupied peering through the, now infra-red, scope of his rifle.

Joey and his partner silently disappeared over the edge of the cliff using repelling ropes which passed through their harnesses. Each man carried what he could on the decent, including their weapons with silencers attached. Safeguarding against the rope hitting the roof and setting of the suspected alarm system, they descended the last 100 feet or so by being lowered from above using the microphones and receivers.

After what seemed like an eternity, but in reality was only about ten minutes, the word came to lower the two hinged receiving brackets and the pitons along with the hard rubber hammer. This particular hammer was going to be used as a precaution against noise as the pitons were struck to secure the brackets to the side of the cliff. Then, the ultimate test. The request for the bridge came. "Send the bridge and don't knock any rocks off to fall on the roof as you get it over the side," Joey ordered.

Sound advice, thought Brad, the consequences not having even entering his mind. He does think of everything. Slowly, Brad, Evan, John and the team member carried the bridge to the edge. With the supporting cable now attached to the bridge, they slowly slid the roughly three foot wide by twenty foot structure over the side and released it. The cable had been first fed through a device anchored on the top of the cliff. Through use of a cranking device, one man could lower the bridge slowly and safely.

During all of this activity, Sniper remained off to one side, peering though his scope for potential targets. Through minimal conversation with Joey below, the bridge was maneuvered into position for attaching to the hinged support brackets. This completed, the instruction came from below to continue lowering slowly. Eventually, came the final instruction from Joey. "In position, level, tie it off. Lower the platform and backpacks. Give us five minutes and proceed in pairs to bridge."

The platform was very lightweight, but sturdy, and measured nearly four foot by eight foot. Once unfolded, it attached to the bridge and allowed them to join up at the base of the cliff for last minute instructions before proceeding across the roof.

Once the platform and backpacks were on their way over the cliff, an impressed Evan asked, "That's it? That's all there was to it?"

"I guess so, buddy. You want to go with me as a twosome?" asked John.

"Why not, man. I only wish you were asking be to play a round of golf instead of dangling 300 feet in the air," responded Evan nervously.

"Don't worry, buddy. With this kind of harness and gear, it's pretty damn simple; and, safe," replied John giving Evan's a tug for reassurance. "We'll get a round of golf in tomorrow. I promise."

After fifteen or so minutes, with the exception of Sniper, all stood in silence on the platform. Brad, Evan and John were amazed what had been accomplished in such a short period of time and were admiring the stability of the structure. The brackets, secured to the face of the wall behind them, would not allow the structure to sway from side to side; however, Joey warned them some minimal movement might occur at the end of the bridge nearly thirty-five feet away in the darkness.

Then, they were instructed to change from black to quiet. After cleaning the blackout from their faces and hands, they discarded the outer dark clothing and donned a more normal attire from their backpacks. Business suits and sport coats to make their presence inside appear normal and specially designed to conceal their weapons was the new attire. Joey also instructed them to cover which meant placing the foam rubber bags over their shoes and tying them around the ankles to prevent noise as they proceeded through the metal ventilation system.

"Everyone ready?" whispered Joey. Seeing all thumbs up, an action Brad recalled as a signal of unity among friends, Joey continued. "Once I remove the cover, I'm going to proceed on in. According to the blueprints of the system, I should get to the return air vent in the south corridor in about five minutes. I don't know how dark it'll be, so make sure you don't lose hold of the line I drop along the way. And, for God's sake, absolutely no noise. I assume everyone understands the reason for that."

Without another word, Joey moved onto the bridge and towards the cover of the ventilation system. The six men remaining on the platform and Sniper, still on top of the cliff, could do nothing but wait for the signal from Joey to follow. In near silence they waited, the butterflies circling in the pits of their stomachs. Finally, Joey's team member gave the thumbs up signal as he heard through his ear piece that all was well. Brad pulled a miniature transmitter from his inside pocket and placed its receiver in his ear.

"We're on our way," was all he said.

"So are we," was the response from Phil back at the hotel, acknowledging receipt of Brad's message. "And, good hunting."

Brad raised his thumb into the air signaling that Interpol would begin their actions, coordinated through Ben and Abe, in one hour's time. Sixty short minutes to figure out where they'd find what they were looking for. Damn, thought Brad, we don't even know how big this place is or its layout. Hopefully, the entire place could be quickly secured so the fear of being caught wouldn't hamper their efforts.

The six men made their way across the make-shift bridge and into the ventilation system with the sturdiness of the structure a pleasant relief to Evan, The last man leaving the roof said one word to Sniper on top of the cliff. A simple "go", with the one word response of "roger" to acknowledge the command, meant that Sniper was now repelling down the cliff.

One by one, as they stealthily dropped to the floor of the dimly lighted southern hallway, they were summoned to an open door by Joey at the end of the corridor. All inside and with one man keeping watch for activity in the hallway through the door's small window, they turned on their small flashlights to take a view of the room.

"How did you know it was safe to drop into the hallway without setting off an alarm?" asked Brad of Joey.

"You're never 100% certain but I've checked for video cameras, motion detectors and light sensors before. This little can here," he continued, holding it up, "emits a fine smoke which reveals any light sensors. Rarely, do hallways have pressure sensitive floors and hell, I could tell before I dropped down that this room had a simple, easy to pick, door lock on it. I doubt what we're looking for is in this section of the building. It's not protected very well."

"Well, look at this," said Evan, shining his flashlight on the wall. "It looks like a plan to expand the facility."

"I think your right buddy," said John, "we must be some sorta facility planning office. That chart on the wall over there shows scheduling for deliveries to be made and, they're not talking about file cabinets. They're talking about laboratory items."

"Shit, man, these items are used in a sterile environment. Looks like Sam was right."

"Christ," said Evan, as he raised the plan he was looking at to reveal the existing structure underneath. "Look at the size of the existing place. It goes way back under that hill. It's four or five times the size of the original building."

"The addition, that's where the real security will be," stated Joey.

"And that's where the damn file will be," added Brad.

"Ohhhhh, will you look at this. A computer on the desk," said John slyly. "I think I'll turn it on and see what I can find out."

"Do your thing, John, while we try to figure where we are and where we have to go from the floorplan Evan found," said Brad.

After about five minutes to determine the route they must take to the one and only entrance of newest section of the facility, John interrupted the planning. He'd been silently hitting the keys of the computer and pulled up a couple of files which proved to be interesting. "This may help us," he said to the others.

"What did you find?" asked Joey.

"A couple of things. First, there is a personnel file for this facility. In total, there are about 125 people working here ranging from cooks to research chemists. Along with each individual, it gives their level of clearance for the facility. It appears they have four levels of security here. It's color coded on the badges they wear. Yellow is designated for corridor access only, probably cleaning and maintenance personnel along with the dining room staff. Personnel with a blue badge are restricted to single lock doors, like this one, still basically uncleared, but allowed access to offices to perform their duties. The guy that works in this office is probably cleared to a blue level." Glancing around the room quickly, using his flashlight, John continued, "Look, this office has simple key locks on its file cabinets and desks, not combination locks." Returning to the monitor's screen he continued. "The green level of clearance looks like primarily for the research chemists and lab personnel. And, black is reserved for the key personnel of the facility, the director, chief of security and his immediate supervisors, and a few of the biological researchers. These folks would probably have access to every inch of this place if they needed it."

"John, isn't the door we came through into this room, blue?" asked Evan.

"I don't remember, Evan, I was in such a hurry to get through it. What're you getting at?"

"I think he's saying the color of the door might equate to the level of clearance required of personnel entering the room," said Brad. Moving to the door and peering through the window up the hallway Brad could see a total of five doors, one yellow and four blue. "I think, Evan may be right. There are four blue doors out there and one yellow. Five bucks says the yellow door is a storage area for cleaning equipment and supplies."

"It is," informed Joey. "I checked it out before coming in here. Doesn't even have a lock on it. One thing I don't understand though. Why would they need a black level of clearance. They could accomplish the same thing with the green. Those badge holders would have access to the entire facility."

"Unless," said John, "there's a black door someplace which allows a very limited access. That would explain why a couple of the biological researchers have the black clearance badges assigned to them. There must be a limited access lab somewhere."

"That's where the file we're looking for would be, for certain," added Evan, "in the most secure area. They wouldn't store the Tuatara File anywhere else, would they?"

"I sure as hell wouldn't think so," said Brad.

"So what we're saying is we're looking for a ahhhh, black door," concluded Joey.

"Pretty much, that's it." To John, Brad said, "you mentioned a couple of things. What was the other?"

"Only that for the higher the level of clearance required for designated areas the more sophisticated the security system used to protect it becomes."

"That sounds reasonable to me," remarked Joey. "Just how extravagant of a system is being used."

"It looks like what they have installed for the green and black areas requires the badge to be inserted into a slot to activate the system."

"Then we go find someone with a black badge and the problem's solved."

"It's not that simple, Joey. Once the green system is activated, to gain entry requires a thumb print match against the badge that's been inserted."

"So, now we need a badge and a thumb print?" asked Evan.

"Or, a badge and a thumb," said Joey.

"Man, you're gross Joey," said Evan.

"Hold on minute. If you want to see the prize behind the black door, sounds sorta like *If The Price Is Right* with Bob Barker, doesn't it. Anyway, entrance into a black area requires a retina match."

"A what?" asked Evan.

"Basically, a fingerprint of the badge holder's eye," explained John.

"I love this high-tech shit," said Evan. "Now we need a thumb and a God damn eyeball, right Joey?"

"Looks like they'd help, Evan," said Joey. To John, he continued, "is there a duty roster anywhere in there?"

"Hold on a minute."

John manipulated his fingers on the keyboard with the speed and ease of a court reporter. The flashing light of the screen changing displays highlighted John's face and showed his determination to find what Joey had asked for. After a couple of minutes, he said, "Here it is folks."

"Any black badgers on duty now?"

"Ahh... it looks like the only one scheduled is a guy named Schultz. He's the security supervisor on duty now."

"Then we have to find this guy Schultz," said Joey.

"Another option is to find someone off duty and sleeping."

"We wouldn't be able to recognize who we were after. Schultz is the guy we need. We can identify him by his badge."

"It's your call, Joey," Brad informed everyone. "Schultz it is."

"Ohh, look at this. There are some visiting black badgers here. For Christ's sake. It's... a... small... world," John said slowly.

"Who are they?" asked Brad.

"The same damn three guys Mal pointed out back in Colorado Springs. The ones whose hands carry the damn file to and from. The guys responsible for all the corporate blackmailing that's been going on for the past decade or so. Schmidt, Garvey and Nettles."

"Those guys are actually here?"

"According to this file, they were logged into the visitor access list on Saturday and haven't been logged out yet. Probably means those bastards are still here, wouldn't you think so?"

"That I would. Either dropping off or picking up whatever they need to blackmail another company into joining Swiss Technology. At least, it means that everything we need to blow these bastards out of the water is the prize behind the black door as you put it, John."

"Then, I suggest, we proceed to get it," said Joey. "We only have about a half hour before Interpol does their thing all over the world. Once the shit hits the fan, you can bet your ass this place will get a phone call."

*****

As they approached the security office where they expected to find Schultz as well as the facility's communications system, they heard approaching footsteps from beyond the last corner. The seven men quickly ducked out of sight behind one of the unlocked yellow doors they'd just passed, a room full of supplies ranging from bathroom tissue to computer paper. Brad sneaked a look through the window as the security guard turned the corner and began down the hall towards him.

"Is he a black badger?" whispered Joey.

"No. Green," Brad returned. "And, he has a weapon of some sort slung over his shoulder."

"Shit, it means the bastard isn't Schultz. Of course, that would've been too damn easy. Move aside, I have to do something," said Joey.

Changing position with Joey, Brad could here the man's footsteps pass by the door. That's a relief, he thought, his heart pounding in his throat. With the precision and intensity of a cat stalking a bird, Joey slowly opened the door and stepped outside. Pursuing his prey from behind, the man didn't know what hit him, as the butt of Joey's weapon struck just behind the ear. With seemingly no effort, Joey dragged the limp body into the room where the man was quickly undressed. Joey and his two men, one now wearing the uniform of the security officer, departed for the office. Brad, Evan and John were instructed to remain behind.

After they'd left, Evan said, "Brad, someone's missing."

"What?"

"Where the hell is Sniper?"

"I mentioned that to Joey and he assured me, as he put it, he's around. Something about not putting all your eggs in one basket in case something goes wrong. I took that to mean, he's kinda watching our backs."

"That's encouraging. He sure as hell doesn't talk much. I don't think I've heard him say more than two words the whole time."

"I don't give a shit if the man is a deaf mute. I couldn't think of anyone I'd rather have backing me up."

"You got that right," said Evan, fully convinced.

Not even five minutes later, Brad saw Joey come around the corner and give a thumbs-up sign. To enter the office, they had to step over the body of one guard laying prone on the floor. Another guard was leaning backwards in a chair with his eyes and mouth still open and a third, black badge and all, was being held in an upright position with a silenced weapon pressed tightly against his temple. It became apparent that Joey had been checking badge colors as he'd entered the security office. The two dead men's badges revealed holes from the single shots that had killed them. Schultz's badge was black and unmarred.

Joey walked over to Schultz and said, "Open your mouth." After Schultz obliged and Joey rested the silencer of his weapon roughly on what Brad though must've been Schultz's tonsils, he said, "Schultz, I'm only going to say this once. I'm not going to waste a lot of time on you. Am I getting through to you so far?" Schultz nodded that he understood so, Joey continued. "Good. Now, we know what it takes to gain access to what we want and we also know where it's located. We know we need your badge, your thumb print and a print of your retina for the scanner to identify. Now, neither I, nor, any of my companions here, are willing to carry your ass all the way to the black area so we can have access to the aforementioned body parts we'll need. Understand?" asked Joey waiting for the acknowledging nod which didn't take long. "As I see it, you have two choices. One, you can lead us to the area under your own power," Joey quietly said, pulling out a knife and revealing the shiny blade to Schultz, "or two, you can remain here and not accompany your thumbs and God damn eyeballs on the trip. Also, understand I don't know which one we might need, left or right, so you see, I need the pair of each. Now if you want option number two, I suggest you do your final praying, because if you prefer option number one, that being joining our team effort here, you only have five seconds to give us your nod of approval."

Joey hadn't even finished and Schultz was nodding vigorously, even with the weapon jammed in his mouth. "Good decision," concluded Joey, "you saved another piece of your anatomy, your fucking ass. Now let's get moving and by the way, if you even give me a hint of being uncooperative, you're history. Understand?" Again, the familiar nod was given. "Good, is anyone in the lab areas now?"

"No. No one at all," responded Schultz dryly, the weapon having been removed from his mouth and placed back at his temple.

"Shouldn't have any problems then, right Schultzee?" Joey mimicked. "Let me answer that on your behalf. There sure as hell better not be."

The men exited the security office, left the team member dressed in the security uniform behind as a safeguard and proceeded to the entrance of the connecting tunnel they'd noticed earlier. The first true test of Schultz's undying devotion came and went. He'd placed his badge in the appropriate slot and followed with the thumb print required by the scanner. They'd passed through three green security clearance check points and now were inside a highly sophisticated laboratory.

"God damn," said Brad, looking around the room. "They sure as hell haven't spared any expense in putting this place together. What a damn set up." Passing by a large expanse of glass, they realized it was a window allowing vision of the adjoining room with all of its caged animals, obviously recipients of the testing being performed in the complex. At one end of the interior zoo, as Evan had called it, was a cage with a reptile of some sort. "The Tuatara Lizard, right Schultzee?" asked Brad.

"You're right. You guys have really done your homework," he responded dejectedly but remained in a cooperative state as he remembered Joey's promise.

"There it is, the black door," said John, pointing to the rear of the enormous lab facility.

They approached the door and Schultz inserted his card into the slot. Back came an instruction to look into the retina scanner. Schultz placed his right eye against the soft rubber provided and in within seconds, the door began to slide open. Five of the six men immediately spread out, looking for the filing cabinet housing the suspected Tuatara File and other documentation used in blackmailing companies.

"God damn," said Evan. "There's stuff here on everything. It must be the storage area for all the illegal activities of Swiss Technologies, the whole damn company. Here are the files on Ebola and next to that are the ones for Small Pox. Interpol should've raided and confiscated all the files of this place and forgotten about the locations in the states and Europe."

“That would be kind of hard to determine up front, Evan. We only found out about this place two days ago, remember? We'll carry what we can but I'm not leaving here without the Tuatara File. It should be here under the Cancer category some place.”

“Got it,” yelled John from the other side the room. “I've got the son of a bitch.”

Excited beyond all description, Brad ran to the other side where John was spreading out the file on a table. Quickly scanning over the documentation within the file, Brad said, “Joey, we can leave any time. This is what we came after,” he said, holding up the file over his head as if in victory.

“I'll give you a couple more minutes to see what else you want to take and then we have to blow this place. They're going to be contacted somehow especially, if this is the main classified storage area for this damn company.”

“Brad,” called Evan. “I think you'll want to take this as well. It's the file documentation for LANCES, the one we couldn't figure out.”

“Grab it Evan, and let's get going Joey. This shit is to important to risk getting caught and not getting outta here.”

“Schultzee, do your thing, eyeball that damn security device.”

Inserting his card in the slot again, Schultz placed his right eye against the scanner. This time however, came back the message, “Exit denied, you have 30 seconds to correct error before alarm sounds.”

“Schultz, what God damn mistake did you make?” asked Joey, placing his weapon under Schultz's chin.

“Sorry,” replied Schultz, “when you enter, everything must be right and when you leave, everything must be left side. I should have used my left eye for identification to exit. I'm kinda nervous and forgot.”

“My man,” continued Joey as he made certain Schultz heard the bullet drop into the chamber of the gun aimed upwards through his head, “you have one, only one God damn chance left to open that door. Don't screw it up!”

The second attempt made by the security supervisor opened the door immediately. The men were now rushing against time and the inevitable warning that would most certainly be forthcoming. They had to be clear of the building and in front for the chopper to carry them off the island, before this entire complex was aroused. Being as cautious as time permitted, they quickly made their way back to the security office at the front of the building.

As they entered, a voice immediately said, “Surrender your weapons.” Glancing over to his team member who'd been left there as a safeguard, Joey noticed the customary gaze of a dead man's eyes. From around the corner of the office appeared three other uniformed men, weapons drawn and ready to fire at the appropriate command from the voice behind them. Everyone turned in the direction of the voice giving the instructions to see three additional men dressed in suits and weapons held waist high enter the room from the adjacent communications center. They were wearing black badges, with the familiar oval shape housing their pictures and, although Brad couldn't read the names, he knew the men were Schmidt, Nettles and Garvey.

“What did you bring me, gentlemen?” asked the Garvey, yanking the files away from Brad and Evan. “How nice. You saved me a trip all the way back to get these. I was on my way when I thought, hell, he's not the guy that was on duty here about one o'clock this morning when I was arranging the files for pick up. I called the other security guards, the ones behind you and determined something wasn't quite right. Sorry about your man here, but that's the way the game goes. And Schultz, using the wrong eye on the scanner, tipped us off when you were leaving the classified area. Good thinking. Problem is, you shouldn't have allowed access to the room at all.” As the man speaking nodded to one of the other security guards, Brad noticed Schultz beginning to cringe downward, almost in a pleading fashion. Nothing further was said, the only sound being that of the silenced weapon eliminating Schultz, a bad employee, at least in the eyes of Garvey.

“You think this is some God damn game. Who the hell are you guys anyway, the fucking co-captains of your team. Did you toss a coin to see who'd get to be spokesman?” asked Joey. “I don't like playing games with people who cheat.” Motioning with his head towards his compatriot slumped in the chair as if he had bad posture, he continued, “that wasn't really necessary, was it? Or Schultz either, for that matter? Your days are nearly over, pal. Why not cut your losses and get the hell out of here and find some damn rock to climb under.”

Joey received a solid blow to the side of his head from the butt of one of the guard's weapons and slumped to his knees. Kneeling beside him, Brad said to Garvey. “What he said is right, you know. As we speak, Interpol is raiding every major office of Swiss Technologies. When the operation is completed, they'll have enough dirt on your operation to bury it and you. If

I were you, I'd be making my retirement plans and hauling ass to where ever it is people like you retire."

Nettles interrupted the proceedings to say, "You must be Bradford Claxton. You've really come up in the world since your dad died."

"If you're talking about my association with the likes of you, then, I certainly haven't come up in the world. The three of you disgust me. The very thought of what you've done over the past ten or fifteen years makes me want to puke. The only thing remotely good about you is that you knew my father."

"Pity, him dying like that and all. And, right when you were in your glory at the Olympics."

"Your pity is the last thing he'd have wanted. Maybe your neck in a noose but never, in a million years, your pity. You're sickening. A man, like my father, who fought against the pain of the damn disease like he did, doesn't deserve the humiliation of accepting pity from the likes of someone like you and never would have."

"You guys think you know so damn much. Those offices you claim are in the midst of being raided by Interpol... well, I'm afraid there isn't one damn thing in them that's incriminating to the extent you might think."

"You forget that we're here because of things we found in those files," said John. "Something pointed us in this direction and the same information will lead the way for others."

"Exactly my point. You *are* here. If you'd found anything to bring my organization to its knees," he said, noticing Joey and Brad getting off theirs and standing again, "then you wouldn't have bothered to come here. You would've found a way without this macho, 007 bullshit. By the way, who do you work for?"

Taking the pressure of Joey to answer, Brad said, "We have plenty of data to bury your asses. The only reason we came on this trip was to recover the Tuatara File so it could be shared with the rest of the world for a change. Something you guys haven't seen as the civilized thing to do."

"Excuse us for not being humanitarian while we were making a fortune," said Schmidt. "You could've saved yourself the trouble though. You see, as it turns out, the day after tomorrow in Melbourne, at the annual conference, I personally will have the honor of announcing to the world community we've concluded final testing of a drug which will eradicate Cancer. That's one hell of an announcement, don't you agree?"

"Yes, it is," said Evan. "It's also one that should've been made fifteen years ago you bastards."

"Come, come. What's a few years in the grand scheme of things."

"How many people have suffered and died with Cancer in the last fifteen years, like my father, you son of a bitch," yelled Brad.

"Brad, Brad my boy. Calm down a little. Your father didn't die of Cancer. You see, at least as far as he's concerned, the extent of what you just said doesn't apply."

"What the hell are you talking about. Of course he died of Cancer."

"No, I'm afraid he didn't."

"Then, how did he die you smart ass."

"He died of this," he responded, holding up one of the files they'd confiscated.

"What's that?"

"It's Lances, a replacement for Cancer, if you will."

"A replacement?"

"Yes, a replacement. You don't think we'd announce the cure for cancer to the world and lose all of our organization's client list, do you?"

"You mean all the companies you're blackmailing for a million dollars a month?" asked John.

"My, my, you have found out quite a bit," came the response. You see, in the infinite wisdom of Swiss Technologies, it was decided that some very large profits could be made if we marketed a Cancer cure, which we do have as you know, and at the same time maintain our client base. This would be impossible without something to assure our clients would remain under the fold. Hence, after some lengthy developmental efforts, Lances was born as the successor to Cancer."

"You purposely developed a disease to take the place of Cancer."

"You could, put it like that," Garvey nonchalantly stated. "We've toyed with the idea of using strains of Ebola, for example, but, our clients products wouldn't be useful. Death from Ebola is too rapid to serve the purpose we were looking for. Our latest attempt last year in Africa with the new strain proved futile."

"That would be the activity out of BioMed in Chicago."

"Yes. Unfortunate about Rick Riddel. He had a promising future as a research biologist. Didn't want to ahh... fit in, so to speak, so he was out."

"So, you tried to find strains of AIDS and Small Pox, for example, that would provide a lingering, agonizing state of being for the unfortunate people who contracted it, making your client's products remain in need?" asked John.

"That's pretty much it. Ingenious idea, don't you agree?" Schmidt proudly questioned. "There's a hell of a lot of money to be made out there, my friends."

"Have you ever heard of the Mayan's?" asked Brad.

"If you mean the ancient Indians of South America, I have, " acknowledged Schmidt.

"Then you probably know they believed that whatever day you were born determined what you were going to be in life. Everyone born on one particular day would be, say an automobile mechanic, all persons born on another day would be a ahh... research chemists and so forth."

"No, honestly I hadn't realized that part of their culture. Thank you very much for the insight, Brad, however; I fail to realize what that has to do with anything."

"Only that you three guys," he said motioning to Nettles and Garvey as well, "must've been born on the same identical day, because, all three of you are assholes and have been your whole lives."

It was Brad's turn to be knocked to his knees by the guard's weapon, something, which in hind sight, wouldn't have occurred it he'd thought of what he was about to say for more than a micro second. After the dizziness cleared from his head, he struggled to his feet with the help of Joey and continued, "I don't suppose you're going to announce the development of Lances at the conference the day after tomorrow are you?"

"That, without a doubt, will never happen."

"Never say never," said Joey.

"What's that mean?"

"Absolutely nothing of any importance to you."

"Lances," informed Garvey, "will be introduced in South America later this year and blamed on a bacteria unearthed through destruction of the rain forest. It's completely different, biologically, than Cancer, but, invades and destroys cells the same way, only slower. The longevity of patients with the disease is longer, which creates a larger market place for our client's products. The Tuatara antibody can't crack the cell membrane but we've developed another one which works. Lances will be around only as a predecessor to the next manufactured disease to take its place. You see, we have thought of everything to keep the cycle going and the profits up."

"You guys are lower than shark shit," said John. "Should I go to my knees on my own or do you want to be real tough and do it for me?" Climbing back to his feet, his head throbbing badly, John found the answer to his last question not to be one bit to his liking.

"Brad, while were playing the game of who can piss off who the most, you'll be most appreciative of this," said Garvey. "Like was explained to you earlier, your old man didn't die of Cancer. Shit, we completely cured him of that with the Tuatara cure. He was as clear of Cancer as the day he was born, thanks to us. Unfortunately, for him, he never realized it. You see, Brad, as he was recovering from the Cancer, we introduced Lances into his body as one of our final tests on our new product. Like I said before, to make certain the Tuatara wouldn't cure it at the same time. And, luckily for us, it didn't. Brad, your old man died of Lances, not Cancer, you smart-mouthed little bastard. Does that piss off your ass a little?"

"Noooooooooooo," yelled Brad, not wanting to, but, fully believing what he'd just heard Garvey utter. "You actually, murdered my father!"

"A court of law would probably call it that."

With John, Evan, and Joey and his remaining team members in awe of what was just revealed, Brad said softly, almost under his breath, "It's a real sin you can only die once, Garvey. You deserve a hell of a lot more than that."

Brad didn't say much as they were herded towards the lobby of the facility. If looks could kill, Schmidt, Nettles and, especially, Garvey, would've been no concern. The lobby was small, considering the size of the facility, with only a few chairs scattered around on the, highly polished, tile flooring. Only one table was evident, littered with outdated newspapers and magazines. The few potted plants, present to add some color to the dullness of the setting, appeared in dire need of watering. Probably, making them suffer the way they make humans suffer thought Brad. Through the glass doors of the entrance, he could see the concourse to the gate house and the lone guard maintaining watch.

"Brad," began Nettles, "would you prefer to walk to the chopper that's picking us up or, would you and your friends prefer to be carried?"

"I would say that it depends on what state we're in when we're being carried. We've had a hell of a day and would appreciate a lift."

"Still the smart ass. You have no idea how much I'm going to enjoy the hell out of dumping you and your buddies on the way back to Invercargill."

"Someone like you, Nettles, I don't have the slightest problem imagining your enjoyment at doing that. Getting back to your question you slimy bastard, do we have time to take a vote?"

After hitting Brad across the mouth with the back of his hand, Nettles said, "take your time, son. I was just hoping that you'd make it easy for us, not having to lug some dead bodies around and all that."

"Were definitely willing to cooperate," broke in Evan nervously. "Why would you even bother to kill us, if you're so convinced we don't have anything that would tarnish your reputations in the world. Seems, kinda like ahhhhh..."

"Overkill?" questioned Schmidt stopping Evan in mid-sentence.

"Exactly, although, I would like to take exception to your choice of words. Isn't it totally unnecessary from what you've said."

"You people have caused us a hell of a lot of trouble, nothing we can't handle mind you, but, it's just the way we ahhhhh... do business. It's the way the game's played, by our rules. Put bluntly, you pissed off the wrong people and now your going to pay the price."

"I don't understand something here," said Brad. "You three guys, after destroying the medical practice of Malcomb Bowers in Colorado Springs by framing him for mal practice law suits, which you were involved in and not him, proceeded to a position with Swiss Technologies, is that right?"

"Yeah," said Garvey boldly, obviously proud as a new father about his actions over the years. "Malcomb... how do I say this, was too much of an honest individual. He couldn't appreciate the big picture and the rewards that it would bring to him. He was actually a damn good doctor, right George?" he asked of Nettles looking for confirmation of what he'd just said.

Noticing Nettles nod in agreement, Brad continued, "How high are you guys in Swiss Technologies? I mean, who gives you clearance to do the things you do?"

"There's nothing you can do with the information over the next half hour or so, so why not enlighten you before you join others that have become warts on the asshole of progress. We're members of the board of governors of the corporation. There are four others and any actions taken are decided by the seven of us. And, I might add, your elimination, Claxton, has always been a seven to zero vote."

"It's nice to be considered important." To Joey, Brad said, "I think we have enough, don't you?"

"I believe we've accomplished everything we wanted to," replied Joey, not certain as to what Brad was talking about but playing along.

"What's going on," asked Garvey with a little concern in his voice.

"May I show you something?" asked Brad.

"Why not?" responded Garvey.

Slowly reaching into the inside pocket of the jacket he was wearing, he extracted the miniature transmitter and earplug. "Everything you've said, is on tape back in Invercargill. Your ass is mine you son-of-a-bitch."

"Bullshit," said Garvey, not taking the time to hit Brad across the mouth again, "not through that little thing. We have protection in this facility, in the walls and roof. The only way to get a transmission out of this building is using the antennae system."

"Do you really think we're stupid," asked John. "We knew about your so called protection and overcame it by using an ultra high frequency and a super intensified miniature antennae. We tested it before we came," he lied, not knowing if the transmitter would in fact penetrate the walls of the facility. "Isn't technology wonderful?"

"UHF doesn't carry that far, son. It'd never reach a receiver in Invercargill."

"It would it it were relayed by a boat off shore, the same one that brought us here," stated John truthfully for a change.

"You're bluffing. Besides, tape isn't allowed in a court of law."

"Depends on what country you're talking about," informed Evan. You three guys, with all your escapades over the last dozen years or so, I'm sure there's a country we can ship your asses off to for prosecution that accepts taped evidence."

"I think you've forgotten who's holding all the fire power here. And quite frankly, I still don't believe you've taped anything."

"The taping doesn't really matter as far as the three of you are concerned," said Joey. "Don't think for a minute the status quo hasn't changed, at least as far as you and your two buddies there, Garvey. You three have already been designated to receive a bullet, unless, that is, you decide to cooperate and take your chances in a court of law." Seeing he had all of their attention, he decided to play it to the hilt and continued. "You know how that goes for Christ's sake. Your God damn board of governors has designated Brad to receive a bullet, a bomb, an avalanche, or whatever, as well as his friends, and you haven't stopped pursuing them! Don't fool yourself into believing that I don't have contacts that are just as dedicated to fulfilling their objective as your people. One big difference between your assassins and the guys I have access to. Mine, although I'm biased a little you understand, I feel are much more efficient." Joey had the attention of everyone in the room now, even the security guards were listening intently. "You see, Garvey, they aren't required to make it look like an accident like your guys. My guys are independent contractors, if you will. They have no allegiance to anyone or anything except the performance of the duty they've been assigned. They don't give a shit, *how* you die, just that you *do* die. They'll find you no matter where you go. It may take them a day, a week, a month, hell, who knows how long to find each one of you? But, find you, rest assured, they will. And when they do, your history my man. A single shot through the head when you'er alone, or in a crowd, doesn't matter to these guys. Commitment to duty you might call it. Doesn't matter whether you get rid of us or not. Doesn't matter if you're on tape or not. By the way, you... are... on... tape," he said slowly. "Believe it. You know how it is when your organization targets someone for elimination. You can't call them off, even if you wanted to. You mentioned making an announcement about what's in the Tuatara File being able to eradicate Cancer. These guys are devoted to eradicating another type of disease, Garvey, slime like you and your buddies and they are very, very proficient at what they do."

"As proficient as your buddy lying in the office beside Schultz?" asked an unconvinced Schmidt.

"Schmidt, if you had a brain in your head, you'd have recognized how young that guy was. Shit, he was a rookie at this sort of thing. It was his first mission. I don't know what happened, but he obviously didn't follow my orders or he'd be standing here next to us this very second and you'd be lying in there in his place. Mistakes happen. Mistakes cause lives. You know that. He made one, part of the game you've been referring to. We knew, all of us here including Brad, John and Evan, this could turn out to be a one-way ticket, but, felt the potential end result far outweighed the risk factors. We knew if we were caught, we'd eventually be confronted by the three of you," Joey lied. "Christ, man, we knew you were here before we even came on this mission and also, with you around, no one would do anything before asking the bosses. You see, Schmidt, you haven't given us much credit for doing our homework. We also knew if we didn't return with you in tow, you'd be hunted down and eliminated, no question about it. The only thing we didn't recognize as a problem, was none of you having a brain large enough to determine how much shit your in. Sure, you could go to wherever it is you have decided would be safe for you if it came to this but, not a minute would go by for the rest of your lives man that you weren't looking over your shoulder or questioning each and every new face you came across. Hell of a way to live. Sure as hell glad I'm not in your shoes. I'd rather be dead or serving life in some prison than to live with that weight on me every minute. Surely, I'm not speaking to three no-brainers here."

"Jesus Christ," responded Nettles. "I can't believe you have the audacity to stand there, under gun point, and say *we* don't know how much shit *we* are in to the guys holding the weapons for God's sake. Unbelievable! Personally, I don't think there is any tape. Claxton give me that damn thing," he ordered. Taking the transmitter and ear piece from Brad, he inserted the receiver in his ear and said into the miniaturized transmitter, "Anyone there?"

Surprisingly, especially to Brad, it was evident by the look on Nettles' face, someone was answering. "Only someone that hopes you *don't* surrender, because if you do Nettles, I'm unemployed," came back Sniper's voice.

"You have this stuff on tape then?" asked a definitely aroused Nettles.

"I probably should lie and say no so, I would be gainfully employed for a week or so hunting your ass down. That's about all it would take to find you. You know, you're not in the middle of Europe or the states. Shouldn't be too hard to find your ass in New Zealand. Getting back to the tape thing, Mr. Nettles, we do have you, Schmidt and Garvey dead to rights on this tape," he lied. "Sorry about the choice of words. My suggestion to you is to allow yourselves to be brought in and try to swing a deal for life in prison. The only other choice, at least from my vantage point, and you understand exactly how I'm looking at this, is death, my profession, and I graduated at the top of my class with honors."

Nettles slowly removed the ear piece and looked with wonderment at the tiny transmitter, now fully believing this minuscule electronic device had just forced him into early retirement. "Who the hell missed this when they were body searched in the office?" asked an enraged Nettles.

"It was so small, it was simply overlooked," stated the guards in near unison. "We were looking for weapons, not transmitters."

"Do you have any idea what missing this little contraption in the search has caused?" Nettles said, holding it up for them to see and then slamming it to the floor. "They have tapes of everything we've just said you God damn idiots."

Suspecting what was coming, one of the guards, wanting to get the last word in, said, "With all due respect, Mr. Nettles, the three of you were the one's with the big mouths. Yours are the voices on the damn tape, not ours," he concluded beginning to raise his weapon to fire in self defense.

Poor guys, thought Brad, *too slow, much too slow*. Before the guards could get the proper aim, numerous reports of silenced weapons were heard, coming from Schmidt and Garvey. *Shameful,* thought Brad, *three more bad employees dismissed from duty.* These guys had never even received a performance appraisal with the box checked that says "needs improvement". *I suppose they save a lot of paper work this way,* thought Brad. Looking at the mess on the floor, he also realized two of the potted plants had been put out of their misery.

"What the hell did the guy on the other end say, George?" asked Garvey, as he slid a fresh clip in his weapon.

"Let's put it this way. I think it's time the three of us retired. The guy on the other end, I think he's responsible for the contract on us. The hit this guy was talking about," he said pointing towards Joey.

"You're saying, the organization is going to come down?" asked Schmidt.

"You know, these three guards here," Garvey slowly said, "were right. We allowed these bastards to get to us to the point where we became pissed off and told them everything they wanted to know. They've really done a hell of a job on us. Gentlemen, I congratulate you for a job well done. But, the only thing you have really accomplished is to force us into a very prosperous retirement, just a little earlier than we'd planned. Hell, I'm ready to retire now anyway."

"I take it to mean you're not going to turn yourselves in then," asked Evan.

"Do you think we're nuts? You've just witnessed us kill four people in the last 30 minutes."

"You are totally nuts and make that five people," said Joey, reminding him of his man lying dead in the office.

"You didn't see that one."

"My mistake."

"So you see, as far as we're concerned, we wouldn't have a chance for life in prison as long as you guys are around as witnesses. The best thing for us to do is dispose of you and deny any knowledge of your little visit here. If we're caught later on, it's basically our words against ahh... well, no one's. As far as this hit squad or whatever, I'm certainly willing to take my chances with all the arrangements we've made for identity changes. Shit, look how long the Nazis lived in South America after World War II, and in relative luxury I might add. Everyone who knows anything, is well aware Israel has funded hit squads to hunt down these guys, a large number of whom have never been found. They disappeared without a trace, something we've prearranged to do. You guys up to it?" he asked of Nettles and Schmidt.

They both nodded in agreement as the sound of a chopper could barely be heard landing in front of the perimeter fencing. Looking out the front door, Brad could see the guard at the gatehouse picking up the phone. Within seconds, the phone on the small table in the lobby began to ring. Stepping over one of the guards lying near the table, his back blood-soaked from bullets exiting his body after they'd done their damage, Schmidt picked up the receiver.

"Yeah," he said and shortly concluded with "be right there," returning the phone to its cradle. "Let's get going, our ride's here. Everyone, out the front door," he ordered.

Schmidt led the way with Nettles and Garvey bringing up the rear, an appropriate place for them, thought Brad, considering they were two of the biggest assholes he'd ever encountered. The third largest was walking a few paces in front of him.

Brad was moving slowly and staring at the back of the man's head walking in front and wishing he could do something, anything. Time was growing short and his thoughts kept returning to Sam and the times they'd enjoyed. He knew it to be normal for someone to think of the people they loved when they were about to die, but, somehow, he believed he was thinking of her because he was going to see her soon. Call it a premonition. Call it anything. All Brad knew was, he didn't feel his days were over.

As they approached the gatehouse and with the sound of the rotor blades turning at an idle speed in his ears, the back of Schmidt's head exploded. Blood, bone fragments and pieces of his brain splattered across Brad's entire body, some hitting Evan who was walking behind him. *Sniper, where the hell is he,* wondered Brad. It didn't really matter, he "was around". As Schmidt was falling to the ground, Brad instinctively dove to find cover and as he hit the ground at an awkward angle, he felt his shoulder go out of place. After all he had been through, this was a hell of time for this to happen. In excruciating pain, Brad retrieved Schmidt's weapon and rolled along the grass beside the walkway.

As Joey turned quickly and tackled Nettles, Garvey crouched down and looked for the shooter who'd ended Schmidt's early retirement. With Garvey's weapon still pointing in their direction, there was nothing the others could do to help Joey. Even if Joey won his tussle with Nettles, he'd certainly be the loser with Garvey awaiting the outcome.

Then, Garvey noticed Brad painfully, because of his shoulder, trying to take aim with Schmidt's lost weapon. In a prone position and hugging the earth as if he wanted to bury himself, Brad noticed the grass in front of him fly into the air as the bullets from Garvey's weapon made a trail toward him. As he squeezed the trigger of the weapon he was holding, he felt the burning, painful sensation of bullets entering his body. One struck him in his separated shoulder and another in the calf of his left leg.

As he rolled once again to escape the line of fire, he saw the guard running towards him from the gatehouse with his weapon in a ready to fire position. As Brad made another attempt to raise the weapon, the guard kicked it out of his hand. He'd bought the farm, barn and all, and he didn't even like living in the country he thought as he passed out from the pain.

Not realizing only a few seconds had passed his eyes opened and he saw the blurred vision of the guard kneeling over him and patting his face to revive him. As his eyes became more focused, he recognized the familiar face of Sniper, slightly smiling. "Sorry I kicked you, man, but, you were about to blow my ass away. Had to."

"What happened?" asked a dazed Brad.

"Can you get to your feet?" asked Sniper.

"I'm not sure, I'm beginning to feel numb."

"That's normal," said Sniper, a man who'd been through a similar situation. "It's your brain interacting with your body to relieve the pain you're going through."

After Brad was helped to his feet and with Evan's help who'd run over, he asked for the second time, "What happened?"

"I guess when Garvey saw Sniper run over and give you a kick," Evan explained, "and raise his weapon, he thought he was doing so to cover us. He must've thought he was the real guard. It was the biggest mistake of his life. Sniper put a little hole through his forehead, dead, I mean, dead center."

"Shit," replied Brad as he remembered Joey saying that he never missed. "That son-of-a-bitch was supposed to be mine."

"At least, we have Nettles in tow. It wasn't even a contest between he and Joey," Evan said. "I sure as hell wouldn't want to take him on now after what I saw him do to that bastard."

"Let's get moving. We don't want someone coming out of the building?" said Joey as everyone else arrived beside Brad.

"How do you suggest we do that?" asked John. "We just can't wait here for our ride to show up."

"We'll take that one," was the rapid response, "out in the parking lot. Sniper's all ready made the arrangements and ahh... kinda okayed it with the crew."

"They're going to fly us out?" asked a confused John.

"The crew's dead. I'll be doing the flying and before you ask, John, yes, I've flown one before. To Sniper and the two remaining team members, Joey said, "take up positions in the gatehouse and cover us while we get aboard. Then, hall ass and join up."

Evan and John picked up Brad to carry him as he screamed in pain. "Get the God damn files," yelled Brad.

"I'll get them," said Joey. "Now get moving."

As Joey retrieved the files, he noticed some men entering the lobby of the building. Running now, files in hand, he passed back through the gate house and with one of his men, roughly grabbed Nettles and began dragging him towards the chopper and leaving Sniper as the lone line of defense. He and Nettles arrived at the chopper at nearly the same time as Evan, John, and the still screaming, Brad. No sooner had they scrambled inside, than the sounds of automatic weapons fire could be heard. Grabbing the weapons from the dead crew members, John and Evan began to give supporting fire to cover Sniper's retreat. Brad was holding a weapon on Nettles and wishing he'd make a stupid move, but, he didn't budge an inch.

Sniper was approaching the chopper when John noticed him violently spin around and fall hard to the tarmac surface. Joey had already increased the power of the aircraft and was beginning to lift off when through the side window, he noticed John, jumping out and running to Sniper's side. With bullets ricocheting around him, John, in one adrenaline-aided motion, pulled Sniper up and over his shoulder. Sniper was snatched from John's shoulder into the interior by Evan and as he was climbing in, a bullet struck him in a place that he'd never live down for the rest of his life. "Son-of-a-bitch," he yelled, "they got me right in the God damn ass. They shot me in the ass. Son-of-a-bitch, does that ever smart," he continued as he finally got inside and laid on his stomach to relieve the pain. "How's Sniper look?"

"I'll make it man, thanks to you. You shouldn't have gone back. You broke one of Joey's cardinal rules of operation."

"I never was a bird lover," said John, wincing in pain.

With the sound of bullets glancing off the skin of the helicopter and some smashing through the wind shield, Joey quickly lifted the craft off the ground and swung the tail around towards the oncoming stream of death. Joey piloted the craft out of range and hovered. Turning around, he yelled to the men behind him, "hell of a job, one hell of a job." Looking back at the instrument panel, he continued, "damn, I think we have a problem. They must have hit an oil line or something. I'm losing pressure. I'm going to fly this piece of shit towards the airfield."

"Will there be anyone there?" questioned Evan.

"Not supposed to be. It doesn't have lights so during darkness, there's no need for anyone to be there. John," Joey yelled. Hearing no response, he yelled louder, "John!"

"Yeah, buddy. What you want?" John yelled back, trying to find a position to relieve the pain in his backside."

"I need the frequency of that damn transmitter they smashed so I can contact our guys to pick us up. What was it?"

"Never mind," said Sniper. "Use mine, it should still work. Pass it up to him Evan."

After a brief discussion, Joey yelled to the back of the helicopter, "they'll be there in about 45 minutes. How's everyone doing back there?"

"Everyone's going to be fine, boss," yelled Sniper. "Brad's going to be sore as hell for a while. The bullets that hit him passed clean through. I've got the bleeding stopped and a dressing on both wounds."

"What about the shoulder separation?"

"He talked me in to yanking it back in place. Better him than me. This guy has one hell of a threshold for pain." About John's wound he said, "and, John's wound? Let's just say he's being a real pain in the ass. He won't even let me look at it. All I know is, I wouldn't want to be him trying to take a shit for the next couple of months. He's probably going to have to do it standing up, if that's possible."

"Sorry about Hutch, Sniper," yelled Joey.

"No need, Boss. He knew well ahead of time what he was getting into. Just didn't do what he was supposed to, that simple."

"Who's Hutch?" asked Evan.

"He is... or was my younger cousin. He was the casualty we suffered back there."

"Christ, I'm sorry to hear that Sniper. Damn."

"I was never really that close to him, but, he was still family, you know? He kept bugging me to get him into this type of shit. Guess he saw too damn many Sean Connery films, you know, the good guys never getting killed. I finally put in a word for him, mainly because of his father, my dad's brother." After what Evan thought was a sigh, Sniper continued, "this was his first mission so we attempted to give him the easiest task there was. I guess when it came to killing someone, he must not have had it in his heart when it really mattered. It cost him his life, which I am really sorry about, but, he also placed the entire mission in jeopardy. I don't really know what all happened in there, I couldn't hear anything, but, someone must have been doing some pretty inventive talking to get them so riled they'd shoot their own guards."

"I think the final touch was your persuading these assholes that you had a tape of what they'd been saying," informed Brad. "Letting them think you were the designated hit man, responsible for hunting their asses down if they didn't turn themselves in pushed them over the edge. George over there, got pretty pissed at the guards for missing the transmitter during their search so they became history."

"You mean to tell me, that was you on that damn transmitter," asked Nettles who was lying tied up with his back to one wall of the chopper. "Damn it! You mean there isn't any tape and all of this shit was for nothing!"

"For nothing you say? You egotistical bastard," said Brad. "With the exception of you and your pals, it seems to have turned out pretty well for everyone. All I want from you is a reason, any reason to force your ass into the same type of retirement your buddies just entered. I understand that where they are, the view sucks and the company funding their monthly retirement checks just entered bankruptcy. The best you can hope for is three hots and a cot for the rest of your pitiful life."

"Almost there," yelled Joey to the back.

"You know something, Nettles, we should leave your ass in this helicopter and just before we leave, blow the God damn thing up with you in it." said Brad.

"You can't kill me in cold blood."

"Why not, asshole. It's the only kind you have in your whole damn body," concluded Brad as the chopper was setting down on the landing strip of the airfield.

All except Nettles stood outside the helicopter as the rotors spun to a stop. Brad was being supported, with the only arm he could raise, thrown around the shoulder and neck of Evan. John looked hysterical as he attempted to walk, each step he took bringing him closer to the ground as he tried to take as much weight as possible off the pain in his buttocks. The men spent the next few minutes recapping what they'd done and congratulating each other on the quick thinking which had saved their lives and made the mission successful. Successful that was, with the exception of Hutch.

"Here it comes," said a relieved Evan, "I can hear it."

"Everyone, take cover over here just in case," instructed Joey.

"Just in case what," asked Evan.

"Either they made damn good time getting here or that chopper is someone else. They're about fifteen minutes early. And, it's also coming from the wrong direction."

As the sound of the approaching helicopter became louder, they first noticed landing lights turn on and then, a search light illuminated the idle chopper on the runway. Next came the familiar trail of smoke and, as if in slow motion, the rocket made its way to the aircraft. The resulting explosion was deafening and the resulting fireball made them turn away from its brightness. Small, smoldering pieces of metal landed all around them.

"God damn, Brad, you were right," said Joey. "These bastards don't give up. And, Nettles was inside the damn thing."

"Cheated again" said Brad dejectedly, as the sound of Sniper's weapon nearly scared the shit out of him. "God damn. That was loud," Brad said as he looked towards the hovering chopper, the search light now extinguished. "Hell of a shot, Sniper. Just tell me your going to do it next time, man. You scared the hell outta me."

"Sorry, Brad, I didn't have the time," he replied, as he took careful aim once again.

After Sniper's second round, the craft began to veer from side to side and then, fell from a height of about 50 feet and crashed on its side onto the runway. After a minute or so, with no one apparently in any condition to make their way out of the death trap, it exploded in a violent display of fireworks and lay there, a crumpled heap of scrap iron, burning ferociously.

"Damn Sniper, you don't miss do you. And you don't even have the scope on the damn thing," replied Brad.

"Don't tell Joey, but, the first shot, I did miss. I wasn't aiming for the damn light, I was trying to hit the pilot."

"I don't believe it. Even when you miss... you make it look good. My lips are sealed."

"I guess I'm getting too old for this shit," said Sniper.

"Not in my book, buddy."

The men all stood, including John who appeared to be six inches shorter than his normal height, and watched the raging fire. Shortly, the sound of another helicopter was heard approaching from the opposite direction. Not even taking cover as a precaution, the men waited in silence as it landed twenty feet away, knowing the mission was nearly over.

They slowly, almost methodically climbed into the craft, each taking a sitting position, except John who was lying on his stomach. As the craft lifted off, they were leaning against its interior walls, finally able to relax. Through the open door, Brad noticed the side of the chopper laying on the ground and still slightly burning. There, in all its grandeur, in the dawning light, was the charred remains of a black oval, inside of which were the scorched words of Swiss Technologies slogan, *TOMORROW'S NEEDS TODAY. Ironic as hell,* thought Brad. His thoughts and subsequent dreams, returned to Sam, waiting for him back in Invercargill. Still in pain, he dozed off, remembering trips with his father in the 1965 red Mustang where, it seemed as if he slept, they'd arrive sooner. And, the sooner he returned to her, the better.

*****

Brad and Sam were again sitting on the balcony and looking at the vista they'd so much enjoyed before the mission to the island. Although, it was late in the morning, they'd only been there for about fifteen minutes. Most of the morning had been taken up by more pleasurable items on their agenda. Remaining in bed to make love, they'd again missed breakfast, but who cared? Skipping breakfast was the norm. Seated on the settee, Brad's arm was draped around Sam and his hand was beneath her robe slowly massaging the firmness of her breasts.

"This is really relaxing," said Sam. "I wish we didn't ever have to leave. I love it here. It's so tranquil."

"Honey, we could move to New Zealand if you want to."

"It's quite a distance from everyone we care so much about, but, I suppose we could try it for a while."

"Sam, honey, we have the rest of our lives together. We don't have to make the decision right away. There's plenty of time."

"It was nice of the New Zealand Government to allow us to use this place again," she said as she peered down at the sparkle of the diamond engagement ring she had received the evening of the Gala back in DC. Next to it, on her finger and adding to its brilliance, was the matching wedding band which made the ring and her life complete. It was now mid-May and they'd finally made it to the backyard alter of Sam's parents in Charleston. They had left immediately following the ceremony and were now, honeymooning in New Zealand and enjoying every minute of it.

The guest list for the ceremony had been enormous including family and relatives as well as the most important people of their lives. Al and his wife had flown back from Europe for the occasion and he was still trying to talk Brad into being a coach on the US Ski Team. Ben Butterfield and Abe had attended with their wives, after they had coordinated and wrapped up all the reports necessary with Interpol to conclude the fall of Swiss Technologies. Ron Riddel, with his wife and his murdered brother's wife, attended.

Because she had grown so fond of Ron during their short meeting in Crystal City, Virginia, Sam insisted to be the one to contact him and let him know that all the problems had been resolved.

Evan and Terri, now husband and wife, were there, of course, having been married the next day after the mission. They "tied the knot" back in Wellington, shortly before the departure to the conference in Melbourne. Her parents had arrived while Evan was out the previous evening having all the fun. He never did find out if the roof of that building had a pressure sensitive alarm.

At the World Health Organization conference, Brad took the place of Nettles, who was "unavailable" to make the announcement. Holding up the Tuatara File, Brad, in a short speech, his arm in a sling and walking with a limp, had announced that Cancer was a disease of the past and, as he remembered Hutch, that the audience had no idea what sacrifices had gone into finding the cure.

Both Joey and Sniper attended the wedding and remained in the United States as the newest employees of Brad's Center in Georgetown. Sniper, jokingly, took the position on one condition. He was to be allowed four weeks' leave a year to hunt. Brad informed him after what he had witnessed, he wasn't about to give him an argument.

Doc was there, wishing them both well. Brad, personally invited him but knew he would be there unannounced regardless, kind of the way he entered his office at the Center.

Malcomb and Sybil attended. Although, cleared of any wrong doing concerning the mal practice suites and able to re-open an actual practice in Colorado Springs, Mal opted not to, turning his attention back to the lab and finding cures for other diseases.

Phil and Chantal were there, Chantal beginning to show the tell-tail signs of Brad becoming "Uncle Brad" this coming September. *A Virgo,* thought Brad, *just what this family needs.*

Brad's mother, he noticed, was beaming with pride as he awaited for Sam to make the wedding march down the aisle. She made the both of them promise to come to the estate outside of Denver again this year for Christmas and jokingly informed them, she had reserved the pool for them. Actually, she had invited everyone, especially Evan, who Heinz was anxious to see.

What would the wedding have been without John, seated beside Abbey, yelling out on occasion, "Go for it." John, as painful as his wound must have been, thought Brad, didn't let it interfere with the normality of his life. Abbey was expecting in early September as well. *Another Virgo, just what he deserved,* Brad had told him.

"Hungry?" asked Brad.

"Only for you, big guy," Sam responded with an inviting smile and a wink. "I love you, Brad."

"Love you back, sweetheart," concluded Brad.

They slowly rose from the settee and proceeded hand-in-hand through the open French doors of their room and back to the warmth of their sanctuary. They both knew, their love for each other was so strong, it would be a lifetime endeavor to prove it to one another, a goal, they each would attempt to attain every second of their lives.

The End

Printed in the United States
1907